Pra...

"A lively, delicious ..."
—Karen Ha... ...night Surrender

"Amanda McCabe w... ...s an excitingly sensuous yet darkly haunting tale of love and human frailty that is sure to engage readers' full emotions." —*Romantic Times*

"An unusual heroine and a nicely done and different setting . . . a most promising debut novel."
—*The Romance Reader*

Praise for *The Spanish Bride*

"An unusual plot, interesting characters, and an intriguing mystery make for a delightful Regency read."
—June Calvin, author of *The Ruby Ghost*

"*The Spanish Bride*, by the immensely talented Amanda McCabe, brings us the bittersweet tale of two people who believe that all of their chances at love have died in the ashes of war, only to find that the warmth of true love can thaw even the coldest of angers." —*Romantic Times*

"[Amanda McCabe] re-creates the world of Regency society with a sure hand . . . [and] provides a sweet and moving romance. I heartily recommend *The Spanish Bride*."
—*The Romance Reader*

continued . . .

SCANDALOUS BRIDES

Scandal in Venice
and
The Spanish Bride

Amanda McCabe

A SIGNET ECLIPSE BOOK

SIGNET ECLIPSE
Published by New American Library, a division of
Penguin Group (USA) Inc., 375 Hudson Street,
New York, New York 10014, USA
Penguin Group (Canada), 90 Eglinton Avenue East, Suite 700, Toronto,
Ontario M4P 2Y3, Canada (a division of Pearson Penguin Canada Inc.)
Penguin Books Ltd., 80 Strand, London WC2R 0RL, England
Penguin Ireland, 25 St. Stephen's Green, Dublin 2,
Ireland (a division of Penguin Books Ltd.)
Penguin Group (Australia), 250 Camberwell Road, Camberwell, Victoria 3124,
Australia (a division of Pearson Australia Group Pty. Ltd.)
Penguin Books India Pvt. Ltd., 11 Community Centre, Panchsheel Park,
New Delhi - 110 017, India
Penguin Group (NZ), 67 Apollo Drive, Rosedale, North Shore 0632,
New Zealand (a division of Pearson New Zealand Ltd.)
Penguin Books (South Africa) (Pty.) Ltd., 24 Sturdee Avenue,
Rosebank, Johannesburg 2196, South Africa

Penguin Books Ltd., Registered Offices:
80 Strand, London WC2R 0RL, England

Published by Signet Eclipse, an imprint of New American Library, a division
of Penguin Group (USA) Inc. *Scandal in Venice* and *The Spanish Bride* were
previously published in Signet editions.

First Signet Eclipse Printing, March 2010
10 9 8 7 6 5 4 3 2 1

Scandal in Venice copyright © Ammanda McCabe, 2001
The Spanish Bride copyright © Ammanda McCabe, 2001
All rights reserved

SIGNET ECLIPSE and logo are trademarks of Penguin Group (USA) Inc.

Printed in the United States of America

Author's Note

I am so excited about this reissue of *Scandal in Venice* and *The Spanish Bride* and having the chance to catch up with these characters! These were the second and third books I ever wrote, and my first Regencies. I had been addicted to the Regency period ever since I was nine years old and came across some books by Georgette Heyer, Joan Smith, and Marian Chesney in a dusty box at my grandmother's house. Even though I've since branched out with some stories with Renaissance settings, the Regency will always be my first love and I think I will always return to it. It has endless facets to explore—and I'm sure I have more scandalous characters to unearth!

I hope you enjoy reading these stories as much as I enjoyed writing them. And be sure to visit my Web site for some research tidbits and resources I used for these books.

Scandal in Venice

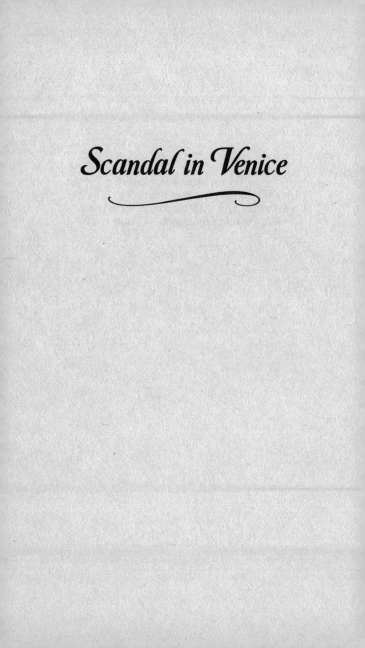

*To my very dear friends
Anne Wright Backus and Laura Kay Gauldin,
for putting up with me for all these years.
What would I have done without you?*

Prologue

H e was dead.

Really, deeply, *profoundly* dead.

And she had killed him.

Lady Elizabeth Everdean nudged cautiously at the prone body of her affianced bridegroom with the toe of her slipper, moving one massive, flaccid arm all of two inches. He did not appear to be moving at all, and the stream of crimson that flowed from the back of his bald head was a very bad sign indeed.

Still, she wasn't absolutely certain. It seemed entirely impossible that someone who had caused such violence, such terror only an instant before should suddenly be so . . . still. Choking back a terrified sob, she clutched her torn chemise around her naked breasts and knelt beside him.

Slowly, slowly she leaned forward, half afraid the closed eyes would suddenly fly open and the cold hands would reach for her again. She stretched out one finger and touched the pulse point on his wrinkled neck.

Nothing. Not a movement, not a breath. The ancient Duke of Leonard would never, could never, hurt her again. Not in this world. Elizabeth almost murmured a prayer of thanksgiving, before she realized that she was now in serious trouble.

She stumbled to her feet and fell back onto the rumpled bed, shaking with sobs. Right next to the murder weapon itself. With a small shriek, she shoved the bloodstained chamberpot onto the floor and buried her head in a pillow.

"Damn you to the furthest reaches of Hades, Peter!" she choked out, consigning her stepbrother to flames of torment with a furious swipe of her fist. "This is all your doing. Yours . . . and mine."

She peered at the unmoving body of her "betrothed" through the tangled curtain of her black hair. And to think, when Peter had told her he had arranged a marriage for her she had been happy. Happy! As darkly comical as that seemed now, she had seen marriage as a way to leave Peter's household, a way to escape from the cold stranger he had become since his return from the Peninsula, a way to escape from their quarrels and icy silences—so different from the laughter of her childhood. She had dreamed of a handsome young gallant, who would take her to London where she could become the portrait painter to the *ton*, the Toast of the Town.

Ha! Had there ever been a more naïve chit than she had been? Those dreams had died a hard death when she had come downstairs for their dinner party that very night and seen the duke waiting for her, ancient and portly and drooling. She would have run away right then and there, barricaded herself in her room, if Peter's iron grip on her satin-covered arm had not prevented her. She had had no choice but to bow her head and allow the duke to take her hand in his scaly palm.

She had thought she knew the worst life had to offer when she sat beside him at dinner, watching him down champagne and lobster patties as if they were nearing extinction. What very little she knew. What had happened after she retired, and the duke paid her a little "call," had been inestimably worse.

It had been, in fact, like a painting she had once seen of the Last Judgment. Elizabeth now knew what those poor, doomed souls, flayed alive and shrieking, had felt when they were thrown to torment. Those snakelike hands had shoved her to the bed, the bed her mother and stepfather had once shared, and reached for her hem.

"You are mine now," he had panted in her face, his breath hot and reeking of garlic. "Your brother thinks he has the better of me, but he can think again, my pretty little whore." And he had latched his teeth onto her earlobe.

Elizabeth screamed then, screamed in mindless terror. Not even his slaps could silence her—she did not even feel them. As he turned to reach for a discarded petticoat to shove into her mouth, her desperate fingers had groped across the slippery sheets for something, *anything*, she could use in her own defense. She had only one thought now, desperate as a wounded animal, that she would surely die if this terrible assault went on.

Then she felt the cool, heavy porcelain of the chamberpot.

Thankfully, it was an *empty* chamberpot.

She had not meant to actually kill him. Just stop him from touching her.

Her own loud sobs, and a timid knocking at the door, jolted her into the present.

"Lady Elizabeth!" Daisy, Elizabeth's young maid, pecked at the door again. "Was that you screaming, Lady Elizabeth?"

They knew! They knew what she had done, that she was a murderess, and now she would be dragged off and hanged, and Peter would laugh. All because of a pig like the duke. She was only eighteen—she did not want to die!

Life was so very unfair.

Daisy knocked at the door again, louder. "Lady Elizabeth, please! Is something amiss?"

They did not know! Of course they did not. Not at the moment, anyway. Taking a deep, steadying breath, she called, "I am quite all right, Daisy."

"Truly, my lady?" Daisy's voice was uncertain.

"Truly. I . . . I had a bad dream, that is all." Elizabeth shut her eyes tightly. If only that were true. "You . . . you may go. I will ring for you in the morning."

"Yes, my lady."

Elizabeth listened as Daisy's footsteps faded, then she ran across the room, tripping over her tattered hem, to where her armoire stood open. She scattered ball gowns, tea frocks, parasols, slippers, and bonnets onto the floor carelessly, pushing a change of clothes into a valise along with her mother's jewel case and a packet of letters from an old schoolfriend, the famous artist Georgina Beaumont. Georgie was in Italy now, far away from England, and she had always urged Elizabeth to join her.

Elizabeth felt that now would be an auspicious time to accept that offer.

On top of the clothes, she placed a carefully wrapped bundle of sketchbooks, pencils, and pigments.

"I have to leave," she whispered as she wriggled out of the ruined chemise. "There is no other way."

As she turned to snatch up clean undergarments, she caught a glimpse of herself in the gilt-framed mirror above her dressing table. Purple bruises darkened her pale shoulders and small breasts; blood had caked at the corner of her mouth. She was suddenly disgusted, nauseous, at such vivid proof of what had happened this horrible night. She grabbed up the lethal chamberpot and deposited the meager contents of her stomach.

When the illness had passed, Elizabeth knelt there on the floor, naked and trembling, unable to cry or think or do anything.

She swore, then and there, that no man would have such power over her again. Her father, her stepfather, her brother, the duke—all the men in her life had caused her naught but sorrow. From then on, she would not be Lady Elizabeth, pampered daughter and helpless pawn. She was simply Elizabeth, and she would be fine on her own.

Chapter One

London, Two Years Later

"**B**y the gods, it *is* Old Nick."

Nicholas Hollingsworth, now *Sir* Nicholas Hollingsworth, late of His Majesty's Army and with a knighthood for valor on the battlefield, raised his dark gaze from the cards in his hand. He squinted through the haze of cigar smoke and brandy fumes until he met a pair of cold blue eyes he had never thought to see again this side of hell.

"Peter Everdean." His voice was steady, low, despite the turmoil in his brain, in his soul. "Is it you? Alive?"

"Sorry are you, Nick?" The golden-haired man smiled sweetly, Mephisto disguised as Gabriel.

Around them, the tumult of the gaming hell went on, men laughing and shouting, bottles shattering, smoke billowing, fortunes won and lost, lives changing on the turn of a card. But to Nicholas, as he folded the cards carefully in his long fingers and laid them on the table, none of the London decadence existed any longer.

He was back on a scorching Spanish battlefield, and the smoke was now cannon fire, the smell acrid in his nostrils, the dirt under his worn boots slippery with blood. He felt again the sharp pain in his leg, the wet, sticky warmth of his own blood, the numb sensation of falling, falling. . . .

A pair of blue eyes above him, a voice telling him they would soon reach the field hospital, not letting him fall any further. Not letting him die.

Nicholas shook his head fiercely. He rose to his feet, perfectly steady despite the quantity of brandy he had consumed that night, his knuckles white on the silver head of his walking stick. He moved carefully toward the elegant figure who waited in the smoke, not entirely sure he wasn't more drunk than he had thought. Or dreaming.

"I thought you were dead," he breathed.

"Certainly not." Peter's voice was as cool, as controlled as ever. "I am far too wicked to die. As, I see, are you, Old Nick." He gestured toward Nicholas with his quizzing glass, taking in the long scar on his tanned cheek, the walking stick that was more than a mere fashionable accessory.

"Quite. Just a bit the worse for wear." Nicholas ran his hand through his thick black curls, uncharacteristically bemused. Here he was, standing in a noisy London hell, conversing calmly with the "late" Peter Everdean, as if four long years had been nothing. Peter was still the golden Apollo to Nick's Hephaestus; slender, charming, graceful, still able to gain every girl's eye, be she duchess or Spanish peasant.

And still as cold as a witch's . . .

Hmm.

Nicholas had seen the truth of Peter long ago, when they had lodged together in Spain. Peter was a man with some secret torment, some demon that rode him. He was charming, yes, an excellent companion, but unpredictable.

Entirely the wrong companion for wild Old Nick Hollingsworth, bastard son of the Earl of Ainsley, whose father had bought him a commission in the hopes he would stick his spoon in the wall in Spain and cause the Ainsleys no more trouble with his escapades. Together, Nick and Peter had been the terrors of the army.

And Peter had saved his life, practically carried him miles to a field hospital. Then disappeared. A physician had told Nicholas, when he awoke from his delirium, that his rescuer had died later that day.

Now here he was, alive, whole, the same Peter. With the same flashing, secret torment in his eyes. And Nick owed him so very much. Owed him his very life.

Now Peter smiled at him coolly, swinging the quizzing glass by its long ribbon. "You know, my friend," he said. "You may be just the man who can help me."

A short carriage ride later, Peter sat down behind his massive library desk and waved Nick to a nearby armchair. "I have been living rather quietly in the country since the war, gotten involved with local politics, that sort of thing." He held out a box of expensive cigars, waiting for Nicholas to take one before he chose for himself. "But I am not altogether isolated in Derbyshire. I've heard of *you*."

"Indeed?" Nicholas grinned.

"Indeed . . . Old Nick. I read the scandal sheets."

"Doesn't seem your sort of reading material, Everdean. Or should I say, Clifton." Nicholas leaned back in his chair, enjoying the cigar, the familiarity of Peter's cynical company.

"My . . . someone at Clifton Manor enjoys them greatly. I merely read them when they happen to be lying about, of course."

"Of course," Nicholas replied, all innocence.

"Yes. Your name is always there. Duels, brawls, hearts broken, horse races won. They say you refused to marry the Woodley chit when you danced with her three times at Almack's."

"I only danced with her once, and of course I would never marry her. She has less conversation than my horse, and is not nearly as pretty."

"Ha! And what was the latest? That opera dancer? Celine Lacroix?"

Nicholas laughed out loud, more at Peter's coolly raised brow than at the memory of the fiery mademoiselle. "She stood in front of my house screaming and throwing rocks at the windows. Woke the whole neighborhood, not to mention that she broke five windows."

"You *had* given the . . . lady her congé. Quite understandable that she would be upset." Peter clicked his tongue in mock sympathy. "But really, Nick, you cannot devote your life to tormenting your father's family forever, you know."

Nicholas sighed. "I know, I know. But since the war, there is not much need for the meager skills I possess."

Peter studied him for a long moment. "What have you been doing, besides drinking and whoring?"

Nicholas looked down at the smoldering tip of his cigar. "Forgetting, of course. As I am sure you are. And having a very good time in the process."

"Old Nick, eh?"

"Quite."

"If you ever happen to become bored with that, I have a task that might amuse you."

Nicholas sat up straight, his interest caught by something in Peter's voice, a distant longing perhaps, a hint of steel. "Do tell."

"Perhaps you will recall, two years ago my household was involved in some . . . unpleasantness, which I do not like to recall."

Nicholas frowned. "Yes, of course, Clifton. I did not connect it to you. I was in Paris at the time."

Yet the tale had reached even to Paris. The Earl of Clifton's sister, fleeing her home the night of her betrothal, leaving behind a very elderly, very dead fiancé. Clifton had put it about that the deceased duke had died of a heart attack, hinted that it had come about because of his exertions in the bed of a housemaid, and that his sister had retreated in heartbreak to distant relatives.

Not that anyone actually believed that. But the Earl of Clifton was rumored to be as ruthless as he was reclusive, and the heirs to the dead duke had been hardly prostrate with grief, but rather elated to inherit the title and estates. The scandal had soon died down, and there had been no inquiry.

Peter's eyes flashed a blue fire, quickly hidden by golden lashes. "I need someone, someone I can trust, to find my sister and bring her back to England."

Nicholas almost fell out of his chair. Him, as the finder of lost brides, the seeker of runaway debutantes? Ludicrous. Absurd. "I understood the young lady to be in Cornwall. Or was it Devon?"

Peter's pale hands tightened. "Neither. I've recently received word she may be in Italy."

"And you want me to find her?" Nicholas rose to his feet, convinced completely that his old friend had truly gone mad at last. "Italy is a very large place, Everdean, and there are many locations where a runaway heiress could hide."

"There is no place where she could hide from Nicholas Hollingsworth, surely. It is very important that Elizabeth be brought back here to me. Soon. And there is no one I trust to do it, as I trust you. Remember Spain? We are old friends. Are we not?"

Nicholas looked into those ice blue eyes, and saw there all he owed Peter Everdean. His life might be worthless, wasted in drink and women, but he liked living it all the same. If it had not been for Peter, he would be lying even now in a mass grave in Spain.

Perhaps a sojourn in Italy would do him some good.

He slowly sat back down. "I don't even know what your sister looks like."

A small smile never reached Peter's eyes. "That is easily rectified. And Elizabeth is actually my stepsister. Her mother married my father."

Peter pushed a small inlaid box across the desk. Nicholas lifted the lid, and there was the most lovely woman he had ever seen in his thirty-four years. And he had seen some.

No, he amended, as he studied the miniature portrait closer. She was *not* beautiful. Her sweet, heart-shaped face and narrow shoulders above a purple satin bodice almost gave her the appearance of a child. Her slender neck seemed to bend with the weight of black hair, swept up and entwined with pearls and amethysts. Yet her wide, blue-gray eyes seemed to speak to him in some way. The curve of her shell-pink lips indicated some wonderful, precious secret that she would divulge only to him.

She was a woodland fairy, dark and enticing and elusive as the mist.

Nicholas looked up to find Peter watching him. He closed the box with a loud snap. A beautiful sprite Elizabeth Everdean might be, but Nick owed Peter a great debt. And, rogue though he was, Nicholas always paid his debts. "Where is she now?"

Peter smiled again, a rare genuine smile of . . . what? Relief? Gratitude? Expectation? Whatever, it was gone in an instant. He reached into a drawer and withdrew a slim letter. "A friend who was traveling in Venice says she saw a girl answering to her description in the San Giacometto."

"Venice?" The old soldier in Nick had taken over, pushing aside the indolent roué. His muscles tensed, his mind raced, hungry for the chase again. He sat forward in his chair. "This friend is reliable?"

"Quite. And Elizabeth is very distinctive. She may be dark, like the Italians, but there cannot be two ladies like her in all of Europe." Peter took up the inlaid box and opened it, smiling down at the painted image. "There cannot. And Italy is just where she would have fled. Elizabeth fancies herself an artist, and indeed she is quite good."

Nicholas felt a frisson of unease ripple down his spine as he watched his old friend trace a pale, long finger over the painted dark hair. Shaking his head, he pushed the unease away. "Venice is not so large a place. It should not take very long."

Peter glanced up sharply. "Then you will do it? You will find Elizabeth?"

"I will. For you."

Peter nodded and looked back down at the painted girl. "Then your debt will be paid."

Chapter Two

Venice

"There *he* is again!" Elizabeth hissed urgently at Georgina from behind her fan, barely audible over the raucous music and the laughter of the dancers. The Contessa de Torre's famous masked ball, held every year to begin Carnivale, was famously wild, and this year was no exception. Napoleon was gone, Italy was free (perhaps a bit *too* free), and the Venetians were in the mood for merrymaking.

And Elizabeth had been having an absolutely splendid time, imbibing the excellent champagne and dancing with her quite attractive, if rather somber, sometime-suitor, the sculptor Sir Stephen Hampton. She had laughed and flirted and cavorted, and had been enjoying lingering at supper with a crowd of fellow artists.

Until she had seen *him*.

He had been in the Piazza San Marco that morning, she was certain of it. Watching her as she sketched. Then, when she had made up her mind to confront him, he had been gone.

Like mist.

She had been suspicious, yes. After all, it had been

rather too quiet on the Peter front for over two years, and she had not expected him to simply let her go as easily as he had. But, more than suspecting the man's motives for watching her, she had wanted to paint him. So much so that she had ached with a need to put his features down on canvas.

In her travels with Georgina, Elizabeth had seen many men. Wealthy men, handsome men, well-dressed and witty men, some of whom had shown a more-than-polite interest in her. A few of the models she had seen in artists' studios had been almost god-like in their physical beauty. Her own stepbrother, as annoying as he was, was a veritable Apollo.

But she had never, ever seen a man like this one. When he had vanished before she could so much as trace a rough outline of him, she had almost thrown a tantrum right in the middle of the crowded piazza.

Well, he was not going anywhere now. Elizabeth left off trying to gain Georgina's attention, and forgetting the revels of the night, forgetting even basic good manners, she propped her elbow on the table, rested her chin in her palm, and stared.

He was tall, taller than almost any man there, and much taller than her own diminutive five feet. Despite the fact that it was supposed to be *un ballo in maschera*, he wore modern evening dress, stark black and white, impeccably tailored over his wide shoulders. The only flash of color was a small ruby in his simply tied cravat. His hair was unfashionably long, as black as her own but curling where hers was stick straight.

Not even a white, jagged, wicked-looking scar slicing across his cheek could detract from his powerful, primitive masculine beauty.

How she *would* love to paint him. As the god Hades in his underworld. In a little toga. Or maybe even nothing.

He was just altogether perfect. As beautifully made as the marble statues she had seen in Rome and Florence. Except that those were cold, white marble, and this man was obviously warm, golden flesh. Yet, despite her appreciation for his wide shoulders, it was his eyes that really caught her, that made her completely unable to look away from him. They were the deepest, darkest brown she had ever seen, almost black, and it was like falling into soft velvet to look into them. Warm velvet, that invited confidences, coaxed secrets from a woman's heart, but gave up none in return.

She, who had learned to be adept at reading people through their faces, their expressions, their eyes, could tell absolutely nothing about this man. He revealed nothing at all.

Oh, not even dear Stephen, who had escorted her dutifully about Venice, could come close to this man! Elizabeth flashed an apologetic glance at the red-headed sculptor who sat beside her, then looked back to the dark stranger.

Only to find him staring right back at her.

Elizabeth gasped, and dropped her gaze back to her lap in bewilderment. Then she peeked up.

Her eyes dropped again. He was *laughing* at her!

"Fool, fool!" she whispered, pounding her forehead with the palm of her hand. "Gaping like the veriest lackwit."

"Did you say something, Lizzie?" Georgina turned to Elizabeth at last, her cheeks still pomegranate red from the lively debate she had been leading on the merits of oils over tempera.

"Not a thing." Elizabeth snapped open her fan, waving it so vigorously that tendrils of black hair escaped from the gilded netting that held the heavy mass in place.

"Oh. I thought you were just agreeing with me about what a *fool* Ottavio is!"

This released a flood of Italian invective from the slighted Ottavio. Georgina laughed merrily, tossed her gorgeous auburn head, and looked back to Elizabeth.

Her eyes traced to where Elizabeth was peeking, and widened.

"Ahhh," she breathed. "I see."

"See what?" Elizabeth dared another look. The object of her admiration was deep in conversation with their hostess. The contessa, every buxom inch of her almost exposed in her silver satin Cleopatra costume, was pressed against his arm, laughing up into his eyes.

One of the sticks of Elizabeth's abused fan snapped in her fingers.

Georgina smiled. "I see, Lizzie, that that is just the sort of man you need."

"What!" Elizabeth gasped. She had traveled with Georgina for two years, had heard every imaginable risqué remark issue from her friend's crimson lips, but she was still moved to blush at times. "Wh— whatever do you mean?"

"That man there. The one you are ogling as if he were a particularly delectable cream puff in Seganti's bakery window." Georgina pointed with the jeweled dagger of her lady-pirate costume, waving the sharp

tip around erratically until Elizabeth grasped her
wrist and forced her to cease. "He is just what you
need."

Elizabeth blinked in confusion. Had Georgina, always a bit eccentric, slipped into complete madness
and begun to procure men to satisfy Elizabeth's
"lusts"? "Need for what, Georgie?"

"For your secretary, of course! Your man-of-affairs,
your *aide-de-camp*. Don't you remember our conversation yesterday? What did you think I meant?"
Georgina's brows rose. "Oh. Oh! Never say *you*, our
little nun, were thinking of other affairs besides accounts payable when you saw this dark mystery
man!"

Their small circle guffawed loudly, drunkenly,
banter flying as Elizabeth felt herself slowly turning
crimson.

"How the mighty have fallen!" Georgina said.
"The nun is in lust!"

Elizabeth groaned, and buried her face in her
hands.

"Really, Georgina!" Sir Stephen sniffed. "Must you
always be so crude?"

"Really, Stevie!" Georgina mimicked. "Must you
be such a prig? We're only teasing Elizabeth a little.
A very little."

"Stop it!" Elizabeth cut off her friends' familiar
squabbling with a wave of her hand, and managed
to lift her champagne glass for a comforting swallow.
She only wished it were something a bit stronger.

Georgina slid her gold brocade–clad arm around
Elizabeth's shoulders. "I am sorry I embarrassed you,
Lizzie, but do admit it. You did feel something, er,

less than pure when you looked at that handsome bit of manhood."

Elizabeth blushed anew. "I . . . really, I thought no such thing. I merely thought I should, well, paint him."

Liar, her conscience screamed. *Paint him in honey, mayhap, and lick him from chin to toe. . . .*

No! Elizabeth fanned herself with the mangled fan again, trying desperately to appear unaffected and unconcerned.

"Oh, Lizzie, dear, of course you want him! And who could blame you," Georgina whispered. "So handsome. And that wicked scar. Very piratical."

Elizabeth gave in to Georgina's gentle teasing with a giggle. "Shall he make me swab the deck, do you think?"

"Only if you are very fortunate. Or walk the plank?"

Elizabeth laughed outright at that, leaning helplessly against Georgina's shoulder. "That does sound intriguing!"

"What exactly is the plank, Lizzie?"

"Why, whatever I want it to be, of course!" Elizabeth blithely reached for a nearby champagne bottle and poured the last of it into her empty glass.

Georgina nodded approvingly. "It is time you showed such an interest, my cloistered friend." She speared a chunk of roast duckling with her dagger and popped it into her mouth, chewing thoughtfully. "I had begun to despair of you, Lizzie, especially when you turned that heavenly Marchese Luddovicco in Rome down flat." She pointed the dagger at an oblivious Sir Stephen. "I had thought Monsieur

Sculptor over there would be as lusty as you were going to get!"

"Georgie! Stephen and I are merely friends, as you well know."

"And I know he would like to be more! He is all wrong for you, Lizzie."

Elizabeth felt it best to turn the topic. "You are one to talk, Georgie! I have not seen you 'take such an interest' since that model in Milan. What was his name? Paolo?"

Georgina speared another piece of duckling. "Bah! Men. Who needs them?" She seemed totally unaware of the irony of this. "I had two worthless husbands in five years—worthless but for their money, that is— and Paolo was becoming far too bossy. For all his gorgeous dark eyes, I felt it was kinder to . . . remove myself from the situation. Why did you think we left Milan in such a hurry?"

Elizabeth giggled into her champagne.

"But you, Lizzie," Georgina continued. "You need to have some fun. You are so young, and you act like such an old matron sometimes. I would wager that handsome rogue over there is just what you require. For the present, anyway."

Elizabeth rolled her eyes. "There is no talking sense to you tonight, Georgina Beaumont! So I am going out onto the terrace for some fresh air."

"Shall I accompany you, Elizabeth?" Stephen rose to his feet, rather awkward in his Caesar costume. He kept attempting to pull the toga down to cover his knees, and his laurel wreath was askew over his brow.

Georgina reached over, grabbed a handful of that toga, and pulled him back down into his chair. "Of course she does not need you to accompany her, nod-cock!" She totally ignored his icy glare, and waved her fingers at Elizabeth's retreating figure. "She is going outside completely alone, I am sure. That is the best way to, ahem, take the air."

Elizabeth, feeling very childish, stuck out her tongue at her laughing friends. Then she turned, swept out onto the terrace . . . and immediately tripped over the boots of the dark stallion.

It *was* her.

When Nicholas had first seen the woman, garbed as Juliet in forest-green velvet and gold lace, laughing and talking, he had known. Just as he had known that morning, when he saw her sketching a group of giggling Italian children in the Piazza San Marco, a beribboned straw hat half-hiding her face.

He had found Lady Elizabeth Everdean. And she was not precisely what he had been expecting.

Oh, she *was* pretty, just as her portrait had promised, small and delicate, pale and midnight dark. He had been told she was interested in art, but he had never expected to find her actually making her fortune in the medium, much less surrounded by a racy crowd of champagne-flushed artists.

When her partner, a tall, patrician-looking man dressed as a Roman with wreath and toga, had put his hand on her arm with obvious familiarity, Nicholas's fingers had reached convulsively for the pistol hidden in his velvet jacket.

For one shattering instant he had forgotten the debt he owed Peter Everdean. He had forgotten everything, and only seen this Elizabeth as a woman.

A lovely woman he wanted for himself.

He wanted to feel her small, pale body naked against his, to breathe in her scent, to ease into her welcoming warmth, and hear her sigh and cry out his name. . . .

He needed some air.

Nicholas evaded the clinging arms of his hostess, and retreated in haste to the darkness of the terrace, to breathe in the quiet, the solitude.

He was not to be solitary very long.

No sooner had he lit a thin cigar and leaned back to enjoy it, than a bundle of green velvet and lilies-of-the-valley scent tumbled through the doors and landed at his feet.

"H—hello," the bundle whispered.

Nicholas found himself gaping like the veriest green lad at the lady's stocking-clad calves and slim ankles above high-heeled green satin shoes. He blinked and quickly raised his eyes to her face. She was half in shadow, yet he could still see the flush across her high cheekbones, and the way she was, in turn, gaping up at him.

"Signorina," he murmured, automatically making a polite leg. "Or . . . is it signora?"

"It . . . it is signorina," she answered, still whispering.

Nicholas's smile was white and predatory in the darkness as he looked down at her. *At last—Signorina Everdean.*

Chapter Three

Elizabeth silently willed the marble beneath her bottom to open up and swallow her whole. When it chose not to oblige, and instead left her sprawled inelegantly at the feet of the most attractive man she had ever encountered, she slowly opened her eyes and dared a peek up at him.

"Good evening!" she chirped, then closed her eyes again when she heard how mortifyingly high-pitched her voice had suddenly become. Coughing as delicately as possible, she tried again. "Delightful party, is it not?"

"Delightful," the man answered, his voice warm and rough, dark as the night around them. Indeed, he seemed almost a part of the night, his black hair and attire blending into the midnight darkness, leaving only the glow of his eyes as he looked down at her, unsmiling.

Elizabeth resisted the urge to titter, something she had not been at all tempted to do since she left the schoolroom. Instead, she leaned back and said coolly, "I do not believe I have ever seen you in Venice before, signor."

"No. I have only just arrived."

A man of few words. Excellent. Then Elizabeth's

eyes widened, as she registered that the man's words had been in perfectly unaccented English. "You are English!"

"Indeed I am."

"I thought I knew all the English who were staying here." She ran through all her acquaintances in her mind, but all of them, even the most eccentric poets and painters, seemed far too, well, *ordinary* to be associated with this man. And no one had mentioned they were expecting a new houseguest. "But then, we have only been here three months ourselves, though Venice is so wonderful it feels only days! We were in Milan before. Have you been to Milan?"

"No."

"You ought to go. It is quite fascinating. I learned a great deal there. In fact, I did not want to leave, but Georgie—Georgina—insisted we come here for Carnivale."

Elizabeth almost slapped herself. She was babbling—*she*, who could fend off every overbold swain with a sharp word and a snap of her fingers! She, who a disappointed suitor had once dubbed the Ice Duchess. She was rattling on like a sapskull, all because a handsome man was looking down at her in the moonlight. She snapped her mouth shut and fell silent.

He held out one hand to help her to her feet, quite startling Elizabeth since she had forgotten she was sprawled out on the cold marble with her skirts about her knees. She reached up tentatively and took the proffered hand; his slightly callused palm felt warm and cool against her skin. She did not want to let go, even when she was firmly on her feet again.

And he seemed quite willing to let her go on holding his hand.

"Where were you, before you were in Milan?" he asked softly, so close that his breath stirred the loose curls at her temples.

"What?" she murmured absently, quite absorbed in the smell of him, evergreen and starch and something darker, richer. She wanted to bury her nose in his satin waistcoat and inhale him.

"I said . . . where did you live, before you were in Milan? In a rose petal?"

"A . . . what?"

"A rose petal. Is that not where all fairy princesses curl up to sleep?" His aged-cognac voice was lightly amused, as if she were a diverting child he was attempting to humor.

A child was the very last thing she wanted to be in this man's eyes. Fairy princess, however, sounded slightly more promising. "I don't know about fairies, signor, but I sleep in an ordinary feather bed."

"Indeed? And I thought I had found an escapee from fairyland, with eyes the color of the stormy sea."

Elizabeth giggled despite herself. She looked down, turning his hand between both of hers, and imagined raising the bronze flesh to her lips, pressing kisses along the callused ridge of the heel of his palm, where he would grip a sword. Suddenly lightheaded, she dropped his hand and stepped back, forcing herself to take in deep breaths of the cool night air.

But her lungs were still filled with the scent of him.

It was just the champagne, clouding her very judgment, making her behave foolishly. That was all. She was only tipsy. Really.

"We lived in Rome," she answered finally, turning her back on his disturbing presence to look down over the Grand Canal and the gondolas filled with revelers that floated there. One couple, cloaked and masked, waved up at her and she waved back. "In rented rooms, remarkably free of any resemblance to a rose petal. Before that we were at the small villa Georgie owns, at Lake Como."

"We?" He had moved silently closer, and she could feel his warmth against her velvet-covered back.

"My . . . my sister and myself. We are artists, and must travel to find patrons."

"Women artists?"

Elizabeth stiffened, bracing for the inevitable mockery. *Please, not him, too.* Yet there was only curiosity in his voice, and an odd sort of tension, waiting. "Yes," she answered. "Georgina, my sister, is becoming quite well known. In England she painted Mrs. Drummond-Burrell's portrait. Perhaps you have heard of her? Mrs. Georgina Beaumont?"

"I have indeed." He leaned against the marble balustrade behind him, his velvet sleeve brushing lightly against her hand. "She was quite the *on dit* in London. Even from afar she excites much interest."

Elizabeth couldn't help but laugh. "Every bit of it true, I assure you! Georgie causes a stir wherever we go."

"I was not aware she had a sister who is also an artist."

"Oh, I am still a student, really. I *am*, however, working on a new commission at the moment."

"Indeed?"

"Yes. A portrait of Katerina Bruni." She glanced at him from the corner of her eye, gauging his reaction to the name of the infamous, and very beautiful, courtesan. "Another scandalous lady, *n'est-ce pas*?"

He laughed, the rich sound of it flowing through her like creamy chocolate. "The mistress of the Marquis of Rothmere *is* well known everywhere, yes. She is a famous beauty, and notoriously particular about who paints her portrait. You are doing very well for a mere student."

Elizabeth shrugged, secretly pleased at the compliment. "The Italians are very friendly, and quite receptive to new artists. Much more so than the English." As the moon appeared from behind a bank of clouds, she turned back to her companion, to study his beautiful, scarred face. "That does not, however, mean they are any more prompt in paying their debts. And my name is Elizabeth Cheswood. It was quite rag-mannered of me not to introduce myself earlier."

"I am very pleased to meet you, Miss Cheswood."

Elizabeth waited expectantly, but no reciprocal information was forthcoming. "You have not told me your name, signor, or where *you* were before you came to Venice."

He shrugged, the dark cloth of his coat rippling impressively across his back and shoulders. "I am not at all interesting, Miss Cheswood. I fear I would bore you with the mundane details of my life."

"I am not bored yet," she answered quietly.

A muscle clenched in his smooth-sculpted jaw. "My name is Nicholas, and I was in London before I came to Venice . . . and found you." He smiled at her tightly. "There you see, Miss Cheswood. Quite ordinary."

"Oh, I hardly think you could be called ordinary, Nicholas of London." The champagne seemed to be making her bold. She traced the jagged scar on his cheek lightly with her fingertip, and, though his entire body was tense as a cracked whip, he did not move away. "Quite the opposite, I would say."

"Oh, yes?" His voice was hardly more than a rough whisper, and he reached out to lightly caress her cheek.

"Yes." Elizabeth hardly knew what she was doing. She had never in her life been so very close to a man, a stranger. But she went on tiptoe, her palm flat against his cheek now, their breath mingling. His arm crept about her waist. "Have you ever had your portrait painted, Nicholas?"

"Never. Should you like to be the first to paint it?" His mouth almost, barely, delicately touched hers. Her eyes drifted shut. . . .

"Elizabeth! What are you doing out here?"

"Blast!" she breathed, jerking out of Nicholas's embrace and turning to glare at the interloper. "Stephen."

"Elizabeth!" Stephen said sternly, waving his shield at her. "Your sister wishes to speak with you, and she feels you have been out in this cold air long enough."

"Georgie sent you?" Elizabeth fumed, her tiny fists planted on her hips. "I hardly think that is the situation! What do you—"

Her words ended in an indignant squeak, as Stephen seized her arm in a surprisingly strong grasp and marched her from the terrace. Her feet did not even touch the floor as he swept her back inside the doors and into the midst of the noisy, overheated party.

She only managed one frantic glance over her shoulder at the shadowy figure, who blew her an impertinent kiss. She did not see Georgina lurking behind a potted plant, twisting her brocade sleeve thoughtfully as she watched the man who, shaking only slightly, was lighting a thin cigar and turning to watch the canal again.

"Signor!" she called, rustling forward. "Signor, we have not been formally introduced, but my name is Mrs. Georgina Beaumont. I could not help but notice that you were just in earnest conversation with my sister. . . ."

"Ah. So you are the famous Mrs. Beaumont?"

"I am. And you are . . . ?"

"Nicholas Carter." He made an elegant leg. "At your service."

Georgina flashed a roguish smile. "I do hope so, sirrah. Or rather, that you are at my sister's service."

"I am afraid I do not understand."

"Would you perhaps be in need of employment, Mr. Carter? While you are in fair Venice? Something I think you would find . . . amusing."

His dark eyes flashed down at her. "Just what are you suggesting, Mrs. Beaumont?"

Chapter Four

"Bianca! How can I draw if you persist in wriggling about so?" Elizabeth snapped. "You swore you would remain still this time."

The little Italian maid, garbed in classical draperies formed of sheets and a braided curtain cord, twisted about again, pouting extravagantly. "But, signorina! Someone is knocking at your door, and it is my duty to answer it! I am maid."

"Your predominant duty at the moment is to be my model," Elizabeth muttered. As she lowered the drawing pencil clutched in her fingers, she finally heard Georgina pounding on the bedroom door. Georgie sounded far too cheerful by half, considering it was not even noon yet.

"Yoo-hoo! Lizzie!" she sang, beating a pattern on the door. "Are you there, dear?"

"Come in, if you must," Elizabeth answered, bending back over her sketchbook. She had spent a sleepless night, going over and over in her mind the encounter with the dark Englishman, coming up with witty repartee she should have made instead of the nonsense she had spouted. As a result, she was bleary-eyed and cranky, with no patience for Georgina's shining good cheer.

"Oh, Lizzie." Georgina tsked, peeking around the door with bright eyes and perfectly coiffed auburn curls. "You are still in your night rail! And here it is almost time for luncheon."

"I am busy. And are you not supposed to be working?" Elizabeth pushed a tangle of black hair out of her eyes and watched, disgruntled, as Georgina bustled about, opening the armoire and searching through the jumble of Elizabeth's gowns.

"Indeed I do have work to do, a sitting with that tiresome old contessa and her nasty poodle. But right now I have a much more amusing task!"

Georgina was fairly vibrating with the need to tell something, so Elizabeth gave in with a sigh, and set aside her sketchbook. "Very well, what is it?"

"You have a caller."

"What? Who? At this time of day? If it is Stephen, you can tell him to go away. I am *still angry* with him over his high-handed behavior last night. We are not engaged, and the fact that—"

Georgina sniffed deprecatingly. "No, it is not that fussy old Stephen! I do not know why you bother with him at all, Lizzie. He is a talented sculptor, I admit, but he is so very *English*! We came to Italy to get away from that, did we not? There are so many attractive men in Venice. You could do ever so much better."

Elizabeth rattled her sketchbook impatiently at this oft-repeated refrain. "Enough, Georgie! I already know your opinion of poor Stephen. He and I are merely friends, in any case. So, if he is not downstairs, who is?" Her lips thinned. "Not a bill collector!"

Georgina paused to examine herself in the full-length looking glass, and straightened the green spencer that matched her green-and-gold striped walking dress. She was too obviously enjoying Elizabeth's impatience. "For once, Lizzie, it is not. You ought to pay more attention when those past-due notices arrive, dear. And you know I will loan you anything you need."

"I have more important things to worry about than bills, and you know I cannot take any more of your money." Elizabeth waved her pencil significantly. "And there is this sketch I am working on."

"Oh, I *know* you have better things to do than bother with ledger books and bills and contracts. And this caller is the very one to solve your problems."

Elizabeth frowned suspiciously. "Yes?"

"Yes. It is someone come to inquire about the position of your secretary."

"I told you, Georgie, I have no need of a secretary! We do well on our own, do we not? This hiring of an extra man was all your idea. And I could hardly pay another set of wages, could I? Not since my advance from Signora Bruni is almost gone, and Bianca costs so much."

The maid rustled her draperies in a great show of Italian indignation. "I am not just maid, signorina, I am *model*! Is very hard work."

Georgina merely smiled the smugly secretive smile that had been infuriating Elizabeth since their long-ago days at Miss Thompson's School for Young Ladies, when Elizabeth had idolized the sophisticated older girl. "Oh, believe me, Lizzie, you will want to meet with this person."

Elizabeth froze. *No.* It could not be. Could it?

"It is the dark lord from the ball last night!" Georgina crowed dramatically.

Elizabeth let out a tiny squeak. Her pencil fell from numb fingers, scattering parchment every which way. "Nicholas," she whispered.

Georgina clapped her hands, dancing around the room on her small green half boots. "Is it not wonderful, marvelous?"

"But . . . how?"

Georgina suddenly whirled to a stop, and looked innocently down at her fingernails. "Fate, Lizzie. It was meant to be."

Elizabeth clicked her tongue knowingly. "Um-hm. Fate. A redheaded fate."

"Oh, Lizzie, don't fuss! What does it matter *how* he came here? It was obviously meant to be." Her eyes narrowed. "It is just such a pity you look as if you had been dragged through a cow pasture, dear. You are not a charwoman, you know."

Elizabeth's gaze flew to the mirror. She did indeed look like the proverbial beggar-girl. Her hair straggled from its loose plait, falling over her face and her nightgown-clad shoulders like limp black linguini, and her face was chalky and hollow from lack of sleep and a surfeit of champagne. She dragged the nightgown over her head, and fled to her dressing room clad only in a silky chemise.

"Fear not, Cinderella!" Georgina sang, producing a comb from her pocket. "Your fairy godmother is here."

The Elizabeth who finally emerged from her room was completely unrecognizable as the shrieking ragamuffin she had been not fifteen minutes before. Her hair was neatly plaited and coiled in a gleaming coronet atop her head, fastened with ivory combs. She was freshly attired in a blue sprigged muslin morning gown, and she smelled of her favorite lilies of the valley. Bianca and Georgina waved her off like proud mamas at a night at Almack's.

And if she was tugging on stockings and slippers as she hopped one-legged down the stairs, who was to notice?

She paused at the foot of the stairs, half hidden by the newel post as she peered through the open door of their small drawing room. It *was* Nicholas. The dark man who had almost kissed her in the moonlight, and who had haunted her night. She had almost come to the conclusion that he had only been a dream, an enchantment of the night. Night in Venice could be quite intoxicating, after all; it could make things, and people, who were really quite ordinary seem almost earth-shattering.

Now she saw she had been quite wrong to suppose he could ever be ordinary in any light. He was impossibly, piratically elegant amid the comfortable shabbiness of their rented furniture. Today, his unfashionably long hair was held back in a neat, black ribbon-tied queue, revealing the clean, strong line of his throat and jaw as he tilted back his head to look at a painting on the wall. His blue coat and buff breeches fit him like a second skin; his boots were glossy with a champagne polish.

And she felt like the lowliest beggar-girl, despite Bianca and Georgina's efforts. She longed to run back and out in her violet silk, her best day dress. But he had already turned, and seen her lurking there, watching him.

With a deep breath, Elizabeth pasted on her brightest smile and stepped forward, hand outstretched. She just hoped he would not notice the smudges of charcoal across her knuckles, or the paint beneath her nails. "Mr. Nicholas! Such a surprise."

He lifted her proffered fingers to his lips, his breath warm and sweet on her skin. "I had heard that you were in need of a secretary, Miss Cheswood."

Secretary? What could that be? Every thought had flown out of her head at the sound of his voice. "Where could you have heard that?" she answered, surprised that her voice sounded so steady and normal when her heart was bursting.

"Shall we say, a small bird told me? A small *red* bird."

She could not help but laugh at the wicked glint in his dark eyes. "Oh, I see. Yes." She seated herself as regally as possible on a threadbare chaise, attempting to tuck her feet beneath her so that he could not see that her stocking had slipped from its garter and fallen to her ankle. Kicking off her slipper, she tried to pull the tube of silk up with the toes of her opposite foot.

"You did not mention that you were in need of a position," she said. She gestured to the fine cut of his clothes, the unscuffed boots. "Indeed, you do not look as if you need to work at all."

"Appearances can be deceiving, Miss Cheswood. You would do well to remember that." Nicholas turned back to the painting he had been studying when she came in. "Is this your work?"

Elizabeth's mouth softened as she examined the painting, a portrait of a young mother and her infant. "Yes. The woman was a peasant, who brought us fresh milk and eggs when we were at Lake Como. She was beautiful, like a Madonna. It is one of my favorites, but it is an early work of mine, very rough."

Nicholas tilted his head, taking in the smiling, golden-haired mother and her fat bambino. The lines *were* rather rough, the background of rolling hills and trees clumsily drawn, but the woman's vibrant personality shone like a fine red wine on a summer day. The vivid blue of her skirt shimmered. It was obvious that Elizabeth *saw* people, saw their true essence, and captured that on canvas. It was remarkable.

Then his gaze shifted from the smiling peasant woman to another mother, painted on a smaller canvas. This mother was pale, her red-gold hair falling over silk-covered shoulders, her blue-gray eyes smiling at the toddler beside her. There was something about those eyes. . . .

"She looks remarkably like you," he blurted out.

"She should. She was my mother." Elizabeth ran her eyes over the woman's painted green gown, the fall of her hair. "She died when I was nine, long before I ever picked up a paintbrush. This was from memory, it was . . . I don't know. Fantasy? I simply . . ."

Then she came back to herself, to the dark eyes intent on her, and she could have bitten her tongue for running on so. Whatever was she thinking, to be babbling on about her mother so? And to a man who, no matter how devastatingly attractive, was a stranger. An *English* stranger. His eyes, those black, fathomless pools, the way he focused on her every word as if it were the most vital thing that had ever been said, they were enormously seductive. He made her quite long to tell him everything, every ugly secret she carried inside, to unburden her soul and move forward, free from guilt and pain and the whole rotten past. This man had enormous power, she sensed, but whether for good or evil she could not tell.

He was probably quite the rake back in England. Just like someone else she knew.

It would be so very, very foolish to give him such power over her. If he was not to be trusted, then news of her whereabouts would find its way back to England so very quickly. Peter was still her legal guardian. He would come for her, drag her away from the tenuous happiness she had found for herself in Italy.

That Elizabeth could never bear. She could never go back to being Lady Elizabeth of Clifton Manor again. She had put all that behind her that awful night. The night she became a murderess.

It had been folly to even paint that portrait of Isobel Whitman Everdean, the Countess of Clifton, Incomparable, Diamond of the First Water, and mother. Anyone could have recognized her.

She would have to be very careful around this intense, unreachable man. She would be quite foolish to hire him, bring him into their household, make him privy to their secrets.

Really.

She couldn't do it.

She could not!

"We were not speaking of my painting!" she snapped suddenly, turning her head away from her mother's smile, the smile that seemed to say *You are my daughter after all.* Isobel had always had a keen eye for masculine beauty.

Nicholas seemed unfazed by her small fit of temper. He simply looked at her with faint amusement in his handsome eyes, and came to stand beside her. He towered above her, enveloping her in his warmth and the spicy scent of his soap, surrounding her in an inescapable cocoon of . . . of sheer *maleness*.

Not that she especially wanted to escape, she found.

"Were we not?" he mused, quite serene and unaware of her faintly gasping breath, the flush on her cheekbones. "And here I thought that your painting was the very reason I am here."

Elizabeth relented, and waved him to be seated on the chair beside hers. Anything so that he would cease looming over her, and she could think clearly again. "How *did* you discover I was in need of . . . assistance?"

He shrugged. "Venice is small. One hears things."

So it was Georgie, Elizabeth thought. A small pang of unwelcome jealousy pierced her heart with the vision of her exquisite friend laughing and whispering with this man.

This man continued. "Despite what you may think, Miss Cheswood, I *am* in need of this position. I am a long way from home. Do you not want to help a fellow English patriot in need? A weak cripple, helpless and in need of an employment?" He brandished the silver-headed walking stick he had been leaning on.

He was about as helpless as a prowling lion on the savanna, Elizabeth knew, but oh, he *was* lovely with that teasing gleam in his eyes. He swept his waving hair back from his forehead in one silky movement, and she almost melted into a puddle at his feet. A great, oozing puddle of female giddiness.

She also thought more pragmatically of the pile of unpaid bills stuffed into her desk drawers, of the hours of work that were going unrewarded because no one thought it important to pay a mere woman promptly. There were so many things she needed, such as pigments, canvas, new clothes. And she could not go on forever living on Georgina's generosity.

If anyone could get her rightful earnings quickly, it was this man.

Oh, but to see him every day! To look at him, talk to him, smell him. Could she do that, without throwing herself at him in some hoydenish fashion?

Could she?

Did she even have a choice in the matter?

No. She did not.

Elizabeth rose and went to the unshuttered window, staring unseeing at the crowded alleyway below. Never, ever had she felt about a man as she did this one, this mysterious stranger with the roguish glint in his eye. There was something in him, an energy, that drew her inexorably.

She had always associated the sex act with her mother and stepfather's frequent noisy couplings and equally noisy screaming fits. With the rough hands of her ancient "fiancé" tearing at her clothes. With the intense way Peter would sometimes watch her, after he came back from Spain a sunburnt stranger. All of it had seemed so very repulsive. The few times she had become a bit tipsy and allowed Stephen or another artist to kiss her, she had been overwhelmed with fear and pushed them away. Even with Georgina's assurances of the joy of the act, she had not been convinced.

Elizabeth felt none of this fear around Nicholas. From the first instant she had glimpsed him in the Piazza San Marco, she had felt only delicious warmth, giddiness, like lying in the grass on a hot summer day. She had dreamed of him in her sleep after the ball, dreamed of kissing him. She had bitterly regretted the fact that they had been so rudely interrupted on the terrace.

Was she in truth becoming the "wanton artist" she had been labeled by the more respectable society they had encountered?

She turned away from him now in abject confusion, her palms pressed to her hot cheeks. It was all so odd! Of all the men she had met in her travels, she should feel the least safe with this one. His presence was overwhelming in their narrow house, his silences intense and watchful, as if he waited for something from her. She knew almost nothing about him.

Nothing except the way she felt when he was near. And for now, that was enough.

"Very well," she answered at last, turning back to him with a smile. "You are engaged."

He did not answer, merely watched her. His hands moved over the head of his walking stick.

"But you should know," she continued, "that I cannot afford to pay you until . . . well, until after you begin your duties. I have no ready blunt at the moment." She had used the last of it on new ball gowns for Carnivale.

"Actually, Miss Cheswood," he interrupted, "you have something I would much prefer to . . . ready blunt, until I have begun my duties and you are able to pay my wages."

Elizabeth stiffened. Had she misjudged this man after all? Was she not safe in his presence? She frowned. "What, pray tell, might that be, sirrah?"

But he surprised her yet again. "One of your paintings. Any you choose."

She felt her jaw begin to sag, and snapped it shut. "My . . . paintings?"

"Yes. I have an idea they will be worth a great deal one day. If, however, you would rather not part with one . . ."

"No! I am quite willing to pay you in paintings. I am simply surprised that you would choose that over coin."

He smiled at her again, that flash of white teeth and dimples that left her dazzled. "Maybe you should give me your account books to look over, Miss Cheswood, so I may begin my duties."

"I have one duty for you already."

"Indeed? And what might that be?"

She laughed at the naughty tilt of his grin. "Nothing terribly interesting, I'm afraid! You must call me Elizabeth."

"Only if you, in turn, call me Nicholas."

She nodded. "Done. We are very informal here, as you shall soon find."

As she went to retrieve the books from where she had shoved them beneath a table, Bianca came in bearing a tea tray, still wearing her bedsheet draperies. Her eyes rolled in approval at the handsome man, and she almost tripped over her train while trying to swing her hips in his direction.

Close on her heels was Georgina, a smart feathered

bonnet on her auburn curls and a green velvet cloak folded over her arm. She clapped her gloved hands at the sight of the dusty ledgers. "Excellent, Lizzie!" she said. "I see you are finally showing good sense, and have hired Mr. Carter. So lovely to see you again, sir." She held out her fingers, and Nicholas gallantly raised them to his lips.

Wonderful, Elizabeth thought wryly, turning away from their giggling and smiling. *Two unrepentant flirts in one household*. And Georgie had even known his surname!

But the jealousy quickly melted away under her friend's familiar smile, her airy kiss on Elizabeth's cheek. "Now, dear, I must be off. After you have your tea, Bianca can show Nicholas to his room."

"R—room?" Elizabeth stuttered. Nicholas was to sleep *here*, under the same roof?

Oh, dear.

"Is that quite proper?" she asked.

"Oh, Lizzie, we are already a scandal! This one tiny thing cannot do us harm. And it is just the small room on the third floor. It will make things ever so much more *convenient*, will it not, Nicholas?" Georgina winked—winked!—at him.

"Oh, quite, Mrs. Beaumont." He winked back.

Bianca wriggled and giggled.

Elizabeth almost moaned.

Then she laughed hysterically when the drawing room door banged open to reveal Stephen, whose face was every bit as red as his hair, except for some modeling clay stuck to his forehead.

"You!" he roared, pointing a trembling finger at the tea-sipping Nicholas. "What are *you* doing here, annoying these ladies?"

"Stevie, dear," Georgina clucked. "He is hardly annoying us. He is Elizabeth's new secretary." Then she poured herself a cup of tea, and sat back to watch *commedia dell'arte* being played out in her very own drawing room.

Bianca snickered.

There was only one thing for a sensible girl like Elizabeth to do. She caught up her skirts and ran to the kitchen to fetch a pitcher of ice water to fling over their heads before they could destroy her drawing room.

Nicholas leaned back on the narrow bed of his third-story room, examining the calling card Georgina Beaumont had pressed into his hand the night before—the card that had begun this entire crazy odyssey of playing secretary. It was almost dawn, and the drunken party who had congregated in the alleyway below his window had at last departed, leaving him alone in the grayish silence just before light.

God's blood, but this task had been meant to be so very simple! A spoiled miss who had imprudently fled the protection of her stepbrother, was to be found and summarily returned to where her best interests would be looked after. He was merely to snatch up the silly girl and deposit her back on Peter's doorstep before he could have time to become at all deeply involved in this Everdean family drama. His debt to Peter, long unpaid, would be canceled when he delivered the girl, and he could return to his old life in the gaming rooms and courtesans' boudoirs of London.

He had a good life. He did. He was wealthy, a member of several interesting if disreputable clubs, and despite his scar women were drawn to him. He was the despair of his high-stickler stepmama and the father who only wanted to forget the reminder of his wicked youth that Nicholas was. He needed no complications, even when the complication was as delectable as Lady Elizabeth.

Nicholas reached beneath his pillow and withdrew the miniature that Peter had entrusted him with. Even in the dim half-light her painted eyes glowed a pale silver, as misty and deceptive as a Yorkshire moor or a London morning.

He could not deceive himself much longer. He had thought this would be the most simple of tasks, a jaunt across Italy, a mere trifle after years of warfare in Spain. An elfin beauty Elizabeth might be, and not silly and spoiled as he had thought. But she was still Peter's sister, and for some unfathomable reason, he wanted her back in his house. It was Nicholas's task—his *only* task—to see that that happened.

And playing at being a secretary seemed the simplest way to accomplish that.

Chapter Five

When Nicholas came downstairs for breakfast he was still a bit pale from his thought-filled night. Yet he managed a gallant bow and a bright smile.

"Good morning, Mrs. Beaumont. Miss Cheswood," he greeted. "It is obvious that nothing disturbed your beauty sleep. Venice could have no two fairer flowers in any of its gardens, by my faith."

It was a weak bon mot at best, but it made the women laugh, particularly Georgina. She waved him to the empty place setting at the small table, which was laden with plates of toast, pots of tea and chocolate, and small jars of marmalades and jellies.

"La, sir!" she said. "You obviously share my liking for the novels of the Minerva Press. I vow I read those very words in *Lady Charlotte's Revenge*. Quite an excellent work. Have you read it?"

"I fear I have not."

"I shall lend you a copy." Georgina poured out a cup of tea and passed it to him. "And did we not say you must call us Georgina and Elizabeth?"

"Indeed you must," said Elizabeth. She was engaged in buttering her toast, but paused to smile at him. "As you can see, we are hardly formal here."

Indeed they were not. Nicholas studied the small, sunny breakfast room while he sipped at the strong tea. Blank canvases were stacked along the walls, amid empty crates waiting for completed paintings to be packed in them and sent off to patrons. Plates and glasses were piled haphazardly on the sideboard, and linens peeked out of its almost-closed drawers.

Even the women's garments were unconventional. Georgina actually wore a dressing gown of burgundy velvet and had stuffed her auburn curls up into a snood, while Elizabeth was slightly more dressed in a yellow muslin round gown and paisley shawl.

Nicholas had never been in such a household. Even an army tent was carefully organized and regimented, and his mistresses' houses had been untidy and informal in a very studied way, their hair carefully coiffed even when they wore lingerie.

This home was strange, almost exotic.

It was wonderful.

"We were just discussing your first task," Elizabeth said, interrupting his ruminations.

"Oh, yes?" he answered. He smiled at her over the rim of his teacup.

She smiled in return, and blushed a very becoming peach. She even seemed more at ease with him this morning, after dousing him with water yesterday. Her eyes were clear and bright, her manner full of assurance.

She might very well be shy in matters of flirtation, but she was obviously a woman in full charge of her work. When she spoke of it, or even prepared to speak of it as she now did, her shoulders straightened and her cheeks grew bright with excitement.

"Yes," Elizabeth answered. "I did a very large

charcoal sketch some months ago for Signor Visconti, of his children. I have not yet received the promised payment. If you can collect it, you will have made a very promising beginning indeed." She pushed a small stack of papers toward him. "Here is the contract, and a description of all dealings I have had with Signor Visconti."

Nicholas nodded, and placed the papers carefully inside his jacket. "I will see to it at once."

"You should be warned," Elizabeth added, "that Signor Visconti is a dreadful old miser. He would rather crawl on broken glass than part with a single sou."

"He is also an old lecher," interjected Georgina. "He pinched my backside at a ball last month, and I could not sit for a full day!"

Nicholas laughed. "Do not fear, fair ladies! I am certain I can deal very effectively with both the miser *and* the lecher."

"Well," said Elizabeth, "I shall certainly be eternally grateful if you do."

Nicholas merely smiled.

Elizabeth was acutely conscious of Nicholas hovering at her shoulder, watching her as she painted, for several long moments before she lowered the brush and turned to face him.

Her hand was trembling far too much, and the leaves on the sun-drenched trees of the canvas were beginning to look rain-hazy.

"Yes?" she said, trying not to appear too calf-eyed as she looked up at him.

"That is a lovely portrait," he answered. "It is almost complete?"

"Yes." Elizabeth eyed the little girl's likeness proudly. It was indeed some of her finest work yet. The child's mischief shone in the glowing colors. "Fortunately. Beatrice is a beautiful girl, but I do not think she is destined to be an artist's model. She is rather . . ."

"Hoydenish?"

"No!" Elizabeth laughed. "I believe 'spirited' was the word I wanted, but hoydenish is even more accurate. This portrait would have been finished a fortnight ago if she had not been up and into mischief every five minutes."

"If her doting mama had disciplined her, instead of sitting in the corner eating bonbons . . ."

Elizabeth nodded wryly at the memory of Signora Farinelli's complete ineffectiveness. "I suppose, however, that it is a fond mama's way to be indulgent. Perhaps even overindulgent at times."

Nicholas's handsome face hardened, and he turned away. "Some mamas, perhaps."

Elizabeth's curiosity was piqued. "Yes. I know mine was, terribly. She let me wear party frocks all day long if I liked, and even let me drink from her wineglass at supper."

"Hmm."

"Yes. I was such a horrid brat." She wiped her hands on a rag and went to stand beside him, watching as he rifled through a pile of her sketches. "What was your mama like?"

He did not look up. "My mama?"

"Yes. Come now, you must have had one. I have serious doubts you sprang from your father's head fully grown, like Athena, and I am long past the age where I will be placated by stories of cabbage patches and storks."

That finally won a reluctant smile from him. "Yes, I had a mama, for whatever she was worth. She was not very much at home."

"Oh." Elizabeth sighed sympathetically. "And I suppose you were sent off to a school very young, too."

"Oh, yes. A horrid school where they beat us with birch branches and forced us to take cold baths."

Elizabeth glanced suspiciously at the dimple that had appeared in his cheek. "I do believe you are telling me a Banbury tale, Nicholas!"

"Indeed I am. There were only ever warm baths at my school."

She sat down on the red velvet chaise she used for models, and drew him down beside her. "What school did you go to?"

"Not one you ever would have heard of."

Elizabeth did not hear the evasive tone in his voice at all. She was far too busy admiring how good his dark hair looked against the red velvet, and how very beautiful his long-fingered hands were. With his hair falling in waves to his shoulders he looked like some pagan god of old. Dionysus at the feast.

How she wanted to paint him! She would place him in some ancient ruins, wearing only a coronet of laurel leaves. . . .

A giggle escaped before she could catch it.

"Is there something amusing?" he asked.

"No! No, I merely, well, um."

"What is it, Elizabeth?"

"Have you ever had your portrait painted, Nicholas?"

"You asked me that the night we met."

"Yes, but we were . . . interrupted, before you could answer."

"Well, I have not. Except once in miniature."

"For a girl who waited while you went away to war?" A jealous pang pierced her heart.

His dimple froze, and disappeared. "What makes you think I was at war?"

Elizabeth shrugged. "That is usually the purpose of a miniature, in these times. And I have thought that you have something of the bearing of a soldier, even if you never sit up straight. And there is your scar."

She prodded at his slouched shoulders, and he immediately shot up poker-straight.

"Yes," he said, "I was at war. But that was a very long time ago, and I have applied myself most diligently to forgetting it."

"Yes. Of course."

They fell silent, listening to the sounds from the street and Bianca singing in the next room. Elizabeth was all-too conscious of the sound of his breathing, of the warmth of his leg against hers. She imagined reaching her hand out to him, touching the silky fall of his hair, pressing her lips to the dimple in his cheek. . . .

She leaped up from the chaise.

"I . . . I just remembered an . . . an appointment." She gasped, not looking at him. "Very important. I must be going right away."

He stood up next to her, the sketches he had been looking at still in his hand. "I wanted to speak to you about the accounts."

"Yes, but I simply cannot now. I . . . I have to go!"
She turned on her heel and whirled out of the room.

Nicholas watched her go, a bemused expression on
his face.

"I asked Nicholas to accompany us to the opera,
Lizzie."

Elizabeth paused in brushing the snarls from her
black hair to turn and look at Georgina. Her friend
was lounging on Elizabeth's bed, already dressed in
her gown of gold tissue over bronze-colored satin,
and eating chocolates.

"You did what?" Elizabeth said, her brow raised.
"You asked him to go with us to the opera? But
Stephen is escorting us! After the other day . . ."

Georgina kicked her bronze satin shoes in delight.
"Wasn't it glorious, dear? Two men fighting over
you, in our very own drawing room. It is just too bad
you had to break it up like that, ruining the carpet
with all that water."

Elizabeth tugged harder at the brush, yanking out
several knots of hair in the process. "They smashed
up two chairs, Georgie! And they are not even *our*
chairs to break."

"Oh, pooh! They seem great friends now, Lizzie.
Did you not see them talking at Lady Lonsdale's tea
this afternoon? I only hope they can sober up enough
to get us to the opera in one piece." Georgina slid
off the bed and came to take over the brushing.
"Here, let me do that or you will soon be quite bald,
and that would never do. Not with the dashing Nicholas about."

Elizabeth smiled faintly, soothed by the hypnotic

glide of the brush through her hair. "He *is* handsome, is he not?"

"*Mais oui!* I knew he would be perfect for you."

"Um-hm." Elizabeth couldn't help teasing just a bit. "He *is* going to straighten out accounts for me. Very useful."

"Pah! Lizzie, if you think all a man like that is useful for is accounts then you do not deserve him. I have half a mind to steal him from you."

"Georgie!"

"I am only teasing, dear! He obviously belongs with you. I couldn't turn those marvelous dark eyes away from you if I ran through the Piazza San Marco in my chemise." Georgina laughed, and deftly twisted Elizabeth's hair up with black and silver ribbons. "Now, what will you wear?"

"That." Elizabeth threw off her dressing gown and picked up the black velvet and satin gown laid out on the bed.

Georgina clapped her hands. "Perfect! He will absolutely swoon when he sees you in that."

The black gown was quite the most daring thing Elizabeth had ever owned, bought on a whim in Rome and never worn. Transparent black tulle formed the long sleeves and draped at the décolletage, which dipped across the very rim of her bosom. If she were to so much as shrug, all her secrets would be revealed. It was as black and soft as the best kind of sin.

It was quite the gown a "scandalous artiste" would wear. And it was absolutely perfect for a gardenia-scented night in Venice.

Elizabeth had barely stepped into her black velvet

shoes when a slightly off-key rendition of "Plaisirs d'amour" floated up through the half-open window.

Giggling, Georgina and Elizabeth threw open the casement and leaned out to see Nicholas and Stephen balanced precariously in a gondola, evening capes thrown back to facilitate their serenade. Nicholas held aloft a bottle of fine brandy in one hand, while the other held Stephen back from falling into the canal headfirst.

"What are you doing?" Elizabeth called. "I would wager some gondolier has reported his vessel stolen tonight!"

"Oh, lady fair!" Nicholas answered. "I assure you that your chariot was most honestly come by! And your loyal charioteers await your bidding."

Elizabeth laughed down helplessly as his white grin lit up the night.

She had never, ever felt so giddy, so reckless, so *wonderful* in all her life as she did this instant. An evening of revels ahead of her, a handsome man waiting to be her escort, and the most beautiful gown ever created on her back. She did not need a gondola—she could fly.

Nicholas *did* almost swoon when he glimpsed Elizabeth in her black gown. Black was supposedly only for mourning, but on her it gained a new life.

She leaned forward from the window, her creamy bosom spilling from the bodice, and he very nearly pitched into the canal right beside the already-tipsy Stephen. She was all black and white, perfect elegance against the gray-pink stones of the house. She wore no jewels around her throat or in her ears, and only ribbons threaded through her hair, yet she shone.

During the long years in Spain, the months of waiting, he had harbored a secret fantasy, one he could never have shared with his carousing friends, or even with Peter. He had dreamed of a woman, an Englishwoman, soft and sweet-scented and wide-eyed, who had smiled a secret, gentle smile only for him. He had dreamed of sharing laughter with this woman, of dancing with her under an English moon, of a gaiety untinged with desperation. This dream had kept him going when all seemed covered by dust and death.

Perhaps, when he had gone ceaselessly from party to party after his return from the war he had been only seeking this dream woman. He had looked for her among English duchesses and English whores.

Yet he had had to travel to another land, to a place completely different from the England he knew, to a place of contradiction and enchantment, to find this dream. To see, in one fleeting moment, the truth of himself in the silver eyes of a woman who was as complex, as un-English, as Venice itself. Elizabeth Everdean was not at all what he had bargained for when he embarked from England on this wild chase.

She was certainly no milk-and-water miss, who would be easily led.

And then the brief flash of . . . *something* was gone, as a whiff of incense on the breeze. Elizabeth waved down at him then withdrew, shutting the window behind her. He was once again just a crippled bastard Englishman, alone in a foreign city and playing a role that he sensed could quickly become most irksome.

Elizabeth, magical Elizabeth, was going to hate him so.

"I hope you have saved some of that brandy!" she cried gaily, emerging from the house engulfed in a black velvet cloak, her features hidden with a white half-mask.

"You are late." Stephen hiccoughed. But the hand he held out to assist her was steady enough.

"Pooh! The opera has not even started yet. And who arrives on time in Venice?" Georgina answered him. She leaped aboard in a flurry of spangled skirts, nearly capsizing them all. "Now, hand me that bottle, and row, *mes amis!*"

Nicholas obeyed in silence, dipping his pole into water that now seemed as black and bitter as his own heart, and sent them off into the laughter-soaked night.

"Are you not enjoying the opera?" Elizabeth nudged her elbow into Nicholas's side, bringing his gaze from the stage where *The Coronation of Poppea* was being played out.

Things were becoming just the merest bit fuzzy around the edges from the two thimblefuls of brandy she had drunk, but even so she could see that he was troubled by something. There was a disturbing flatness to his eyes, a stillness about him when he always seemed to be in restless motion. At first she had feared that he disapproved of her, considered her the veriest hoyden in her daring gown and her brandy drinking.

It was more than that, though. He was acting just a bit like Peter had, when he had returned from the war so silent and searching . . . and haunted.

She gave Nicholas her sunniest smile, and leaned gently against his shoulder. It was a lovely night, and she was bedamned if she was going to allow a man's dark mood to ruin it! "I can see you do not," she whispered. "But never fear, Mr. Carter. We shall go on to the Princessa Santorini's ball after, and it is certain to be livelier. I have heard she is to have living statues, *naked* and painted white. I intend to do a great deal of sketching while we are there."

A faint but promising gleam broke through the opaqueness of his eyes. He raised her gloveless fingers to his warm lips and kissed them, one by one. "This morning you called me Nicholas. And I am not entirely sure you could even hold a drawing pencil. That brandy was very potent."

Elizabeth sighed at the delicious feelings invoked by the touch of his lips. "Are you implying that I, a *lady*, am foxed . . . Nicholas?"

"Not a bit. No one could ever be drunk from the miniscule amount you had. A little . . . happy, mayhap."

"Hmm." *I could be drunk on you*, she thought with a small smile. He tucked her hand into the crook of his arm, and she propped her chin on his shoulder. The feel of his soft hair against her cheek was absolute heaven. Deeply content, Elizabeth closed her eyes and listened to the music.

And reflected that never, if she had stayed in England and married into the *ton* as her brother wished, would she be allowed to behave so.

Suddenly, the music was interrupted by a brawl forming at the back of their box.

Georgina and Stephen had procured a bottle of champagne somewhere, and had begun the princessa's ball a bit early by steadily draining it. Now they were quarreling in fierce whispers.

Eventually Georgina lost her temper completely and actually pushed Stephen so hard he fell off his gilded chair with a resounding crash. Scandalized opera glasses turned in their direction, and even Nicholas was startled out of his sophistication enough to gape at them.

"It appears your suitor is being murdered by your sister," he murmured.

"Indeed." Elizabeth didn't even raise her head from his shoulder. "Georgie is my dearest friend in all the world, but at times she can be a bit, well, odd. I should absolutely know better than to take them about in public together. Something untoward always happens—a fire, a flood, a plague of locusts." She lifted one finger to his jaw and turned his eyes back to the stage. "Simply ignore them, and they will cease to make a spectacle of themselves."

The furor was indeed already dying down. Georgina had stopped giggling behind her fan, and helped Stephen to once again sit upright in his chair. He pretended to study the program.

Nicholas once again wondered just what he had embroiled himself in, getting involved with *artists*. Quarrels at the opera, maids dressed in bedsheets, what could happen next? His London friends were not precisely high sticklers for the proprieties, but this was something new again.

And, once again, something fascinating.

"I do think they might have shared that champagne with us," Elizabeth whispered. She kicked at the empty bottle that had rolled beneath her chair. "It would have been the polite thing to do."

"Shall I go fetch you some?" he asked.

Elizabeth considered, weighing the empty bottle at her feet against the warmth of his shoulder beneath her cheek. She decided she should have both. "Only if you will agree to share it with me."

He pressed a quick kiss into her palm, and stood. "I will return soon. Do not move, and do not get into trouble."

She laughed aloud, unmindful of the stares being directed once more at their box. "I will not, Nanny."

Somehow, Nicholas could not quite believe the angelic smile on her face.

"Nicky! Yoo-hoo, Nicky!"

Nicholas groaned at the sound of that silver-bell voice, light tones straight from the deepest reaches of his nightmares. He would have fled into the crowd flowing in and out of the opera house if heavily bejeweled fingers had not already latched onto his arm.

"It *is* you, Nicky!" Lady Evelyn Deake's violet eyes sparkled up at him from under darkened lashes. Her smile, carefully bright, was so brittle Nicholas almost expected her powdered cheeks to crack beneath it.

Long ago, when Nicholas had been newly home from Spain and feeling quite the monster with the red wound on his cheek and his stiff leg, Evelyn had briefly been his mistress.

He had been overly eager for a woman.

This was not at all a good thing. In point of fact, it was the very thing he had feared most, to encounter someone who had known him in London, before he could even decide what to do about Elizabeth. Though he should have realized it was a distinct possibility, with all the English who were flocking abroad.

But *Evelyn Deake*, of all people!

"Darling!" she cooed, smoothing back her golden ringlets. "I should have known it was you when I heard that someone was cavorting with those scandalous women artists. It is just your style!"

Nicholas debated pretending that he did not know Evelyn, that he had never heard of anyone called Nicholas, that he was Luigi and spoke no English. Yet even as the desperate thought flitted through his mind he dismissed it. He deeply regretted his long-ago, brief liaison with Evelyn, for now she knew him far too well to be put off by such flimsy deceptions. It would have to be a very good lie indeed to get past *her*.

"What a surprise, Evelyn," he said coolly, his dark lashes sweeping down to cover his dismay. He raised her jeweled hand, barely brushing the knuckles with his lips. "I would never have expected to see you in Italy. What can Lord Deake be thinking, to let himself be without your charming presence for so long?"

"You have not heard?" Evelyn fluttered her lacy fan and smiled her pointed cat's smile at him over its edge. "Dear Arthur went to his eternal reward last spring. Right in the very midst of the Season. Inconsiderate to the very end."

This explained the silvery gray of her gown. Evelyn used to favor the brightest reds and blues to be found in any modiste's. "My condolences. I had not heard. I was in Paris in the spring."

"Yes, so I heard. Political aspirations? Or merely wreaking havoc among all the little mademoiselles?"

Nicholas just bowed, as she trilled over her own wit.

"And now you have turned to the signorinas," she continued. "I suppose all the London beauties are wise to your charm now, Nicky."

Nicholas's gaze wandered over her shoulder to the handsome Venetian youth who stood a few feet from Evelyn, his Italian eyes practically smoldering with jealousy. "I see Italy is agreeing with *you*, Evelyn."

She threw a laughing glance at her escort. "You mean Alfredo? Yes, he *is* diverting. I am enjoying my stay in Venice enormously."

Nicholas forbore to point out how very mild the "scandalous" antics of Elizabeth and Georgina were in comparison with blatant dalliance with smooth-faced boys. "So you will be staying here for a time?"

She laughed again, that silvery artificial laugh that so grated on him. "My dear, I have purchased a house here. The Ca Donati. It is absolutely charming, if a trifle *old*, and, as you said, the Italians are treating me very well. I may never go back to London. Are *you* here for very long?"

Nicholas shrugged. "Only for a brief errand, I fear."

Evelyn pouted prettily. "How sad. I was so looking forward to renewing our acquaintance."

That would be when Venice sinks into the sea, he thought, but he said nothing and only swung his quizzing glass by its ribbon and watched her.

"But perhaps we can find time for a small tête-à-tête before you depart," she said.

"Can I confide a seceret in you, Evelyn?" he asked, his voice low and intimate.

Evelyn swayed toward him. "Oh, yes, darling," she breathed. "I do so love secrets!"

Nicholas smiled inwardly in satisfaction. The queen of the scandal-broth had not changed a bit. "I am here incognito. On a wager."

"A *wager*? Oh, darling, how too delicious!" Evelyn giggled, obviously planning the many letters she would fire off to her friends back in England. "Can you tell me the particulars?"

"Not at present, I fear. But I do need your assistance."

"Of course, darling!" Evelyn put her hand on his arm, drawing so near that he was made nauseous by her sweet perfume.

"You must not divulge my identity to anyone. It would make the wager null and void."

He could almost see her mind spinning, longing for a glimpse of the betting book so far away in White's. "Do you mean no one in Venice knows your true identity but me?"

"No one but you, Evelyn."

"Not even Mrs. Beaumont and her little sister?"

"No." *Especially not Mrs. Beaumont and her "little sister."*

Evelyn laughed again. He gritted his teeth and smiled.

"Marvelous, Nicky! And of course you can count on my discretion. Only do tell me one thing."

"What?" he asked warily.

"Which sister is it? The widow or the little gypsy?" Then Evelyn's gaze shifted, her smile turned sly. "Never mind, darling. I believe I can hazard a guess."

Nicholas looked back to see Elizabeth in the crowd,

watching them, poised for flight. Her shocked face, openmouthed and wide-eyed, was at such odds with her daring gown that he almost laughed.

Almost.

"Hell and damnation," he muttered, and ran a shaking hand through his black curls. With a swift farewell, he broke away from Evelyn's grasp and rushed after Elizabeth's swiftly disappearing figure.

Evelyn's violet eyes narrowed as she watched him go.

Chapter Six

Elizabeth could not forget the image of Nicholas deep in conversation with the blond woman, their heads bent close as she looked up at him with dewy eyes and stroked his sleeve with her be-ringed hand.

Elizabeth had fled the opera house in confusion, leaving him behind in her mad dash to find a gondola to take her to the ball.

The princessa's ball was delightful. She did indeed have living statues, though artfully draped in loincloths rather than completely nude, and there was an abundance of champagne. Georgina and Stephen had left off their arguing by the time they caught up with her, and all her artist friends were there and bombarding her with questions about her coveted Katerina Bruni commission. Nicholas, who had at last shown up on his own, was quite attentive, bringing her delicacies from the supper buffet and dancing with her awkwardly on his stiff leg.

It should have all been quite perfect, and would have been if she could have forgotten about the woman at the opera house, ceased wondering who she was, what they had been discussing so intimately.

She was *not* jealous. She wasn't. How could she possibly be? She did not even really know Nicholas. He was her employee, her secretary. A very tall, very attractive secretary, to be sure. . . .

Perhaps therein lay the difficulty, a tiny voice whispered in her mind. She did not really know Nicholas, and she wanted to. Very much.

All she truly knew was that he was English, and, by his voice and manners, not of a lower class. An impoverished or adventurous younger son of gentry, perhaps.

She had no idea of what his past held, how he had really come by his scar, what had driven him to seek employment in their eccentric household. He *could* be a criminal, though she sensed this was not so.

Elizabeth wanted to know all these things. She wanted to pierce the armor of his reticence, see past his dark eyes, know his secrets. She had always been deeply curious, and he was by far the most intriguing mystery she had ever encountered.

But knowledge could come with a high price—the revelation of her own secrets. That she was a runaway, a murderess. And that was a price she simply could not pay, not even to satisfy that burning curiosity.

What a conundrum! She almost wished she had never seen him at all, never been faced with this dizzying jumble of jealousy, curiosity, excitement, lust, fear. She had been happy before, traveling and honing her craft, and not feeling so lost and lonely as she had in England. Yet if she had never met him, she would never have heard his laugh, seen his dimple when he smiled, or watched the admiration in his eyes when he looked at her work.

Elizabeth buried her face in her hands, the music and champagne and confusion making her head ache abominably.

"Lizzie, are you ill?" Georgina laid her cool hand against Elizabeth's brow. "You feel overly warm."

Elizabeth managed a small smile. "I am just tired, Georgie. Truly."

"*Pauvre petite!* You have been working too hard, and here I have dragged you about to too many parties this week. Shall we go home?"

"No. You are having such a good time, I could never forgive myself if I took you away so early."

Georgina bit her lip. "I'll fetch Nicholas to take you home, shall I?"

"No! Not Nicholas. He is dancing with our hostess, see? I can go alone. It is not far."

"Alone? In Venice? I should say not!" Georgina tapped her chin thoughtfully. "I shall get your fussy old Stephen to see us both home, then, and I will come back when you are settled. Yes?"

Elizabeth nodded in relief. She was aching for her bed, for dreamless sleep, for a cessation of the mad whirl of thoughts in her head. "Yes."

But their escape was not to be so easy. As they prepared to step into the gondola that would carry them home, a silvery voice called . . .

"Yoo-hoo! Oh, are you going toward the Giudecca Canal? May we ride with you?"

Elizabeth groaned and shrank back into the hood of her cloak.

It was the golden-haired woman Nicholas had been speaking with at the opera, and with her a glowering, beautiful young Venetian man. The woman was waving and coming toward them. It was all far too much a coincidence—Elizabeth had never see this woman before in her life, and now here she was twice in the same night.

And Georgina was smiling and saying that that was precisely the direction in which they were going.

Lady Evelyn Deake was just the sort of English abroad Elizabeth most disliked encountering. And not simply because she had been seen in intimate conversation with the all-too-alluring Nicholas, either.

Their journey home, though not a great distance, was made longer by crowds of vessels filled with merrymakers. The shouts and screams and loud music were causing Elizabeth's head to throb, and Lady Deake's conversation was only making the situation worse. Even Georgina, usually so adept at deflating British pomposity, was only able to stare at Lady Deake in amazement while occasionally rolling her eyes in Elizabeth's direction.

Lady Deake had apparently been in Italy for several months, since the death of her "dearest Arthur," and found nothing to be to her exacting standards (except, to all appearances, for the sullen-mouthed Alfredo, whose hand never left her leg). She chattered about her home in London, which was *ever* so much larger and brighter and grander in every way than the crumbling old Ca Donati, which she recently purchased from the *very* disagreeable Marchese Donati. The servants in her London home were also a great deal more efficient than these lazy, dark Italians, who lounged about all day doing absolutely nothing to earn their wages. Italian food was so very upsetting to the digestion, and Italian women knew *nothing* about fashion (this said with long glances at

Elizabeth's and Georgina's gowns), and some of them could not even speak *English*. . . .

Elizabeth gradually drifted from the vivacious stream of complaints, leaning back on the cushions and studying the masked and costumed figures of the other groups, who were unfairly having fun. She had heard similar opinions many times, from English travelers from Milan to Messina, and now she merely smiled at Lady Deake while not hearing a single word she was saying.

She longed to, just this once, lose her temper and snap, *Cease your prattling at once, you silly woman!*

Unfortunately, she was no longer Lady Elizabeth Everdean, sister of the Earl of Clifton. She was Elizabeth Cheswood, scandalous artist who had to earn her bread. And she had heard of the Veronese fresco cycle in the Ca Donati, which was in dire need of restoration. Rumor had it that the new owner—now revealed to be Lady Deake—was looking for an artist to complete the task. It was a plum of a commission, and Elizabeth had wanted it.

Truth be told, she still wanted it.

She was quite aching to get her brushes on the Veronese, and that was the only thing that kept the prattling Lady Deake from plunging headfirst into the canal at Elizabeth's hands. That and her curiosity about Nicholas.

". . . do you, Miss Cheswood?"

Elizabeth blinked at the sound of her name, floating back down into the reality of their overcrowded gondola and the overpowering scent of the other woman's perfume. "I beg your pardon, Lady Deake?"

Evelyn tittered. "Lost in some artistic rapture, no doubt, Miss Cheswood!"

"Um, quite."

"Venice is *so* full of *scope* for the imagination."

Elizabeth somehow doubted that Lady Deake's imaginative scope had ever gone any further than matching bonnet to redingote, but she merely nodded and tried to look romantically artistic.

Evelyn continued. "I was just asking what you, as another Englishwoman, have found most intriguing about the Italian . . . landscape."

Elizabeth thought of Nicholas's velvet dark eyes, and blurted, "The men."

Evelyn tittered again, running one polished fingertip along Alfredo's arm. "Oh, yes, I quite agree! Englishmen have nothing to the *mystery* of the Italians." She smirked. "Most Englishmen, that is."

The gondola at last bumped to a halt before the looming shape of the Ca Donati, and they were soon on their way again, sans two passengers, amidst a trilled "Ciao!" from Lady Deake. Elizabeth was not sure if she was profoundly relieved or rather disappointed. The conversation had just been growing interesting.

Georgina burst out laughing as soon as the great brass doors shut behind Evelyn and her Italian. Elizabeth fell against her in helpless mirth, the two of them chorusing "Ciao!" under Stephen's bewildered gaze.

"I thought she was very . . . vivacious," he said.

That only made them laugh louder, the gondola swaying with the force of their hilarity.

"Oh, the mystery of Italian men!" Georgina simpered. "Not as *tidy* as Englishmen, of course, and so dark, but what eyes, what hands!"

"What backsides!" Elizabeth crowed. "But, Georgie, *you* were the one who let her accompany us. This is all on your head."

"Someone at the ball told me she was the new owner of the Ca Donati, and I wanted to hear about her Veronese. But alas, the woman is too silly to realize what she has." Georgina sighed. "Lady Deake quite reminds me of why I left England in the first place. How do those London misses ever tolerate it, Lizzie? All that money—all that lack of sense."

"I never *was* a London miss, Georgie, just a country mouse. After you left Miss Thompson's School to run away with Jack, I never had any excitement at all. The same people, the same parties, all the time." Elizabeth closed her eyes, listening to the soft slap of the oars in the water, the laughter all around her. The sweet-sick smell of the canal, smoky torches, perfumes, and flowers was thick in her throat and nostrils. She was suffused with Italy, and England, the place of secrets and silly people like Lady Deake, seemed quite far away.

Or perhaps too dangerously close.

Elizabeth inadvertently cried out, pressing her fist against her mouth.

"Lizzie!" Georgina cried, reaching for Elizabeth's cold hand. "What is it? Are you feeling ill again?"

"No, no, nothing like that." Elizabeth tried to smile reassuringly. "It is only . . . oh, Georgie, promise me we will never leave this place! Never go back to England."

"Dearest, what has brought this on? Is it merely

Lady Deake and her prattling? Or . . . have you heard from your brother and you did not tell me?''

Elizabeth shook her head. "I did not mean to alarm you, dear. I simply love our life here so. I like not having to be so careful all the time of what I say or do, for fear of being censured by some dowdy old duchess. I like wearing gowns like this one instead of fusty pastels, and drinking champagne, and painting all day. I . . .'' She broke off in a sob.

"Lizzie! Shh!" Georgina gathered her into a hug. "It will not change. We will never go back. Even if we did return to England, as we very well may one day, it would not be like that again. We are different. We will always be free.''

"Promise me?''

"I promise. Why do you think I ran away with Jack all those years ago?''

Elizabeth sniffed, and gave a watery smile. "His dashing red regimentals?''

"Well, yes. But more than that, he offered to take me away from the tedium of Miss Thompson's and away to Portugal. You were the only bright spot in that gray cloister, Lizzie, and I was soon to finish and leave you anyway.'' Georgina patted her hand consolingly. "It is only that silly Lady Deake upsetting you. But you are safe here, Lizzie.''

"Safe," Elizabeth whispered. "Yes.''

That night, for the first time in many months, Elizabeth dreamed of Clifton Manor. Of Peter.

It was hardly surprising, since she had been dwelling on England and the past so much of late. Not even a glass of warm milk liberally laced with brandy had been able to help tonight, and all those memories came flooding up from where she had so firmly pressed them down and down.

In her dream, she was eighteen again, filled with youthful passion for her art, wild dreams of escaping Derbyshire and running off to a Parisian garret (as soon as Boney could be persuaded to quit the country and make its garrets safe for Englishwomen). The countryside was dull, there was no one to talk with but their neighbors, the giggling spinster Misses Allan and old Lady Haversham, and Peter always seemed so angry with her. Angry, and cold, and beautiful as an ice storm.

In the beginning of this dream, he came to her again in her makeshift studio, sunlight all around them from the high, unshuttered windows. His long fingers were hard on her arms, biting into the soft flesh bared by her puffed-sleeved gown, but she hardly felt it. His voice, rough and low, unrecognizable from his usual patrician tones, came to her as if from a very far distance.

"I cannot bear it any longer." He gasped. "You were put here just to torment me, Spanish harlot. The way you look at me, the way you talk." His eyes swept over her. "Just as she did."

She stared up at him, at his familiar features distorted in almost-painful passion, at the way the sun turned the silver gilt of his hair to a halo. She was shocked, numb, utterly stricken. She wanted to scream, to cry, to run, but she was paralyzed. She could only stand there in his grasp.

His hands pulled her against him, raising her on tiptoe so that his watch chain pressed into her tender belly. His breath was warm as his lips trailed across her cheek.

"No!" she cried out, her voice dismayingly faint. "No, this is wrong. You are my brother!"

"What new trick is this? Your *brother*?"

And she knew then that he did not see her, Elizabeth. But she did not know what it was he did see. She broke free, running behind her easel, her breath bursting from her.

"Then you will have to marry someone else," he murmured, almost to himself. "You must go away from here, because I cannot look at you anymore."

He reached for her again, but his long, pale hand became the Duke of Leonard's twisted, arthritic claw, pinching at her. She looked up at Peter, but his face was horrible now, wrinkled, the spittle flying from the corner of his mouth as he cackled, "Whore! Murderess!"

She heard a woman's shrill laughter, and looked to see Lady Deake, golden and perfect in a white gown, laughing with malice.

The spittle at the duke's mouth became blood, a great scarlet flood of it, and she was drowning, drowning, awash in the blood and guilt and fear. Drowning . . .

Elizabeth came awake with a gasp, sitting straight up amid her twisted sheets. A Venetian moon lit up even the corners of her small room, revealing only the benevolent clutter of gowns and hats and canvases.

The duke was long dead, and Peter was very far away.

"Oh," she whispered, and fell back against her pillows. "Oh."

She had to laugh, once her heart slowed in her breast. It was quite ridiculous, really, to become so overwrought over a dream vision of the duke and Lady Deake behaving like bad street fair players. Silly.

If only that horrid scene in her studio at Clifton Manor had not really happened, once in another lifetime. If only she could forget it now.

If only she did not truly have blood on her hands.

Elizabeth lay on her wide, white-curtained bed, the blankets kicked into a heap at her feet, moonlight and a cold breeze flowing from the open window, her eyes focused on the plastered ceiling above her. And she allowed all those memories to wash over her, the beautiful ones along with the ugly. She let herself be Lady Elizabeth Everdean again.

Chapter Seven

Elizabeth had been six years old when her mother, Isobel, a dashing widow and a true Diamond of the First Water, had left merry widowhood behind to marry the equally dashing Charles Everdean, the Earl of Clifton. Only six when they left their crowded town house for Clifton Manor, and what Isobel called "Your new father and brother, darling."

Elizabeth had liked Charles, who had allowed her to take his name, and she had idolized Peter. Twelve years her senior, he had been everything she could have wanted in an elder brother. He had taught her to ride her pony, had read her books from the vast Clifton library, had protected her from their parents' many noisy quarrels.

After Isobel and Charles died when Charles's high-perch phaeton had overturned during a race, Peter had cared for her tenderly. Mourned with her, encouraged her budding interest in art, arranged for her education at Miss Thompson's School, and even taken her to London once to visit the Elgin Marbles.

Then he had purchased his commission and been off to Spain, to be shot at and send her infrequent letters. Until the letters trickled to a mere handful, and then ceased altogether.

When he returned, he had not been at all the same Peter. Her golden, laughing brother had been replaced by a bitter stranger. A stranger who drank far too much, who lurked in his dark library, and forbade her to give parties until her very few local friends dropped away. A stranger who stared at her with glowing blue eyes and yet seemed not to see her. He even provoked quarrels with her, until the temper she had inherited from Isobel would loom up, and she would scream and throw things like the veriest fishwife.

After that horrid scene in her studio, Elizabeth realized she could not live with Peter any longer. She agreed to the betrothal with the Duke of Leonard, some political crony of Peter's, only to escape, thinking that nothing could be worse than the prison Clifton Manor had become.

How very, very wrong she had been.

Elizabeth was torn from her memories by a sound from the small terrace outside her open window. The tap of a cane, as soft as cat's paws. She pushed back the blankets and slid out of bed, threw on her dressing gown, and crept outside.

"Hello, Nicholas," she said, somehow not at all surprised to see him awake so far past the witching hour. There was, after all, a sort of fatedness about a moonlit night during Carnivale that made all things seem possible.

He was barefoot, clad only in an open shirt and black trousers as he leaned back against the marble balustrade. The red tip of his thin cigar glowed in the darkness, and the moonlight gleamed off the half-empty crystal snifter of brandy balanced next to him.

The night was chill, but he did not seem to feel it, and neither did she.

"I did not mean to wake you," he said, his voice rough with smoke and brandy. "Georgina said you were feeling unwell."

"I am feeling much better. And I was already awake." Elizabeth saw the brandy, and gestured toward it. "May I?"

He wordlessly held the snifter out to her. They stood in companionable silence, with Nicholas looking down at the canal and Elizabeth looking at his bare chest. At the way the light dusting of black hair across the smooth muscles disappeared into his waistband. His skin looked like Georgina's gold satin dress, and Elizabeth longed to rub her palm across it and see if it was as sleek as it looked, to press her lips against the joining of his neck and collarbone. She wanted to bury her nose in that hair and inhale deeply of his clean, spicy scent.

That clean smell that seemed to wash away all the wickedness she had seen.

Elizabeth shook her head fiercely to clear it. "I had such dreams," she said. "I could not go back to sleep."

Nicholas took a long sip of brandy before he answered. "It is this place."

"This place?"

"Venice." He waved the red glow of his cigar at the houses, sleeping pale gray in the twilight. "There is witchcraft in it. It must have enchanted your dreams."

She was startled. She would never have thought him the poetic sort. Intelligent, flirtatious, and even appreciative of art, yes. But not poetic. "That it has. But a very good sort of enchantment."

"Even though it disturbs your sleep?"

"Even then."

"And the same enchantment is not to be found in England?"

"No. That is exactly why I love it here. It is like no place else—especially *not* England."

"Do you ever think of going back there?" he asked. "To your home?"

Elizabeth narrowed her eyes as she looked at him. There was a sort of tension in him now, a stillness, a waiting. This was not just idle chatter, she felt. He wanted something from her, wanted her to say something, but she could not begin to fathom what. She reached for his brandy and took another fortifying swallow before she answered. "I *am* home."

"Yet surely you miss England. Surely your life there was easier than it is here, wandering like a nomad," he pressed.

"Easier!" The memory of her recent dream, of Peter and the dead duke, was still fresh and powerful, and she lashed out at this gorgeous man who seemed strangely intent on bringing all that ugliness into the light. "Easy, to be nothing but a prisoner, to be helpless and never free to be myself? You know nothing of me, Nicholas, or my life in England. You don't know what it was like when Georgina left. You don't know what Italy, what being here, means to me."

"No," he answered quietly. "I do not."

"No." Elizabeth was suddenly tired, achingly tired to her very toes. And appalled at how very much she had almost revealed.

"Will you tell me, Elizabeth?"

"Tell you?"

"About your life in England." He placed his hand over hers where it rested on the balustrade, his palm warm and comforting. He was a cipher to her, but he was so large and solid. It was tempting, just for a moment, to lean against him and put all her worries onto those wide shoulders.

But only for a moment. To give up her hard-won independence would be so dangerous. What if this man came to hear of what she had done? He would hate her, and could even turn her in to the authorities.

She wiped at her damp cheeks, and stepped away from his tempting warmth.

"Please," he said softly. "I want to know."

"There is not much to tell," she answered, forcing a lightness she was far from feeling into her tone. "I had a very ordinary life there, one some women would find enviable."

"Not you." It was not a question.

"No. I could not breathe," she admitted. "I was . . . drowning. I had to leave, or lose myself completely. I had a certain security, but it was not enough."

"You had family there?" His voice was tight.

For an instant, Elizabeth thought of Peter as he had once been, golden bright and laughing, swinging her into the air to hear her childish giggles. She shook her head. "No. Georgie is my only family."

"You left a secure life in England for the uncertainties of a life abroad? You and your . . . sister?"

"Yes. It sounds insane, I know. Perhaps it *is* insane."

"No. Not insane. I understand the need to escape."

Elizabeth studied the glow of his eyes in the night, and somehow she knew. "You *do* understand. You understand why I left comfortable respectability to become an artist, a professional artist and not some drawing room dabbler. Why I won't go back."

He gave a sharp bark of singularly humorless laughter. "Respectability is quite overvalued, my dear. You were absolutely correct to run in the opposite direction."

"Is that what you are doing, Nicholas? Running from something?"

"Isn't everyone doing that, in one way or another?"

"Yes. But everyone's *something* is different." Elizabeth turned to him, giving in to the temptation to place her palm against his skin, against the strong beat of his heart. "What is your something, Nicholas? What are you running from? And what does your heart want more than anything else?"

"I do not know." He put his hand over hers, pressing her paint-stained fingers into his skin. "Perhaps to escape from myself. To cease being myself, for just one day, and become someone . . . better."

"I told you why I left England," she whispered. "Will you tell me why you left?"

"I was searching for something. A lost object."

"What was it?"

He smiled crookedly. "Maybe it was you, sweet Elizabeth."

She tried to push back. "Don't tease."

He held her, refusing to let her leave. "I am not teasing. Far from it."

Then he bent his head and kissed her, softly at first, his cool lips barely brushing hers. But when she offered no objection, he deepened the pressure, bending her back over his arm as he kissed her deeply, warmly, seekingly. She had never, ever been kissed like this before, and it was utterly delicious.

Elizabeth finally drew back slightly, drawing the breath deeply into her starved lungs. She stared up at him, dazed. Slowly, details like the cold marble balustrade against her back, his hand on her hip, began to penetrate the pink haze of her passion.

She trailed one fingertip over his features, his glistening lips, the pale scar. "Oh, Nicholas," she breathed, unable to say anything else. "Oh, Nicholas."

Chapter Eight

"Oh, *cara! Molto bene!*" Katerina Bruni, the famous courtesan, purred. She stretched on the red velvet chaise, her emeraldlike eyes never leaving the figure of Nicholas, who was bent over the account books at Elizabeth's desk and taking no notice of anything else.

Even when the loose sleeve of Katerina's blue velvet robe slid off her shoulder and she took her own time shrugging it back into place.

Elizabeth couldn't help but giggle just a little. She turned away to mix a bit more of the blue pigment.

"Where *did* you discover him, Signorina Cheswood?" Katerina continued. "I never saw him before the princessa's ball last night."

"And you know every man in Italy?" Elizabeth teased.

Katerina laughed. "I do, I do! All the ones worth knowing. It is my business. But your new—secretary, is it?"

"Yes."

"He is something different. Very handsome, very mysterious." Katerina tapped at her chin with one pink fingernail. "Yet very serious at the moment. Must be English, no?"

Elizabeth giggled again. Nicholas, serious? She truly liked Katerina Bruni, not something to be said for most of her clients. Signora Bruni showed up as scheduled for her sittings, sat still, and her "patron" always paid the bills on time. She was also an amusing conversationalist, and Elizabeth valued her opinions on men and business. But obviously her powers of observation were not so acute where Nicholas was concerned.

"He *is* English. But, between us . . ." Her voice dropped to a whisper. "Seriousness is not among his many qualities."

It was Katerina's turn to laugh. She covered her mouth with her white feather fan, the sapphires in its handle catching the sunlight from the windows. "So what are some of the qualities he *does* possess? Or is that too, um, private?"

Elizabeth thought of the previous night, of their kiss on the terrace, of his hands on her back, his lips warm and soft on hers. She could feel her cheeks pinkening. "Oh, assuredly private, Signora Bruni!"

Katerina pouted a bit. "*Cara*! And after all I have told you about the marquis. Am I not your friend?"

"Well . . ." Elizabeth glanced at Nicholas from the corner of her eye. "He *does* have the grandest . . ."

"Is there something amusing over there, ladies?" Nicholas called out.

Elizabeth and Katerina both started guiltily and looked away. Katerina fanned herself vigorously, and Elizabeth busied herself mixing more pigment.

"Oh, not at all!" she answered. "Signora Bruni was just telling me a bit of interesting gossip she heard at the ball last night."

"Oh? And would you care to share it?"

He sounded so very much like the stern Miss Thompson at her old school that Elizabeth laughed out loud again. When she turned to him to share this, however, he looked so very forbidding that she merely shook her head. "It would not interest you, Nicholas."

"Hmm." He shut the account book he had been perusing, and rose to his feet. "I must run an errand. I will see you after tea."

Elizabeth frowned. "Very well. Don't forget about the Vincenzis' party tonight."

"I will not. Good afternoon, Elizabeth. Signora Bruni." He bowed, and was gone.

"Now, then, Signorina Cheswood," Katerina said. "He is gone, and you can tell me all. Is that *dolce* man your lover? And if he is not, would you object if I tried my luck?"

"No!" Elizabeth cried, appalled at the thought of Nicholas in the very alluring arms of Signora Bruni. "Well . . . that is, he is not my lover. Not precisely. We have . . . kissed, that is all."

"Ah, but some kisses are enough, yes?"

"I . . . yes. Some kisses are quite enough." Elizabeth shook her head. She had not stuttered so very much since she had learned to talk.

"Then," Katerina continued, "you must want him as your lover."

"No. I . . ." *I want him as my husband.* Elizabeth almost dropped her paintbrush in shock at the unbidden thought. As it was, she trailed a long streak of blue over the creamy expanse of painted shoulder.

"I see." Katerina nodded wisely. "Well, *cara*, it is simple enough. I shall loan you one of my black silk chemises. They are always successful."

Elizabeth placed the brush carefully into the jar of turpentine, her hands shaking so much she feared for the rest of the painting.

"Are we finished for the day, Signora Bruni?" she said.

"Hmm? Oh, yes, I must be at the dressmaker's in half an hour. Shall I see you on Tuesday?"

"Yes, Tuesday."

After Katerina had departed, Elizabeth busied herself tidying up, cleaning off the ugly blue streak, but her mind was miles away.

Nicholas, a *husband*? She, Elizabeth, a *wife*? It was such an absurd idea!

She had vowed never to marry, to put her art first. Now here were visions of country churches. And large, cozy marriage beds.

"Stop that right this moment!" she told herself sternly, as she struggled to push the chaise back against the wall. "You are being a nodcock, and it must cease now before it begins to affect your work."

She collapsed onto the chaise, and stared up at the ceiling in utter confusion.

All the worry and fuss was probably for naught, anyway. Nicholas had been very distant and preoccupied ever since he had come to breakfast that morning, not looking at her, not speaking to her directly if he could avoid it. He seemed, in point of fact, to be thinking of something far away, and not her and what had happened between them at all.

That kiss, that wonderful, glorious kiss had obviously not affected him as it had her. She had longed to run to him as soon as she awoke that morning, to feel his arms around her, keeping her safe.

He had appeared to want to run *from* her.

"Perhaps I made far too much of a small thing," she mused aloud.

That was, unfortunately, entirely possible. She did not have the experience Nicholas did. What was earth-moving to her was probably a mere diversion to him, a pleasant interlude.

"Oh!" she whispered in abject confusion. "Why can love not be simple?"

She needed advice—badly.

Benno ("No last names, signor") was a very disreputable character indeed. His hair fell in greasy black hanks from beneath a battered hat; his coat was full of holes; and his stench rivaled that of the fetid alley where Nicholas stood speaking with him. Still, Benno did seem to know his business. And he had been highly recommended by the people Nicholas had been talking to in the tavernas in the previous days.

"So, signor." Benno's bloodshot gaze shifted around them, always searching. "You require a kidnapping. Of a lady."

Nicholas did not at all like the way Benno licked his lips at the mention of the word "lady." "I require *assistance* at a kidnapping. I will stay with the lady the entire time."

"Eh?" Benno's eyes narrowed in disappointment. "Then what do you need Benno for, if you do it all yourself?"

"You are more familiar with Venice, the back ways, the . . . more flexible officials. I need assistance in making certain the lady is taken safely out of Venice, out of Italy, without being detected by her friends."

"Benno *does* know the back ways of Venice, true." His grimy face still reflected dismay at the loss of being alone with his abductee. Yet other, more mercenary, concerns soon took over his disappointment. "Benno does not come cheap, signor."

"No, indeed. I never supposed Benno did." Nicholas reached into his many-caped greatcoat and withdrew a hefty purse, clinking invitingly with coins. Benno snatched at it, but Nicholas deftly held it out of his reach. "This is a small payment. There will be another purse when our task is complete and the lady is out of Italy."

"Signor . . ."

"If you accept this payment, Benno, I expect service. If you take it into your head to cheat me, I will find you and you will regret it. Are we understood?"

"Oh, yes, signor, yes! Benno would never cheat you. Never. I am an honest businessman."

An honest extortionist and kidnapper. How novel. "Good. See that you remain so." Nicholas delivered the purse into Benno's eager hands. "Then listen closely. This is what I require. I want a gondola, a covered gondola, waiting tomorrow afternoon at a location I will send you word of. I will need blankets, and a quantity of laudanum."

"Oh, yes, signor. Benno will take care of it all."

"Excellent. Now get out of here. I will send you word shortly."

Benno's shuffling footsteps soon died away, and Nicholas was alone in the dark, stinking alleyway. But he did not see the tottering piles of refuse, or the rats who peered at him from the shadows. He only saw Elizabeth, as she had been on the terrace, pale in the moonlight, smiling up at him after he had kissed her so improperly.

He felt again the way she had leaned into him, the way her mouth fit so perfectly with his. The cool silk of her hair in his fingers. The trust shimmering in her eyes.

She was extraordinary, unlike any woman he had ever known before. Sophisticated but with a glowing innocence still in her eyes, alluring and beautiful but totally unaware of it. The way she moved, and laughed, and thought was utterly unique. He could have spent months, *years*, watching her, studying her, and still never have discovered all the facets of her. She was always surprising him.

He knew she would be beautiful and fascinating when she was ninety.

And it was when he realized this, last night, that he had known he had to move. He had to make this business over and finished before he could not do it at all. Before he snatched up Elizabeth and ran with her, to Turkey or China or America, or anyplace where they would never be found and where he could spend all his days watching her.

He had to forget about her. He had to think only of Peter, and his promise. He owed the man his *life*! And all Peter wanted in exchange was . . .

Nicholas's very heart.

"Elizabeth," he whispered. "My dear. I am so very, very sorry."

But only the rats were there to hear him, to watch him cry for the first time in years. The first time since he had been told Peter was dead in Spain.

*　　*　　*

That afternoon, with no warning, the heavens opened and a deluge poured down. And Venice was impossibly dismal.

Georgina lay on the settee, wrapped in her warmest dressing gown after being caught in the rain on her way home from a sitting, and became engrossed in the latest horrid novel from England. Elizabeth sat in her corner, attempting to work some more on the Katerina Bruni portrait. Her brush moved over the canvas methodically, but she could not seem to concentrate on the courtesan's pouting expression, or on giving her green eyes the sparkle that was so much a part of her.

Elizabeth's thoughts kept flying to the kiss again, and Nicholas's strong shoulders beneath her hands. When she tried to shade a long curl, she instead saw him smiling down at her as they floated on a sun-drenched canal while he tried to steer their gondola.

Her brush moved of its own accord, and she soon found she had painted in the margins of the canvas, not the dusky Katerina, but a laughing Nicholas.

"Oh, no!" Elizabeth stared, aghast, at her painting. "This must cease!"

"What?" Georgina looked up from her book. "Did you say something, Lizzie?"

Elizabeth tossed her brush aside and went to look out the window at the unceasing rain. The gray torrent had driven all the merrymakers indoors, and the city was deserted. Only a few bedraggled streamers and blossoms gave a tiny splash of color.

"I said this rain has to cease," she said, tracing one fingernail through the mist on the windowpane. "Or it will ruin the Vincenzis' party tonight."

"Indeed, it was meant to be in their grand gardens.

Such a shame if it is spoiled, and you do not get to dance under the stars with the divine Nicholas!"

"Oh, Georgie, really." Elizabeth's rebuke was faint. She *had* daydreamed of dancing under a star-strewn sky in Nicholas's strong arms.

"Is that all that is worrying you, Lizzie?" Georgina put her book aside, and sat up.

"What else could it be?"

"I do not know. Nicholas? The two of you looked so happy at the opera yesterday. You could not stop looking at each other."

"Oh, yes, it was lovely!" Elizabeth paused. "And . . . and last night, he kissed me."

"Lizzie, how marvelous!"

"Yes. Marvelous." Elizabeth's voice was small, even to her own ears.

"Then what is wrong, dear? You are attracted to him, he is attracted to you, you are spending time together. . . ."

Elizabeth left the window and went to sit next to her friend, tucking an extra lap robe around her chilled shoulders. "Georgie, I need your help."

"Whatever you need, Lizzie. You only need ask."

"I need you to tell me about your marriages."

Georgina's eyes widened. "My marriages? But, Lizzie, you know all about them! And none of them lasted long enough to be really interesting."

"I know their names, but I do not *know* about them. About your feelings for them. Your letters when we were apart were always about your work, the people you were meeting. Never about your husbands."

"Well." The unflappable Georgina Beaumont somehow seemed at a loss for words. Her mouth opened and closed a few times before she spoke again. "Well, Lizzie, you know I will tell you whatever you want to know, but why this sudden desire to know this?"

"I do not know! I thought perhaps, oh, this is so foolish . . . I . . . I wish to know more about men."

"Oh." Georgina fell back against her pillows. "But, Lizzie, you know about men! There is Stephen, as silly as he is; Paolo; Luigi; the Duc d'Evagny, who wanted to give you carte blanche . . ."

"Oh, them! I never felt the least bit tempted to confide in them. To be intimate with them."

"As you do with Nicholas."

"I may be. Yes. But . . ."

"But what?"

"But if I give in to my feelings, will he turn on me? Betray me, as Peter did? Are all men like Peter?"

"I see." Georgina chewed thoughtfully on her thumbnail. "Dear, it is quite understandable that you should feel this way, that you should be so wary of giving your trust again. Peter treated you shockingly. I knew he was a bad 'un, even when we were at school. It is a miracle you can even think of being close to another man."

"Yes! That is just what I fear."

"Well, Lizzie, let me assure you that not all men are like Peter Everdean. They are out there, oh yes, and you must be careful of them. Like my second husband, Sir Everett."

The two women shuddered in concert. The late, unlamented Sir Everett had been quite wealthy; indeed, his wealth had paid for the small villa at Lake Como. But he had also been quite fat and quite temperamental. He had bred yappy French poodles on his country estate, and Georgina had often been compelled to tend their kennels.

"You must always avoid men who wear corsets and gorge themselves on fig pudding at all costs," Georgina now admonished. "I would never have looked twice at him, if I hadn't been so desperate when Jack died. And then, you see, there *are* men like Jack."

The friends sighed in remembrance. Captain Jack Reid had been tall, blond, charming, dashing in his regimentals. He had been a younger son with few prospects, but all the girls at Miss Thompson's had been quite in love with him. Georgina, older than Elizabeth and quite dashing herself, had been the envy of the school when she had eloped with him to Gretna Green and then gone with him to Portugal. He had been killed there.

"Oh, Lizzie," Georgina said. "Our rough months in those drafty billets were . . . perfect."

"Jack *was* handsome," Elizabeth answered.

"And as good as he was handsome." Georgina twisted on her wrist the narrow pearl bracelet he had given her, which never left her person. "He was not the most intellectual man, true, but he loved that I wanted to be an artist."

"What of Mr. Beaumont?"

"Ah, well, Lizzie, you needn't fear that Nicholas will be another Mr. Beaumont." Aloysius Beaumont, wealthy cit, had been all of seventy-six when he had married Georgina, and seventy-seven when she buried him. He had been elderly, but generous.

"And rather nice, when he could recall who I was," Georgina said. "And if it were not for him, we could never have had the things we do on the pittance Sir Everett's children allow me."

"And what a shame *that* would have been! Every grocer and dressmaker in Italy would be destitute," Elizabeth teased.

"So, my dear, perhaps you should take a chance with Nicholas. You need not tell him quite *everything*, even if you are lovers. He may turn out to be your Jack. Or at least an amusement."

Elizabeth hugged Georgina, but in her heart she was screaming, *But what if he does not want to be my Jack?*

Chapter Nine

"You are very late."

Nicholas paused at the sound of Elizabeth's voice, still poised over the candle he was lighting. Slowly, he turned to look at her.

Elizabeth sat, very still and pale, in the corner of the dark foyer, hands folded in her lap as she watched him. She was dressed for a party, in sky-blue muslin trimmed in white satin ribbon, her hair plaited and caught up in ivory combs.

She looked like the Parmigianino Madonna, all slender neck and mysterious, downcast eyes.

"I thought perhaps you had had a contretemps with an irate client," she continued, coming to take the flint from his frozen fingers and lighting the candle herself. "You are not one to forget a party."

He slapped his open palm against his forehead. "The Vincenzis' party! I was to escort you. I am sorry, Elizabeth. I was just . . . walking. I lost track of the time."

"That is quite all right. As it is raining, we can't go out into their lovely gardens anyway. Everyone will be smothering in their tiny ballroom. Georgina has gone ahead." She smiled up at him, her mouth turning suddenly down as she saw his hair dripping onto the carpet. "You must be frozen through! Come into the kitchen where there is a fire, before you catch the ague."

Nicholas allowed her to lead him into the warm kitchen, and fuss over him with towels and warm kettles. But he, who had never had a modest day from the time he could toddle away from his nurse and pull off his nappy, balked when she asked him to remove his shirt.

"Wh—what?" he stammered.

"I said you should remove your shirt," Elizabeth answered calmly, stirring at the brewing tea. "It is soaked through."

"I am not certain that is a very good idea."

Elizabeth laughed. "Oh, please, Nicholas! Do not go missish now. Your teeth are chattering, and if you make yourself ill I will not see a farthing of payment for a month." She slanted him a sly smile. "I already saw a great deal on the terrace last night, you know. I promise to use my artistic detachment and refrain from ravishing you here in my kitchen."

Nicholas couldn't help but laugh at himself. He *was* behaving rather like a spinster aunt, shivering in wet clothes in order to preserve a doubtful modesty. This, after all, was a woman he had held, kissed . . . planned to kidnap. He pulled off the sodden shirt and leaned back in his chair, relishing the heat of the fire and the cozy sounds of Elizabeth's tuneless humming and the soft patter of the rain.

"Here we are!" Elizabeth arranged the tea service on a small table, and sat beside him to pour. "A nice pot of tea, some brandy if you need something a bit stronger, and even some sandwiches Bianca had put away in the pantry."

"It looks lovely," Nicholas answered, gratefully accepting the liberally laced cup of tea she offered. "But I do not want you to waste your evening waiting on me. You should be at the party."

Elizabeth waved away his protest. "Not at all. This is ever so much nicer than yet another party. I'm quite enjoying the quiet. And the company."

"So you tire of the social whirl?"

"A bit. I love the gatherings—Venice is a delight, and there are so many artists here." She paused to take a thoughtful bite of sandwich. "But at times it can be rather overwhelming, and I forget the perfect pleasures of a good fire on a rainy night."

"Carnivale will soon be over."

"Yes."

"What will you do then? Stay and watch Venice in its Lenten solemnities?"

"Settle down to my work, you mean?" Elizabeth chuckled. "Yes, I do need to do that. The Bruni commission will not wait forever, and I have a few things I am working on for myself. Georgie has suggested we take a villa in the country for Lent, somewhere nearer Venice than her home at Lake Como."

"Do you approve of this plan?" He listened to her carefully, straining for a glimpse of wistfulness, longing for a return to English aristocratic country life. If she could be persuaded to return on her own . . .

"Oh, yes. The country would be very conducive to my work."

"So you do tire of city life?"

"Not a bit!" She poured herself another cup of tea. "I am having a wonderful time here. So many patrons eager to spend their money! And we must come back here in the spring, anyway."

"Return? Why so?"

"I received a letter this afternoon, a new commission. To restore the Veronese frescoes in Lady Deake's Ca Donati. I am to begin work on them in April, when Lady Deake returns from Rome."

"What?" Nicholas almost fell from his chair in his shock. "Lady Evelyn Deake—you will be working for her?"

"Yes." Elizabeth frowned. "Nicholas, whatever is the matter? This a perfect commission; every artist in Venice has been vying for it. It is a great honor to be so singled out, even by someone as thoroughly irritating as Lady Deake."

"Elizabeth." Nicholas knelt before her, her hands between his. If Elizabeth spoke with Evelyn, if Evelyn told her who he truly was . . . all would be lost. "Listen to me. You have traveled all over Italy. You have seen so much."

"Yes, that is true." He voice was puzzled, her forehead creased in concern as she looked down at him. She obviously thought him moon-mad.

Still he plunged on, hardly knowing or caring that he was babbling. "Perhaps it is time you expanded your experience, discovered a new culture."

"A new culture? Such as France?"

"Perhaps. Or even . . . England."

She snatched her hands from his. "England!"

"There are many fine artists there . . ."

"Absolutely not! There is nothing to be learned there. This is my home, and here I will stay." She took a long sip from the brandy bottle, sitting there marble still, eyes closed, until she visibly composed herself. "Oh, Nicholas, do sit down. What is wrong with you tonight? First you walk about in the rain, and now you are full of England for some reason."

Nicholas reluctantly sat back in his chair, watching her, the glitter of her eyes as she suppressed tears, the mulish set of her dainty jaw. Never had he known such desperation before. He had thought himself quite prepared to do anything to take her back to England and Peter, and then go on with his life. Now he trembled with something very like fear that she would discover the truth from Evelyn's painted lips, that her laughter and kisses would be lost forever when she knew.

As they would when she was kidnapped by himself and the nasty Benno.

He did not want that, he saw now. He only wanted to go on like this always, sitting beside her in a firelit kitchen with the rain whispering at the windows.

"There is no reason," he said, smiling at her in reassurance. "No reason at all."

Elizabeth lay awake for long hours that night, watching the silvery fall of rain outside her window and thinking of Nicholas's words that evening.

She knew him so little. For all his charm, his dimpled grins, his wondrous kisses, he was yet a stranger. She knew nothing of his motives, his past. She had not wanted to ask, for fear of opening the Pandora's box of her own past. And he was such fun, so good at his job, that it had not seemed all that important.

Until now. Now, when he had shown her such seriousness, such barely veiled desperation. She had never thought to see that in his merry countenance. He had been so earnest when he urged her to give up Lady Deake's patronage and return to England. His intensity as he had gripped her hands had been almost frightening.

Could he truly miss England so much himself that he hoped his employment with her would take him back there? That seemed so flimsy an excuse. She would not have thought him such a patriot as all that. In her speculations on his past, she had supposed him to be fleeing England like herself, in search of adventure and fortune. Or perhaps fleeing a broken heart . . .

"Of course!" Elizabeth whispered to herself. "It was the mention of Lady Deake that brought on this rage to leave Venice."

They *had* been conversing so closely at the opera. Elizabeth shuddered at the memory of Lady Deake's bright curls nodding near Nicholas's shoulder as she giggled up at him.

Lady Deake must have been a part of his past, or had at least known him before. And if he had been moving in such a smart set as that, he was not the middle-class soldier she had supposed him to be. What a coil!

He had been living under their roof, eating his meals across the table from her, watching her paint, teasing Bianca, bantering with Georgina. He was not intrusive, did not at all mind their erratic ways, and was very good at his job, willing to deal with very unpleasant people to collect what was owed to her.

In his short tenure, he had persuaded no less than three clients to pay their accounts in full, leaving only two particularly stubborn ones in arrears. Elizabeth had bought a dashing new blue velvet cloak, paid

Georgina her share of the rent, and still had coin left over.

But more than that, clients now looked at her with a different air, a respectful air, a professional air. There were no more lewd remarks, no more agreeing on one price then paying another when the work was complete. It was quite marvelous.

And entirely due to Nicholas. In their household, he was charming, witty, a little silly, a little roguish. In public, he was every bit a commanding military man, stern and uncompromising with all who owed her money. The hard glint in his onyx eyes could even make Elizabeth stand up straighter.

Yet he never spoke of himself. Georgina was an unrepentant snoop, with a positive gift for ferreting out people's secrets whether they wished her to or not. All her leading questions over the breakfast table only earned a grin, a "That is far too dull a topic to discuss over these superb scones," and perhaps a suggestive comment concerning one of her late husbands.

Elizabeth's more delicate inquiries had fared no better. Their conversations were always interesting; he was a very intelligent man, and witty as well. But they always concerned business, Italian art, or gossip about the people they met at social gatherings. He never inquired about her own past, except for that night on the terrace; he never spoke of his own.

"I *will* find out the truth." Elizabeth climbed out of bed and lit a candle, searching through her cluttered writing table for a sheet of notepaper. "I will simply write and ask Lady Deake to tea, before she leaves for Rome."

Chapter Ten

"He has settled well into secretarydom." Georgina paused in sipping cognac and sketching in her book to glance at Nicholas, who had crossed the crowded terrace at Florian's Café to speak to one of Elizabeth's clients who was in arrears.

Elizabeth popped a small tea cake into her mouth and chewed absently, watching with avid interest as Nicholas's gleaming white grin flashed in the sunlight. He really was an utterly handsome specimen of manhood, despite his odd behavior.

Yes, gorgeous but mysterious.

Elizabeth was, in fact, becoming utterly and dizzily obsessed with her secretive secretary who kissed like an angel. She was becoming like a schoolgirl mooning over the dancing master. It was completely ridiculous, but there it was.

She was blushing fire red just thinking about it; she could feel the color creeping down her throat. Nicholas looked up then, caught her staring at him with cake crumbs on her chin, and grinned his wonderful, infuriating grin.

"Oh!" She groaned, snatching up her napkin and scrubbing furiously at the crumbs.

"Blast it all, Lizzie, just bed him and get it over

with!" Georgina muttered. Her gloved hand reached out for another of the cakes.

"If only I could." Then she would know what *it* was like, would know what Nicholas looked like with no clothes at all, and she could then go on with her life.

Perhaps.

"Why can you not?"

"You know perfectly well why, Georgie."

Georgina shook her head hard enough to set the feathers on her bonnet bobbing. "Tell me, dear."

"I ought not to get so very close to someone, particularly an Englishman. He may know someone who knew me in Derbyshire."

"What does one thing have to do with the other? He won't necessarily guess your secrets simply because he sees you in your chemise."

"Georgie! Some women may be able to take a lover and not spill all their secrets at once, but I could not. I would feel I had to tell him all, silly me."

Georgina nodded. "You do have rather a revealing face."

"I already feel horrible about deceiving him so. And he is only the secretary now." The secretary she kissed passionately.

"Lizzie, you are making far too much of this! You must simply steel yourself and keep silent. And if you talked too much you would not have enough time for the amusing bits, anyway. That is what an affair is for, after all."

The amusing bits. That sounded rather promising. Still, Elizabeth shook her head. "I wish I could feel as you do. It would make things so much simpler.

But Nicholas would have to know he was bedding a *murderess*."

"Shh!" Georgina squeezed her hand, her forehead creased in a fierce frown. "I told you never to use that word, Lizzie. It is utterly untrue. You were merely defending yourself against a monster. And when I think of it, I could go and murder that stepbrother of yours myself for putting you through that!"

"Georgie . . ."

"No! What occurred was entirely his fault, not yours. You deserve happiness, Lizzie. But that is not all that is keeping you from Nicholas, is it, dear?"

Elizabeth bit her lip and glanced away. "No. I . . ."

"Nicholas!" Georgina looked up with a too-bright smile as Nicholas appeared beside them. "We were just speaking of you. Care for some cognac?"

"Thank you, Georgina, cognac sounds perfect. And I hope you were only saying very interesting things about me."

"Georgie only ever says interesting things," Elizabeth commented. "Particularly about handsome men."

Georgina rolled her eyes. "I was only remarking on what a consummate businessman you are, Nicholas. Exactly what Lizzie needed."

Nicholas laughed, his head tipped back to reveal the strength of his tanned throat above his snowy cravat. "I certainly hope that may be the case, madam."

Elizabeth smiled reluctantly. It was always thus when he was about; no matter what her fears or worries, he could make her laugh or smile. Simply by his presence. "Absolutely."

"Then perhaps this will help solidify my position." He tossed a small velvet pouch into Elizabeth's lap.

She opened it, and gold spilled onto her palm. Enough, more than enough, for a daring blue silk gown she had coveted in a dressmaker's window. The gown she had hoped could entice Nicholas into another indiscretion. "What . . . ?"

"The last of what Signor Visconti owes you for that sketch of his children. He just paid me."

"That stubborn old goat?" Elizabeth squealed with joy, and leaned forward to kiss Nicholas's cheek in impromptu thanksgiving. "You are a wonder, Nicholas!"

His arm tightened around her waist, clinging. Elizabeth drew back a little to look up at him, puzzled.

He was watching her, his eyes narrow and opaque, no hint of his rakish smile. He stared at her as if he had never seen her before, and had not the least notion of how she had come to be half on his lap.

Perhaps he was not so unaffected by their kiss as he had seemed. Tentatively, Elizabeth reached out her thumb to wipe away the trace of tinted lip salve she had left on his cheek. His jaw tightened, but he did not move away. Instead, he leaned, just barely, into her hand. His silken curls brushed against her fingers.

It was the most intimate moment Elizabeth had ever known, and it was over in an instant. Like the sun crawling from the clouds, Nicholas laughed, pressed a hasty kiss into her palm, and deposited her firmly back into her own chair.

If not for the lingering warmth on her hand, she could have said she imagined the whole incident.

Nicholas's brief intensity was gone, and he was laughing with Georgina.

Elizabeth forced a smile to her own lips, and ducked her head over her open sketchbook.

"Well, *mes amis*, I must be away!" Georgina gathered her sketches, her parasol, and her reticule, and rose to her feet in a rustle of butter-yellow silk skirts. "I have a new model I am interviewing for my scene of Apollo and Daphne."

"Not another Paolo!" Elizabeth cried. More than one handsome model, lovestruck for Georgina, had turned their houses head-over-ears with midnight serenades, lavish bouquets that blocked the corridors, and even, on one memorable occasion, a gift of a squealing piglet. Elizabeth had quite enjoyed the respite from models.

"Certainly not, Lizzie! I am through utterly with Paolos." Georgina kissed Elizabeth's cheek, then, giggling, Nicholas's. "I will see you tonight. Do not forget our theater engagement, my dears—*The Merchant of Venice!*"

With a twinkle of her fingers, she was gone, leaving Elizabeth quite alone with Nicholas. If one considered a table in the most crowded café in Venice quite alone.

It felt as if it were to Elizabeth.

Nicholas helped himself to the last cake. "And what are *you* going to do with this fine afternoon, Elizabeth? No models to inspect?"

Elizabeth laughed. "Not a one, I fear! No sittings, either, since Signora Bruni canceled. I was thinking of taking a tour of Santi Giovanni in Brogana," she said, mentioning the fifteenth-century church she had often seen but never gone inside.

"Why that? Sounds dusty."

"Because, pagan, an artist should never pass up an opportunity to observe a church or palace. It may prove most edifying. Or at least something to do of an afternoon, while waiting for the night's festivities to begin!"

"Hmm, well, in that case, *Madame Artiste*, I shall accompany you. You have quite convinced me of the charms of old churches. And you need an escort."

An unwilling little thrill made Elizabeth's heart beat just a tiny bit faster. An entire afternoon, alone with him! "Well," she said, a teasing reluctance in her voice, "if you feel it would be quite dangerous for me to venture to the church alone . . ."

"Oh, yes, it is. One never knows about those vicious nuns. And you could educate me on the finer points of Gothic architecture."

"You could not be such an infidel if you know that Santi Giovanni is in the Gothic style. There is an intellectual hiding inside of you, Nicholas."

"You have found me out again!" He drank the very last of the cognac, and smiled at her. "I must send off a quick message, and then we can be on our way."

Elizabeth smiled and nodded, telling herself that the strain in his voice, the light in his dark eyes, was surely all in her imagination. He was quite her merry Nicholas again.

". . . domed and columned in the Gothic style. It was once the funeral church of the doges, including . . ."

Elizabeth leaned against Nicholas's shoulder with a suppressed sigh. An historical outing had seemed such a good idea. Churches usually fascinated her, and Santi Giovanni in Brogana *was* quite magnificent. But somehow the warmth of the incense and the beeswax candles, along with the droning voice of the guide and the cakes and cognac she had consumed at Florian's, were conspiring to put her to sleep where she stood.

"You are not attending," Nicholas whispered. "Should you not be writing all of this down?"

"Shh," she answered. "I am contemplating."

"You are drowsing. Come, I have a much better idea for our afternoon."

Elizabeth brightened a bit. "What?"

"Come along, and I will show you."

"But the tour is not finished!"

"We will just slip around that candelabra, see, and out that door, and be gone in a trice. That old tour guide will never even notice."

"But where . . . ?"

"Just come with me! You will not regret it, Elizabeth, I swear."

So she went.

He could not do it.

Nicholas took Elizabeth as far as the secluded canal where an empty boat was waiting, only to find that he could not possibly force her into it and take her away. It was not just because of their passionate interlude on the terrace. He could not put fear and disillusionment into the silver-gray eyes that were laughing up at him now.

He had done horrible, terrible things in his life, but this he could not. Elizabeth quite simply deserved better than to be hauled off summarily like a bundle of freight, like a possession. She deserved . . .

Well, what she *truly* deserved was to be left to live her life in peace, to be allowed to have her career and make her choices with no interference. It was a realization that quite startled Nicholas. He had always liked women, of course, but he had always put them into tidy compartments in his life—young things in white at Almack's who were not to be touched, and courtesans and daring widows who were safe to trifle with. And then, in a compartment all her own, was his mother.

This was a new way of seeing the world, to consider that a woman was a *person*, with thoughts and talents and wishes all her own, and a right to make choices.

It had taken extraordinary women, like his wonderful Elizabeth and her outrageous, independent "sister," to make him realize this. And yet it was too late.

He still owed Peter a great debt. He was still obligated to take Elizabeth back to England, by some means. But not this way. Not by force and fear.

He would simply have to think of something else.

"Well?" Elizabeth said, tapping her half boot impatiently and interrupting his moment of epiphany. "What are we going to do?"

He had to think quickly. What did ladies like to do? "Shop!"

"What?"

"Shop. On the Rialto."

"Oh!" Elizabeth laughed, obviously thinking of the bright new coins in her reticule that were simply burning to be spent. "What a grand idea! And what a unique gentleman you are, Nicholas, to think an afternoon of shopping would be all the crack."

"Oh, my dear." Nicholas half turned her, so she would not see him wave off the lurking Benno. "You do not know the half of what I think the 'crack' is."

Later that evening, when he had deposited Elizabeth at the house with her new purchases so she could dress for the night's festivities, Nicholas drifted aimlessly through the narrow walkways of Venice. He was quite unmindful of the light rain that had begun to fall and that soaked his bare head and dripped onto the collar of his greatcoat. He didn't heed the passersby who knocked into him and hurried on, or the beggar children who sometimes appeared underfoot. He did not see the buildings, some magnificent and some squalid, or the piles of refuse and the lines of sodden laundry.

He could only see Elizabeth.

Never in his life had Nicholas Hollingsworth, war hero, dedicated rogue, and nobleman's bastard, felt so completely out of sorts. Even in battle he had had a sword and pistol to defend himself with. Yet before a pair of quiet gray eyes he was utterly defenseless. What little was left of his honor was vulnerable to her smile.

He had paid off a very irate Benno, who had not been at all happy that his carefully planned trap had come to naught. Nicholas had sent the odious little man away, and now he was left with no plan at all. No ideas for taking Elizabeth to England and into the care of her stepbrother.

He could only now admit that he did not *want* to

take her to England. And for one very selfish reason. He was happy. Truly happy.

Nicholas loved living in the narrow house on the canal. He loved breakfasting with Elizabeth and Georgina, sharing the English newspapers with them, and listening to their laughter and their plans. He loved the smells of turpentine and chalk that floated down the corridors, watching a blank canvas come to a true and sparkling life under Elizabeth's brush. He loved dancing with her at a ball, or just watching her across a room as she talked with her friends, her elflike face alive with enthusiasm. And yes, he even loved to spar with that ridiculous Sir Stephen, who still imagined he might have a chance with Elizabeth.

"This is horrendous." He groaned and leaned back against a damp wall. "Of all times for me to become disgustingly content. Of all places! Of all women." Nicholas closed his eyes.

Peter had been the best friend Nicholas had ever known, until he found Elizabeth. Peter had not always been so cold, so unbending. He had lived with Nicholas through the terrors of war, the deaths of comrades, and the deadly dull times of waiting in dusty Spanish billets. He had saved Nicholas's life, not just on that battlefield, but numerous times, with his company.

Yes, Nicholas was happy in Elizabeth's company. He could stay for eternity in that chaotic house and never want to leave. Surely he owed the woman he could love a happy life, a life of her own choosing. And, for whatever reason, she very clearly chose not to live that life with her stepbrother. There were secrets in her life, he knew.

His honor told him that he owed it to Peter to keep his word.

Nicholas opened his eyes and stared up at the slate-colored heavens, letting the rains pour down over his face.

"Tell me what to do!" he shouted. "Tell me what is right."

It was the closest he had ever come to a prayer.

Chapter Eleven

London

"What is wrong, *mon chèr?*"

Peter Everdean, Earl of Clifton, turned from the fire to glance at the woman who reclined in his bed. Her hair spilled sun gold over the brocade sheets and her fetching white shoulders, but he was unmoved. Detached.

"Go back to sleep, Yvette," he murmured.

"But, *mon chèr!*" She pouted prettily, stretching against the pillows. "Eet ees very lonely here in this huge bed, and I cannot sleep when I am lonely."

"Yvette!" He slapped his palm against the arm of his chair, startling awake the greyhound that slept by the hearth. "I said go back to sleep. I am trying to think, and your egregious false French accent is not helping matters."

Yvette slid beneath the bedclothes, wide-eyed, and Peter returned to his absent contemplation of the red-orange flames.

He had thought, hoped, that bringing the oh-so-talented Yvette to his London town house would help him to forget, if only for an hour or two. It had not. Even her soft moans, her practiced sighs as she moved beneath him, had not erased Elizabeth from his worries.

Where *was* she, by Jove? It had been weeks, *weeks*, since Nick Hollingsworth had gone to Italy, and there had not been a single message from him. Not a word as to whether she had been located, what she was doing, if she was well or ill.

He had to see her again, to see that she was alive. To bury his head in her cool hands and beg her forgiveness for his monstrous behavior. He had been insane when he came home from the Peninsula, tormented by memories and nightmares, by the ever-present sound of gunfire in his ears.

During the years he had been gone, fighting, Elizabeth had represented all that was good about life and home. Her girlish, long-awaited letters, scented with lilies of the valley, had meant Clifton Manor to him—home and safety and quiet.

After Spain, after Carmen, he had wanted only the green sweetness of home, the sound of his sister's laughter.

He had somehow thought she could make him whole and pure again, but instead he had come back to England to find that she looked so . . . Spanish. So like Carmen. And she had not been the sweet girl of his memory; she had been independent, defiant. He had been overcome by the crazy thought that she *was* Carmen, that she was there to torment him.

But now she was gone, and he had spent two long years resting, recovering, and most of all regretting what had passed between them.

"Oh, Lizzie," he whispered. "How can I ever make you understand if you are not here? How can I make you see the truth?"

He, who had always sworn to protect her, had driven her to murder and life in exile. *Elizabeth*, his sister, whom he had taught to ride a pony and danced with at country assemblies. His dear, talented Lizzie. He had driven her away.

He wanted so much to tell her the truth, to restore the easy affection, the trust that had been between them so long ago.

It was becoming increasingly obvious that Nicholas, the greatest hope he had had in these two years, was not about his job properly.

Peter would simply have to travel to Italy himself.

"I was *so* very happy to receive your note, Miss Cheswood!" Lady Evelyn Deake practically glowed with sweetness and light as she welcomed Elizabeth into the vast marble foyer of her Ca Donati. "I do so want to become better acquainted with you."

Elizabeth somehow doubted that. She was a mere hired artist, a servant. Surely not someone Lady Deake would wish to be bosom bows with. But Evelyn's artificial amity suited Elizabeth's purposes very well indeed, so she allowed her arm to be taken as Evelyn led her into a sumptuous green-and-gold morning room.

"I am happy it was not an inconvenient time to view your frescoes, Lady Deake," Elizabeth said, as she seated herself on a satin slipper chair by the fire and arranged the pink skirts of her walking dress.

"Not at all, not at all. Venice is so very *dead* in the afternoon. No teas or card parties at all." With an airy wave of her diamond-bedecked hand Evelyn dismissed the crowded canal of afternoon revelers outside her window. "Before I show you the ever-so-adorable paintings, we must have some tea."

Elizabeth opened her mouth to reply, but Evelyn quickly interrupted.

"No, I insist! I get so few chances to talk with another Englishwoman these days."

Elizabeth watched as Evelyn fussed with a gilt tea service, and speculated on exactly how to bring the conversation about to the topic of Nicholas. She did not want to arouse Lady Deake's suspicions, after all. Finally she said, "You must miss your life in England very much, Lady Deake."

Evelyn sighed dramatically. "Oh, indeed! I have a great many friends in London, and they are ever so much more agreeable than most of the people I have encountered here thus far. But then, London is quite dull at this time of year, and I absolutely abhor the country. So I decided to come abroad. So stylish now, to be on the Continent. And Italy *does* have its charms."

"To be sure," Elizabeth agreed.

"Has it been very long since *you* were in England, Miss Cheswood?"

Not long enough, Elizabeth thought. "Oh, yes. I hardly remember it. Yet I feel I know it very well. My new secretary has such vivid stories of English life."

"Ah, yes. The beauteous Nicholas. He *would* have fascinating things to tell, I'm sure." Evelyn's smile had turned distinctly feline.

Elizabeth nodded calmly and sipped her tea, concealing her anticipation behind a conspiratorial giggle. Lady Deake must surely have known Nicholas before! "Were you possibly acquainted with Mr. Carter in England, Lady Deake?"

"With Mr. Carter?" Evelyn visibly started, as if she had suddenly recalled something, and she stared down into her cup. "No, no. I have never seen him before the night at the opera, ever. He just . . . I just . . . well, I am rather a connoisseur, you know. Of handsome gentlemen. Like your Mr. . . . . Carter." Evelyn laughed nervously. "Would you care for more tea, Miss Cheswood?"

"Yes, thank you." Elizabeth watched Evelyn with a thoughtful frown. Something was definitely in the air. Lady Deake was a very silly woman, but she was a very poor liar. She *had* known Nicholas before that night at the opera, it was quite obvious. It was also obvious that she was concealing something very interesting indeed.

"Perhaps, Lady Deake, you could show me the Veronese now?" Elizabeth said, with her warmest smile.

He was going to have to tell her. Yes. This very moment, he would go to her and tell her the truth, before she could hear it from the mouth of someone like Lady Deake.

Elizabeth would very likely hate him. She would cast him out of her life, out of her golden circle. But perhaps, just perhaps, she would first listen to him, and would come to understand at least a bit of what he was about.

Perhaps she would even consider agreeing to see Peter again.

But perhaps he should wait just one day more, until Carnivale was over. Then he would have one last ball at her side, a time to dance with her and be next to her.

Nicholas groaned and rolled over on his narrow bed, lying on his bare stomach to watch the shadows lengthen across the floor. His dilemma seemed perpetual, never-ending. Peter and his promise stood for the honor that was all that he could truly call his own. Elizabeth was all the things he had scoffed at, claimed could not exist—things such as pure talent and unselfish friendship.

Growing up in his mother's house, cold and dark, and then at a succession of schools noted for their strict modes of discipline, his life had been distinctly devoid of such things as laughter and art. He had always been in the shadow of his father, the illustrious Duke of Ainsley, who was forever attempting to control his bastard son's life—despite his abandonment of that son's mother so long ago.

Nicholas had suffered under his father's dictates, under the scorn of his stepmother and his proper half sisters, until he had gone to war to escape them—to escape himself.

In Spain he had found a certain rough camaraderie, a shallow sort of friendship based on shared danger and determined debauchery. It had been different with Peter Everdean. They had talked together a great deal, of hopes for the future, memories of England, and of women. Yet Peter had never been much for laughter, except for the brief reign in his life of a dark-eyed senorita named Carmen.

It had taken Elizabeth to bring Nicholas all he had missed in life. She gave freely of her affection, her laughter; she had let him into the charmed circle of her life. She never asked about his past, his fortune and connections—she had no need of such things. She was concerned only with *him*.

He would tell her the truth. She deserved that. Tonight. Or perhaps tommorow morning. . . .

A country villa!

Elizabeth stared down at Georgina's hastily scrawled note, sent off from an estate agent's office before she dashed away to a sitting. A country villa, dreaming in the sun, sounded like Paradise after the social wildness of the past weeks. She could truly work there, complete the Bruni commission—and the sketches of Nicholas she had been working on secretly late at night. Rather naughty sketches, if she did say so herself, of a heavy-eyed Nicholas, half dressed, and clearly in love. . . .

She giggled then at her own folly, and fell back onto the bed without even removing her bonnet or shoes. She watched the patterns of the sun move lazily across the ceiling.

Of course he was not in love with her! As much as she did wish it, with a force that almost frightened her, men as handsome as Greek gods did not fall in love with small, dark women with paint beneath their fingernails.

No, they fell in love with blond, angelic, proper misses who painted polite watercolors and never, ever drank too much champagne at balls. Nicholas might laugh and even flirt with her, but then he laughed and flirted with everyone. Even Georgina and Bianca, and Katerina Bruni, who flashed her green eyes at him during sittings.

Elizabeth sighed and rolled over, reaching beneath the mattress to retrieve the sketches that were hidden there. She leafed through them, smiling. He *was* lovely, especially when he smiled at her, his head bent toward hers as they spoke together. It was very difficult to remember why she had sworn off men when she was near him—he melted away the walls of ice around her soul when he smiled.

He was not like any man she had ever known. He was intelligent, though he tried so hard to hide it behind silly grins, and he respected intelligence in her. He listened to her, appreciated what she was trying to do with her work.

And he was a divine kisser. Absolutely top of the trees!

Once, frightened and cold, she had vowed never to believe what any man said to her. Yet here she was, beginning to trust, to *love* a man as dashing and mysterious as Nicholas.

Perhaps in the country, far away from the distractions of sittings and social gatherings, she would discover the true man behind Nicholas's façade. She would draw him out, about the past and the future.

Perhaps she could even tell him a little, a very little, of her own life.

Filled with the rosy glow of hope, Elizabeth pushed the sketches back into their hiding place, and went to tell Nicholas of their travel plans.

Chapter Twelve

"Can you see it yet, Lizzie? What is it like?"

Elizabeth leaned further out of the carriage window, one gloved hand clapped firmly onto her bonnet to prevent it from flying away. "I cannot see it yet, Georgie," she called back over her shoulder.

"Well, what *do* you see?"

Elizabeth looked about her. The narrow road they were traveling hugged a precarious cliff that looked out over an impossibly blue sea. White breakers crashed and roiled on the rocks below.

"Only sea," she answered. "Oh, it is glorious! It's as if we were flying above the water on bird's wings. You should look, Georgie!"

Georgina waved a handkerchief in front of her green-tinged face. "No, I thank you! It is certainly bad enough to be riding in here without *seeing* what is outside. Can the driver not go slower?"

"You asked him to hurry." Elizabeth sat back in the carriage, and pushed the tendrils of loose hair back beneath her bonnet. "Perhaps some fresh air is what you require, Georgie. If you would lean your head out of the window—"

"No! I shall be well by the time we arrive, I vow. Perhaps some cool water would help, though."

"Let me get it for you." Elizabeth pulled their hamper from beneath her seat and rummaged about for the flask of water and a cup. Poor Georgina—it was ever thus when they traveled, she reflected. It seemed her friend's only weakness.

Georgina gratefully accepted the water and sipped at it carefully. Soon her color seemed a bit more pink than green. She even smiled a little. "I *am* glad Nicholas has gone ahead to be certain the villa has been properly aired. I vow I shall go directly to bed, and eat only custard and clear broth for a week."

"We are supposed to do *some* work at least, Georgie, while we are here."

"Oh, yes, yes. Work. There will be more than enough time for that, with no balls or routs to attend. But I daresay we will have *some* fun."

"No models, I beg of you!"

"Certainly not! Nicholas will be the only man we will see. And as I am sure you will not share him, the rest of us will be quite nunlike." Georgina sighed dramatically.

Elizabeth laughed. "He is not mine to share!"

"Is he not? Then why were you such a mooncalf these three days he has been gone?"

"I was not! I have been far too occupied in packing our trunks to concern myself overmuch with his absence."

"Um-hm." Georgina just smiled. "Would you hand me those biscuits, dear? You have so diverted me that I no longer feel even a twinge of illness."

Elizabeth passed Georgina the tin of biscuits, hoping for silence. It was not to be.

Georgina nibbled a bit at the biscuit; even her eyes seemed to sparkle now with some of her usual vitality. "You *have* missed him, have you not, Lizzie? Just a bit?"

"Perhaps, just a bit," Elizabeth replied, with a small sigh. "Venice seemed so very much . . . quieter without him there."

"Hmm. That may be due in a very small way to the fact that Carnivale is at an end, and we have had no parties to go to."

"That is only a small part of it!" Elizabeth laughed. "Our own house has been quieter, as well. It is nice to have someone about to give a male opinion every once in a while. Yes, I missed him."

"Lizzie." Georgina frowned a bit, suddenly serious. She reached out and touched Elizabeth's hand. "Are you in love with Nicholas?"

Elizabeth laughed again, nervously. She drew her hand away, and patted at a strand of hair that had strayed to her neck. "Love? Oh, Georgie, what a thing to ask!"

"Yes, I know. Are you?"

"I . . . I hardly know. I have only known him a few weeks."

"Sometimes only a few hours will suffice," Georgina murmured. "I know you are fond of him; that is obvious. But are your feelings deeper than that, dear?"

Elizabeth stared down at her folded hands for a long moment, a realization slowly growing in her mind. She could scarce admit it, even to herself, but . . . "Yes. I suppose I am falling in love with Nicholas."

"Oh." Georgina turned to look out of the window.

"Georgie, what is it?" Elizabeth cried. "You like

Nicholas, do you not? You have urged me to spend time with him."

"Yes, dear, I have, and I do not feel I have been wrong in that. I feel he is a good man, as well as a handsome and charming one."

"Then what is wrong?" Elizabeth caught her lower lip between her teeth. "Is it . . . is it that you fear he does not return my regard?"

"No, Lizzie! Quite the opposite. But I sense . . ." Georgina paused.

"What?"

"I sense that Nicholas, for all his virtues, is not all that he appears to be."

"Whatever do you mean—not what he appears to be?" A growing panic seemed to climb from Elizabeth's stomach to her throat. "Have you heard something concerning him?"

"No, Lizzie! It is only a sense. I cannot explain it, it is simply a . . . feeling."

"You think I am foolish to have this regard for him?"

"Not at all. I am merely saying—be cautious. I know I told you to follow your heart, dear, and so you should, but at the same time do not let your love blind you completely." Georgina took Elizabeth's hands again, and smiled reassuringly. "I have a great deal more experience with men than you, for good or ill. I like Nicholas, truly, but I must advise you now not to be too rash, Lizzie. Yes?"

Elizabeth squeezed her friend's hands in return. "Yes. I will do as you advise."

"Very good! And remember—one can be cautious and still be merry. This time is for you to rest, to think, to be comfortable with people who care about you. Such as me—and Nicholas."

"Oh, Georgie!" Elizabeth kissed Georgina's cheek. "I am the most fortunate woman in the world to have a friend such as you."

"Not half as fortunate as I, dear Lizzie." Georgina held her close for an instant, then sat back with a smile. "And now, I think I will just rest a moment, before we reach the villa."

Elizabeth nodded and returned to her contemplation of the landscape. "We *will* be isolated here. I have not seen a structure, a person, or even a goat for fully half an hour."

Yet even as she spoke the road turned and they faced a downward slope into a wide green valley. Tiny cottages and a spired church were laid out below like a toy village. They seemed to sparkle in the afternoon sunlight, a fairy kingdom.

And set above the storybook hamlet on a verdant hillside was a villa, its white stucco and red-tile roof softened by climbing ivy and pots of red and pink flowers lined up on the terrace.

A man was waiting on that terrace for their arrival, his black hair undulating like a satin ribbon in the light breeze.

Elizabeth leaned out of the window again when she saw him, and waved madly.

"Oh, Georgie!" she cried. "It is beautiful! It is going to be such a wonderful month."

When the carriage drew to a halt, Nicholas was there to open the door and help them down.

His hands lingered warmly for just a moment longer than was proper on Elizabeth's waist.

"Welcome to your new home," he said, and kissed

her cheek. "I hope you will like it. I filled every room with flowers, just for you."

"Then I am sure I shall." And over his shoulder, she smiled at Georgina.

"If you do not stop fidgeting, Nicholas, I will not be able to finish before the light changes!" Elizabeth waved her paintbrush at Nicholas, and stamped her bare foot on the grass.

Nicholas settled back into his pose, lounging against some crimson cushions laid out on the ground, and laughed up at her. "So very sorry, Madame Artiste! We cannot have the light change, can we?"

Elizabeth frowned at him, but she could not truly be angry. Not on such a very splendid day. The sunlight filtered through the budding branches of the trees, casting a pale golden glow over the scene before her. The carpet spread on the ground, the array of fruits and cheeses and wines, and the man who laughed up at her were all sparkling in the Italian sunlight.

In the distance, she could see their villa, and Bianca airing the laundry out of an upstairs window. Georgina had set her easel up on the terrace, and she was near enough that Elizabeth could make out the pink of her shawl. But it felt as if she and Nicholas were all alone in some enchanted land out of time, with only a few sheep to watch the progress of her portrait.

The subject of the painting rolled onto his back and beckoned to her with one long, tanned hand. "You have been working far too hard for such a lovely day, Madame Artiste. Should you not take a respite and try one of Bianca's delightful apricot tarts?" He picked up one of the pastries, and bit into it with such relish that some of the apricot ran down his beard-shadowed chin. He had not shaved for two days, since Elizabeth had arrived in the country, and it gave him a delightful, piratical air she was trying to capture on canvas.

"Mmm!" he murmured. "Do try one!"

Elizabeth could not resist leaning down to kiss away the sticky fruit, but she pulled back with a laugh when his arm encircled her waist. "I should take a rest before you eat them all! You have already devoured all of the sandwiches."

"And who ate every bit of sole almondine at supper last night, before the plate even came to my end of the table?"

"*Touché.*" She wiped her hands on a paint-stained rag, and sat down beside him, tilting her head back to let the warmth of the sun flood over her face.

When Nicholas shifted to rest his head on her lap, her fingers crept into his silky curls. She closed her eyes and inhaled deeply of the fragrance of wine, grass, paint, and Nicholas's own evergreen soap.

She had never been so deliciously, madly full of scream-out-loud joy. Not simply ordinary joy, as when she completed a particularly fine painting or held a baby against her heart and smelled its milky scent, but dance-around-naked, full-to-bursting, life-is-perfect joy.

A warm day, a canvas on her easel, and this man's head on her lap was all it took to make life absolute perfection.

"Have you ever been so happy?" she whispered, almost to herself.

His hand swept gently around her waist, warm and secure. "Only once before."

Elizabeth's eyes opened. "Once?"

"With Mariah." His lips curled in a smile that was sweet with remembrance—and with teasing.

"And who is Mariah?"

"Oh, the love of my life. She was an angel of perfection, with golden curls and adorable freckles, right *here*." He lazily tapped the end of Elizabeth's nose.

Freckles! "Oh? And where is this angel now?"

"I have no idea. We had a hideous falling-out, and she left me flat." Nicholas sighed. "My life has never been the same." He buried his nose deeper in her muslin skirts. "It is too pitiful to recall."

Elizabeth frowned suspiciously. "Just when was this falling-out with the love of your life, precisely?"

"I was seven, she was nine. An older woman. I put a mouse down the back of her dress and she never spoke to me again."

"You beast!" Elizabeth laughed, beating him across the shoulders with a folded napkin. "Here I was all prepared to feel sorry for you, and you were telling such a Banbury tale!"

"Every word is true, I assure you. My life has been desolate of romance since Mariah."

"Now, why do I doubt that? Was there ever truly a Mariah?"

"Certainly there was. She was our cook's daughter. I was quite mad for her."

A silence fell. "You had a cook when you were growing up? Servants?"

"Yes, of course. There was the butler . . ." Too late, Nicholas saw the trap he had laid for himself. He sat up, and looked at her warily. "Yes. We had servants. My pockets were not always to let."

"Are your pockets to let now?"

"Of course. I am working as your secretary, am I not?"

"Of course." Elizabeth framed his face in her hands, forcing him to look at her steadily, not laugh and turn away. "Nicholas, tell me about your family."

He did try to turn away, but she had him well and truly caught. "It is not very diverting," he answered.

"I do not care about being *diverted*. I simply want to know about your family, your home."

Nicholas moved away from her. "I am a bastard," he abruptly announced.

Elizabeth's eyes widened in shock. "A . . ." She shook her head. "I take it you are not speaking metaphorically."

"Quite literally, I'm afraid. My father neglected to marry my mother."

"I see."

He rushed on in the face of her silence, before he could lose all his nerve. "My father was already betrothed, you see, when my mother came up *enceinte*, and he refused to break off his engagement. His fianceé was the daughter of a marquis, you see, and my mother's father was only a well-to-do cit. But my father did his duty to us, oh yes. When my mother's family cast her out, he set us up in our house in London. I had tutors, a pony, and later Eton and Oxford, a commission in the army. He even acknowledged me, gave me a place in Society. He did his duty; more than his duty, some would say."

Nicholas spoke evenly, perfunctorily, but his features were tight with the strain of recalling his youth. Elizabeth wiped at her eyes with the napkin. "I would say not! Your father had a duty to *love* you! To be your father. And in that he failed miserably."

Nicholas shook his head. "He had another family to be father to, a wife and three respectable daughters, who all married well and set up their nurseries, just as they ought. I was an embarrassment, a mistake who refused to fade quietly into the background. I was wild, I flaunted myself all around Town with my racing curricle and my mistresses. I decided if he was going to hate me, it would be for a damned good reason."

"No!" Elizabeth was crying in earnest now, her heart breaking for the lonely boy he had been, the lonely man she was only now being allowed to glimpse. She knew all too well the heartbreak families could cause one another, when they were meant to be the ones who loved each other the most. So upset was she that she did not even blush at the mention of his mistresses. "He could not have hated you, Nicholas. No one who knows you could hate you."

"You should hate me, Elizabeth."

"Why? Because you were not born in wedlock? Believe me, my family is hardly of pristine reputation." She threw herself upon him, clinging when he would have moved away. She forced him to look at her. "And you should know me better than that, Nicholas! I never judge people by their appearances, their families, or their fortunes. I have seen that in my own life, and it caused me nothing but pain. I can only judge by what is in a person's heart. You have a beautiful heart. You have made the sun shine in my life every day since I met you."

"Elizabeth, no . . ."

She pressed her fingertips to his mouth, stopping his protests. "No. Your father was wrong, very wrong to treat you as he did, and one day he will know that. But I would never play you false, Nicholas. I would never push you to the background. I know too well what that is about. You and I, we are meant to live in the forefront of life, always."

"Elizabeth! Beautiful Lizzie." He crushed her against him, his face buried against her neck, his tears wet on her skin. "You should know how much I deserve your scorn, but I could never bear it if you looked at me with hatred, God forgive me."

"I could never look upon you with hatred. I love you."

He looked up at her shining face, her eyes glowing silver. "Say it again!" he begged.

"I love you." She turned his face up to hers and kissed him on his cheek. "I love you, Nicholas, come what may. We are two of a kind, I knew it when I saw you at that masked ball. I have been waiting for you forever."

"I love you, too, my Lizzie. Always remember that, always. My heart is yours no matter what may happen."

Elizabeth turned to the sun, and laughed and laughed. "And my heart is yours, whatever comes. But what can come between us now? We love each other, do we not? Nothing can change that."

"I pray you are right."

"I am right. Unless you have a mad wife in the garret, as in one of Georgina's horrid novels?"

Nicholas laughed reluctantly. "No wives of any sort."

"Then we shall be together always. Nothing can part us now that you have given me your heart, and I have given you mine."

"Nothing." And Nicholas clutched her close against him.

Chapter Thirteen

"Shall you go out tonight, my lord?"

Peter did not even turn from his window, where he was watching people gather around one of Rome's famed fountains as night drew near. "Out? Where would I go out to?"

"I merely saw the letters on the table, my lord, and thought perhaps . . ."

"Ah, yes. Lord Braithwaite is in residence here, and invited me to a small dinner he is having tonight. I had not thought to attend, but perhaps you are right, Simmons. I should renew his lordship's acquaintance."

"Very good, my lord. Shall I lay out the blue coat?"

Peter nodded briefly, and turned away again.

He had decided to make the brief stop in Rome on his route to Venice. Carnivale was over in the Serene City, and most of the English in residence there had fled the somberness after the recent bacchanalia. There were many English in Rome, and he had had hopes that someone would know Elizabeth, tell him where she had gone.

Thus far he had found no one who recognized Elizabeth's miniatures, and no one he could claim an acquaintance with except the corpulent old Lord Braithwaite.

Thus this evening's festivities, though he was not feeling in the least sociable. *Someone* had to have seen her at some time. She could not simply have vanished, though it appeared to be so. Elizabeth was just . . . gone. She could be in India or China, for all he knew. Along with Old Nick Hollingsworth.

"Damn him," Peter whispered. "If he thinks he can thwart me, he is much mistaken."

"I could scarce believe it when dear old Braithwaite told me you were in Italy! Imagine—an *earl*, right here in the midst of our little society."

Peter grimaced, and nodded vaguely to his dinner partner. Lady Evelyn Deake, yellow curls bobbing and jeweled fingers flashing, had not paused for breath during the soup or fish courses. She showed absolutely no signs of slowing now that the roast lamb was on their plates. Not even Peter's distant replies and glazed eyes could stop her.

It was his most dreaded nightmare, being trapped at a dinner party with indifferent food, watered wines, an overheated room, and a dull dinner partner. It was almost worse than Spain.

"Of course, we *have* met before," Lady Deake continued, pausing only for a refreshing sip of wine. "At the Borthwick ball last Season. You were there with that dashing Lady Ashby!"

"Oh?"

"Yes. That was before my dear Arthur's passing. It was quite the crush, but I distinctly remember your arrival. Lady Ashby was wearing . . ." One long, varnished nail tapped at her chin. "Red velvet! Yes.

And those famous rubies of hers.'' She tapped playfully at Peter's wrist with one of those nails. ''Which you were rumored to have given her!''

''Oh?'' Peter vaguely remembered the ball, one of many he had plunged into after Elizabeth's departure in the hopes that activity would distract his mind. He remembered Angela Ashby, and her cloying French perfume. But, fortunately, he had no recollection of this woman.

''And here you are tonight! Such a coincidence.'' Evelyn popped a sugared almond into her mouth and tried to smile at him alluringly as she chewed. ''And I hear you are for Venice after this! I live there. What takes you to my corner of Italy?''

Peter doubted she could claim quite all of Venice as ''hers,'' but he merely smiled tightly. He saw their host's prized Leonardo painting of the Madonna over Lady Deake's head. The Holy Mother's dark hair, parted sleekly in the center and brushed behind her ears, reminded him of Elizabeth. ''I am here for art, Lady Deake.''

''Indeed! Well, this is certainly the place for paintings and such. You must visit my home when you are in Venice. There are some fine frescoes in the main drawing room.''

''Yes?''

''Yes. They are by . . . oh . . . I can never recall his name. V something.''

Peter had never in his cynical life so longed to snicker impolitely at someone. He touched the damask napkin to his lips. ''Verrocchio?''

''Oh, no, that is not it. I am quite sure.''

''Vignola?''

''No. . . .''

"Veronese." Peter was swiftly running out of V names.

Evelyn brightened. "Yes! That is the one. I have just engaged an artist to undertake the restoring of them; they are in quite shocking condition. They are old, you know."

"I guessed."

Evelyn tittered. "It is a *female* artist I have engaged!"

Peter froze. His fork, laden with lamb, was suspended in midair. For the first time that evening, he gave his full attention to his dinner partner. "Female artist?"

"It is very scandalous, I know. But she and her sister are all the crack now. Simply everyone wants them to paint their portraits."

"How very fascinating, Lady Deake." Peter gave her one of his rare, prized smiles. "Or may I call you . . . Evelyn?"

Evelyn gaped at him. "Well . . . yes, If you like—Peter."

"Now, Evelyn, do tell me more about these sister artists."

"Well. The one I have engaged is the younger. She is quite small and plain, with hair as dark as these Italians. She is not at all like the elder, who is as tall as an Amazon, with wild red hair. I hear she is quite well known in England, though. And they have this secretary, who everyone knows must be more than simply the secretary . . ."

Chapter Fourteen

Supper at the villa was a merry one.

Bianca had quite outdone herself, preparing a divine risotto with prosciutto, and a fine lemon trifle for desert. Georgina and Elizabeth had worn two of their prettiest dinner gowns. There was a good wine from the neighboring vineyard, and it flowed amid much conversation and laughter.

When the trifle had been eaten, the ladies did not retire and leave Nicholas to his port. Instead, they joined him, and sipped at the ruby-red wine while enjoying the soft breeze from the open doors.

"Ah, Georgie." Elizabeth sighed. "Is this not better than going to Rome, as you originally wished?"

"It is." Georgina swirled the port in her glass, its depths the same color as her velvet gown. "Rome would be much too crowded at this time of year, and we would have had far too many social obligations. I like this—dinner *en famille*."

Elizabeth, too, liked the idea of that—family. She had not felt a part of such a thing since her mother and stepfather died, perhaps not even before that tragic accident. She had felt herself apart, alone. Now she felt alone no longer. All the shattered, scattered pieces of her life had now seemingly come together to form a new, wonderful whole.

She laid one of her hands over Nicholas's, and smiled. "Yes, this is very nice indeed. I can't recall a nicer supper, ever."

"But perhaps Nicholas finds us rather dull," Georgina said, laughter in her voice. "Perhaps he is quite missing the gay life of the city?"

"Not at all, I assure you." Nicholas lifted Elizabeth's hand for a brief kiss. "The energy of you two lovely ladies has exhausted me utterly. I am glad of the country respite."

"But do you not miss all your admirers, Georgie?" said Elizabeth. "All the posies and billets-doux? As the post comes only once a week here, we shall hear nothing from Signor Franco or Mr. Butler, or any of the others, for several days at least."

"Excellent! If I *never* hear from either of them again it will be far too soon."

"But I thought you quite liked the signor!" Elizabeth exclaimed.

"I did rather, when I thought him merely an amusing dinner partner. That all ended when he proposed to me at the Vincenzis' party."

"Oh, no!" Elizabeth groaned.

Nicholas was a bit puzzled. He was accustomed to young English ladies, such as his half sisters, who schemed and plotted and would stop at almost nothing to procure proposals from gentlemen.

But then, when had Georgina and Elizabeth ever behaved as his half sisters did?

"This is a bad thing?" he said.

"Terrible!" answered Elizabeth. "It means that Signor Franco will never see the inside of our drawing room again."

Nicholas looked at Georgina. "Do you never wish to wed again, Georgina?"

Georgina shook her head. "Have you ever been married, Nicholas?"

Elizabeth glanced at him sharply.

"No," he replied. "I do not believe so."

"Then never do so," Georgina said firmly. "Unless it is to Lizzie. Marriage to her would be quite out of the common way."

"Georgie, please!" Elizabeth laughed.

"It is true," Georgina protested. "And I suppose everyone should be married once, if only to see what it is like. But as for me, I shall *not* marry again."

"Georgie is quite determined to end her days the merry widow," said Elizabeth, tipping the last of the port into her glass.

"Yes," said Georgina. "I shall spend my dotage in . . . oh, Bath, I think, painting awful seascapes and shouting rude things at handsome young men in the Pump Room."

"And may we join you in your dignified retirement?" Nicholas asked, with a great grin.

"Oh, yes, certainly. Lizzie and I shall push you about in your bath chair, and play matchmaker to your ten children."

"Georgina Beaumont!" Elizabeth protested with a blush.

"I am merely teasing, Lizzie. I am certain you will have only three. And by the time we are doddering about Bath, it will be time for your grandchildrens' come-outs." Georgina drained the last of her port, and rose to her feet. "Now, I must retire or I shall fall asleep in what is left of this excellent trifle. Good night, my dears."

"Good night, Georgie," Elizabeth called.

Nicholas resumed his seat, and took Elizabeth's hand between both of his. "Your sister is an extraordinary woman."

"She is. And, despite her protestations, I do believe she will wed again."

"Do you?"

"Yes. She is far too romantic not to. It will take a very special man indeed, though."

"Oh? And do you have a candidate in mind for her?"

"Hmm. But not you, Nicholas. You are already spoken for."

"I am that." He leaned closer to her, so close that she could feel his warmth through her gown and shawl, against her skin. Her eyes began to drift shut.

But to her great disappointment, he did not kiss her.

"Will you walk with me in the garden, Elizabeth?" he asked instead.

"I thought you would never ask."

Arm in arm, they strolled out of the dining room and down the terrace steps to the garden. It was almost a full moon, and the trees and the barely awakening flowers were bathed in silver. Their footsteps crushed blossoms into the walkways, releasing their sweet scent into the air.

A small, cool breeze had crept up, and Elizabeth leaned closer to Nicholas for warmth in her thin silk dinner gown.

"It is almost like the night we met," she mused. "The moonlight, the scent of the flowers."

"But there is no canal," he said. "No masked ball, no gondolas."

"This is much more pleasant. It is only us."

"Elizabeth." He stopped and caught her arm, turning her about to face him. "I brought you out here to talk to you. I must . . ."

She stared up at him. His face was drawn and serious, not a hint of sparkle in his dark eyes. "What is wrong, Nicholas? Are you ill?"

"No. I simply must . . . must speak with you, before we can go on. There is something I must tell you."

Her eyes dropped. This was a moment she had been dreading. A moment of revelation. Of judgment.

"I must tell you something, as well," she said.

"You, Elizabeth?"

"Yes." She turned from him, and went to sit on a marble bench beside a statue of a cavorting Cupid. She stared up at the moon, and thought of Peter and of the dead duke. She hardly knew where to begin.

And she did not truly want to begin at all. She wanted their lives to go on as they had been ever since they had met, full of laughter.

She had suffered so much, and only tonight had she come to feel truly secure, truly in the midst of a real family at last. Did she not deserve this time of joy, however fragile, however brief?

"Yes, I do," she whispered. *And I cannot allow anything to harm this time, to spoil it.*

"What did you say, Elizabeth?" Nicholas sat beside her on the bench.

"I merely said—I *do* have things to tell you. Many

things. But not tonight, please. Tonight is too beautiful."

"But, Elizabeth . . ."

"No." She pressed her finger to his lips. "Tomorrow is time enough for reality. Or the day after. Tonight I only want you to hold me. Please, Nicholas, just hold me against you, as if you would never let me go."

Nicholas gathered her against him, his cheek pressed to the softness of her hair. He inhaled her sweet, precious scent, and all seemed peaceful and perfect in their small corner of Eden.

But his mind was shouting one word—*Coward*.

"Someone seems very happy this morning!" Georgina said, around a mouthful of hairpins. She smiled at her friend as Elizabeth leaned against her open window, humming and plaiting her hair.

"Someone?" Elizabeth said. "You could not mean me!"

"Oh, no. You are just the little lark singing love songs all morning long."

"It must be all the fresh country air."

"*And* a fine gentleman. What did happen in the garden last night?" Georgina pushed the last of the pins into her coiffure of deliberately disarranged curls, and stood to button up her morning dress. "I know when romance is afoot in my very house."

Elizabeth laughed aloud. "Oh, Georgie! He *loves* me. He told me yesterday on our picnic, and I have been aching to tell you ever since."

"Oh!" Georgina shrieked, running to clasp Elizabeth in an exuberant embrace. "I knew it! I absolutely knew it. I could tell from your faces at dinner last night. Tell me, how did you answer him?"

"Well . . ." Elizabeth sat down on the edge of Georgina's unmade bed and kicked her bare feet idly. "Actually, I declared myself first."

"You didn't!"

"I did, and I have no regrets, not a whit. He had just confided in me, you see. About his past. You were right that there was more to him than seemed, Georgie. He had such a miserable childhood. I was crying, and he had his head on my lap, and I just could not seem to help myself. The words just poured out."

"And?"

"And then he said that he loved me, too, and that nothing could ever be allowed to come between us. And it will not."

"What of your fears before? About your brother, and your true identity?" Georgina sat down beside her, her forehead creased in concern.

Elizabeth waved an airy hand. "That is all forgotten."

"Then you told Nicholas of what happened?"

"Well, no. Not precisely." Elizabeth looked away. "I tried to, last night in the garden, but it was so wonderful. I didn't want to spoil it."

"Then you will tell him?"

"Oh, yes. Of course. When the right time presents itself. But I am far too happy here to bring that ugliness to this lovely place. What harm can it do to wait just a bit longer? Until we are back in Venice?"

Georgina looked doubtful, but all she said was, "Whatever you think best, Lizzie."

"Yes. And I will have to tell him soon. My real name will be on the marriage lines, will it not?"

"Marriage?" Georgina gasped. "Has he . . . ?"

"Not yet! Not yet. But I think he very soon will."

They shrieked in unison, and threw their arms about each other in a flurry of ribbons and lace.

"The yellow silk we saw in Signora Benini's shop window last month!" Georgina cried, ever the planner. "It would be utter perfection, Lizzie, with yellow roses in your hair."

Elizabeth giggled, and swept the sheet off the bed. She twirled it over her head like a bridal veil and marched about the room humming a stately pavane. "It would be wonderful! Oh, but we mustn't plan yet, Georgie. It would be ill luck."

"Hey-ho!" Nicholas's shout floated up through the open window. "Is someone being murdered up there, with all that shouting?"

Elizabeth ran to the window, the sheet still clasped about her head, and waved down at him. He was handsome and smiling in the morning sunshine, his strong throat revealed in the open-throated peasant shirt he wore with a simple knotted red kerchief. He was her gypsy prince. "Not at all!" she answered. "I was merely deciding on what to wear today."

"I think what you are wearing now is charming."

Elizabeth looked down, and saw she still wore her night rail under the trailing sheet. She stepped back. "Rogue! Wait right there. I shall be down directly."

"Do not be very long. The light is just right for viewing the ruins."

"I said I would be there directly! Be patient."

" 'Tis twenty years till then!"

"You have been reading Shakespeare again!" She

blew him a kiss from her fingertips, and withdrew from the window, closing it against his protestations.

"Such a rake." She sighed and reached for the blue dress of Georgina's she was borrowing for the day. Pausing only to button it up and reach for her slippers, she waved at Georgina and danced out the door to where Nicholas was waiting with their picnic hamper.

"There she is at last, my Juliet." He lifted her by her waist, twirling her about and about until the sky tilted drunkenly and her skirts flew about her knees.

"You shall have to set me on my feet, Romeo, before I cast up my accounts all over your fine shirt!" She laughed, clutching at his shoulders in her dizziness.

"And we can't have that, now can we?" Nicholas lowered her to the ground, his hands warm and safe on her waist. For a moment, he clasped her to him, so close and tight it was almost painful.

"Nicholas?" Elizabeth stepped back a bit, frightened that whatever had been about to be said last night was going to haunt their day again. "Is something amiss?"

He only smiled faintly, and wrapped a long strand of her black hair around his finger. He studied it closely, as if he had never seen such hair before. "Amiss? What could possibly be amiss, on such a day as this? I have apricot tarts in my hamper, and a lovely girl on my arm, and the Italian sky above me." He laughed, and danced her around in a circle. "You see, dear, I have even begun to wax poetical today."

Elizabeth laughed obligingly. "Byron need have no fears of his new rival, I think." She linked her arm in his, and led him toward the pathway that went to the old Roman ruins. "It *is* a fine day, just as every day has been since we came here. I vow I have never stopped smiling, even in my sleep! I even have sweet dreams here."

"Then we shall have to come here very often indeed."

"Yes, we shall." Elizabeth paused to examine an oleander bush. "But sometimes, Nicholas, I . . ."

"Yes, dear? You. . . . ?"

It had to be said. "Sometimes I feel as if you did not completely share in this happiness."

Nicholas was silent a very long moment. He held Elizabeth's hand but he did not look at her. "Wise Elizabeth," he said at last. "There is . . . something. But you were correct last night in saying that this is not the place for such things. It is far too lovely. *You* are too lovely to have your holiday marred in any way. And what I have to say is not so urgent."

"But you will tell me?" she whispered. *Just as I must tell you.*

Instead of answering, he raised her fingers to his lips. "We are being far too serious for such a day! This is a day meant for frivolity of the most blatant sort. Were we not going to view the ruins?"

Elizabeth looked around at the warm sun, the sapphire sky, the flowers just beginning to peek from the ground. It *was* a lovely day. Misgivings still lurked in her mind, but she shrugged them away and smiled. "I have a much better idea."

"Oh? And what is that idea?"

"A swim."

"Now?"

"This instant!" Elizabeth hurried off down the

twisting pathway that led to the sparkling sea, tugging Nicholas by the hand behind her. "Or are you frightened?"

That was a challenge Nicholas had never been able to let pass by. "Scared? I was a champion rower at school, I will have you know. And I took more than one spill into the Thames, which was considerably colder than this little pond."

"Good. Then perhaps you can keep up with me!"

They reached the shore, where gentle pale blue waves, tipped with white, lapped at the rocky sand. Elizabeth shed her shoes and stockings, and reached for the buttons of her gown.

Nicholas laughed at her utter audacity. "Are you going in the altogether?"

"Certainly not! I am a lady." Her gown joined the pile of clothing, along with her single petticoat. "I will wear my chemise."

Nicholas was utterly unable to look away as she turned and waded into the water, disappearing little by little until only her seal-dark head was visible above the waves.

Nicholas had seen her bare legs that night on the terrace in Venice, and her décolletage was revealed in many a ball gown, but that had always been at night, dark. In moonlight, Elizabeth was lovely.

In sunlight, she was incomparable.

Her legs were not long, but they were slender and white, her feet elegantly arched as they kicked behind her. He wished he had her skill with a paintbrush; then he could capture her forever, just as she was this moment. A mermaid frolicking in the Mediterranean surf.

"Are you not coming in, champion rower?" she

called. "The water is cool, but wonderful!" She beckoned to him, revealing the enticing sheerness of her wet garment.

Nicholas, frozen in place for those long moments, suddenly sprang into motion. His clothes joined hers on the sand, and he swam out toward her until he could grasp her waist. He lifted her high against him, kissing the seawater saltiness of her lips until she gasped.

"I love you," he whispered, staring up into her shining eyes, the sunlit corona of her hair. "I love you, and I wish that this day, this moment, would never end."

"It won't." She pulled his head back to hers, kissing him in return. "We will not let it end. Ever."

Chapter Fifteen

Venice

"Signorina! Signorina, you must wake up!"

Elizabeth burrowed deeper beneath the bed-clothes, trying to escape from Bianca's ever-more insistent voice. Since their return to Venice three days ago, when Nicholas had carried her, giggling, over the threshold, she had not retired once before dawn. She had been sitting on the terrace the night before, drinking champagne and gossiping with Nicholas and Georgina until the sun had been quite high. It felt as though she had only just fallen asleep, and she was loath to have her delicious dream interrupted.

"Oh, do go away, Bianca!" She groaned. "It is hardly morning."

"But, signorina, there is a visitor! *Such* a visitor!" Bianca rolled her eyes.

"A visitor? So early?" Elizabeth groaned again. It was very likely some patron who was not happy with their portrait, or one of Georgina's spurned suitors. All their artist friends would be still abed, as all sensible people should be. "Go and wake Georgina. Or Nicholas."

"Signora Georgina is already downstairs, and Signor Nicholas is not at home."

Georgina, awake and downstairs before noon? And Nicholas out already, after their late night? Very odd. "Where is Nicholas, Bianca?"

"I do not know. He said he had an errand, and would be back for breakfast."

Elizabeth opened one eye to peer up at the maid. "And who is this caller?"

Bianca shrugged. "I do not know. He would not give his name, but he is *molto* handsome."

"He?"

"Yes, and he is asking for you, but Signora Georgina, she says you are not to be disturbed and he must go away."

Curiouser and curiouser. Elizabeth swung her legs out of bed and reached for her dressing gown. "What does this man look like? Aside from being *molto* handsome."

"Oh, tall, as tall as Signor Nicholas. And golden. And very elegant."

Tall, golden, and elegant. Could it be . . . ?

Elizabeth turned quite as white as her sheets.

"I must be found out," she whispered.

"Signorina?"

Elizabeth shook her head. "Hand me my slippers, Bianca. I must greet our guest."

As if in a daze, she brushed her hair and tied it back with a piece of ribbon, donned her slippers, and made her way down the stairs with Bianca fluttering behind her.

It was as she had feared, as she had dreamed on many a disturbed night. Georgina stood before the empty grate, still wearing her night rail, and brandishing a fireplace poker at the Earl of Clifton.

Peter *was* elegant, every bit as elegant as she remembered. He quite overpowered their rented room in his doeskin breeches and many-caped greatcoat. He stood behind her writing desk, his hat and walking stick resting atop some of her sketches of Katerina Bruni. His gloves slapped rhythmically against his thigh.

He quite looked as if he owned the place, and they were merely his recalcitrant servants. Two years might almost never have passed.

Except that *she* was different now. She no longer would stammer and blush and cry before his coldness. She was free. She was a woman who had made her own way in the world, and was no longer a little girl.

Was she not?

"Good morning, Peter," she said coolly, as if it had not been so very long since they had seen each other; as if they might have dined just the night before. She took the poker from Georgina's hand, placed it back beside the grate, and drew her glowering friend firmly to her side. "And what brings you to Venice at such a quiet time of year?"

"Why, the charming weather, of course." He gestured with his gloves to the steady, silver rain outside the windows. "Such a vast improvement on English rain."

"I am certain you will notice no difference when you have returned to England." *Where you belong*, she added silently. "When will you be returning?"

"I shall be back beside my own cozy hearth very soon. When you have packed your trunks, dear sister, we shall be gone from here."

Georgina surged forward. "Why, you bas . . ."

Elizabeth grasped Georgina's hand tighter, holding

her back from scoring Peter's golden features with her wicked nails. "I am afraid that is impossible, *brother dear*. My home is here now, and I cannot abandon my work."

"Oh, I think not."

A knot of ice slowly formed in Elizabeth's belly as she watched Peter remove a sealed document from inside his coat. She watched in a haze as he laid the paper on the desk.

"I am still your guardian, Elizabeth. Until you reach your twenty-first birthday, which, if I am not mistaken, is almost a year away. Those were the terms of our parents' will."

"This is absurd!" Elizabeth whispered.

"Oh, my dear, it could not be less absurd. I have here a magistrate's order, giving you into my care." He glanced about their dim, dusty drawing room, littered with canvases and sketches. "And you obviously need my care, Elizabeth. No gently reared woman in her right mind would choose to live such a . . . disordered life. If you do not come home with me now, your friends could be brought up on charges of kidnapping."

"What?" Elizabeth cried, utterly shocked. All the times she had tried to imagine what would happen if Peter found her, she had never envisioned this, threatening her friends.

"No, Lizzie!" Georgina seized Elizabeth's arm, and drew her into the empty corridor, whispering furiously, "You must not go with him. Who knows what will happen? Something quite dreadful, to be sure. He cannot be in his right mind to come here like this, barking unreasonable orders, taking over your life."

"Georgie, I must. I have no choice. I would never

see you in such trouble for my sake. The scandal could mean the end of your career. If I go away quietly, you can put it about that I am ill and have gone away to—to Switzerland or someplace, to recover."

"Never! I do not care about all that. What are some old portraits I'm finishing to your safety? You are my own sister, Lizzie; I would die if any harm befell you. And you are not *safe* with that man!" Georgina shook her head fiercely. "I never liked him, even when all the girls at Miss Thompson's were swooning over him. He was too cool by half."

Elizabeth turned away and leaned her forehead against the wall, closing her eyes tightly. What to do, what to do? Of course she could not stay and see anyone arrested and put in clink on her behalf. Yet how could she simply pack her things and leave meekly with Peter? How could she leave her work, go back to Clifton Manor, where so many memories waited?

How could she go back to that staid English country life, after Italy?

She shuddered just to think of the old vicar, the Misses Allan, Lord and Lady Haversham with their deadly dull "salons."

And, worst of all, how could she ever leave Nicholas?

Nicholas.

Elizabeth slowly opened her eyes and stared sightlessly at the white plaster of the wall as the worst, the most hideous thought fluttered through her mind like an insidious whisper.

No. Nicholas could have nothing to do with all of

this. Simply because he had disappeared from the house the very morning Peter appeared . . .

But Nicholas loved her! Did he not? Those weeks in the country had been the most glorious of her life, and his adoring attentions had told her he felt the same. Surely his kisses, his sweet words, did not lie?

And then, how could he even know Peter? An artist's secretary, a bastard son, would never have occasion to meet the Earl of Clifton, let alone conspire with him in such a way. Surely.

However . . .

How well did she truly know Nicholas, a tiny voice whispered in the back of her mind. She knew the feel of his arms, his kisses, how he moved with her so perfectly when they danced. He had told her of his father, but she did not know who that father was, how Nicholas had come to be in Italy, how he dressed so fashionably if he had to seek employment.

She sank onto the nearest chair, her knees suddenly too weak to support her, her head in her hands as these unwelcome thoughts chased around her mind. If she loved Nicholas, how could she even suspect him? She had given him her heart and her very soul; she could not be such a poor judge of character. No artist could be.

It all had to be a ridiculous coincidence.

But then how *did* Peter know where to find her? She had been so very careful all these years.

Apparently not nearly careful enough.

"It cannot be," she whispered. "He loves me."

"What did you say, Lizzie?" Georgina leaned over her. "Are you quite well? Shall I have Bianca fetch some brandy?"

"No, no brandy. I must keep my head about me. I shall be well presently."

"Are you certain?"

"Yes. Georgie, have you seen Nicholas at all this morning?"

Georgina frowned in thought. "No, not at all."

"Bianca told me he went out quite early."

"Blast! If only he were here . . ." Georgina's voice trailed away. "No. Oh, Lizzie, no, of course it was not Nicholas who betrayed your whereabouts. He . . ."

"He what? He *loves* me?"

"He does love you! I know the way he looks at you, Lizzie. He would never conspire with Peter Everdean against you this way."

Elizabeth shook her head. "I do hope you are right. But I cannot be sure of anything now, the world is so havey-cavey all of a sudden."

"You can be sure of me. I will not let him take you away, not when your career is so promising before you."

"Georgie, my dearest friend, what choice do we have? He only wants me to go to England with him, for some unfathomable reason. He doesn't really want you arrested. And it is only until I am twenty-one, less than a year away. A year of rusticating could hardly do me any harm. Then I can come back here. Or maybe go to India, or America!"

"America! Oh, Lizzie, we should go there now. He will lock you up. He will force you to marry. He will . . ."

"Georgie," Elizabeth interrupted firmly. "I escaped him before, I will again. All will be well." She clung to her friend's hand. "All will be well."

Georgina was quiet for a long moment. "You will write every day?"

"Every, every day! And I shall paint every day, even if I have to do a portrait of Lady Haversham's poodles." Elizabeth stood and smoothed back her hair, trying to bring some composure back to her countenance. "Now, I shall tell Peter to return to his hotel, or wherever he came from, and wait for us to send him word that I am ready to depart. That should bring us a little time, at least. Bianca is such a slow packer."

"Yes. And if all else fails, we could always have Nicholas challenge Peter to a duel!"

Elizabeth could not help but laugh at the vision of Peter and Nicholas, in their fine coats and polished boots, facing off across a Venetian square filled with pigeons.

Her composure lasted only until she had dismissed Peter and gone up to her bedroom. As she closed the door behind her, the first sight she saw was Nicholas's half-finished portrait, propped on its easel in the corner.

She went to it, and traced the painted dark curls with her fingertip, moving over his eyes and his smile.

His wonderful, dazzling, mischievous smile. She turned away from the painting. Even if he were a deceiver, she could not stop loving him just like that, in an instant. He had brought true laughter into her life, brought *life* into her life, when she had thought her whole self given over only to art. That could never fade, no matter what came. Could it?

"Forever, you said," she murmured. "But I have not time for such fancies now. I must think. Think!"

She took her small traveling trunk, only just unpacked from the country, and began carefully, slowly folding her undergarments and night rails and tucking them inside. Her day dresses went in, her hats and slippers. All her gowns had been taken from the wardrobe and piled on the bed when the longed-for, but dreaded knock came at her door.

And when she opened it to see Nicholas's pale, haunted face, she knew the truth.

His wild gaze went past her to the open trunk, the pile of gowns. "What are you doing, Elizabeth?" he croaked, his voice hoarse and broken, nothing like his usual laughter-filled tones.

She turned from him and went back to slowly folding her clothes, her mind a careful blank. She forced herself to concentrate on the dresses in her hands, the feel of silk and muslin, the scent of the lavender sachets she tucked into the folds. She did not want to think of the man behind her. She did not want to either love him or hate him.

"I am packing, of course," she answered. "Surely you must know I am going on a voyage, Nicholas. *If* that is your name." She clutched a fur-trimmed pelisse to her bosom dramatically, feeling more and more like some melodramatic Minerva Press heroine.

"It *is* my name, blast it!" Then his stillness shattered. He grabbed her shoulders, forcing her to face him, to look up into his eyes. "I did not lie about that."

Elizabeth wanted to sob, to collapse on the floor and howl with the agony of it. She wanted to beat him with her fists, to kick him until he felt as much pain as she did. Until that instant she had clung to hope, but now it was irretrievably gone. "You did come here because of Peter."

Nicholas's hands tightened on her arms, as if he feared she would disappear in a puff of smoke if he let her go. He nodded slowly.

"Did he pay you?" she asked softly.

"No! Lizzie, it was not like that . . ."

She did cry then, at the sound of her nickname on his lips; hot, silent tears that fell unchecked down her chin and spotted her bodice. "Then what was it like, Nicholas? What could possibly have induced you to be so unspeakably cruel? To ruin all my hopes? Tell me! Damn you, tell me why."

Her careful control was quickly slipping away. Nicholas led her to the dressing table and forced her to sit, kneeling before her like the veriest supplicant before his empress. He held her hands between his, and she was too wrapped in misery to snatch them back.

"I knew Peter years ago," Nicholas began. "In Spain."

"Spain."

"Yes. We were in the same regiment, and we became friends."

Had anyone ever really been friends with Peter? Elizabeth sniffed, and wiped at her eyes with her sleeve. "So that is your reason? Friendship?"

Nicholas pressed a handkerchief into her hands. "More than mere friendship, Lizzie. Peter saved my very life."

She snorted inelegantly. "Peter? A hero?"

"Yes, he was. I was terribly wounded. You have seen my leg, when we were swimming." He had the grace to blush at the mention of just how much of him she had seen that day. "I would have bled to death there on the battlefield, if he had not carried me miles to the field hospital, fighting off the French every step of the way."

Elizabeth nodded a bit. "I see."

"Do you?" A reluctant hope lit in Nicholas's eyes. "Do you see, Elizabeth, how very much I owed Peter? I thought he was dead, that my debt would forever go unpaid. Until last winter, when I met him again in London."

She drew her hands from his, and turned to the gilt-framed mirror above the dressing table. The white-faced woman there seemed a veritable stranger. "So you discharged your debt. My life for yours on that battlefield."

"Elizabeth, please!" he cried, trying to take her hands again. "I had no idea . . ."

"No idea of what?" She held her hands away from him, folded them before her to still their trembling.

Nicholas sat back on his heels. "That you are who you are."

"What could that possibly mean? Of course I am who I am."

"I was a different person then, Lizzie. I was selfish, wild. I thought surely you had run away in some spoiled pique, that it was all a misunderstanding. That it would be a simple thing to persuade you that it would be best for you to return to England."

"What occurred to make you think otherwise?"

"You, of course. I saw your life here. Your work, your friends. I saw that you were not some pampered, petulant miss; you were a strong-willed person who would not be easily persuaded."

Elizabeth's fist suddenly came down on the table, rattling bottles of scent and pots of rice powder, as anger finally melted the knot of horrible numbness. "So you concocted this ridiculous scheme to insinuate yourself into my life, to pretend to care about me!"

"That part was *not* a lie." His voice was low and intense, in counterpoint to her white-hot anger. "I do love you. I think I have loved you since I first saw you at that masked ball. You are so unlike anyone I have ever known."

"You say you love me, yet you planned to hand me over like some piece of merchandise to my brother, knowing how I felt about my life here."

"I do not know! I do not know what I would have done, had the issue been forced on me. I tried to tell you, but I was a coward, I let you put me off. But I vow this to you, Elizabeth—I did not bring Peter here. I have not even been in contact with him since I left England."

Elizabeth's head ached unbearably. She closed her eyes against all the pain, but it would not be shut out. "I do not know what to believe. I am far too tired to sort all this out right now."

"What will you do?" he asked quietly.

"Go back to England, of course. To spend the next year at Clifton Manor, until I reach my majority and can rejoin Georgina here."

"Lizzie, you don't . . ."

"Yes. I do. I may even decide I want to. There is something rather soothing in the English countryside, is there not? Perhaps I can really think while I am there."

"But I can't let you just leave me like this!" he said softly.

"Oh, Nicholas." She turned back to him, and laid her fingertips against his beloved face. "You have no choice in the matter, and neither do I."

He grasped her fingers, pressing them to his lips. "I will do whatever you say. I only want what will make you happy, you know that. Will you write to me at least?"

"I do not know if I can. I don't even know your true name."

"Sir Nicholas Hollingsworth." A ghost of his former dashing smile whispered across his mouth. "At your service."

Her eyes widened. "Old Nick Hollingsworth?"

"One and the same, I regret to admit. But how did you know of my unfortunate sobriquet?"

"I used to read all the London scandal sheets when I lived at Clifton Manor. You were a favorite subject." She laughed, a mirthless, hollow sound. "Now I understand about Lady Deake and her odd behavior. She threw a glass of champagne in your face at a ball once, did she not? And then fled the scene in tears?"

He looked down at the carpet, his ears crimson among his black curls. "That was a very long time ago."

"Yes," Elizabeth agreed. "A long time ago. I do regret not being the one to restore her Veronese. Perhaps she will hire Georgina." She looked back to the mirror, to watch his reflection in the glass. "I may write to you, if only to hear about the oh-so-dashing life you led, and will probably lead again."

"Will you, Elizabeth? Will you write?"

"Perhaps." She stood and went back to her packing, her spine very straight. "Now I do think you should leave. Before Peter returns, or Georgina comes after you with the andirons."

Nicholas also stood. "I do love you, Elizabeth. That was never a lie, not for an instant. I will always love you."

She sighed. "I don't know how to believe you."

"No." He turned to leave, but she stopped him with a word.

"Nicholas?"

"Yes?" He swung around in hope, but she merely held out a rather rumpled letter, folded and sealed.

"You are not the only one who has harbored secrets," she said. "And for that I am sorry. Please, read this when you are alone, and you will understand."

Nicholas swallowed hard, searching for the words that would make things right between them, that would prove to her the depths of his feelings. But in the end, there were no words. He pressed a single kiss on her averted cheek and left her standing there, the door clicking shut softly behind him.

"I love you, too, Nicholas," Elizabeth whispered. "And that is the very damnable thing."

"Nicholas! Where are you going?"

He was almost out of the door, his valise in hand, when Georgina flew downstairs to grab his arm in an iron grasp. She wore a nightgown and a shawl; her feet were bare and her hair loose. She had obviously been crying, as her cheeks were puffy and as red as her wild curls.

Nicholas had never thought to see Elizabeth's

glamorous friend so disheveled and distraught. It was another black mark against his character; another life he had wreaked havoc in.

"I am leaving, Mrs. Beaumont," he answered her.

"Leaving? Now?"

"I think it best. Under the circumstances."

"Whatever are you talking about? You must help Elizabeth! You cannot leave now, we need you."

"You have no need of me."

Her eyes were wide, bewildered. "But you love her, do you not? You are to marry her?"

Nicholas almost laughed aloud with the bitterness of it. "I doubt Elizabeth would care to marry me now, since she thinks I have brought such disaster on your house."

Georgina stared up at him in utter disbelief. "This is *your* doing? You were working for Peter all the while?"

Nicholas was too tired to explain again, too exhausted to justify what had truly been unjustifiable. He drew a small velvet jewel case from his coat and pressed it into Georgina's cold hand. "Please, give this to Elizabeth, Mrs. Beaumont, and accept my deepest apologies."

Even when the heavy front doors were between them, he could hear her screaming curses at him in English, Italian, and French, vowing grotesque vengeances on him and all his descendants, like some Amazon of old.

He could tell that all those horrid novels had not gone to waste.

He believed he now knew how Adam had felt, when he was expelled from Paradise by an angel with a flaming sword.

* * *

"Well, well. If it isn't the *secretary*."

It was quite the last voice Nicholas had wanted to hear, aside from Georgina Beaumont's, when he had come to Florian's with the express wish to become drunk as a bishop. He knocked back his brandy, and closed his eyes against the warm sting. "Get away from me, Peter."

"Or what? You will challenge me to a duel, perhaps?" Peter slid into the chair next to his and signaled to the waiter for another brandy. "I would hardly recommend it. You are quite foxed already, and obviously suicidal. It would be no challenge for me at all, and no way to get back into Elizabeth's good graces. She is quite fond of you, I see, though I scarce could say why."

Nicholas did not answer, or even look at his friend. He stared fixedly out the window at an arguing couple who had paused beneath the portico. The dark-haired woman threw back her head; her hands gesticulated wildly in the air. If there had been a heavy object to hand, she would no doubt have thrown it at her hapless partner's head. The man listened to her in stony silence.

If only Elizabeth had flown at him like that! If she had only railed at him, cursed him, thrown paint pots at his head. Instead she had confronted him in chill calm, icy dignity, her lovely silver eyes grave and dark as slate, unforgiving. He knew from his own experience that such anger, pushed deep down inside, was the very worst sort. It would only fester there, getting colder and larger until her hatred for him overcame all her love.

"You knew," he said, still watching the couple. "You knew that I would fall in love with her."

Peter shrugged. "Certainly I did not *know*. Contrary to popular belief, I am no sorcerer possessed of the dark arts. Even I cannot know what a person's foolish heart will do."

"Yet you suspected."

"Um, perhaps, yes. I know Elizabeth, and I know you. Or at least I did once. I knew that your spirits were the same. Wild, and perhaps a bit misguided, but well meaning."

Nicholas's fist clenched around the snifter of brandy. "So this was some sort of test you devised."

"Not at all. Really, Nicholas, you always did make things out to be far more complex than they are. Because you would understand what she was about, I thought you were the one who could persuade her to see reason and give up this silly gypsy life."

"I hardly think her life is *silly*," Nicholas snapped. "She is a fine artist, a great one even, and she has many clients and a brilliant future."

"You see, my friend? You do understand her."

Nicholas took a deep, steadying breath. "What will you do now? Drag her back to England?"

"I hardly think 'drag' is the right word. That conjures up such images of cavemen. And yes. She will come back to England with me. Was that not the point of this absurd exercise?" Peter sighed, and seemed almost pensive as he looked down into his own glass. "I can try to make her understand, perhaps even forgive me, for my behavior, only if we are at home where it is quiet. Here she is too caught up in her wild ways."

Nicholas's fierce anger, his desire to plant Peter a

sound facer, had subsided to a dull roar behind his eyes. All he really had now was an ineffable sadness. He had lost so much in one morning. He had lost everything—his love, his honor, his future. "How am I to make her forgive *me*?"

Peter gave a strange half smile. "That, Nick, I cannot tell you. Will you also be returning to England?"

"Yes. I could not stay in Venice."

"No. That would not be wise. I hear that Elizabeth's Amazon friend can shoot the ace from a card at fifty paces. I should not like to encounter her in some dark alleyway." Peter drained his brandy and stood. "I want you to know, Nick, that I bear you no ill will for how all this turned out. You will always be welcome at Clifton Manor, should you ever choose to call."

With that, he departed, fading into the milling crowd and leaving Nicholas alone with his drink and his thoughts.

"*You* may bear me no ill will, Peter," he muttered. "But what of your sister? And what of myself?"

As Elizabeth prepared to step into the boat that would carry her from her one true home, Georgina caught her in one last farewell embrace.

"Georgie," Elizabeth said in a strangled voice. "Write to me very often, and tell me all your doings, every detail. All your commissions, and parties. And tell Stephen I said good-bye."

Georgina wrinkled her nose. "I will tell him, if that is what you want. And you must write to me of all *your* doings."

Elizabeth laughed. "Oh, yes, I shall tell you of the sheep and the grass growing!"

"No, tell me of your painting. I will send all of your work on, and you must not neglect it."

"I will not neglect it. I couldn't."

"Elizabeth," Peter called impatiently. "It grows late."

Elizabeth kissed her friend's cheek one last time. "I will see you soon, Georgie."

"Yes. Perhaps sooner than you think!"

"Do not do anything foolish, such as follow me to Derbyshire! You would hate it there."

"Do something foolish? Me? Never!" Georgina pressed a small box into Elizabeth's gloved hand. "Here."

"What is this? A gift?"

"Yes, but not from me, I fear."

"Then who . . . ?"

Georgina's lips tightened. "It is from Nicholas. He asked me to give it to you before he left, right before I lost my temper at him utterly and said some very rude things."

Puzzled, Elizabeth opened the box, and stared down in astonishment.

There, flashing in the late afternoon sunlight, was a sapphire-and-diamond ring. A betrothal ring.

For one instant, Elizabeth wanted only to cry out all her grief and disappointment. Then she wanted to fling the thing into the canal.

In the end, she just closed the box and stuffed it into her reticule. Perhaps, one day, when some of the pain had faded, she would want to take it out and remember how, for a brief while, a man had made the sun shine in her life every day.

Chapter Sixteen

A new volume of poetry lay open on the lap of Elizabeth's new bishop's blue carriage dress, and her eyes were cast down upon it, but she had not really read a word in ten miles or more. Nor did she see the green glories of the English countryside that flew past the carriage windows, palest blue sky and hedgerows glistening in the morning mist.

She did not see or feel anything at all. She hadn't since the last of Venice's golden spires had faded from her view, and she had sensed herself leaving Elizabeth Cheswood behind and becoming Lady Elizabeth Everdean again.

The voyage had been uneventful, a series of ships and carriages and inns, meals she didn't want to eat, too much wine drunk, and no conversation.

"We should arrive very soon," Peter commented. He looked stylishly bored, as he had for their entire journey, never dusty or rumpled or insulted by her silences. But now his hands twisted and untwisted on the golden head of his fashionable walking stick.

"Yes. I can recognize some of the countryside." Elizabeth cut another page of her book.

"I hope you will be quite comfortable there, at Clifton Manor. Your rooms are just as you left them."

"Yes." Her gloved fingertip traced the printed lines that she did not see.

"And your maid is still employed there. The silly chit refused to leave, even when Lady Haversham tried to hire her away."

"Good. I did miss Daisy." *And nothing else there.*

Peter smiled coolly, almost as if he sensed the unspoken words that hung bewteen them. "No one to dress your hair properly in Italy?"

"I am quite capable of dressing my own hair, thank you. Daisy was always so very cheerful, though. A great comfort in such a gloomy household." Elizabeth knew she was behaving childishly, but she could not seem to help herself. It was either that or weep.

A heavy silence fell in the carriage, broken only by the steady rustle of Elizabeth's pages turning and the tap of Peter's stick on the floor. Suddenly, he leaned forward and grasped her wrist.

Elizabeth was so startled that her book fell from her lap with a clatter. She clutched the penknife in her fist. To cover her confusion, she pulled her hand away and bent to retrieve the book.

"It will not be like that at Clifton anymore, Elizabeth," he said, his voice almost . . . was it beseeching?

"Like what?" Elizabeth murmured, completely taken aback.

"As it was before you left. I was wrong, very wrong to have behaved as I did towards you. The quarrels, that business with the duke . . ."

Elizabeth held up her hand to stop the bewildering flow of his words. "Please. Let us never speak of that again."

"No. Of course." Peter sat back, and she could see

the old coldness descending on him like a cloak. "I have no excuse. I was not myself when I returned from the Peninsula."

That Elizabeth could agree with wholeheartedly.

"But you have been gone a long time, Elizabeth," he continued. "Things have changed. I know that Clifton is not Venice . . ."

Elizabeth snorted.

Peter went on as if he had not heard her lapse in manners. "But I am certain you can be happy here again. I only wish to make amends to you."

Elizabeth was quite sick of men who felt they knew what was best for her, who thought they could order her life to suit themselves no matter what her own feelings were. "Oh, Peter." She sighed. "The only amends you could have made was to have left me to my own life and not have sent your flunky after me."

"Elizabeth, you are wrong about me. I am your brother; I want only what is best for you."

"You cannot even begin to know what that would be! Only I know what is best for me."

Peter merely shrugged. "We shall see." Then he added, very gently, "And you are also wrong about Nick Hollingsworth."

She was saved from answering when the carriage drew to a halt on the gravel drive curving in front of Clifton Manor. Elizabeth peered out from behind the wispy veil of her bonnet. The house had not changed at all, the grand Tudor façade with its incongruous pillared Georgian side wings, which had been added by her stepfather. It was a good deal tidier than when she had last seen it, however, and a bit less forbidding. The ivy was trimmed back, and the stone front steps gleamed beneath the feet of the servants assembled there.

Despite the polishing, the new flowers spilling from the beds, the crisp curtains behind the windows, the aura remained the same, a miasma of the living of so many generations. So much of her own past was there. The laughter of her beautiful mother, as she let her little daughter try on her gowns; her stepfather carrying her piggyback down the grand staircase; Peter dancing with her at her very first ball. There was also the dead duke. It was all there, waiting for her to take it back up again as if no time had passed at all.

"Are you ready?" Peter asked. "They are waiting to greet you."

Shaken from her fancies, Elizabeth nodded and hastily tucked the book into her traveling case. "Yes, certainly."

Jenkins, the elderly butler who had been at Clifton since Elizabeth had come there as a child, was the first to step forward and welcome her as Peter assisted her from the carriage.

"Lady Elizabeth," Jenkins said. "May I say what a great honor it is to welcome you home again?"

The twinkle in his faded eyes belied his formal manner. Elizabeth smiled as she recalled how he had slipped her extra plum cakes at childhood teatimes. "Thank you, Jenkins," she answered. "It is very good to see you again."

"And Mrs. Smith is also quite eager to greet you," Peter added, indicating the black-clad, rosy-cheeked housekeeper.

"Mrs. Smith!" Elizabeth cried in delight. "Do you still make that exquisite chocolate trifle?"

"I do, my lady, and there is some just waiting for your tea this afternoon."

Elizabeth kept her careful smile in place as she was introduced to a myriad of unfamiliar housemaids, kitchen maids, footmen, and gardeners. She had quite forgotten how very many people it took to run such a great house, after two years with only Bianca.

When they reached Daisy, and Elizabeth saw the tears shimmering in her lady's maid's eyes, her composure slipped, and all the tension of her long voyage melted. She forgot decorum and position entirely, and threw her arms around Daisy's small figure.

"My lady!" Daisy cried in shock.

"Oh, Daisy!" Elizabeth sobbed. "How I have missed you!"

"I missed you, too, my lady. I knew you would come home one day, so I never let that Lady Haversham entice me away, even when she wanted to send me to London with her daughter."

"You will never know how I wished you were with me in Italy. You would have adored it, after all those romances we read together! So many ruins and black-eyed counts." Disregarding propriety even further, Elizabeth took Daisy's arm and led her into the house, leaving Peter behind. She turned automatically toward the great staircase. "My rooms are ready?"

"Yes, my lady. I supervised the airing of them myself; it's just as you left it."

It was indeed. The pink silk curtains and bed hangings, the lace-skirted dressing table with its gilt Cupids cavorting around the mirror, even the porcelain doll (Martha) propped on the marble mantel were all just as she remembered. Even the paintings on the walls, her own early efforts, had not been moved.

"Oh, Daisy, I would vow I was sixteen again!" Elizabeth removed her bonnet and sat down on the cushioned window seat that looked out at the gardens. "And the view is quite unchanged."

Daisy shooed away the maids who had already set to unpacking Elizabeth's trunk, and began to shake out the gowns herself. "Italy must have been ever so exciting, my lady."

"Oh, yes. Italy was . . . heaven."

Daisy held up the black velvet and satin gown Elizabeth had worn to the opera on that far-off night, when she had thought to entice Nicholas with its daring neckline. "And these were angel's robes, my lady?"

Elizabeth laughed. Now she remembered exactly why she had hired Daisy so long ago—her irreverence. "So they were! I wore gowns like that to operas, and balls, and breakfasts, and on gondola rides that lasted all night. And I saw art that only gods could have created. Art everywhere." She thought with a pang of the unrestored Veronese. "It was heaven."

"Well, my lady," Daisy answered, briskly hanging the black gown up in the wardrobe. "Things can be lively around here, too."

"Yes?"

"Yes. Lady Haversham's poodles escaped and tried to *eat* some of the vicar's prize hydrangeas a month ago. Ever since then we have heard about nothing but greed and stealing in the Sunday sermons. And the Misses Allan just returned from wintering in Brighton, just bursting with all the gossip they heard there and eager to spread it about. It's almost Venice, without the art."

Elizabeth giggled helplessly. "Daisy, you always could lift me from my sulks! How is it you did not marry while I was away?"

"It was like this, my lady—no one asked me."

"Me, neither." Elizabeth sighed. "Except for Ottavio Turino, but that does not count. He asks every lady to marry him when he is in his cups. We are better off not married, anyway, believe me."

It was Daisy's turn to giggle. "Oh, Lady Elizabeth, what people you met! But what shall you wear to supper? Jenkins says the vicar is coming to dine."

"Reverend Bridges? Oh, something very wicked I should think. Something to welcome myself home properly. What about that green velvet with the gold lace? And do be sure to tell Jenkins to have plenty of wine on hand."

"My lady!"

Elizabeth looked back out at the garden, sunset pink now. "I know that everyone here is expecting a scandal now that I have returned; I may as well oblige them. I've nothing better to do."

Two hours later, a new woman from the travel-stained, weary waif emerged to greet the vicar in the Blue Drawing Room. She had missed supper, but had no intention of missing the Vicar altogether.

She had exchanged her modest carriage dress for green velvet and gold lace, which Bianca, in a fit of economizing, had created by modifying the Carnivale costume Elizabeth had worn the night she met Nicholas Hollingsworth. Her hair was swept up from her bared shoulders and held by golden ribbons; a faintly glistening powder had been dusted across the daring décolletage.

In the firelight of the drawing room she almost glittered, like a strange Italian painting dropped into the decorous manor.

She was not the pastel-clad miss Mr. Bridges, the esteemed vicar of Clifton village, remembered from two years ago, who had stood quietly in the corners of assemblies and always seemed to have paint streaks on her hands and clothes. His last view of her, cringing at her betrothal ball, was quite lost in this dashing lady. He gaped, and could scarcely contain his eagerness to rush out and spread the news among his parishioners.

Peter's lips thinned.

"Mr. Bridges!" Elizabeth cried gaily, holding her ungloved hand, her new sapphire ring sparkling on her ring finger, out to him. "How very long it has been, yet here you are, the same as ever."

"Lady Elizabeth," he answered slowly. "I must say you are *not* the . . . same as ever."

"Am I not?" Elizabeth laughed merrily, trying to imitate Georgina at her most flirtatious. "It is this gown. I am far too old to don white in the evenings now." She wagged her finger playfully at the silent Peter. "Why, brother dear, are you not going to offer your sister something to drink? I vow I am still quite parched after that long journey!"

Peter bowed shortly. "There is ratafia, if you like, Elizabeth. Or I could ring for tea."

"Oh, pooh, no! Is that not brandy I see in your glass?"

"I hardly think . . ."

"I will have brandy. Thank you."

Her voice was also new, steely with determination under a smile. Even Peter took heed of the warning. He bowed again, and went to fetch her a brandy.

Elizabeth settled herself on a chaise by the fire, and smiled up at the vicar. "Now, Mr. Bridges, do sit beside me and tell me all the local news. I am quite perishing to hear if Miss Gray ever married her London viscount, and if Lady Haversham's daughters are all settled."

She whipped open her gold lace fan, and peered at the elderly vicar over its edge.

Lady Elizabeth Everdean had, quite momentously and dramatically, come home.

Chapter Seventeen

Elizabeth watched in the mirror as Daisy looped a long strand of pearls through her elaborate coiffure. She had remembered Derbyshire as quite lacking in social amenities, but in the weeks she had been back they had attended several assemblies, dinners, musicales, and card parties. Many of the local families were in residence before departing for the London Season, and it was considered quite a social coup to have the odd and faintly scandalous Lady Elizabeth at their gatherings.

And Elizabeth had the distinct sense that Peter was trying, with a grim determination, to cheer her up by dragging her hither and yon, from tea party to dance without a pause in between.

In her more dreamy schoolgirl days, when she had imagined an exciting Continental life, she would never have thought the fantastical, golden Venice would seem a solid reality and England a bizarre dream. Yet it had happened.

Clifton Manor, a beautiful house filled with fine furnishings, seemed an uncomfortable place, inhabited by the kind of people who should have been familiar but instead seemed to have strange ideas of what proper behavior should be. They were kind to her and always polite, to be sure, but she seemed not to be what they expected of their Lady Elizabeth, and they watched her closely to see what odd thing she would do next. She felt she was always on exhibit, like a tiger in a menagerie.

At night she would sometimes dream of floating free in a gondola, dappled in buttery sunlight while her handsome gondolier flirted with her in fluid Italian. She dreamed of rich wine on her tongue, almond cakes at Florian's, the scent of incense in the dim splendor of San Marco.

She would wake from these dreams sobbing with homesickness. The old stone church in the village, while lovely, couldn't rival the almost-pagan splendor of a Byzantine cathedral. The servants looked quite scandalized when she drank more than a thimbleful of sherry before dinner, or wore one of her Italian gowns to a party.

Not that her life at Clifton Manor was bad in any way. The servants, despite their curiosity, were most happy to have a lady in residence again, even if she did nothing that was expected. Daisy adored the stories of the odd Venetian maid Bianca, and the narrow gray-pink house she had tended to so poorly. Daisy even posed for her own portrait, after an initial hesitation, and made over all Elizabeth's old pastel frocks by lowering the necklines and removing the excess furbelows. She even delighted in bringing in Georgina's letters on the morning trays of chocolate and toast.

Two footmen had cleaned out her old studio on the third floor, and Georgina had sent on all her works in progress. Elizabeth dutifully set up her easel, and even ground some pigments, but somehow she could not paint. The brushes would just hang from her fingers, and the colors and images that used to flood her mind and make her forget all else refused to come to her. Her mind was a blank. Aside from the portrait of Daisy, she had not finished one work.

Even her appetite was gone. Mrs. Brown, the cook, tried to make her "Italian" meals, to no avail.

Elizabeth could not do anything but think of Nicholas, and the life she had left behind.

Every day, rain or sun, she would go walking through the fields and woods, striding along aimlessly. She hoped that if she could walk far enough, fast enough, she could leave *him*, the taste of him, the sound of his voice, far behind. She felt almost a physical pain in the pit of her stomach whenever she remembered his pale face revealing his betrayal.

She had loved him truly; indeed, she loved him still. Despite his lies, and the lie they had lived together for so many weeks. He lived in her heart, and he would not easily be dislodged. Even distance did not dim the memories.

One moment she would curse him, and vow that if she ever saw him again she would spit in his face for leaving her to this, for lying to her and then never even writing to her. In the next instant, she would cry at the thought of never seeing his face again. It was like a never-ending "delicate time of the month."

One night, unable to sleep, Elizabeth built up a fire in her bedroom grate and tried to feed all her sketches of him to the flames. She could not bring herself to do it. Instead, she brought out her hidden bottle of brandy, drank it, and cried until dawn.

All that came from that experiment was a raging headache.

She had grown thinner, paler; she could see that now in the mirror. She knew that she could not go on in this stupid manner forever, but she didn't know how to stop it. She missed Nicholas; she missed Georgina and all their friends. She hated the fact that Peter set footmen to follow her wherever she went, hated sitting across from him at the dinner table, listening to his cool voice talk to her of inconsequential matters like the weather and the last gathering they had attended.

Most of all, she hated the Elizabeth she had become. The merry girl in Italy, so independent and confident in her abilities, would never have cried such a sea of tears. She would not have been so very indecisive over a mere man. Especially such a man, such a rake.

"Old Nick, indeed," she murmured, not realizing that she spoke aloud.

"I beg your pardon, my lady?" Daisy said.

"Oh, not a thing. I was merely thinking of a painting I am composing in my mind."

"Well, that is good that you are thinking of painting again! And what do you think of your hair, my lady?"

Elizabeth dutifully turned her head to examine the elaborate whorls and waves. "Exquisite, as always. You are more the artist than I am, Daisy. I am not so very certain about the gown, though."

"What is wrong with it, Lady Elizabeth?"

"I loathe white." She fluffed out the skirt of the silk and tulle gown, a creation left over from her days before she left. "It looks rather silly on a woman of nearly one-and-twenty! If only I had not already worn all my Italian gowns."

"White or not, it looks well on you, my lady. And you have your lovely Indian shawl to wear with it."

"Hmm, and quite appropriate for supper and cards at the Havershams'." Elizabeth dug under the dressing table for her discarded silk slippers. "I have half a mind to plead a megrim and stay home with a good book."

"I wouldn't want to do that, my lady. Not tonight, anyway."

"No? Why not?"

"I hear tell the Havershams have a new houseguest."

Elizabeth sighed. "Oh, lud! Not another pimply faced nephew, dangling for an heiress?"

"Oh, no, my lady." Daisy's voice dropped to a whisper. "I heard that this one is a sculptor. Newly arrived from Italy."

Elizabeth stood in the doorway of the Havershams' grand drawing room, surveying the company assembled amidst the overstuffed, overdecorated chinoiserie that Lady Haversham was currently infatuated with. There were the Misses Allan, spinster sisters and arbiters of county morals, dressed in rusty black and surveying everyone through their lorgnettes; the vicar, enjoying a very large glass of fine Madeira; Mr. Taylor, local eligible bachelor and heir to the Viscount Drake, dressed in the pink of London fashion and surrounded by giggling misses.

And conversing with their hostess was the person she sought. Sir Stephen Hampton, her old friend and one-time halfhearted suitor, looking just as she had last seen him in Venice.

He saw her as well, and gave a tiny nod in her direction. Elizabeth waved her white lace fan.

Peter took her arm in a firm grasp. "Shall we go in, my dear?"

Elizabeth did not look at him. "I suppose, since we are already here and have no hope of retreat."

The room hushed just a bit as they made their entrance, as it always did. Local society had grown accustomed to seeing the "odd" Lady Elizabeth, who had vanished from their midst so mysteriously two years ago, in company, but they were still wary of her. It was almost as if they expected her to sing bawdy songs at the pianoforte, or dance barefoot across their ballrooms.

She merely smiled and nodded as Peter escorted her to their hostess, and the hum of conversation slowly resumed.

"Ah, Lord Clifton, Lady Elizabeth," Lady Haversham cried, the feathers on her puce-and-lavender turban bobbing. "You must meet the newest addition to our little society, Sir Stephen Hampton. He is quite a renowned sculptor, and has only recently returned from Italy."

Peter raised a golden brow in Elizabeth's direction. "Italy? Indeed?"

"Yes," Lady Haversham replied. "I thought Lady Elizabeth would be particularly interested in meeting him. She was always so very *artistic*."

"Indeed I am very happy to meet him," answered Elizabeth. She held out her gloved hand for Stephen to bow over. "Your fame has quite preceded you, Sir Stephen. Even in the wilds of Cornwall, where I have lately lived."

"How do you do, Lady Elizabeth?" Stephen gave her hand the merest squeeze.

"Sir Stephen is on his way to begin a commission for the Duke of Ponsonby, for his late duchess's memorial," Lady Haversham interjected. "And speaking of marble, Lord Clifton, I do want to ask your opinion of the ruin I am thinking of having constructed in our park. . . ."

Lady Haversham led Peter away, leaving Elizabeth providentially alone with Stephen.

"Would you care for some refreshment, Lady Elizabeth?" he inquired politely.

"Oh, yes, thank you, Sir Stephen."

They did not speak again until they found a secluded alcove behind the refreshment table.

Elizabeth threw her arms around his neck. "Oh, Stephen, you dear old thing! I have never in my life been so very happy to see anyone."

His arms tightened briefly. "*Are* you glad to see me, Elizabeth?"

"Terribly! I have missed you all so much." She sat down on the velvet bench, and smiled up at him. "Tell me, how is everyone, and what are you doing in Derbyshire?"

"Everyone is well. Georgina sent this on to you." He reached into his coat and withdrew a thick letter. "She has closed up your house in Venice, and I suspect you will see her here soon enough."

"Oh, no! I have told her she must not think of coming here and leaving her work."

"I do not think she could have been stopped. Once your friend has set her mind to something it cannot be turned."

Elizabeth laughed, and tucked the precious letter

into her reticule, to be savored later, when she was alone. "No, that is true. Well, I shall be very happy to see her regardless."

"But how are you, Elizabeth? Are you well?"

"Me? Well enough. As you can see, Derbyshire is hardly Venice, but I am busy. There are dinners and musicales almost every evening."

"I thought you were in costume when I first saw you this evening!" He gestured toward her white gown.

"Oh, you mean this gown? I thought my black velvet not quite suited to the evening!" Elizabeth fluffed up her skirt, and smiled.

They were silent for a moment, listening to the Havershams' eldest daughter mangle a Mozart concerto on the pianoforte, then Stephen said, "You are not happy, Elizabeth."

She let her bright mask slip at last, and the corners of her mouth turned down. "No."

"You are not suited to this life."

"Not in the least! I miss my work desperately."

"I know how you can escape."

"Do you?" Elizabeth laughed mirthlessly. "Then pray tell me, Stephen. I have been racking my brain for a way for weeks."

He knelt beside her, and took her hand in his. "You could marry me."

Chapter Eighteen

It was by no means the most elegant brothel in London.

Smoke hung heavy in the air. The drink was watered, the green velvet upholstery and carpets were a bit shabby and threadbare, and the gilt of the mirrors' frames was chipped in spots. The "ladies" wore far too much paint, and the lace trim on their shifts was quite dingy (not that one could see that in the faint candlelight). Their faces were harsh, their laughter even harsher.

The patrons were scarcely any better-looking. These were not the dandies and the titled gentlemen who frequented Madame de Sevigny's establishment across town. These were low-level tradesmen, dock workers, sailors, smugglers. Baths were a rare occurrence for these men, and brawls frequent.

And the most disreputable sight in the entire room was Sir Nicholas Hollingsworth.

He was ostensibly involved in a game of cards, and winning, much to the chagrin of his odorous opponents. A half-empty bottle of cheap whiskey sat beside his pile of winnings; two of the house's finest, one blond and one a redhead, perched in his lap, one unfastening his shirt and the other giggling against his neck.

He always refused to let any black-haired whores near.

"Oh, come upstairs now, Nicky," the blonde cooed. "Cards are ever so dull!"

"There's a new girl," the redhead added. "We could invite her along, if you like."

Nicholas threw back his head and laughed, reaching out to pinch the blonde's ample bum. "That sounds promising, loves! Let me just . . ."

He was shocked from his inebriated haze when one of his opponents suddenly overturned the flimsy card table, scattering cards, whiskey, and coins in every direction. The two whores fled, shrieking, leaving Nicholas sitting in the ruins, utterly stunned. He fumbled for the dagger hidden in his boot.

A slender fist grasped him by the shirtfront and pulled him unceremoniously to his feet. "I wouldn't go anywhere with those tarts if I were you," a voice, rough with smoke, said. "There is no telling what you could catch . . . Nicky."

Then Nicholas found himself looking down into the glittering green eyes of none other than Mrs. Georgina Beaumont.

"Phew! Have you never heard of a small invention called soap, Nicholas?" Georgina lit the only lamp to be found in Nicholas's lodgings. Her nose wrinkled as she surveyed the damage—clothes scattered on the floor, empty bottles, congealed plates of uneaten food. "There are also things called housemaids, though I doubt you could find one in desperate enough straits to clean this place."

"I don't want anyone here," he answered pointedly, the first words he had spoken since Georgina had dragged him by his shirt from the brothel and shoved him into a waiting carriage.

"Obviously." Georgina removed her battered old felt hat, and shook her red hair free.

"How did you know where to find me? How did you know I would be at Mrs. Barry's establishment?"

"Oh, that was simple enough. I have been following you about for a week."

"Following me!" Nicholas could have hit himself for letting his guard down so shockingly.

"Yes, and that just shows how very low you have sunk. In Italy, you noticed everything and everyone about you."

"Yes, I noticed how very stubborn lady artists can be." He sat down on a pile of dirty clothing, and closed his eyes wearily.

"Oh, Nicholas," Georgina said sadly. "What have you done to yourself?"

"I have not *done* anything."

"Except drink and gamble and whore. I must say, you do not whore very well, either. You flirt and tease, but you never take a girl upstairs."

"You have only been following me for a week. I may have been engaged in all sorts of debaucheries before that."

"No. I doubt that you did anything differently at all before I found you." She paused sympathetically. "Poor Nicholas. None of them are Elizabeth, are they?"

"God's blood!" he exploded. "Why are you doing this, Georgina? Why are you here, and not sporting with the Italian models at home?"

Georgina blinked in shock at this deliberate cruelty. "That is unkind, Nicholas. And unfair. But since I know what pain you are in, I will overlook it. Once. And in answer to your question, I am here to shake some sense into you, you stupid man. And into Lizzie as well."

"I like being unsensible, thank you very much, so you can just be on your way."

"Blast you! I saw the two of you in Italy. I know that you truly care for each other—love each other. Just as I loved my Jack, once upon a time. Probably you would be wed by now, if you had not turned out to be such a lying coxcomb." She pushed some dirty clothing off a chair and sat down gingerly. A piece of stationery crackled beneath her hip, and she pulled it out and read over the familiar handwriting with growing comprehension. "I see."

"See what?"

"This letter Lizzie gave you. You know what happened to her, then? Before she came to me in Italy? Her brother's beastly behavior, and the . . . the unfortunate demise of the duke."

He closed his eyes. "Yes. I know."

"So that is why you will not go to her, Nicholas? The truth gave you a disgust of her?"

"No! It is not that at all. Surely you know that nothing could give me a disgust of her, and certainly not the fact that she was horribly taken advantage of."

"Then what is it?" Georgina cried. "What could possibly be wrong?"

"She would not have me if I did go to her! You are completely right—I am a lying coxcomb. She deserves better than someone who would treat her as shamelessly as Peter and that duke dared to. She is far better off as far from me as she can possibly go."

"Oh. Oh, Nicholas, what a terrible mess we have all made of things." Georgina went and opened the window, leaning far out to breathe of the cool night air. "I have never seen two such stubborn, fatalistic people as you and Lizzie. You will not even try to solve your differences, you just weep and get foxed, and declare that you are nobly letting her go on to a better life without you. Where is the man I knew in Venice? You would never have let her get away from you there!"

"Georgina, it is not that easy . . ."

"Pah! Of course it is. And you are just fortunate to have me as your friend. I will help you to resolve everything."

"Will you now?"

"Yes, I will. But you must cooperate."

"Cooperate. Yes. And just how do you propose to get Lizzie to forgive and forget all that I have done? Will you wave your magic wand?"

"Oh, very witty. Not that you deserve to know, but I am on my way to Derbyshire. I am leaving in the morning, and have a very fast phaeton to take me there. And you, Nicholas, will accompany me."

"Oh, will I?"

"Oh, you will. And please stop saying 'oh.'" She kicked disdainfully at an empty glass, and sent it rolling across the carpet. "The country air will do you some good, I think. Whatever would Lizzie say if she could see you living in this squalid manner?"

Nicholas had the most bemused, dreamlike sensation of being completely overcome by a tidal wave.

His will was no longer his own. "She would probably say that it was no more than I deserve."

Georgina drummed her fingers on the windowsill thoughtfully. "No. Somehow I do not think that is what she would say at all. She would say . . ."

"M-marry you?" Elizabeth blinked up at Stephen.

"Why, yes." Stephen's face was quickly becoming quite as red as his hair. It was obvious that he was not at all accustomed to proposing to young ladies, or to having his proposals greeted with obvious shock and dismay. "It is the perfect solution to your difficulties. If you ran away to Gretna Green with me tonight, you would no longer be under your step-brother's guardianship. You could resume your painting, return to your home in Italy—whatever you like. I would not make, er, um, husbandly demands upon you, I vow that on my honor."

It was quite the longest speech Elizabeth had ever heard him make. She felt the tickle of tears on her eyelashes, and turned away to fumble for a handkerchief. "Oh, Stephen, I do seem to have become such a watering pot since I returned to England! You are quite the sweetest man I have ever met, and I am truly blessed to have you for my friend."

He smiled grimly. "But you are refusing me."

"I must. I think it is the only sane thing to do. Do not think I'm not tempted by your offer, because I am, terribly. I quite long for the Italian sun on my face again."

"Then why not accept me? We enjoy the same things in life; we have the same friends. I could give you a comfortable home. We could be content together."

"Content, yes." Elizabeth had a sudden vision of the two of them, doddering old artists wielding brushes and palette knives in their palsied hands, never speaking to each other because there was no need. She almost laughed. "But never truly happy. I had a truly happy day once, and I know how that can be. I could never ruin your life by depriving you of the chance to find that; that would be poor repayment indeed for your friendship."

"Is it your secretary, then? Nicholas?"

She felt the tears beginning in earnest, and ducked her head into the lace ruffles of her bodice. "I did love Nicholas once, yes. In point of fact, I strongly suspect I love him still."

"Then . . ."

"No! It is of no use to even speak of it. I do not even know where he is, and if I knew I am not sure what I would do about it."

They sat together quietly, listening to Miss Haversham finish off Mozart and a Miss Julian begin a Handel sonata. Finally, Stephen took her hand in his very gently.

"Are you certain I cannot persuade you?" he said.

"Quite, quite certain."

"Then, dear friend, I hope you will still call for me if ever you require assistance." Then he pressed a kiss to her fingers and left her, winding his way through the milling crowd to take leave of their hostess.

Elizabeth dabbed at her eyes and smoothed her skirts. She very much wanted her own fireside and a glass of brandy, but unfortunately a tedious evening still stretched endlessly before her.

"If only I could hide here in this alcove all night," she mused aloud.

"That would be insufferably rude," Peter said from beside her.

Elizabeth spun around. "Really, Peter! Must you creep up on me so?"

"I was merely coming to tell you that Lady Haversham requires a fourth at her whist table."

"You know I dislike whist." Elizabeth hated the querulous tone of her voice, but she couldn't seem to help herself. It had really been a most trying evening, and her head ached. The façade had become so heavy.

Peter observed her flushed cheeks and overbright eyes through his quizzing glass. "You and that sculptor were having a most . . . involved discussion, my dear."

"Yes, we were. Fellow artists are quite rare in Derbyshire, you know."

"And perhaps you knew him before? In Italy?"

Elizabeth's frayed temper snapped. "If I did, it is hardly any of your affair! And now, if you have no objections, I must join our kind hostess." She wrapped her Indian shawl over her shoulders and turned her back on him, stalking away across the drawing room in obvious high dudgeon.

Chapter Nineteen

The next day, Elizabeth went for a very long walk. She ended up on her favorite seat, a large, flat rock atop the crest of a hill, placed fortuitously in the shade of a tall oak. From this vantage point she could see the house and fields of Clifton Manor spread out before her.

It was a lovely, peaceful place in which to be alone to think. She had quite forgotten how beautiful England could be when one was solitary in its cool, green prettiness.

And she had a great to deal to think of. Such as Stephen's surprising appearance in Derbyshire, and his even more surprising proposal of marriage.

It would have been a most convenient solution, to marry him and resume her career. With such a successful sculptor as her husband, she could even attract more patrons, have the possibility of joining more professional societies.

If only she loved him, or even felt more than a sisterly fondness for him. But he could not make her laugh until her ribs ached; he did not make her very toes curl with just the thought of one of his kisses. The only time he had kissed her, once in Rome, it had been distinctly lacking in finesse and passion.

Unlike Nicholas's kisses.

"I do miss you, Nicholas," she whispered. "Was I wrong to go away from you?"

She had been plagued by doubts all through the sleepless night. Did she give in to Peter's demands too easily? Should she have given Nicholas a greater chance to explain his actions?

But what explanations were there? He had lied to her for weeks, about his feelings, his very identity.

"Just as you lied to him, you foolish girl," she said aloud, her voice thick with bitterness at that flash of self-realization. She *had* lied to him, as he had to her, for their entire acquaintance.

"Talking to yourself, Elizabeth?"

Elizabeth looked up with a gasp to see Peter leaning negligently against the tree. He was dressed for riding, and his horse was tethered nearby.

She had been far too preoccupied with her musings to even hear his approach.

"You are always creeping up on me so!" she answered. "And, no, I was not speaking to myself, I was talking to that sheep over there."

"Hmm. May I join you, then, or is this a private moment for you and the sheep?"

She hesitated, then nodded and slid over to make a space on the rock.

"Lady Haversham tells me she asked you if you would paint her portrait," he commented, as he took the proffered seat.

"Yes. We spoke of it last night over the whist table. She wants a new portrait to present to Lord Haversham on their anniversary."

"Will you accept?"

"I don't know. Perhaps. I am rather out of practice."

"I think it would be a very good thing for you to work, perhaps lift you out of these doldrums."

She laughed shortly. "I *was* working, until I came here."

A heavy silence fell, broken only when Peter said, "Would you care to go to Town for the Season?"

Elizabeth blinked, certain she had not heard correctly. "London?"

"Yes. That is the only Town I know that will be commencing its Season in a fortnight. I received an invitation to Lady Ponsonby's ball."

"But . . . you detest London."

Peter shrugged. "Detest is surely too strong a word. I prefer the country, certainly, but I have been spending more time in Town of late. It has many diversions I am sure you would enjoy—balls, theater, lectures, museums, and galleries."

Elizabeth's eyes narrowed. "Why? Is there someone there you wish to betrothe me to? Some ancient duke or marquis?"

Peter clicked his tongue. "How very suspicious you have become! I merely thought you might enjoy a broader society. You may even secure some commissions. London is certainly full of people who have nothing better to do with their time than sit about having their portrait painted."

Elizabeth was still suspicious. London *did* sound tempting, full of more of the amenities of civilization that she had come to enjoy while on the Continent. And she could seek out new patrons, as Peter had said, try to build a new career. If only she were certain of Peter's motives.

"Perhaps," was all she said.

"Elizabeth," Peter said slowly, "I do not want you to be unhappy, as I see you have been."

"I am not *unhappy*. Merely at . . . loose ends."

"Nonetheless, I want you to feel as if Clifton were your true home. I also wish you could forgive me."

"Forgive you?"

"Yes. You were fond of me once; could we not try to rebuild something of that?"

She rose to her feet, almost shaking with disbelief. "Peter, you treated me shockingly when you came home from the Peninsula. You forced me to become engaged against my wishes. Then, when I had found a life, a happiness of my own, you snatched it away."

"Elizabeth, be reasonable . . ."

"No! You *men*—you think you can do the most outrageous things and we will just forgive you, smile, and go on as if nothing had happened. Well, no. It does not work this time. It simply cannot."

"This cannot go on!"

Elizabeth didn't even look up from the sketchbook she had propped up beside her plate of toast and marmalade, though inside she was thoroughly shocked. In the days since their scene on the hillside, Peter had never burst out in such a fashion, or even spoken to her of anything but the weather. Their meals had been silent, her days in the studio solitary. Elizabeth had even begun to bring her drawing to the table.

Apparently, this breakfast was to be different.

"Cannot what?" she asked quietly.

"You know what I am talking about, so do not insult my intelligence by pretending otherwise."

Peter threw his crumpled napkin down beside his untouched plate. "I am speaking of this spoiled, childish attitude you have been exhibiting since I asked if you cared to go to Town."

"Spoiled! Childish?" Elizabeth dropped her pencil and exchanged glare for glare along the polished length of the table.

"Yes. You drift about like a wraith in some bad novel, walking the fields all hours of the day. When we do go out, you insist on shocking everyone with your language and your gowns. You are even refusing to show basic table manners and converse politely."

Elizabeth could only gape at him, astonished. Where had her cool, distant stepbrother vanished to?

"You used to speak with me at breakfast," he continued. "You would tell me all you did with your days."

"That . . . that was years ago, when I was just a prattling girl. Much has happened since then, and I prefer quiet in the mornings. And, in point of fact, you are the one who has been lacking in conversation these past days."

He had the grace to blush a little at the reminder of all that had happened since the days she would chatter through all their meals. He held up a sheaf of invitations for her perusal. "Then if you are so unhappy in this house, why not come to London? We have already been invited to many routs there."

Elizabeth snorted. "I do not feel in the least like being gaped at at balls and card parties more than I already am! If I go to Town, it will be on my terms, and not to go to parties at the Havershams' town house, as if we were still here." She could feel her face turning scarlet, could feel all her loneliness, her anger at the men in her life, rushing up to the surface from the place she had so carefully pushed it down to.

"And," she continued, "if you wish to talk about childish behavior, let us talk about you. Because I refused to live my life according to your dictates, you chased me down. No, worse, you sent a *spy* after me. You took me away from my friends, my work, and to what purpose? To have your own way? *That* is childish, not to mention morally reprehensible, Peter Everdean."

Her temper at last spent, Elizabeth was utterly mortified to feel tears spilling onto her cheeks. She gathered her sketches up in her arms, and turned away. "Now, if you will excuse me . . ."

"Elizabeth," Peter called out softly, "please wait."

She paused with her hand on the door, but did not turn back. "What is it?"

"I did not bring you to England for some petty revenge, though it may have seemed so to you. And even to myself."

"No? Then what was the reason?"

"I . . . I wanted to make amends toward you for my beastly behavior after I returned from Spain. I needed to make you understand that I . . ." He broke off, his own eyes suspiciously bright.

Peter, crying? Elizabeth was utterly bewildered. "To make me understand what?" she asked, her voice gentle. He was seeming more like the brother she recalled from years ago, the brother she had thought long dead. "Tell me, please, Peter. I feel so overturned by this whole affair, but I want so desperately to understand."

"Come with me," he said, pushing back his chair. "I want to show you something."

Elizabeth followed him to the library, the one room where she was never allowed, and watched with wary eyes as he unlocked the bottom drawer of his desk. She saw the flat case that held her own miniature, the one painted on her fifteenth birthday, which Peter had carried with him to Spain. She also saw another box, which he removed from the drawer.

"Come and look," he said, opening the box and carefully laying out a bundle of ribbon-tied letters, another miniature portrait, a dried gardenia, and a woman's ruby earring. "Here are all my secrets for your perusal, Lizzie."

Still unsure, she reached for the miniature, cradling it in the palm of her hand as she examined the portrait painted on the ivory.

It was a girl, a woman, of great beauty. Elizabeth's artist's eye instantly envied her high cheekbones, her delicate jaw. The pale oval of her face was crowned by a heavy mass of black hair; her dark eyes seemed to flash and laugh. Swinging from her ears, peeking from loops of her dark hair, were the ruby earrings.

"She is very lovely," Elizabeth managed to say at last.

"You look very like her."

She looked down again at the dark lady, and shook her head. "No. We both have dark hair, but my face is much rounder than hers. She is so much more . . . exotic than I ever could be."

"I thought, when I returned from the war, that you resembled her very much indeed. In some of my less lucid moments I thought you *were* her. And I took my rage out on you, since she was beyond me forever." He fell silent, twirling the earring absently through his long fingers. "When you fled under those horrible circumstances, I was shaken to my senses. I longed to tell you, *had* to tell you how much I loathed myself for what I had done. I wanted to make amends to you, but you were not here to listen to my apologies. For two years I lived with the knowledge that I had failed you, after our parents entrusted you to my care." He looked up at last into her pensive face. "Lizzie, my dear sister, can you ever forgive me? For everything? It is no excuse, I know, but I was not myself."

Elizabeth did not answer. Instead, she held out the painting. "Who was she?"

An odd half smile curled at his lips. "Carmen. She was a wealthy widow from Seville, but she worked with the partisans against Napoleon. She was a spy for us—until she betrayed us to the French, and your Nicholas was almost killed in the resulting battle. She died, as well." Peter tossed the miniature back into its box. "She was also my wife."

Alone at last in her bedroom, Elizabeth stretched out on her bed to turn Peter's words over and over in her mind. Her entire world had tilted yet again, and she couldn't yet hold on to the idea that Peter was not exactly the villain she had thought him to be for so long. He was not yet her beloved brother again, either. She was not certain what he was.

Except that he was a widower.

"Another love gone awry," she murmured. "Can love never be right in this family?"

For the first time since coming back to Clifton Manor, she remembered the utter magic of her time with Nicholas, untainted by what had come after. She remembered lazy luncheons at Florian's, boat rides in sunshine and starlight that she had never wanted to end. She remembered how they would laugh together, how interested he had been in her work; how they had kissed. She even remembered how he would trail after her in galleries and churches, trying not to yawn and whispering delicious bon mots into her ear to make her giggle.

She remembered that the sound of his laughter was the only thing in all the world that could rival the joy of a blank canvas and a palette full of paint.

She also remembered the portrait, hidden away in her studio, that she had begun that sunny day in the Italian countryside. The portrait she had never wanted to see again.

Barefoot, she padded up the stairs to her studio and searched through the carefully crated canvases Georgina had sent her until she found the one she wanted. She propped it on an empty easel and stepped back to study it.

There, with vineyards and their white villa in the background, was *her* Nicholas. Not the Old Nick of the scandalmongers, or the Captain Hollingsworth of Peter's regiment, but Nicholas. His shirt was open at his throat, baring a delicious V of golden skin and the merest hint of dark, curling hair; his black hair was tousled in the wind. He was laughing at her, the laughter she had always smiled foolishly at hearing. None of that had been a lie.

She did love him. Her heart had not been whole since the day she left him. She needed him as she needed air, water, and art. It was not a choice. And now she saw that she had been a fool to turn her back on that love, even if she had been so angry.

Peter's stories of life in Spain, which he had spun for her into the small hours of the night, had made her begin to see what had made Nicholas go to Italy in the first place. Nicholas owed Peter his life—his *life*.

So, in a fashion, Elizabeth owed Peter her life, as well.

She went back to her room, and took out writing paper and pencil from her desk. After an hour of contemplative nail-biting, she began:

"My dearest Nicholas . . ."

She labored over that letter all night, crossing out lines, trying to sound forgiving and friendly, but not so very forgiving that she became maudlin.

It was a very difficult task, and the fire burned merrily with discards before she at last had a version she was content with. She addressed it to the lodgings she had found among Peter's papers, sealed it—and promptly lost all her nerve. She stuck it hastily into a drawer amid her silk stockings, and went to bed to sleep and try to forget her folly.

Nicholas was probably far away from England by now. And he more than likely did not remember her or what they had shared. It had been too long, and she had been too silent.

And, after all, what chance could there really be for them, after all that had happened?

Chapter Twenty

"You see. I told you that country air was exactly what you needed." Georgina smiled at Nicholas over the rim of her teacup. "Your eyes are much clearer already."

"That is because there is no proper tavern in this entire blighted village. And *this* place only serves watered ale." He indicated the small public room of the Dog and Duck Inn, where he had taken rooms and where Georgina had come to join him for a late breakfast. She, however, was comfortably ensconced in a friend's country manor for the duration of their stay.

"Well," she answered, "the house where I am staying boasts an excellent cellar and a fine chef. I'm sure Lady Overton would not mind in the least if you and Elizabeth were to come to supper some evening soon."

"If we ever actually meet with Elizabeth. I think Peter must have her cloistered in that house."

"Not at all. I have heard that she is out and about quite a great deal. And we shall see her very soon, I am sure. We must be careful, and approach her when she is away from that horrid stepbrother of hers. I do not want to cause her any more trouble.

In point of fact, I have often wondered if I did her more harm than good when I took her in two years ago." Georgina set her cup aside and lowered the veil of her fashionable hat. "But that is all past. I am taking tea this afternoon with a woman named Haversham, and I am quite hoping Elizabeth will be there. Care to escort me?"

Nicholas shuddered. "Tea with someone named Haversham? No, I thank you. Besides, I am not at all certain Elizabeth has forgiven me, or even begun to think of me in a more kindly fashion. She might very well flee in horror if she saw me at the tea table with no warning whatsoever."

"Hmm, yes, quite right. But you *will* attend the assembly tomorrow evening with me?"

"I shall certainly try. I have no previous engagements, I believe."

"Ha ha."

"In the meantime, Georgina, do behave yourself. We are meant to be inconspicuous, remember?"

"Of course!" Then she stood, shook out her purple-and-gold-striped walking dress, unfurled her ruffled purple parasol, and swept out amid the stares of every person in the room. "I shall see you this afternoon, Nicholas!"

"Inconspicuous, indeed," Nicholas murmured. The thought of having that woman as a de facto sister-in-law for the rest of his days was indeed a daunting one—but not enough to keep him from begging Elizabeth on hands and knees to marry him.

Daisy hummed as she tidied Elizabeth's bedroom, even sang a bit as she hung freshly pressed gowns in the wardrobe and laid bonnets away in their boxes. It was a lovely spring day, and Clifton Manor seemed quite bright and fragrant since Elizabeth had emerged from her cocoon and taken an interest in the housekeeping—and in painting.

All the servants, even the tweenie, had sat for sketches, which Daisy now gathered up and put away in a portfolio. Work seemed easier, somehow, when artistic endeavors broke up the monotony of dusting and polishing.

Even the earl smiled, laughed sometimes even, and went walking with his sister in the gardens after supper. There was talk of a grand ball to be held at Clifton Manor, of a trip to London.

Daisy sang out again as she opened one of the dressing table drawers and started to straighten the tangle of stockings there. A sealed letter fell from a knot of pale pink silk.

"Oh, no!" Daisy picked up the square of vellum and squinted down at the scrawled direction. "Lady Elizabeth must have forgotten to post this."

She considered taking it up to the studio where Elizabeth was working, but then shrugged and slipped it into her apron pocket. She was going into the village to buy some ribbon, anyway; she would simply post it while she was there.

Nicholas stood for a very long time outside the Dog and Duck, attracting many a curious stare from the passersby, who were not accustomed to gentlemen dressed in quite that height of fashion standing about on the streets. He heard the whispered speculations on the style of his cravat, his scar, and his walking stick and most of all from young ladies, his "romantic" air of "melancholy."

One brave soul even asked him outright if he was Lord Byron "in disguise."

Nicholas simply observed. He watched the people who passed him, shopkeepers and farmers and nannies with their charges, even one grand lady in her carriage. He had never lived in the country; he was very much a product of London, with its soot and its excesses. And the sun-baked hamlets he had seen in Spain in no way resembled this place, full of Tudor architecture and muddy streets.

Somehow he could not envision Elizabeth ensconced here, amid all this Englishness. He could not see her gossiping over bolts of muslin at the draper's, or taking tea with these silly young girls who giggled at him from the tiny tea shop across the way.

His love belonged under sunnier skies than these, with paint under her nails, plenty of champagne to drink, and lots of artists to chatter with at parties.

"Oh, Elizabeth," he murmured. "I should have snatched you up and run very far away with you when I had the opportunity. I should have taken you off and made you marry me, despite what you said."

Too late, his conscience chided. *You were a complete fool and now you are paying the price.*

So deep in his own thoughts was Nicholas that he did not even see the cloaked young woman scurrying along the walkway until she had collided with him and sent them both tumbling to the ground. Papers and ribbons flew from the woman's basket.

Nicholas immediately sprang to his feet and held out a hand to assist her, brushing ineffectually at the dirt on her dark-colored cloak. "I do beg your pardon, miss! So very clumsy of me."

"Oh, no, not at all, sir!" she answered breathlessly.

"It was my fault. I was in such a hurry to catch the post." She stuffed the papers back into the basket, gave him a merry smile, and hurried on her way. "Thank you, sir! Good day to you!" she called back over her shoulder.

"Good day," Nicholas said to her retreating back.

That was the most excitement he could expect of the day.

As he bent to retrieve his hat, he glimpsed one of the girl's letters, stepped on and half covered with mud. He started to shout after her, but she was out of his sight. Then he held the letter up and read the direction: "Sir Nicholas Hollingsworth."

"Oh, where can it be!" Elizabeth overturned the drawer onto the carpet, tossing stockings every which way in her frantic search.

The letter was nowhere to be found, even after she had turned every sheer bit of silk inside out.

"My lady? Are you lookin' for somethin'?"

Elizabeth glanced up to see Ellie, one of the junior housemaids, watching her curiously from the doorway.

"Yes," she answered, and brushed a stray stocking from her head. "A letter. I seem to have misplaced it."

"Oh, Daisy must have it, my lady. She went to the village not half an hour ago to post the letters and fetch some ribbon."

"Post them!" Elizabeth wailed. "Oh, no! She can't!"

She was utterly aghast that everything that was in that blighted letter, all the love and longing she had poured out from her pen, was now floating free in the world. She was especially aghast that Nicholas might actually receive the letter and read it.

She did love him, yes. She was even rather close to understanding what he had done. But that did not mean that she was ready for *him* to know that!

"This is terrible."

Ellie watched in bewilderment as her mistress ran past her, down the staircase, and out the front door, slamming it loudly behind her.

Elizabeth hurried across the damp lawn and down the road that led to the village, clad only in an old yellow muslin round gown she wore for painting and thin kid slippers, her hair falling from the ribbon she had tried to catch it up in.

She was almost halfway to the village, a cramp forming in her side, when she saw him. Standing by a hedgerow, watching her run toward him.

"No," she gasped. "You are just a dream."

Nicholas knew that he had never seen anything more beautiful in all his pitiful life than Elizabeth Everdean running across a country lane.

She was hardly a graceful runner, moving at a painful, gasping gait. Her black hair had half tumbled from its ribbon, and her hem was muddied.

Yet no Incomparable, no Diamond of the First Water, could compare. He had tried to forget her in his wild ways since they had parted so painfully in Venice. Now he knew that he could never have possibly forgotten her, if he had caroused for a century.

"No," he said. "I am not a dream."

She moved slowly closer, so close that he could smell her lilies-of-the-valley perfume. "Then why are you here, Nicholas? Rusticating?"

He smiled at her crookedly. "My dear, you know me better than that. I am only here in this wilderness because of *you*."

"Me?"

"Yes. I have been a week at the Dog and Duck, all because of you."

"An entire week?" She looked up at him, her eyes wide and astonished. "In the village? Why did you not come to Clifton Manor, to call on me?"

"I was afraid you would have thrown me out on my ear."

Her lips thinned. "And so I would have, you rogue!"

He held out her crumpled and stained letter. "Would you truly, Elizabeth?"

She sat down on a fallen log, her face buried in her hands. "Oh, Nicholas. I have been quite desperate these past weeks."

"Oh, my dear, I . . ."

"Sh," she interrupted. "I do love you. The time we had together in Venice was everything I wanted in life. But I am not certain that we can have that again. That we can come to trust again."

Nicholas sat beside her, his knee barely brushing her skirts, but not daring to touch her in any other way. "I cannot blame you, Elizabeth. You have been through so very much already, and what I did was unforgivable."

"You lived a lie with me for weeks, Nicholas."

"Yes. I felt I had no other choice. Your letter says that Peter told you of what happened in Spain, so you do know what I owe him. And finding you was all he asked of me, even if I could not fulfill my promise to him."

"You could have told me! I might have railed at you at first, but I would have come to understand. You know that I am far from being a saint. I have made mistakes in my life, too, horrible ones. We could have helped each other."

"I know that, my love. Now I can do everything just as I should have done it. But then I was too scared."

"Scared? Of what?"

"Of you, of course."

Elizabeth snorted in disbelief. "Me?"

"That is a very bad habit you have gotten into, Elizabeth, and yes. I was scared of you, of what you would do. I was in love with you almost from the first moment I saw you, and I could not give that up. I did not want you to look at me with anger and disappointment, as you did that last day. I kept putting off the inevitable—because being with you made me happier than I ever thought anyone could be. Because I love you, Elizabeth."

She turned her face from him, and his heart sank. He thought she was disgusted with him, with his professions of love. Then he saw her shoulders trembling. Slowly, still wary of rejection, he put his hands on her shoulders and turned her back to him.

She was crying, perfect, precious, diamondlike tears that glistened in her eyelashes and on her cheeks. She grabbed him by the collar of his coat and pulled him down to her.

"You utter idiot," she whispered. "I love you, too."

Then, much to Nicholas's shock and delight, she kissed him.

*   *   *

Elizabeth was a bit shocked herself at her hoyden-ish behavior. The shock was quite buried, however, beneath her delight at having her lips on Nicholas's again.

It was every bit as wondrous as she remembered. Finally, so dizzy she feared she might swoon, she drew back and gently touched his cheek. "You never wrote to me."

"You told me not to," he answered, his voice deeper than usual, his eyelids slumberous.

"And you believed me?" She laid her cheek against his shoulder, and breathed deeply of his ever-green soap scent. "I have been aching to know what you were doing all these weeks."

Nicholas almost blushed. "Pining for you, my love, of course. What were you doing?"

"Oh, ever so many fascinating things." Elizabeth thought of whist at the Havershams', where she was meant to be taking tea right that moment, carriage rides with the Misses Allan—and Stephen's proposal.

"Well, you must tell me of all of them across our breakfast table when we are married."

Elizabeth sat straight up. "Married!"

"Yes. I want you to be my wife, Elizabeth."

"I never said I would *marry* you, Old Nick Hollingsworth."

"Madam! Are you offering me carte blanche? I am shocked."

"Oh! You . . . you popinjay!" Elizabeth stood and turned her back to him. "How can I marry you? You have not even asked me yet. Properly, on your knees."

She glanced back over her shoulder to find him kneeling at her feet. She laughed aloud at the comic sight he made, mud covering his fine trousers and polished boots. "Whatever are you doing, Nicholas?"

"Kneeling, of course. Or is this better?" He fell face forward into the mud. "I am completely prostrate before you, Lady Elizabeth. Please marry me. I am quite desperately in love with you."

Elizabeth laughed even harder, so hard that she fell over beside him in the mud and muck. "How could I say no to such a gallant proposal? Yes. I will marry you."

"Dearest!" Nicholas attempted to plant a muddy kiss on her lips, but she held him off.

"I am still angry with you, you know," she said. "I feel I must tell you that right now. You hurt me terribly, and it will take many years for you to make amends to me. Perhaps even an entire lifetime."

"What if I were to begin making the amends right this moment?" He began softly kissing her neck.

"I would say—you are doing an excellent job of it thus far."

"I can do even better."

"Oh, yes?"

His dark eyes were serious as he looked down at her. "I can take you back to Italy."

Her smile froze. "Italy?"

"Yes. If that is what you want. Or we could go to India, or China, or Canada. Anywhere you want, that is where we will go."

"You would do that? Give up your place in London society simply so your wife could paint and cause a scandal on the Continent?"

"My entire life has been a scandal, my dear. What could one more be? For you, I would live in a hut in Siberia. I would walk across Egypt, take up residence in a Cairo tomb. You want to be in Italy, I can see it in your eyes when I speak of it. I would be a brute indeed to keep you here, and deprive the world of your talent." He traced a thumb across her mud-streaked cheek. "And perhaps once we are in the sun again the color will come back to your cheeks."

Elizabeth threw herself against him, her tears wet on both their cheeks. "It will, I know it! Once away from Lady Haversham, I will bloom like a veritable garden. We will be happy in Italy—or anywhere, as long as we have each other."

Nicholas clung to her like a drowning man, his face buried in her black hair. "Even if you are angry with me still?"

"Even so." She kissed him again, and then again. "I love you enough, Nicholas Hollingsworth, to overcome anything."

"Then I should marry you very soon, before you lose this conviction."

"Yes, you should." She leaned against him, happily contemplating things she had never thought of seriously before—things like wedding gowns and baby rattles. "Shall we marry here, or in Italy?"

"Wherever you like, as long as you say 'I do.' "

"Here, then. I don't want to give you time to change your mind, though I have so shocked poor Mr. Bridges that he may refuse to perform the ceremony. And then . . ." She stopped, blushing an absolute crimson.

"Then . . . what?"

"Then what of, um, babies?"

Nicholas laughed. "I like babies. Do you?"

"Sometimes. If he has your dark eyes."

"Oh, no, no. *She* will have your gray eyes, and your wondrous smile."

Elizabeth couldn't help but smile that wondrous smile. "So she will. And she will be quite gifted, I'm sure—she will be painting landscapes at age three."

"Two!"

"Perhaps she will even be born with a paintbrush in her hand, so she can start right away."

"My love." Nicholas pressed a kiss against her hair. "I am sure of it."

"There is just one thing you have to do before we can marry, go to Italy, and have this gifted, gray-eyed daughter."

"Oh? And what is that?"

"You must ask Peter's permission."

Chapter Twenty-one

Elizabeth squeezed her eyes tightly shut, trying not to wriggle about as Georgina, Daisy, and a fleet of housemaids fluttered around her.

"Can I not look now?" she said.

"Not yet!" Georgina admonished. "Just one moment more."

Elizabeth could hear the rustle of satin, could smell tulle and roses. She twisted impatiently. "Georgie! Hurry. We will be late."

"My dear, they can hardly begin without you. But you may look now."

Georgina's hands turned her toward the mirror, and she slowly opened her eyes.

"No," she breathed. "That is not me."

"Oh, I assure you that it is!" Georgina laughed.

A vision was reflected in the glass, an ethereal vision. The gown, newly arrived from London, was a soft sea of palest blue-green satin. The tulle overskirt was sewn with tiny pearls and crystals in the form of roses and lilies. The satin slippers peeping from the hem were sewn with the same beadwork.

The vision's hair was a loose river of black, caught up with a wreath of white roses. Perfectly matched pearls, her betrothal gift from Peter, gleamed in her ears and about her throat.

"You are the most beautiful bride," Georgina said. Tears shimmered on her cheeks.

"As beautiful as you, when you married Jack?"

"Oh, ever so much more beautiful! I wore a rumpled carriage dress over the anvil at Gretna Green." Georgina dried her eyes, and turned to pick up a nosegay of roses that matched the hair wreath. "Here are your flowers, Lizzie."

"I picked them from the garden just this morning, Lady Elizabeth," said Daisy.

Elizabeth inhaled deeply of their sweet, early summer scent. "They are perfect. This is a perfect day."

"And it has only just started!" Georgina checked her own reflection in the mirror, straightening her feathered hat and smoothing the bodice of her pale yellow silk gown. "It can only grow more perfect as it goes on. Such as when you see Nicholas waiting for you at the church."

Elizabeth giggled into her flowers.

A knock sounded at the door. "Elizabeth?" Peter called. "Are you quite ready? The carriage is waiting."

"Come in, Peter," she answered.

Peter entered the room impatiently, shaking his watch by its gold chain, but halted abruptly at the sight of his sister standing there.

"Elizabeth," he said softly. "You are the very image of your mother."

Elizabeth smiled. She was not a bit like the blond Isobel, even in her stunning new gown, but it was a very nice thing to hear. It seemed to bring her mother closer to her on this most important day. "Thank you, Peter. And you look very like your father, even that waistcoat you are wearing. I have never seen you wear red brocade before!"

"It is a festive day, is it not? A time for new beginnings. Ivory satin just didn't seem appropriate." He took her arm and slowly, as if afraid she would pull back, kissed her cheek. "If my father were here, he would be filled with pride at the thought of escorting you down the aisle. I hope that you will accept me in his stead."

"I would be delighted if you would give me away." She gave him a small, ironic smile. "After all, if it were not for you, Peter, I would never have met Nicholas, and this day could never have happened."

"*Touché*," he said, with an answering smile. "I know that you are not certain of your feelings toward me, Elizabeth."

"Peter, I . . ."

"No, please, let me finish. I know that I have a great deal of work in my future to make you forgive me completely, for us to make a new sort of friendship. But I do love you, Lizzie. I want to be your brother again, if you will allow me to."

"I want that, as well," Elizabeth answered slowly. "I cannot say that the past will be fully forgotten. But, God willing, the future will be a long one, and we will have many new roads to travel together. And my children will have great need of their uncle."

He lifted her hand to his lips and kissed it. "Thank you. I vow that I will never cause you to doubt me again."

"I do believe you. Now, we should not keep the vicar waiting."

"No. We have a wedding to attend."

* * *

The stone Norman church in the village was full, every pew taken and a few unfortunate latecomers standing at the back. Lady Haversham, her poodles, and all her pink lace–clad daughters had claimed one pew all for themselves. The Misses Allan had left off their black just for the occasion and wore dark green.

On the bride's side of the church, a flurry of artists from Italy and London and Paris were seated in a sea of bright colors, laughing and gossiping and finding out who had gained what plum commission.

Yet even they fell silent as the organ swelled with the processional, and Georgina swept down the aisle with her bridesmaid's nosegay held elegantly before her.

Then Elizabeth appeared, her fingers clutching Peter's arm, her eyes only on her bridegroom, unhindered by a veil.

Nicholas was the most handsome she had ever seen him in his blue coat, his smile wide and white as he watched her come to him, as he took her hand in his, and kissed her cheek much to the disapproval of the vicar.

Then Mr. Bridges intoned, "Dearly beloved . . ."

And Elizabeth smiled.

The Spanish Bride

*To the finest mentors a fledgling writer
could ever ask for—Tori Phillips,
Karen Harbaugh, Linda Castle, and Martha Hix.
I truly could not have done
this without all your help and advice.
Thank you!*

Prologue

Spain, 1811

"I pronounce you man and wife. In the name of the Father, of the Son, and of the Holy Spirit. Amen."

Carmen Montero, known in her Seville home as the Condesa Carmen Pilar Maria de Santiago y Montero, trembled as the priest made the sign of the cross over her head. Her fingers were chill in her bridegroom's grasp.

It was done. She was married.

Again.

And she had always sworn to herself that she would never again enter the unwelcome bonds of matrimony! She had relished her widowhood, the freedom to live as she pleased, apart from restrictive Seville society. The freedom to work for the cause of ridding Spain of the French interloper.

Her husband, Joaquin, Conde de Santiago, had been good for nothing in life. She shuddered still to think of his cold cruel hands, his rages when, every month, she was *not* pregnant with a son and heir. At least in death his money had proved useful, working to help free Spain from the French.

Yes, she had sworn never to marry again.

Yet she had not foreseen that there could be anything like this man in the world.

When she had first seen Major Lord Peter Everdean, the Earl of Clifton, her heart had skipped a beat, just as in the silly novels her friends had slipped into their convent school so long ago. Then it had leaped to life again. He was just as handsome as she had heard whispered by her friends at balls in Seville, the Ice Earl, as the ladies gigglingly called him.

But it had not been only his golden good looks that drew her. There was something in his beautiful ice-blue eyes: a loneliness, an isolation that she had understood so deeply. It had been what she had felt all her life, this sense of not belonging.

Now perhaps she had found a place she *could* belong, even in the midst of war. Perhaps they both had.

Carmen peeked up through her lashes at the man beside her, only to find him watching her intently, a faint smile on his lips.

She smiled slowly in return, once she could catch her breath. The only word that could describe Peter was *beautiful*. He was as elegant and golden as an archangel, his fair hair and sun-bronzed skin gleaming in the candlelight of the small church. His broad shoulders gave a muscular contour to his red coat and his impossibly lean hips looked charming in tight-fitting white pantaloons. His rare smiles enticed women the entire length of Andalucia, and every place he went.

Now his ring was on *her* finger. Tall, skinny, bookish Carmen. This extraordinary man was her husband, her lover, even her friend.

It was all suddenly overwhelming, the incense in the church, the emotions in her heart. She swayed precariously, only to be caught in her husband's strong arms.

"Carmen!" he said. "What is it?"

"I just need some fresh air," she whispered.

Nicholas Hollingsworth, Peter's fellow officer and their only witness, hurried down the aisle ahead of them to throw open the carved doors. "She is probably exhausted, Peter," He pointed out. "She rode all day to get here!"

"Yes," Carmen agreed. "I am just a bit tired. But the air is a great help."

Indeed it was. Her head was clearer already, in the cool, dry night. She leaned her forehead against her husband's shoulder and closed her eyes, breathing deeply of his heady scent of wool, leather, and sandalwood soap.

"I am a brute," he murmured against her hair. "You should have been asleep these many hours, and here I have insisted on dragging you before the priest."

Carmen laughed. "Oh, I do not think I mind so very much."

"It was past time for the two of you to make it respectable," Nicholas said. "You have been making calves' eyes at each other for weeks, every time Carmen comes into camp. It was quite the scandal."

"Untrue!" Carmen cried, laughing. "You are the scandal, Nick, chasing all the *señoritas* in the village."

"I do not have to chase them! I stand still and they come to me." Nicholas saluted them smartly, and turned to make his way back down the hill to the lights of the British encampment. "Good night, Lord and Lady Clifton!"

Carmen and Peter watched him go, silent together in the warm, starlit night, and in the sense of the profundity of the step they had just taken.

They had known each other only about two months, in intermittent visits Carmen made to the various encampments of Peter's regiment. Yet Carmen had somehow *known*, the moment she had seen him, that he was quite special.

"I remember when I first saw you," she said.

"Do you?"

"Yes. The day I rode in from Seville to speak to Colonel Smith-Mason. You were playing cards with Nicholas outside your tent, in just your shirtsleeves. Most improper. The sun was shining in your hair, and you were laughing. You were quite the most handsome thing I had ever seen."

"I also remember that day. You were riding hell-for-leather through the camp, on that demon you call your horse. You were wearing trousers and that ridiculous hat you love so much." He laughed. "I had never seen a woman like you."

"Hmph, thank you *very* much! I will have you know that that hat is the height of fashion right now."

"I stand corrected, Condesa. But I could not believe that anyone so very lovely, so refined, could be a spy."

"I am not a spy," she corrected him. "I simply sometimes overhear useful information that could perhaps aid you in ridding my country of this French infestation."

"So that is not spying."

"No. It is—helping."

Peter laughed, the rumble of it warm against her. "Then, I am very glad indeed that you have decided to help *us*. You, my dear, could be a formidable foe."

"Not as formidable as you." Carmen fell silent, turning her new ring in the moonlight to admire the flash of the single, square-cut emerald. Peter had told her that the ring had been his mother's, who had died when he was a small child. "This war cannot go on forever."

"No." Peter's hand covered hers, tracing the ring

with his thumb. "Are you sorry now, Carmen, that we married so hastily? Are you having second thoughts about sharing your life with mine after the war?"

"No! Are you?"

"Of course not. You are the only woman I have ever loved."

Carmen's brow arched doubtfully. "Really?"

His laugh was rueful. "I did not say the only woman I have ever *known*. You would see that for a sham immediately. But you are the only woman I have ever loved."

"Then, you did not ask me to marry you out of some sense of obligation, after—well, after what occurred last week?"

"Are you referring to the fact that we anticipated our wedding vows?" Peter clicked his tongue. "My dear, how indelicate!"

Carmen couldn't help but blush just a bit at the memory of that night, when, tipsy with brandy and kisses and a dance beside a river, they had fallen into his bed and done such incredibly wonderful, wicked things. Peter's hands, his sorcerer's mouth . . .

A giggle escaped.

"No," Peter continued. "I married you because I think it is so charming that, despite the fact that you can ride and shoot like the veriest rifle sergeant, you still blush at the mention of the, ah, small preview of our marital bed."

"Small, *querido*?"

"Well, perhaps not *so* small."

"No." Carmen smiled. "Yet have you thought of after the war, when we must leave here and go to England, and you must present me as your countess?"

"Of course I have thought of it! It is almost all I do when we are apart. It will be wonderful. I have a sister and an estate that I have neglected these many years, so we must go there as soon as we can."

"You have been doing your duty for your country 'these many years.' Surely your family must understand that?"

"Yes, but it does not make it any easier to be parted from them. Sometimes, when I cannot sleep at night, I think of them, Elizabeth and Clifton Manor. I can almost smell the green English rain . . ." His voice trailed faintly away.

Carmen looked out over the lights of the camp. She had never been to England, or indeed anywhere but Spain. It was all she knew, warm, sunny, tradition-bound Spain. How would she fare in a new, English life?

She leaned her head against his shoulder, her eyes tightly shut. "Will they like me at your home? Will your sister like me?"

Peter tipped her chin up with one long finger, forcing her to meet his gaze. "Elizabeth will love you; you are very much like her. They will all love you at Clifton. As I do. Believe me, darling, it is much easier to be an English countess than a Spanish one, and you have done that wonderfully. You must not be afraid."

Her jaw tightened. "I am not afraid."

Peter laughed "Excellent! I knew that a woman who does the things you do could not possibly be frightened of the English *ton*." He kissed her lightly on her nose. "Are you ready to return to camp?"

"Oh, yes."

The encampment was uncharacteristically quiet as they made their way hand in hand to Peter's tent. A few groups of men played desultory games of cards around the fires. Outside the largest tent, Colonel Smith-Mason stood with some of his officers, talking in low voices over a sheaf of dispatches.

Peter glanced at them with a small frown.

"Do you think there is something amiss?" Carmen whispered. She had lived long enough with the intrigues of war to know that events could change in an instant, but she had hoped, prayed, that her wedding night at least could prove uneventful.

Outside the bedchamber, anyway.

"I do not know," Peter answered, his watchful gaze still on the small group. "Surely not."

"But you do not *know*?"

He shrugged, "We have more important things to think of tonight," he said, bending his head to softly kiss her ear.

Carmen shivered, but waved him away. "No, you must find out. I will wait."

"Are you certain?"

"Yes. Go on. We have many hours before dawn." He kissed her again, and she watched him walk away, his polished buttons gleaming in the firelight. Then she turned to duck into his tent. *Their* tent, for that night.

It was a goodly size, but almost spartan in its tidiness. The cot was made up with linen-cased pillows and a blue woolen blanket; a stack of papers and books was lined up exactly on the table, and the chairs pushed in at precise angles. His shaving kit and monogrammed ivory hairbrush were flush with his small shaving mirror. The only bit of personal expression was in the miniature portrait on a small stand beside the cot: of his younger sister, Elizabeth. Next to it was a portrait of Carmen, painted when she was 16, which she had given him as a wedding gift.

Carmen laid her small bouquet of wild red roses beside the paintings and went to open her own small trunk, which had been brought there while they were at the church. In it were the only things she had brought away on her journey from Seville: two muslin dresses and a satin gown, a pair of boots, rosary beads, men's trousers and shirts, and a cotton nightrail that was far too practical for a wedding night.

She slipped out of her simple white muslin wedding dress, and took the high ivory comb and white lace mantilla from her hair. She brushed out her waist-length black hair. Then she sat down on the cot to wait.

She was quite asleep when she at last felt Peter's kiss on her cheek, his hand on her back, warm through her silk chemise. She blinked up at him and smiled. "What was it?"

"It is nothing." He sat down beside her and gathered her into his arms. He had shed his coat and shirt, and Carmen rubbed her cheek against the golden satin of his skin. "There were rumors of a French regiment nearby, much closer than they should be."

"Only rumors?"

"Yes. For tonight." He wrapped his fingers in her loose hair and tilted her face up to his, trailing small, soft kisses along the line of her throat. "Tonight is only ours, my wife."

"Oh, yes. My husband. *Mi esposo*." Carmen moaned as his mouth found the crest of her breast through the silk. Her fingernails dug into his bare shoulders. "Only ours."

The bridal couple was torn from blissful sleep near dawn by the horrifying sounds of gunfire, panicked shouts, and braying horses.

Peter was out of bed in an instant, pulling on his uniform as he threw back the tent flaps.

Carmen stumbled after him in bewilderment, drawing the sheet around her naked shoulders. "What is it?" she cried. "A battle?"

"Stay here!" Peter ordered. Then she was alone.

Carmen hastily donned her shirt and trousers, and tied her hair back with a scarf. She was searching for her boots when she heard her husband's voice and that of Lieutenant Robert Means, a young man she had sometimes played cards with of a quiet evening. And fleeced regularly.

"By damn!" Peter cursed. "How could they be so close? How could they have gotten so far without us knowing?"

"Someone must have informed them," Robert answered. "But we are marching out within the quarter hour."

"Of course. I shall be ready. Has Captain Hollingsworth been alerted?"

"Yes. What of . . ." Robert's voice lowered. "What of your wife, Major?"

"I will see to her."

Carmen stuck her head outside the tent. "She will see to herself, thank you very much! And what are you doing running about unarmed, *husband*?" She rattled his saber at him.

"Carmen!" Peter pushed her back into the tent. "You must ride into the hills and wait. I will send an escort with you."

"Certainly not! You require every man. I have ridden about the country without an escort for months. Shall I ride to General Morecambe's encampment and tell him you require reinforcements?"

"No! You are to find a safe place, and wait there until I come for you."

"*Madre de Dios!*" Carmen pulled her leather jacket out of her trunk and thrust her arms into the sleeves, glaring at him all the while. "I will not hide! I cannot play the coward now. I will ride for reinforcements."

"Carmen! Be sensible!"

"You be sensible, Peter! I have been doing this sort of thing for a long time."

"But you were not my wife then!" he shouted.

"Ah. So that is it." Carmen left off loading her pistol to go to him, and framed his handsome, beloved face in her hands. "I cannot give up what I am doing to become a fine, frail, sheltered lady again, simply because I am now your wife. No more than you can stay safely here in camp because you are now my husband."

He turned his head to kiss her palm. "No. Even though I wish it so, you are quite right."

"We shall have many, many years to sit calmly by the fire, *querido*."

He smiled against her skin. "And will you long for your grand adventures, Carmen, when you are chasing babies about Clifton Manor?"

"Never!"

Peter caught her against him and kissed her mouth, hard, desperate. "I will see you at supper, then, Lady Clifton."

"Yes." Carmen clung to him for an instant, an eternal moment, then stepped away. "Promise me you will fight very, very carefully today, Peter."

"Of course, my love." He grinned at her, the white, crooked grin that had won her heart. "I never fight any other way."

Then he was gone.

The men had been gone for almost a half hour when Carmen rode out for the hills, set on her task.

She did not even see the glint of the sun on the rifle barrel as it aimed through the trees. She heard nothing, until the bullet shot from the barrel and landed in her shoulder.

The force of the shot knocked her from her horse, and she lay there in the dust, too stunned to feel pain.

She reached her fingers slowly to touch her shoulder. They came away a bright, sticky red.

"Is this it, then?" she whispered. "*Madre de Dios*, how can I die now?"

Her vision was very blurred when a face swam into view. A broad, sun-burned face, with drooping mustaches and deceptively merry blue eyes. A face she recognized from balls and receptions in Seville, where she danced with French officers and sometimes ferreted secrets from them.

"Well, well, *señora!*" he said. "Or should I say, *Madame la Condesa?* You must allow me to offer my best wishes on your nuptials."

"Chauvin," she whispered.

"Ah, so you are conscious? *Très bein!* You have been plaguing my regiment for weeks, you and your friends the so-called partisans. Now it is my turn, *Madame la Condesa*. There are some small questions I would like to ask you."

"I won't . . . tell you anything," she managed to croak through her parched throat.

"*Au contraire, ma belle chère.* I think you will. But back at my lodgings, where we can speak—comfortably. After I have a glimpse of the little battle that is taking shape. Perhaps we will even see your new husband there!"

Major Chauvin slid his arms none too gently beneath Carmen and pulled her to her feet.

Not surprisingly, she fainted quite away.

"*Nicholas!*" Peter shouted out, unheard over the infernal din of battle, as he watched his friend fall beneath a rifle shot, facedown in the mud and muck.

He fought his way to him, slashing out like a madman at any who dared get in his way. When he at last reached Nicholas, Peter hoisted him onto his shoulder and dragged him out of the very thick of the fighting.

"Hot fighting today, eh, Peter?" Nicholas gasped, choking blood onto the sleeve of Peter's already ruined uniform.

"For God's sake, man, don't talk!"

"Am I . . . done for?"

"Not if I can help it." Peter squinted through the smoke and dust. "Where is the damned field hospital?"

"North of here." Robert Means had appeared beside them, his red hair quite black with gunpowder and mud. "Is he badly off?"

"Bad enough." Peter looked down at Nicholas, who was now slumped in a stupor. "But he can live if I get him to a surgeon soon."

"I'll help you." Robert slipped Nicholas's other arm over his shoulder, and looked about to take their direction. "Bloody hell!"

"What now?"

"Look!"

Peter followed the line of Robert's pointing finger, and saw Major Francois Chauvin, the French leader they had been parrying with and retreating from for months. He was mounted, and his horse was climbing swiftly into the hills above the heat of the fighting. Perched before him, cradled in his arms, loverlike, was a woman.

Even from this distance, Peter could recognize the banner of black satin hair. The hair that had been spread across his pillows only that morning.

It was Carmen in the Frenchman's arms, Peter's one-day wife.

"Ah, *ma chère*. How very thirsty you look, how very much in pain," Chauvin cooed. He poured himself a glass of water from an earthenware pitcher and sipped at it, his cool, hawk-like eyes never leaving Carmen. "It would be so very much easier on you *and* me if you would simply tell me what I must know. Then I could summon the physician, who could give you laudanum. Please, *ma belle*, let me help you."

Carmen, slumped in a straight-backed wooden chair, was almost unconscious from the burning, sticky pain that shot from her shoulder down her entire body. She tasted blood from where Chauvin had struck her repeatedly across the face. She ached for water.

Still, she shook her head.

Chauvin clicked his tongue chidingly. "I was so very afraid you would do that. You Spanish are so very stubborn." He reached for her hand, cradling it on his soft, repulsively moist palm.

One of his fingers trailed over her ring, the emerald Peter had placed there only the night before.

The night before? It seemed a lifetime, an eternity ago.

"Ah," said Chauvin, his hand tightening on hers until she heard the bones grind. "It is the English major who is causing these silly scruples, is it not?"

Carmen just stared at him.

"Yes. Well, *ma chère*, there is no need. The English, he is surely dead by now, and if he is not, he will soon hear of his bride's dreadful perfidy. The jealous one will take care of that for me." He slid the ring onto his own smallest finger. "You will not be needing this anymore, *ma belle*. Madame Chauvin in Paris will be amused by it when I send it to her."

The pain, the gnawing pain, of her wound grew faint as she looked at her wedding ring, Peter's mother's ring, on the fat finger of that French pig. Instead, a rage flared in her heart unlike any she had ever known. Now strength flowed through her, fueled by this white-hot anger. She sat up straighter, her arm cradled against her abdomen.

Then Chauvin made his great mistake.

He half turned away from her to pour another glass of water. His gaze was cast down to the pitcher.

And his sidearm was toward her.

Without thought, Carmen lunged forward and seized the pistol. In one quick, smooth movement, she pulled it up out of the holster, cocked it, and fired it into his heart.

Chauvin fell at her feet, only able to gasp once, his eyes sightless even as they found her pale face, the gun in her hand.

Then he was dead.

She stared down at him for one endless instant, at the blood trickling from his mouth, seeping from his wound. She knelt beside him carefully, and yanked her ring off his finger.

Only when it was safely back where Peter had placed it did all the pain and the fear rush back onto her. She fell back heavily against the chair leg, gasping for breath.

Chauvin was dead, but her troubles were only beginning. Surely someone else in the French encampment had heard the shot; any moment now they would burst through the door, and she would be dead.

Never to see Peter, or hear his voice, or feel his kisses on her skin again.

Still clutching the pistol, Carmen hauled herself to her feet and made her way across the room to the single, high window. It was large enough for her to fit through, if she could only pull herself up to it.

Her shirt was soaked through with sweat and blood by the time she managed to drag a chair beneath the window, climb up on it, and pull herself through the casement. She collapsed from the intense pain when she hit the hard-packed ground, but soon revived.

And began to make her slow, painful way down the hill . . .

A month after the battle, Peter was set to becoming very foxed indeed.

But not quite foxed enough yet. He still saw Carmen in his mind, beautiful and radiant at their wedding; leaning limp against the shoulder of that French pig Chauvin.

He still heard the voice of the Spanish partisan, telling him what he had heard of Carmen's death.

Peter reached for the half-empty bottle of cheap, raw whiskey and, ignoring the rather dingy glass, poured a measure of it straight from the bottle down his throat.

He threw back his head and closed his eyes against the sharp sting of the alcohol. It seemed to him, in his hazy state, that perhaps when he opened his eyes she would be there, sitting across from him, her booted feet propped on the scarred table. Laughing at him, for believing she, the most *alive* person he had ever seen, could be dead.

But when he opened them, there was only the dank *taverna*, crowded with English soldiers waiting for their passage home, rough Spanish sailors, and dark tavern maids in low-cut blouses.

A few of them had already expressed interest in Peter, but he had rebuffed them. There could be solace in the sex act, of course, but now he preferred to find it in a bottle. None of these women had Carmen's elegance, the sharp intelligence that lit her dark eyes, the fine grain of her skin.

None of them *were* Carmen.

He took another pull on the whiskey bottle, and wiped his mouth on the back of his wrist. When he looked up, he saw Robert Means, his arm in a sling, standing in the doorway, looking about the crowded room.

Peter feared he knew what Robert was looking for, and he was right. When Robert's eyes lit on Peter's corner table, he nodded and crossed the room. It took him quite a while, as he had to thread his way through the packed masses of people. Peter debated fleeing while he had the chance, ducking out of the back door; he had no desire to see or speak to anyone.

But he feared his reflexes were too dulled by the whiskey, and he could only sit and watch as Robert reached his table and sat down in the chair across from him. The chair where Peter had imagined Carmen sitting.

"You were meant to be aboard ship an hour ago. We sail at dawn," said Robert. "I said that I would find you before then and bring you back."

Peter shrugged. "Why don't you just sail without me?"

"Are you saying you do not want to return to England?" Robert's tone was deeply shocked. "You wish to stay here?"

"Why not? Here is good. Here is fine. Better than England, anyway. I can't face them there, their pitying glances and their curious questions."

"What would I tell Lady Elizabeth? That I abandoned you in some dockside taverna?"

"Tell my sister any damn thing you want. She's better off without me, in this sorry condition." He took another long drink from the bottle, and held it out to Robert. "D'you want some?"

Robert shook his head, but he took the bottle out of Peter's hand and examined it. "Did you drink all of this yourself?"

"Of course."

"Oh, Peter. I have never known you to lose control in such a manner," Robert placed the bottle at the edge of the table, away from the reach of Peter's grasp. "She is not worth it."

"What? My wife is dead, and it is not worth my becoming disguised?"

"You saw her, Peter! With Chauvin."

Peter shrugged. "What does that signify? It could have been any number of things. Chauvin could have raided our camp . . ."

Robert shook his head and looked away. A faint blush stained the sun-weathered skin of his cheeks. "Oh, my friend."

"What are you shaking your head dolefully about?"

"I did not want to tell you this, not with all that has happened." Robert's voice was low and mournful. "A friend would not add to your grief so."

A cold pit of ice formed low in Peter's stomach; an ice that not even cheap whiskey could melt. "What do you mean, Robert? I could scarce be any lower than I am now. So tell me whatever it is. You are plainly longing to unburden yourself."

Robert nervously licked his lower lip; his hands folded and unfolded on the table. "I did hear, when I was in Seville, that—that . . ."

Peter had never been a patient man. In his cups, he was even less so. He slapped the flat of his hand against the table. "By damn, Robert, say it this instant or shut up!"

Robert looked directly at Peter then, his eyes wide, sad, and guileless. "I heard in Seville that Carmen and Chauvin had been—lovers."

The ice spread at those words, touching Peter's heart. When he was able to speak, the words came out thick and strangled. "What nonsense! I am sure that she gave the impression of flirtatiousness with him at the balls there. That was part of her work. But she would never have shared his bed."

Robert's gaze dropped. "I fear she shared more than his bed."

"What do you mean?"

"She shared secrets. *Our* secrets, English secrets. That is why Chauvin knew of our troop movements at Alvaro."

Without warning, a fire flickered through Peter, melting the numbness of the ice and leaving a blinding fury. Peter lunged across the table and caught Robert by the front of his coat, half pulling him from the chair. "By God, man, if you are lying to me . . ."

Robert shook his head fiercely. "I vow to you, Peter, on my mother's life, I am not lying! I heard it from Carmen's best friend, Elena Granjero. She has known Carmen since she was a child. She vowed to me that this was the truth, that she could no longer conceal it now that—that Carmen is gone. Carmen was a French spy!"

Peter slowly released Robert and fell back into his chair. Then, all at once, the grief, the whiskey, the betrayal were all far too much for him. He buried his face in his hands and wept.

It was a pale, thin wraith of a man who stepped from the ship at Dover. His uniform sagged off his shoulders, and his overlong golden hair flopped across his brow and over his collar.

His sister Elizabeth, though, did not hesitate for a moment. She raced along the dock, her blue cloak flying behind her, and flung her arms around his neck.

"Peter!" she sobbed, her tears wet against his neck. "Oh, Peter, I feared I would never see you again! It has been so very long, and you have not written me in ages."

"So very long." Peter held her to him very tightly, his cheek against the dark swirls of her hair. Then he set her gently aside. "Oh, don't fuss so, Lizzie! I am here now, am I not? Whatever passed before is of little moment."

He turned away from her, and walked away to where their carriage waited, the Everdean crest gleaming gilt-edged in the sunlight. He climbed inside without a backward glance.

Elizabeth turned her bewildered gaze to Peter's companion. Robert Means shook his head sadly, and smiled at her.

"I fear, Lady Elizabeth," he said quietly, "that your brother has had quite a dreadful shock."

Far away, a baby was taking her first breath, filling her tiny lungs and sending a piercing shriek out into the world.

"It is a girl, Condesa!" The midwife placed the squirming new bundle of humanity on her mother's chest. "A beautiful girl."

Esperanza Martinez, Carmen's duenna since her childhood, leaned over to peer into the baby's face, now as wrinkled as her own. "What shall you name her, Carmencita?"

Carmen, exhausted and exultant, wrapped her arms about her new daughter's slippery body and held her against her breast. "I shall call her Isabella. After my mother."

Esperanza nodded. "That is a very good name."

Carmen looked down at Isabella. She could see that her features, though rather squashed at the moment, were fine and lovely. The fingers that curled around her own were long and elegant.

Just like her father's.

Carmen began to cry then, great, large tears that spilled from her cheeks and splashed onto the baby. "Oh!" she sobbed. "If only her papa could see her."

Esperanza's thin mouth twisted. "Yes. If only."

Chapter One

England—Six years later

"Shall we see London very soon, Carmencita?"

The Condesa Carmen Pilar Maria de Santiago y Montero smiled across the carriage at her companion. Esperanza Martinez appeared distinctly green about the edges after all the miles of rough roads they had been obliged to endure. Carmen herself was completely convinced that her bruised nether regions would never be quite the same again.

"Very soon, I am sure," she answered. "You will see the fabled golden spires of London, never fear, Esperanza!"

"Really, Mama?" Isabella de Santiago, who had been very quiet for a six-year-old on their grueling journey, looked up from her doll with a glint in her dark eyes. "Are the spires *really* golden?"

"No doubt, Bella. And streets paved with rubies, just like that book about England we have been reading," Carmen said with a laugh.

Esperanza briefly lowered her handkerchief from her mouth and said, "Your mother is telling you what these English call a 'Banbury tale,' Isabella *niña*. London is no more paved with rubies than Seville or Vienna or Paris was. And it is probably a good deal dirtier."

Carmen shrugged. "Where did you hear such a phrase as 'Banbury tale,' Esperanza? I vow you have been reading those Minerva Press novels again. I knew that those packages from your friend Señora Benitez in London were horrid novels!"

"No such thing!" Esperanza surreptitiously tucked *Lady Arabella's Curse* deeper into her reticule.

Isabella had heard little past the word "dirty." Her tiny nose wrinkled. "It could never be as dirty as Paris!"

"Oh, *querida*," Carmen murmured, putting her arm around her daughter's shoulders. "You liked living in Paris, did you not?"

Isabella thought this over very carefully. "I liked our house, and the carousel in the park. And Monsieur Danet's sweetshop. He always gave me extra *raisins glace,* because they were my favorites."

Esperanza's lips pursed at the memory of smears on dainty white frocks. She loved order and properness above all, and unfortunately Carmen and Isabella were not the sorts to always live by those precepts.

"But it was very dirty," Isabella concluded.

"Well, London will surely be no dirtier than Paris," said Carmen. "And I am certain that you will like our new house, Isabella. The estate agent says there is a small park right across the square, and Esperanza and I will even take you to have ices at Gunter's, and to Astley's Amphitheater. If you are very, very good."

"What is an Astley's, Mama?"

"Come and lay your head on Mama's lap, and she will tell you all about the acrobats and trained bears at Astley's."

Minutes later, lulled by the motion of the carriage and the soft sound of her mother's voice, Isabella was fast asleep, her rosebud mouth open against Carmen's red velvet cloak. Even Esperanza was snoring softly.

Carmen leaned her head back against the leather squabs, and finally let her smile slip away. It *had* been a long and arduous journey, and it was far from over. It would not be over even when they reached London. Not for her.

They had not left Paris only for a change of society, as she had told Esperanza when she had asked her to pack their trunks yet again. The fortune she had inherited from her mother's family, along with the annuity from her first late husband, was vast, and they could have gone anywhere—Rome, Venice, Baden-Baden.

Anywhere but the one country Carmen had so carefully avoided on all their ceaseless travels.

If not for those letters . . .

She reached into her own reticule and drew out the cheap envelope, grubby and creased, sealed with sinister-looking black wax. She knew the words by rote now, the ugly words, but she unfolded it and read it again:

> "If you have no desire for your own, treacherous role in the occurrences of September 1811 . . . Alvaro Hill . . . the deaths of so many fine Englishmen . . . treacherous spies . . . send five hundred pounds to the address which will soon be revealed to you, Countess Shadow."

"Shadow" had been her name on the dispatches of long-ago days, days of great secrecy and danger in Spain. No one could know of that now, or know of that awful day when she had lost her whole world with the speed of a bullet.

No one but this person. This person who sent her nasty letters from England.

She shoved the letter back into her reticule with a whispered curse. There had been three such missives coming to the house in Paris, each becoming nastier as she refused to capitulate. She had nothing to fear from any revelations of her life in wartime Spain. She had only done what she had to do. But a scandal on Isabella's head, when Carmen had worked so very hard to build a place in Society for her, would be unbearable.

Carmen had only the best planned for her little girl. The best schools, the best tutors, the finest marriage. A duke at the very least! Perhaps a prince. It was only fitting for *her* daughter.

Carmen had her own way of dealing with offal that threatened Isabella's golden future. It had to be someone who had known her in Spain, perhaps a member of Peter's regiment. If any of them had survived. When she found this letter writer, he would be very sorry indeed.

But, oh! To go to England!

Her nerves had been on edge ever since their ship reached the English shore. It had been just as she feared. She saw *him* in every red coat, heard him in every aristocratic accent.

Over the years, she had dashed across the Continent so fast that she had almost outrun the sound of an indifferent voice saying, "What, that blond bloke? He's dead, he is. Died back at Alvaro. Din't you hear?"

Dead. Her Peter, her husband, was dead.

Yet he was not truly dead. Not in her heart, not in their child.

Carmen's hand smoothed over her daughter's guinea-gold curls, pushing them back from her small face. Isabella felt so tiny against her, so vulnerable.

"Oh, Peter," Carmen whispered. "If only you were here. I am so tired, I do not know how much longer I can do everything by myself. If only . . ."

But Carmen knew all too well the horrible futility of "if only."

Chapter Two

"Shall I lay out your blue coat for the evening, my lord?"

Peter Everdean, the Earl of Clifton, sat staring down at the papers on his desk, ostensibly reading them. In reality, he had not seen a word in fully fifteen minutes, or heard anything that Simmons, his valet, had said.

He had been contemplating the offer of marriage he was thinking of making to Lady Deidra Clearbridge, a very suitable, pretty, accomplished, and (it had to be confessed) rather dull young lady of good family.

"Hm?" he murmured. "Blue coat?"

"Yes, my lord."

"Why the deuce would I need my blue coat?" He tugged absently at his rather disheveled cravat, which had, only that morning, been a perfectly executed Mathematical. "I am quite well dressed enough at the moment for an evening at home."

"Yes, my lord. Quite." Simmons looked down his rather long nose at the rumpled cravat and shirtsleeves. His lordship's clothes *did* tend rather to wrinkle when he was going over estate business. "However, it was my understanding that Lady Elizabeth arrives this afternoon from Italy, and that she has sent word she wishes to attend the Duchess of Dacey's ball this evening."

Peter looked up at that, his ice-blue eyes almost horrified behind his spectacles. "Elizabeth! By Jove, I had quite forgotten all about her arrival. No one but my sister would ever wish to attend a confounded crush like the Dacey ball after a grueling journey from Venice."

"Yes, my lord. So—the blue coat?"

"Yes, yes, the blue coat. And quickly, man! She could be here at any moment." The sun was setting beyond his library windows even as they spoke.

Simmons bowed and retreated.

Peter cursed again, and tore off his spectacles. He loved his sister, and of course the house was a great deal livelier when she and her crowd of artistic friends and admirers were about. But she felt that when she was in London, she had to attend every rout, every musicale, every ball, every tea in order to find clients and further her promising career as a portrait painter. It was the only reason, she said, to ever leave her sunny Italian home for the gloominess of London.

And, more often than not, Peter's old friend, Sir Nicholas Hollingsworth, would find a way to wriggle out of escorting her and she would insist on dragging Peter along behind her. What was worse, she insisted on introducing him to every pretty, unmarried girl she could find. This was a severe disruption of his purposely quiet life, filled with political discussions at his club, meetings at the House of Lords (when in session) a few respectable parties with serious-minded people, Lady Deidra by his side . . . perhaps a cozy evening or two with Yvette, until their association had come to its recent end.

Peter called his life quite satisfactory, peaceful, and quiet after years at war. Elizabeth called it an early crypt, and saw it as her bounden duty to get him out into the world again.

He sighed, and shoved his spectacles and account books into a drawer. He would just have to resign himself to the social whirl for the next few weeks. And perhaps Elizabeth was correct in her opinions; he *had* played the mourning recluse, the wounded war hero, for too long. It had been six years since he had been invalided home to England; his melancholy, his "spells," had been a very convenient excuse not to live since then. It hurt far less that way.

Well, Elizabeth would surely be happy to hear of his intentions toward Lady Deidra.

"Isabella? Isabella, *querida*, wake up. We are here. Home." Carmen lifted her daughter's sleepy weight against her shoulder. "Can you walk?"

"No." Isabella buried her nose against the fur collar of her mother's cloak.

"Then, I shall have to carry you, even though you are almost too big and heavy for your mama!" Carmen hoisted her high in her arms and stepped down from the carriage.

The house, a narrow, respectable, cream-colored stone on a well-kept square, was shuttered and quiet as Carmen made her way up the scrubbed marble steps. Esperanza hurried before her to unlock the door.

Late afternoon sunlight streamed from the high windows of the small foyer, revealing furniture still shrouded in holland covers. The butler, housemaid, and cook were not engaged to start until the next day, though there were signs that someone had been in to clean for them.

One round, gilded table was uncovered and held a silver tray piled high with cards.

"Look, Carmen!" Esperanza whispered excitedly as she sifted through them. "Look at all the invitations that have already arrived."

"That is most gratifying, Esperanza, but I absolutely must put this child down before I peruse them. My arm is quite numb."

"Oh, Carmen, give her to me! I will find her bedroom."

"Excellent. *Gracias*, Esperanza." Carmen surrendered her daughter's weight with a grateful sigh. "Do you suppose there might be some tea to be had?"

"I will look. A pot of tea would be most soothing." Then Esperanza carried Isabella up the narrow staircase, crooning to her a soft Spanish lullaby, which she had once sung to Carmen as a child.

Carmen unpinned her small fur hat and ruffled her cropped black curls wearily. She sorted through the invitations, mostly from people she had met on her travels and who had known of her arrival in London, without a great deal of interest.

It *was* gratifying that there were so many of them. Her quiet demeanor, her natural sense of reserve, had quite unwittingly created an aura of mystery and elegance about her life that people she met found intriguing, even though she did nothing to foster it. It appeared that London Society would be no different.

That was fortunate. The more balls and routs she attended, the greater her chances of ferreting out the identity of this scoundrel.

One invitation in particular captured her attention. "Look, Esperanza," she called, as her companion came back down the stairs, *sans* child. "I have been asked to the Duchess of Dacey's ball tonight. The *Gazette* said it is *the* event that opens the Season. It is always a mad crush."

"A crush?" Esperanza sounded doubtful as to the charms of such a thing.

"Yes." Carmen laughed. "Perfect."

* * *

"I have heard that she is a *gypsy*."

"A gypsy? Oh, my dear Millicent, no. I was speaking with Lady Treadwell, who was introduced to her in Paris earlier this year. She said that she is an heiress to a great Spanish family. Perhaps even the *royal* family."

"No, no! I heard that she is a Russian princess, fleeing an unhappy love affair."

Peter leaned against the silk-papered wall of the Duchess of Dacey's grand ballroom, attempting to ignore the cluckings of three matrons who were gathered in front of him, blocking his view of the dancers.

The duchess's ball had become quite a crush, as predicted. Excellent for her reputation as a hostess, but a blighted nuisance if one actually wished to move about. Peter was quite trapped between the three women, a potted palm, and a young couple engaged in a deep flirtation involving a great deal of simpering and giggling.

How they could even converse, let alone flirt, above the confounded racket Peter could not say. The ball was a roaring bore, and Lady Deidra had not even attended. Peter drained his glass of champagne, and glanced again at his watch.

It was all of seven minutes since he had last looked.

He sighed as he tucked the watch away. He loathed London during the Season. Every proud mama had their snares out for him, parading their white muslin-clad darlings before him as if they were at a sale at Tattersall's. The newspapers all referred to him coyly as "that elusive bachelor, the Earl of C," and speculated on which young lady he would eventually settle on. It was quite revolting, and one of the central reasons he was thinking of ending it all by wedding Lady Deidra.

He would never have agreed to come to this, one

of the grandest balls of the Season, if Elizabeth had not begged for his escort.

"It would be so very good for my business, Peter," she had said when he tried to demur. "I absolutely must renew my acquaintance with the duchess, she knows utterly *everyone* in the *ton*."

"Where is your husband? Why can he not take you?" Peter had protested, even as he sensed the futility of it. "Didn't he take some sort of vow at your wedding? For better, for worse, for every rout where there could be potential patrons of the arts?"

"He has gone to inspect that country manor we have just purchased, as I wrote you! Evanstone Park, only a short distance from Clifton!"

So here Peter was, in the corner of a crowded ballroom, drinking poor-quality champagne and listening to some silly women prattle on about some gypsy.

He glanced at his watch again. Almost ten o'clock. Surely he could respectably take his leave now. He forced his way out of the corner, past the matrons, and went in search of his sister.

"Look!" one of the matrons hissed. "It is the Ice Earl! I did not know *he* was in Town. Dangling after the Clearbridge chit, do you think? I did hear . . ."

Peter ignored that silly sobriquet of Ice Earl and the reference to Lady Deidra, and hurried onward, intent on his errand.

Elizabeth was found holding court in a small sitting room off of the ballroom, surrounded by her friends. The diamond bracelets fastened over her kid gloves flashed as she waved her feather fan to emphasize some point.

"Peter!" she called. "Do come and join us. I just heard the most remarkable *on-dit*."

"Oh?" He sat down beside her on her settee, and took another glass of champagne from a nearby tray.

"What is it? That that woman over there in the rather egregious orange satin is a princess of France in disguise?"

Elizabeth wrinkled her nose. "Lud, no! That is quite a horrid frock. What I heard is ever so much better. I heard that the Condesa de Santiago is invited to this ball, and that she has accepted! I did not even know she was in England."

"Who?"

"The Condesa de Santiago. My, but you *have* buried yourself in the country, Peter. Simply everyone has heard of her. I even saw her once at a ball in Venice last year."

"Ah. So we have established that she is famous," Peter answered. "What is she famous for doing?"

One of Elizabeth's friends, a young lady in pink silk, interjected helpfully, "I have heard she is a gypsy."

"No, one of those red Indians from America," said a gentleman in a shocking purple waistcoat.

Elizabeth waved all this away with a flick of her fan. "She is almost Spanish royalty, and she makes her way from one European court to another. She is very beautiful, and very mysterious. To have her at one's ball guarantees it will be a great social success." She glanced scornfully at the man who had expressed the Indian theory. "So I daresay the fact that she is Spanish means she cannot be American, Gerald."

"And Santiago hardly sounds Russian," Peter murmured wryly.

"Her whole name is very long and far too complicated. But what is that about Russia, dear?" said Elizabeth.

"Merely another opinion I heard offered when I was trapped beside a potted palm."

"Really?" Elizabeth's brow arched curiously. "What did you hear?"

"Nothing at all of interest, I fear."

"Pooh! I did want some new tidbit to send on in my next letter to Georgina. We are both quite fascinated with the condesa. Georgina wanted to paint her portrait, but the condesa left Venice before we could meet her."

"Oh, well," said Peter. "If *Georgina Beaumont* is interested . . ."

"Oh, hush! I don't know why you hate Georgina so, she is my dearest friend in the world."

"I think the fact that when last we met she chased me with a fireplace poker had something to do with it."

"That was only because . . ."

A woman wearing an astonishing headdress of flowers and fruit interrupted this familiar brother-sister squabble. "I heard that the condesa was the mistress of a duke."

Elizabeth was appropriately distracted. "Which duke?"

"I did not hear that part," the headdress woman said. "Perhaps it was a marquis."

"But what of the rumor that she was seen in Vienna with Lord Riverton?" said the girl in pink silk.

In spite of himself, Peter was beginning to be intrigued with this condesa. The usual gossip at *ton* affairs was usually completely uninteresting to him, perhaps because he was so often the center of it.

But this seemed rather different from the usual elopements of heiresses with dancing masters and who was seen going into whose room at which country house party.

A condesa, a foreigner whose connections were really quite unknown, who was seen at the finest houses in Europe. A woman of mystery . . .

He had not encountered such an intriguing female in . . . well, in many years.

His jaw tightened at the memory of another dark, mysterious Spanish lady. *Her* name had even been similar to this woman's.

"And she is coming here?" he said, carefully indifferent.

Elizabeth blinked at him in astonishment. "Why, Peter. Never say *you* are interested in the doings of this condesa?"

"This fete has been—less than stimulating. A beautiful lady, whether she be Spanish, Russian, or red Indian, would surely enliven things."

"Even if she does appear, I doubt she would be as lively as all that. One could hope, of course, that she might start clicking castanets in the midst of some staid country-dance." Elizabeth tapped her fan thoughtfully against her chin. "I cannot account for it, brother. Usually you just sigh and roll your eyes at our frivolity."

"I never roll my eyes."

"I beg to differ! So—your curiosity is piqued by the condesa?"

"Perhaps a mere soupçon of pique," Peter grudgingly admitted.

"But what of . . ." Elizabeth's voice fell to a whisper. "What of Yvette Montcalm?"

"I am not going to ask how you came to know that name, Elizabeth."

"You needn't try to freeze me with that tone, Peter. People tell things to artists, you know, while they are forced to sit still for a sitting. Delicious gossip—such as your cozy little *pied-à-terre* on Half Moon Street."

"The mere fact that I listened to your tales of some Spanish woman has nothing at all to do with Madame Montcalm." And he would not yet give his sister the satisfaction of knowing he and Yvette had parted ways.

"Of course not." Elizabeth covered his hand with

her own small one. "I am just glad that all this talk of Spain has not brought on unpleasant thoughts for you."

"You needn't fret, Lizzie. I have put all that nonsense quite behind me."

"Excellent! Then, you must let me introduce you to my new friend Lady Halsby. Nick and I met her in Venice, she is quite lovely . . ."

Peter laughed. "No, Lizzie! I have put Spain quite behind me, true, but that does not signify that I am ready for more of your matchmaking efforts. I will come to parson's mousetrap in my own time, thank you."

"Well, if you do change your mind . . ."

Elizabeth's words were lost as a furor arose among the crowd nearer the ballroom doors. Elizabeth stood and tried to peer above the heads of those around her, stretching on the toes of her satin slippers.

"How very vexing!" she cried. "I cannot see at all."

"It is she!" someone said. "The condesa has arrived."

"Look!"

A sudden hush fell as the doors to the ballroom opened, and the liveried footman announced, in ringing tones and an egregious Spanish accent, "The Condesa Carmen Pilar Maria de Santiago y Montero."

Peter, who was considerably taller than his diminutive sister, had an excellent view over the crowd as a figure appeared in the doorway.

She was tall, taller than most women, with a proud, straight carriage and a horsewoman's slim suppleness. She wore a dashing gown of black and gold lace over deep green satin. Antique gold Etruscan bracelets gleamed over long black gloves.

Her head was turned away as she greeted the

Duchess of Dacey, but beneath the pattern of her black lace mantilla could be seen fashionably cropped night dark curls, interspersed with gold ornaments shaped like tiny jeweled butterflies.

Framed by the inlaid doors, she made quite a dramatic and eye-catching picture. Peter silently applauded the condesa's keen sense of theatricality. It was obvious why she had the entire jaded *ton* eating from her silk-gloved palm.

Then she turned to reveal her face, pale as milk, with huge dark eyes that cooly surveyed the crowd laid out before her.

Peter's champagne glass fell from his fingers to crash onto the marble floor, causing the ladies around him to leap back with startled cries, their skirts clutched against them.

The woman who had just made such a striking entrance was not a gypsy, or a Russian.

She was his wife.

Chapter Three

"Ah, Condesa!" The Duchess of Dacey was almost giggling, the orange plumes in her headdress acquiver, as she took her new guest's arm and drew her into the crowded ballroom. "Such an honor you do my humble soiree!"

Carmen inclined her head in what she hoped was a regal manner, striving to keep her features smooth and mysterious, despite her exhaustion and nervousness. "I do apologize for my late arrival, Your Grace," she murmured.

"Not at all! Why, we have not even gone in to supper yet." The duchess linked her arm through Carmen's and smiled brightly. "But you have not met everyone, Condesa! You are surely acquainted with the Marquis of Stonehurst? He tells me you met in Paris."

"Yes certainly. How do you do?" Carmen held out her gloved hand to the portly little marquis and suffered him to drool over it, wondering if perhaps he could be her letter writer. She had met his brother in Spain, who had then conveniently died and left this man the title. But, no—he was so obviously concerned with only his own comforts. He would not have been concerned with his brother's life in Spain; he would never have heard of Shadow or Alvaro.

Yet, as he attempted to peer down her bodice, she

almost wished it was him. It would have been such a pleasure to skewer the little lecher with her dagger.

"Delighted to see you again, Condesa. It was such a pleasure to dance with you at Madame de Troyes's ball last winter." He smiled up at her in a particularly unpleasant manner. "I hope I may have the honor of dancing with you tonight?"

I would rather sink through the floor and die, Carmen thought. Then she smiled sweetly. "I am sorry, but I do not mean to dance tonight. Now, if you will excuse me . . ." With a small nod, she moved away from the odious marquis and their giggling hostess, and made her own progress across the room.

She paused to speak with those people she had met on her travels, and to be introduced to their friends, who were all eager to make her acquaintance. She smiled, and nodded, and exchanged pleasantries, accepted invitations to take tea and to drive in the park.

Though, behind all this exquisite politeness, she was always watching. Wondering if one of these smooth-faced people, who were drinking champagne and attempting to make witticisms with her, could be the one who had either seen her themselves in Spain, or had a son or brother or husband who did. Wondering which of them thought they held so much of her past, and her future, in their grip.

Where could she even begin? It seemed hopeless.

And this ball did not seem the right atmosphere for making inquiries concerning military service. It was an evening of preliminary reconnaissance only.

At last she managed to evade the crowds and find a quiet corner, a tiny nook curtained in by one of the open French doors leading to the terrace and the gardens. Carmen slipped gratefully behind the heavy velvet draperies and let them fall behind her, enclosing her in silence.

The night air was blessedly cool on her face after the overheated, over-perfumed ballroom. She pushed her mantilla back from her flushed cheeks, and leaned her forehead against the door frame, closing her eyes.

She was utterly exhausted. A ball, particularly one of this magnitude, was the very last place she wanted to be after a long journey. All those silly people, eating and drinking far too much, whispering wicked things about one another—it was all so familiar. London was just Paris, Venice, and Vienna with a different accent.

She shuddered.

If she could follow her own wishes, she would be tucked away beside her own fire, with a new book and nice sherry. And she would assuredly be wearing her favorite old dressing gown, the red velvet with the mended elbow, and not this itchy thing from Madame La Tour's Parisian couturier shop! It was said that the condesa (a creature Carmen considered rather separate from Carmen) was a woman of dashing style, but really fashion was a confounded nuisance.

She tugged the close-fitting lace and satin bodice away from her skin and let some of the cool air onto her shoulders. Yes, she would definitely change into her dressing gown as soon as she arrived home.

But for now she had work to do. What she sought would never be found if she stayed at home by her own fire.

"It will not be for long," she whispered. "It will all soon be over."

Carmen straightened her shoulders, and smoothed her bodice in preparation to rejoin the ball.

"Ah, the Condesa de Santiago, I presume. I have heard much about you," a low, velvet soft voice murmured behind her.

Someone had joined her, undetected, in her safe nest. Another who fancied himself an "admirer," no doubt. Carmen pasted on a bright smile and turned.

A gasp escaped her lips before she could catch it. "Peter! *Madre de Dios*, is it you? But it cannot be!"

"My sentiments precisely," he answered, his blue gaze flickering over her in freezing examination. "Carmen."

The room spun about her head; there was such a roaring in her ears, like a dozen rushing rivers. She fell back against the door, hardly able to remain standing. She covered her face with her gloved hands.

"You are not going to swoon, are you?" he said. His voice was exactly the same, just as she heard it so often in her haunted dreams. Like warm brandy.

"No," she replied. And promptly collapsed at his feet.

"By Jove, Carmen! Never say you have become a frail flower of a female." He scooped her up easily in his arms, and nudged open the door with his shoulder.

She felt the cool air on her shoulders and face as he pushed back the lace of her mantilla. "Certainly not," she managed to gasp, still overcome by the hazy sense of unreality. "I am far too tall to ever earn the sobriquet of 'frail flower.' It is only you English and your overheated rooms. I could not even catch my breath." She looked up at him, wondering if everyone talked of such things as the temperature when faced with long-dead husbands.

She rather thought not.

"My apologies," Peter said, "on behalf of all the English who overheat their rooms."

He placed her carefully on her feet, and she leaned against the marble balustrade of the terrace, grateful for its cold solidity.

She studied him in the moonlight, this stranger she had once known so very well. He was as beautiful as ever, an Apollo with hair as bright as winter sunlight, tall and elegantly slim. But there was something there that had not been six years ago. Deep lines bracketed his lovely mouth; his eyes were as flat and still as a millpond, no stirring of emotion at seeing her again. It was almost as if another soul had come to inhabit the body of the man she loved.

How could *her* Peter be behind those eyes?

"I thought you dead," she managed to say. "They told me you were killed that day."

"Ah, my dear. What an impasse. I thought *you* were dead."

"Me? Dead? Whoever told you that?"

He shrugged, the deep blue velvet of his coat rippling impressively over the smooth muscles of his shoulders. At least he had not become soft over the years. He was still sleek and strong as a tiger.

"I do not recall," he answered. "But now I see that you are very much alive." His eyes slid over her dazzling décolletage. "And unscarred. Come to finish the job, darling?"

Carmen started. "Job?" Surely he could not know of *that*. They had not seen each other in so long; he could not know of the letters, of why she had come to England. Despite his sorcerer's eyes, he could not read her mind.

Could he?

She suddenly became very interested in the fan she held in her hands. She opened and closed the gold-and-black lace. "Whatever do you mean? I am here only to enjoy your London Season."

Peter's patrician features were tight, his hands curled at his sides. "I am talking of your job of betraying my regiment six years ago."

If he had suddenly reached out and struck her

across the face, Carmen could not have been more shocked. It seemed one shock too many. Her fan fell from her fingers, its delicate sticks shattering on the marble at their feet.

Major Chauvin had said those many years ago that she would be blamed for the demise of the Fifteenth Light Dragoons, and thus might as well tell him all she knew anyway. Somehow she had not believed him. Had not believed that Peter could ever think such a thing of her.

"Betrayed?" she whispered.

"Yes. You do remember the day after our wedding? Nicholas Hollingsworth almost died that day. Many men did die."

"Nicholas!" Carmen remembered the dark, laughing man, who, next to Peter, had been the most handsome man of the regiment. A wave of nausea broke over her. She turned away from Peter, her hand pressed to her mouth. "No. I would not do such a thing."

Peter took her arm and turned her to face him. His grasp was hard. "I saw you, Carmen! Riding away from the battle with Chauvin, cradled in his arms." He shook her. "You knew of our troop movements. Did you run to him immediately after our wedding, from my bed to his? Did you, Carmen? Is that why you were so insistent on riding off by yourself?"

Six years of anger and grief shone in his eyes as he pulled her against him, drawing her up on tiptoe, her breasts pressed against his chest.

"Have you come to kill me?" he whispered.

" 'Tis you who are killing me, Peter!" Tears coursed unchecked over her cheeks and chin, spotting her expensive bodice. This man could not be her husband! Peter had been hard at times, yes, but never cruel. She pushed futilely against his chest, unable to bear his warm nearness, his familiar scent. "I never did those things you say."

"Then, prove it! Prove you never betrayed me. Betrayed the love we had between us. I have been in torment for so long."

"How can I prove anything? It was so long ago, a lifetime," she sobbed. "You are obviously set against me in your heart, and have been for a long time. Nothing I say now could change that, could it? I claim innocence on my mother's soul. That is all I can do."

"Carmen!" He shook her arm again, and her ivory comb and lace mantilla slipped free from their fastenings and tangled at their feet.

Desperate to be free, Carmen lashed out, slapping him once across the face. He immediately released her, and fell back, trembling.

A thin line of blood had appeared at his lip. He touched it lightly, and Carmen stared down at her left hand as if it did not belong to her at all. Slowly she peeled off the black silk glove, and they both looked down at the ring that had caught his lip. A large square-cut emerald.

She folded her fingers into a fist.

"Carmen," Peter whispered. "I did not . . ." He was as pale as the marble of the terrace as he stared at that ring.

"Peter! There you are at last. I had quite despaired of finding you. It is time for supper, and I am famished. You did say that . . ."

The tiny woman in blue silk, who had glided out onto the terrace behind them, stopped abruptly when she saw that Peter was not alone.

"Oh," she said. "I do beg your pardon."

Carmen bent to retrieve her mantilla, and arranged it carefully over her hair, bringing the lacy folds forward to conceal her tearstained face. "No, no, I beg *your* pardon, *Señorita*. I was just leaving."

"Condesa de Santiago!" the woman cried. She rushed forward to seize Carmen's bare left hand in her own small, gloved ones. "This is such an honor! I have been quite longing to meet you. Have you yet had your portrait painted in England?"

"My portrait?" Carmen glanced in bewilderment over the woman's dark head to Peter, who was still as stone.

"Yes! Oh. I must seem very rag-mannered to you. Since my brother appears to have been struck quite mute, I shall introduce myself. I am Lady Elizabeth Hollingsworth, nee Everdean."

"Brother?" Carmen looked down at the tiny, black-haired elf, who looked not a bit like the tall, golden Peter.

"Stepbrother, actually. I am an artist, and I should so love to paint your portrait." Elizabeth dug about in her pearl-beaded reticule. "Here is my card. Do send me word when you are settled. You must come to Clifton House, to take tea with me."

Carmen blinked down at the small square of pale blue vellum. "Hollingsworth? Such as Nicholas?"

Elizabeth's eyes widened. "Yes! He is my husband. Do you know him?"

"Only—only by reputation," Carmen murmured.

Elizabeth laughed merrily. "Oh-ho, yes! So very many people do."

Carmen smiled slightly and backed away toward the steps that led to the garden. "Do excuse me, Lady Elizabeth, but I really must depart. It grows very late."

"Certainly! But, please, do call on me. Or allow me to call on you."

"Yes, of course. Good night." Carmen picked up her skirts and fled into the darkness of the garden, unmindful of the mud that sucked at her thin slippers. She only wanted to be away from there, so she could think quietly.

Elizabeth watched her flight with a frown, then turned back to her pale brother. "Peter? Whatever did you say to the poor woman?"

Peter shook his head and gave her an odd little half smile. "Why, nothing, Lizzie. I merely complimented her on her—sense of fashion."

"Fashion? Do you mean you complimented her gown?"

"Yes, something of that sort. Shall we go in to supper?"

"Certainly. I hear that the duchess's lobster patties are quite divine."

Yet even as Peter took Elizabeth's arm to escort her back into the ballroom, he could not resist looking back to where Carmen had disappeared into the night.

Then he saw, gleaming against the marble, the carved ivory comb that had fallen from the folds of Carmen's mantilla. He picked it up and secreted it inside his coat.

Surely its owner would miss it.

Chapter Four

Home at last.

Carmen locked the front door behind her and made her weary way up the shadowed stairs to her bedchamber. Esperanza had seen to the airing of the room, and the bedclothes were turned back to reveal fresh linens. A fire burned merrily in the grate, and set on a small table before it was a light repast of tea sandwiches, a pot of tea, and a bottle of her favorite sherry.

Her stomach rumbled, reminding her of the mundanities of life, such as the fact that she had missed supper, and the duchess's fabled lobster patties.

Madame La Tour's stylish gown was rather difficult to remove alone, but Carmen managed to wriggle out of it, and left it and the mantilla in a heap on the floor. She turned toward her full-length mirror, and almost thought a stranger was staring back at her.

She looked like a wraith, silvery-white in the firelight, her eyes huge and her dark, short hair tangled over her ears. Even her nudity, the tall, angular body she had despaired of all her life, seemed not her own. She looked, and felt, quite otherworldly.

Everything had turned top-over-tail, the whole existence she had painfully built for herself, and it seemed certain that it could never go right side up again.

Peter was alive! She had hoped, oh, a thousand times that she could she him again, just once, to touch his face, feel his arms about her. For just a glimpse of his smile, she would have given her own soul.

Now it seemed her prayers were answered. He was *alive*! Yet how he had changed. He seemed so old now, as old as she herself often felt, and so very hard. And his anger toward her was a very powerful force; it had obviously been festering inside him for six years, poisoning all they had once had, and hoped to have, together.

Carmen's hand drifted over her pale midriff, to her belly above the white silk drawers, across the faint stretch marks from when she had been carrying Isabella inside of her. She had been a small baby, but so active, always kicking and turning . . .

Isabella!

Carmen pressed her fist to her mouth to muffle a sudden cry. What if Peter came to hear of Isabella? What if he saw her, this golden-blond child? He would doubtless guess the truth in an instant.

And she, though titled, was a foreigner. She would be powerless against the Earl of Clifton if he decided to take their child.

"That cannot happen," she said aloud, fiercely.

A knock sounded at the door, startling her. She grabbed up her dressing gown and slipped it over her nakedness. "Yes?"

Esperanza peered around the door, her wrinkled face framed by an absurd pink ruffled nightcap. "Carmencita! You are home early."

Carmen forced herself to smile lightly. "It is hardly early, after one."

"That is early for you. You are usually gone until the dawn." Was there a hint of disapproval in her

tired voice? If there was, it was concealed as she
bustled about the room, shaking out the discarded
gown and locating hastily kicked off slippers. "Did
you have a good time at the ball?"

"Hm, not really. It was such a dreadful crush, just
as everyone said it would be. I could not breathe at
all. And so many things happened . . ."

"Things such as what, Carmencita?"

Carmen shook her head. "I will tell all later, Esperanza, but I am too tired now." She sat down beside
the fire and poured herself a liberal amount of the
sherry. "I cannot remember when I was last so
tired."

Esperanza eyed the sherry. "You should eat something before you drink that, Carmencita. Did you
have supper at the ball?"

"No, more is the pity! I heard that the duchess's
lobster patties are delightful."

"Then, you must eat those sandwiches. You look
pale as the grave."

Carmen gave an unladylike snort. "Thank you,
Esperanza, for that encouraging compliment!" But
she did pop a cucumber sandwich into her mouth.

Esperanza nodded in satisfaction, and bent to pick
up the mantilla. "Carmen!"

"Yes?"

"Did you not wear your ivory comb tonight?"

Carmen's hand flew to her hair. "Oh, no! It must
have fallen at the ball."

"How could that have happened? We used ever
so many pins!"

Carmen closed her eyes and shook her head. "It
simply fell, that is all. I will send a note 'round to
the duchess tomorrow, and see if anyone found it in
her ballroom."

"That comb belonged to your mama," Esperanza

clucked. "Really, Carmen, sometimes you are so very careless."

Esperanza was always quick to point out her shortcomings, and had done so ever since Carmen's babyhood. "I am certain someone will have discovered it. But I am far too tired to think of it now!"

"My poor *niña*," Esperanza cooed, her irritation forgotten. "You must sleep. I know something did happen tonight, something terrible you are not telling me. I can see it in your eyes. But I will wait."

Carmen kissed Esperanza's cheek. "I *will* tell you later. Now, dear one, good night."

"*Buenos noches, niña.*"

When Esperanza had gone, Carmen climbed gratefully between her cool sheets and fell into deep, dream-plagued sleep.

At last Peter was alone in his bedchamber. It was nearly dawn; a few gray-pink tendrils were reaching through the curtains. Yet it had still taken several protestations of complete exhaustion on his part to persuade his chattering sister to cease prattling about the ball and retire to her chamber.

He splashed cold water from a basin onto his face, unmindful of the damp spots that appeared on his open shirt and scattered across his chest. When he lifted his eyes to the small shaving mirror, the face that stared back at him was positively haggard. Haggard, and pale, and . . . haunted.

Could Elizabeth have been right when she expressed concern for him in the carriage on their way home? Was his old madness coming back upon him?

Peter pushed away from the mirror with a muttered curse. It could not be. He had fought too hard to overcome his ghosts, to come back to the light and try to make a life for himself where he could not hurt anyone ever again. He would not give in to that darkness again, even if he *had* held a ghost in his arms that night.

The darkness, what Elizabeth called his spells, had come over him when he had returned from Spain, wounded in both body and spirit. *Home* was not as he had remembered it, not the fantasy he had longed for when he had lain alone in a Spanish field hospital. Elizabeth had grown up into a dark beauty in his absence, with an iron will of her own that he had not been prepared to deal with. And her every glance at him had spoken of how frightened she was of the monster he had become. It finally forced her to run away.

Six years ago, on that fateful day, he had thought Nicholas Hollingsworth, his best friend, dead. Yet fortunately he had lived and was now married to his sister. However, Peter had thought Carmen not only dead, but had later learned she was their betrayer.

Now he saw that Carmen was not dead, and the realization was vexing. She was here, in England, healthy and whole, and more beautiful than she had ever been even in his dreams.

Why had she come into his life again, opening old wounds and reminding him of the foolish dreams he had once cherished? Peter could not flatter himself that she had come to England to find *him*. She had been so obviously shocked to see him; as shocked as he was to see her.

To see that emerald on her finger.

Carmen, dead Carmen, was the famous condesa. It was strange, a nightmare—a dream. But he also could not ignore the deep joy that had coursed through him when he had first glimpsed her face.

Then his eye caught on the ivory comb he had tossed onto the bed, gleaming against the burgundy velvet counterpane. He reached for it, turning it over and over on his palm.

Its cool smoothness against his skin, callused from riding, reminded him that this was a nightmare, or a dream, that had become all too real.

Chapter Five

"Look, Peter, here is an account of the ball last night!" In her excitement Elizabeth rattled the newspaper so vehemently that her morning chocolate sloshed out of her cup onto the white damask tablecloth.

"Indeed?" Peter did not look up from his letters, which he had not actually read a word of since he had sat down.

"Indeed! And we are mentioned."

"*You* are always mentioned, Lizzie. You cannot step from the front door without causing a stir these days."

"Hm, but here they have actually gone to the trouble of describing my gown and jewels. Usually they just say I was there. See here, 'cerulean silk trimmed in white alençon lace and satin rosebuds, created by the new couturier Madame Auverge, and the stunning Everdean pearls.' My consequence must be increasing. This is excellent, since I am unveiling Lady Kingsley's portrait at a small soiree next week, and I think it is quite the finest work I have done thus far. The portrait, and my being mentioned at all the right gatherings, should mean even more commissions." She scanned the rest of the column. "Do you not want to know what they say about you?"

"What do they say? That I wore a 'stunning'

blue—no, cerulean—coat, created by Weston?"
Peter smirked.

"No, much better by far! They report that you appeared quite fascinated by the lovely Condesa de Santiago, who is recently arrived from the Continent, and that you were seen escorting her onto the terrace."

Peter's coffee cup slipped from his hand, but he did not even notice the hot stain that spread across his new doeskin breeches. He frowned at his grinning sister, who he wouldn't put it past to have sent that little tidbit in to the papers herself. "Scandalous rag! What is it you are reading, Elizabeth? They shall be out of print by the end of the day."

"Why?" Elizabeth's eyes widened innocently. "Is it not true? Were you not on the terrace with the condesa? Locked in an embrace?"

"It was not like that." Peter's jaw was taut.

"Not like—what? She is beautiful, is she not? And rather familiar-seeming, as well."

"What are you talking about?"

"The condesa, of course. Quite intriguing. I was beginning to have hopes that your tastes are improving. That actress Yvette . . ." Elizabeth frowned. "I have never seen that shade of blonde in nature."

"Yvette is hardly a suitable topic for a man to discuss with his sister, Elizabeth. Besides which . . ."

"Oh, how every vexing! I did so want to 'discuss it,' " Elizabeth cried.

"Also, if you would please not interrupt, I have some other news for you."

"Really?" Elizabeth blithely reached for the butter. "What is that?"

"I have decided to make an offer for Lady Deidra Clearbridge."

Elizabeth's reaction was not at all what he had expected. The piece of toast she was buttering fell from her hand and landed butter-side-down on the lap of her green morning gown. Her jaw gaped. "You are what?"

"Going to offer for Lady Deidra Clearbridge. I thought that would make you happy. You are always harping at me to make a respectable match and set up my nursery. I am going to do so." As soon as he could figure out what to do with the very-much-alive first Countess of Clifton.

"First of all, I do not *harp*! And Lady Deidra is not at all what I could have wished for. She is such a milk-and-water miss." Elizabeth's nose wrinkled.

"Living in Italy has made you bold, Lizzie. Lady Deidra is perfectly proper."

"You would run her over in a month, Peter! I know you. The condesa is much more your style."

Peter tossed down his letters and rose to his feet. "I must go out, if you will excuse me, Lizzie."

"You are avoiding the subject, as usual. Where are you going? And are you going like that?" She looked pointedly at the large coffee stain on his leg.

"I was going to go upstairs and change, but if you think I could start a new fashion . . ."

"You *are* in a mood this morning. But if you do not want to tell me where you are going, I certainly have no wish to know."

Peter laughed and bent down to kiss her cheek. "I am in a 'mood' because of the late night last night, thanks to my social sister! I am an old man, and need my sleep."

"You? Old? Ha! I have more gray in my hair than you."

"You, dear, are eternally young. And when is your husband coming to Town, O Goddess of Youth?"

"The day after tomorrow, thankfully! I need his assistance in planning a house party at our new country manor, since I know that *you* will be of no help."

"Well, do try to stay out of trouble until then." He started to turn away.

Elizabeth caught his hand, suddenly serious. "Peter, dear, are you quite certain you have been well? You look rather pale this morning, and I think that . . . well, I know you said you have not had any spells of late, and I believe you, but . . ."

"Lizzie," Peter interrupted. "I am really quite well. And now I must be going. I have an appointment that I must keep." He kissed her cheek again, and left the breakfast room.

Elizabeth watched him go, worrying with her teeth at her lower lip. "Don't forget!" she called. "We are engaged to attend Lady Castleton's musicale tonight."

Across Town, another pair of eyes scanned the same newspaper over the breakfast table.

"Scandalous!" Carmen hissed. "Deep in enraptured conversation, indeed. I think this paper must employ the same writers that create your horrid novels, Esperanza."

"Mama?" a little voice piped up. "What are you reading? Can I see it?"

"*May* I see it, and no you may not. You do not know how to read yet, anyway, *niña*, and when you can you will read more edifying literature than this rag." Carmen made a concerted effort to smooth the frown from her face. She folded the paper, placed it carefully beside her plate, and smiled at her daughter.

"I can so read! A bit. Esperanza is teaching me to write my name." While her mother's attention had been turned, Isabella had systematically demolished her toast into minuscule crumbs. She carefully picked up one of the crumbs with one sticky fingertip and popped it into her mouth. "But it is a very long name, Mama. Why could you not have named me Mary? It's much shorter."

"Isabella was your *abuela*'s name!" said Esperanza, crossing herself as she always did at the mention of Carmen's long-dead, sainted mother. "You should honor it, Isabella." Then she swept out of the room to fetch the morning post, black bombazine skirts rustling.

Carmen watched her leave, puzzled at her cross behavior. "Indeed, it is your grandmother's name, Bella, and a pretty name, too." She reached out with her napkin to wipe Isabella's small chin. "And soon, we shall find you a governess, to teach you to behave like the fine lady your grandmother was."

Isabella pulled a face. "I do not need a governess! I have you and Esperanza."

Carmen tousled Isabella's already tumbled golden curls. When she made that stubborn, set-jawed face, the child looked so like her father. "Certainly you need a governess. She will be able to teach you so much more than we can."

"But, Mama . . ."

Carmen held one finger to her lips. "No more, Bella. But if you are very good this morning, perhaps we could go to Gunter's for ices this afternoon."

Isabella brightened. "Really?"

"Really. But only if you have a bath and let Esperanza dress you in your new pink frock."

Esperanza came back into the breakfast room at that moment, the letters on a silver tray. She smiled, her earlier dark mood apparently forgotten. "So very many invitations again, Carmencita!"

"Thank you, Esperanza. It would appear so." Carmen surveyed the thick stack of cards and letters. Thankfully, there were no missives sealed with black wax today. "My, but we are becoming popular! Here is an invitation to a supper party at the home of the Marchioness of Penshurst, an invitation to the opera . . . but what is this?" She held up a letter written on rich, pale blue stationery, neatly folded and sealed with an elaborate *E* pressed into darker blue wax. She tore it open and read aloud, "My dear Condesa, please forgive me for writing to you so quickly after our meeting. I know we were not properly introduced at the Duchess of Dacey's ball, but we are women of the world, and can overlook such silliness! If you are not otherwise engaged, could you take tea with me this afternoon? I am quite longing to become better acquainted with you. Sincerely, Lady Elizabeth Hollingsworth."

"Hollingsworth?" Esperanza said. "The lady artist we heard of when we were in Italy?"

"The very one. I met her at the ball last night. She said she would like to paint my portrait; she was very charming. And she was married to one of the English officers I knew during the war." Carmen did not mention the fact that Elizabeth was, in reality, her own sister-in-law. She had told Esperanza, long ago when she had arrived home enceinte, that she had been married briefly. But she had never said to whom, and she had always thought Esperanza only half believed that she had been legally wed. It seemed rather ill timed to bring it up now.

"Carmen, this is wonderful!" Esperanza cried. "This Lady Elizabeth is so well-known."

"Hm, yes, she is. But I really don't have time to sit for another portrait now." She carefully folded the letter. "You are right, though, Esperanza dear, in saying that she is quite well-known. Patrons are lined up to have her paint their portrait, and she does me great honor in requesting I sit for her. So I shall have tea with her. After I look at these letters of application for the post of governess."

After quieting Isabella's protests about the governess, Carmen sent her off with Esperanza to be washed and dressed for the day. Then she retreated to the small room that would be her library, a cozy room with deep, comfortable sofas and chairs, and crates of well-loved books waiting to be unpacked and placed on the empty shelves. From the tall windows, she could see the small park across the way, where children and nursemaids were gathering.

She had hopes that soon this room would feel a haven of quiet from the world.

Today, it was not.

She sat down at her little French desk to pen a reply to Elizabeth's letter, but somehow the polite, simple words would not come. Instead, she sat, chin in hand, and watched that park, watched the children at play.

Was she making a mistake in responding, even in a small way, to Elizabeth's friendly overtures? She genuinely liked her, even on such brief acquaintance. She was merry and charming, unafraid to go after what she wanted; Carmen sensed that they could well be kindred, unconventional spirits. And Carmen remembered well Elizabeth's handsome, funny husband.

But Elizabeth was also Peter's sister.

Peter, who had become so bitter that he no longer seemed the same gallant man she had once known, once loved. The years had changed him so.

Just as they had changed her.

Carmen twisted the emerald on her finger, finding its familiar weight comforting. No, she was not the same idealistic girl she had been then. Despite the disappointments of her first marriage, the horrors of war, she had been so full of romantic hopes and dreams.

Peter had seemed almost a fairy tale then, a knight who would carry her away from the fears and the danger with only his kiss. But, of course, that had been an illusion. He had died and left her alone, and she had carried on as best she could. It had not been a fairy tale by any means, her life of travel and searching, but she had survived. She had even carved out a measure of happiness with her little girl.

If Peter discovered Isabella, he could take her away if he chose. He had seemed quite angry enough last night to so choose. That would be the one thing that could shatter Carmen's life utterly and beyond repair.

Perhaps it would be better if she left England right away, and be damned to the blackmailer. She could go to Russia, or America, or anywhere far away where no one could find her daughter.

And yet . . . she could not ignore the way her heart sang when she saw his face again, his beautiful face. She had longed to throw herself against his chest, to bury her face against his neck and inhale his well-remembered scent, to feel his arms safely around her again.

Those warm Spanish nights they had shared had come rushing back to her in that moment, and it was as if the years had never passed.

She had missed Peter terribly, for six long years. And she had seen the look on his face when he saw the moonlight flash on her ring. He had missed her, too.

Despite the lies and the misunderstandings, he had missed her.

If only the years and experience did not lie between them. And so very many secrets.

Carmen pressed her hands against her eyes, trying

to hold back the flood of futile tears that threatened to flow.

A knock sounded at the closed door.

"Carmen?" Esperanza called. "Are you there?"

Carmen blinked fiercely and scrubbed at her cheeks. She picked up her pen and tried to appear unruffled. "Yes, Esperanza, what is it?"

Esperanza opened the door and came in, her silver tray bearing a single calling card held before her. "You have a visitor. A *man*." Her sniff conveyed her disapproval.

"A man? It is not my at-home day. Whoever can it be?" She reached for the card and stared down at the elegant script printed there:

Peter Everdean, the Earl of Clifton.

She turned it over and read the one word scrawled there in pencil.

Please.

"*Madre de Dios*," she whispered. "What is he doing here? How did he find my house?"

Well. It seemed there was nothing for it. She would just have to see him.

Chapter Six

Carmen smoothed her hair for the fifth time, staring intently into the mirror, but not really seeing the neat fall of short curls bound by a blue satin ribbon. She was only searching for excuses *not* to enter the drawing room.

Peter waited for her there. Peter, here, in her very home.

She was only glad that Esperanza had been able to slip Isabella down the back stairs for her outing, with no questions asked.

She glanced at the small clock on her library mantel, and realized that he had been waiting for almost fifteen minutes. Carmen was many things, but she hoped that *rude* was not one of them! She patted her hair once more, smoothed the skirts of her blue muslin morning gown, and went to meet her fate.

His back was to her as he studied the view out of her windows, but even so he quite overwhelmed the small drawing room. His elegant doeskin breeches, blue coat, and champagne polished boots gleamed among her well-loved, well-traveled, if rather battered Spanish antiques. A mahogany walking stick and a pair of butter-soft chamois gloves rested on a crate of still-to-be-unpacked paintings.

Carmen nudged a doll that lay on the carpet beneath a chair with the toe of her slipper, and gathered her Indian cashmere shawl closer about her shoulders. "Good morning, Peter. Such a surprise to see you."

He turned and smiled at her, an oddly sweet, crooked half smile. One she remembered so well that she almost forgot to breathe.

"Not a very pleasant surprise, eh, Carmen?" he said quietly.

She looked away to conceal her breathlessness and bewilderment, and sat down on the nearest chair, arranging her skirts carefully. "Not at all, I assure you." Then she looked up at him again. He seemed more *her* Peter in the fresh morning light, not so much the intimidating earl as he had been in the modish surroundings of a *ton* ball. Now, when she watched his familiar face, it seemed almost as if they had been apart for only moments, not years.

"Indeed?" His golden brow arched. "I gathered from your rather precipitate departure last night that a visit from the devil himself might be more welcome."

Carmen had to almost sit upon her hands to stop herself from reaching out, from touching him to be certain he was real. "I thought of nothing else last night but our meeting," she confessed.

"Neither did I." He took a step closer to her, so close that she could breathe of his clean, sandalwood soap scent. He reached out his hand, very slowly, to touch her cheek.

Carmen could have wept. She closed her eyes and leaned her head slightly, infinitesimally, into the warmth of his palm.

"Carmen," he whispered, his voice low and agonized. "You are *alive.*"

"Yes," she answered softly. "I am now."

"I thought never to see you again. But—how?"

She opened her eyes and smiled up at him. "I might ask you the very same question."

"Ah, Carmen," he sighed. "What a pair we are."

"I looked for you," she said. "At the hospital. The surgeon who was still there told me that you, or rather 'that bloke,' had died."

Peter's mouth tightened. His hand fell away from her cheek. "The hospital. I was not there for long, and in the confusion, I am sure it was easy to assume my demise. I was wounded while carrying Nicholas to the hospital, but not seriously. They sent me to Madrid, then home."

Carmen remembered well the anguish of that long-ago day when she had stumbled, pregnant and ill, into the almost empty hospital, only to be told of his death, the death of most of the regiment. "Fortune has been against us," she murmured.

"Yes, fortune has not been kind to us, has it?"

She looked up at him, at his smile, so warm only moments before, now sardonic and empty. "Why are you here, Peter? You have never been the sort to dwell on the past in a sentimental fashion."

"No, indeed I have not. Though I must say it is a rather tempting prospect in the present circumstances. I am rather curious as to what the famous condesa has been doing since our little interlude in Spain."

Carmen swallowed a bitter retort. She waved her hand airily, her emerald catching the sunlight from the window and reflecting it back to him. "Oh, this and that. Many amusing things. Nothing of consequence."

"Becoming quite the toast of the Continent, so I hear." There was barely controlled, fierce anger in his voice.

"There *was* that. But if you think me so wicked as to betray the entire Fifteenth to their deaths, then why do you care what I have been doing?"

There. It was said at last, and there was no recalling it.

Peter flushed a dull red. "Yet you claim innocence in the whole affair."

Carmen rose to face him, her own cheeks decidedly warm. "I do not *claim* it; it is the truth! I had nothing to do with that ambush at Alvaro. I was a victim of it."

"You needn't flash that Spanish temper at me! I saw you, riding away with Chauvin. I heard that . . ." He bit his words off abruptly.

"If you have based your suspicions on that flimsy piece of evidence, then you never knew me at all," Carmen interrupted.

"No," he said. "I suppose I did not."

Peter stared down at Carmen, at her flushed cheeks, her long, elegant hands curled into fists, as if she longed to plant him a facer. A surging joy threatened to overcome years of anger.

Oh, dear Lord, this was *Carmen*. Carmen, alive and beautiful, within reach of his arms. Not the elegant condesa, but *his* Carmen. The woman whose laughter and kisses had been his only refuge in the darkest days of war. His love, his wife.

She stared at him now with a flash of rage in her dark eyes. She was so furious, so full of righteous anger.

Could she have been innocent of what he had thought for so long? Could his eyes have deceived him?

"And I never knew *you*," she said quietly, interrupting these tumultuous thoughts. "Not truly."

"Once, you knew me better than anyone else ever did," he answered.

"I thought so, too. Once." Carmen twisted her ring on her finger. "Why did you come here today, Peter? To hurl some more accusations?"

"No, indeed. I came to give you this." He reached inside his coat and took out her missing comb, carefully wrapped in a handkerchief.

"Thank you." She took the comb from him, her fingertips brushing ever so briefly against his palm. "I was afraid I had lost it forever."

"Yes," he said softly. "Some things when lost are irredeemable, are they not?"

Carmen looked up at him steadily. "Yes."

He wanted, with all his being, to say something more, but he knew not what. His hand lifted, just the merest amount, toward her. Then it fell back to his side. "Well, I shall inconvenience you no longer, Condesa. I shall say good afternoon."

Carmen smoothed her skirts carefully again, appearing unaffected and slightly bored with the whole scene. But her cheekbones were flushed. "Good afternoon. And thank you."

"Thanks? For what?"

"For returning my comb, of course."

"Ah, yes. Of course." He gave her a small bow and turned to leave.

"Peter?" she called after him.

He looked back to her, one brow arched inquiringly. "Yes?"

"I . . . well. I just wanted to say . . . good day." Carmen could feel herself blushing again, but she could not remember at all what it was she had wanted so desperately to say.

He smiled then, and nodded. "Good day."

Then he was gone, his footfalls fading on the tiled floor of her foyer and the front door clicking shut behind him.

She waited until she saw his phaeton go past her window and out of sight, then she collapsed onto the sofa, her face buried in a velvet cushion.

"You *widgeon*!" she moaned. "How could you have been so cabbage-headed as to actually *speak* to him?"

She could have kicked her heels in utter vexation. She even did, just a bit.

But it did not make her feel one jot better.

"Oh, Condesa! What a very charming house. And so kind of you to have me here for tea."

Lady Elizabeth Hollingsworth settled herself comfortably on a satin settee, spreading her peach muslin skirts about her. Even the feathers in her fashionable hat seemed alive with enthusiasm.

"Not at all," Carmen replied, carefully pouring out tea from her silver Russian samovar. Her hands were trembling so she feared she would spill some, and that would be quite embarrassing! "I was quite looking forward to your visit. I know so few people in London."

"But you seemed to know everyone at the Dacey ball!" Then Elizabeth leaned forward eagerly. "You have considered sitting for a portrait?"

Carmen laughed at Elizabeth's zealousness, the abrupt change of subject. "Perhaps! I understand that your work is wonderfully fine. But not any time soon, I fear. I have only just arrived, as you can see, Lady Elizabeth. My house is still in chaos."

Elizabeth looked about at the boxes, the disarranged furniture, the paintings propped against the walls. "Pooh! This is hardly chaos. You should see my home in Venice. *That* is chaos. And you must call me just Elizabeth. Or Lizzie."

"Very well, if you will call me Carmen." She offered the plate of Esperanza's delectable almond cakes.

"Well, then, Carmen. What exactly is between you and my brother?" Elizabeth popped a cake into her mouth, and watched Carmen expectantly.

Carmen nearly choked on the sip of tea she had just taken. She blotted with her napkin at the amber droplets that had fallen onto the silk bodice of her gown. "I scarcely know your brother, La—Elizabeth."

Elizabeth smiled sympathetically. "Yes, so he says. He thinks I am completely fooled. But I am an artist, you know; a student of human nature, in many ways. And I would be very surprised indeed if you had truly only met last night."

"Elizabeth . . ." Carmen's voice trailed away as Elizabeth turned her wide gray eyes toward her. Somehow she, who had lived with lies for years, could not lie to this woman. "Yes."

"You knew him in Spain, did you not?"

"Yes," Carmen whispered. "Did you know . . . ?"

Elizabeth shrugged. "I saw a miniature of you once. You have changed a bit since it was painted, certainly. You are thinner, and the short hair makes such a difference. But your eyes are the same."

"Then, you know?"

"Yes. Peter told me, the day he showed me the painting. Quite reluctantly, I might add. He probably wanted to keep you a secret eternally. But that was when he thought you dead. Everything is changed now, of course."

Carmen couldn't help but laugh at Elizabeth's tone, so blithe in such a strange situation. "Yes, everything is changed now. Not necessarily for the better."

Elizabeth munched on another cake. "How can you say that? Of course it is for the better! It is like a—a novel, a romantic novel. He thought you dead . . ."

"As I thought him."

"Yes. It was very sad, Carmen; he almost went insane from mourning you! Yet you have found each other again. It will mean the end of—less satisfactory things, and we shall all grow old and fat together, watching our children play."

If only. "Oh, Elizabeth. What a lovely picture. And so lovely of you to accept me so swiftly. But there are so many complications. Too many, I think."

"Nonsense! What possible complication could override the fact that you have found each other again so miraculously . . ."

"Mama, Mama!" A tiny, golden-haired whirlwind chose just that moment to fly into the drawing room and throw her arms about her mother's waist. Her pink hair ribbons were quite undone, the ends trailing from her curls, and her skirt hem was muddied. Yet nothing, not even hoydenism, could disguise the patrician perfection of her small face.

"Esperanza took me to the park!" she said, oblivious to their guest. "We fed the ducks, and saw lots of other children, and ladies all dressed up. Will you walk with me tomorrow, Mama? I was so very, very good, so can we go to Gunter's now, please?"

Carmen put her arms around her daughter and held her very close, despite the mud. She looked at Elizabeth over the tangle of Isabella's bright curls.

Elizabeth's mouth was agape. "Oh," she whispered.

Carmen pressed a kiss atop Isabella's head. "We will go to Gunter's soon, darling, when you have washed and changed your dress. But right now Mama has a guest."

"Oh!" Isabella spun about, then pressed back into her mother's skirts, suddenly shy.

"Introduce yourself, dear," Carmen prompted.

"I am Isabella de Santiago," the child said, bobbing a small curtsy. "How do you do."

Elizabeth smiled. "How do you do, Miss Isabella. I am Lady Elizabeth Hollingsworth, but you must call me Lizzie. Your mother and I are becoming friends, and I am sure that you and I will be, too."

Isabella took a tentative step toward her. "You are very pretty," she announced.

Elizabeth laughed merrily. "So are you, Miss Isabella!"

"Are you coming to Gunter's with us?"

Elizabeth looked up at Carmen. "Well, that is for your mother to say. But I do adore a strawberry ice."

Carmen hesitated only a moment. After all, Elizabeth had already seen Isabella. Had realized the truth. What harm could come of accompanying them for ices?

And Carmen did truly like Peter's sister. *Her* sister now, she supposed.

"Of course," she said. "We would love for you to accompany us."

Chapter Seven

Carmen watched distractedly in the mirror as Esperanza brushed out her short black curls and bound them with a fillet of amethysts and pearls.

"Am I making a mistake?" she murmured to herself.

"A mistake?" Esperanza answered, herself distracted by trying to make the stubborn curls fall just so. "About your gown? Should you rather wear the blue velvet?"

"What?" Carmen shook her head. "No, the aubergine satin is quite all right. I was merely wondering if I am doing the right thing in accepting Lady Elizabeth's invitation to the theater."

"You love the Shakespeare!"

"I do. But really I invited her to tea in the first place to decline her kind offer to paint my portrait. Then suddenly we were at Gunter's with Isabella, and she was saying I had to meet her husband! Then I agreed to this theater outing. I probably should have gone to Lady Wright's card party instead." Carmen's gaze dropped to the jewelry arrayed before her, her wedding ring winking amid the glittering tangle. She picked it up and slid it onto her finger. "Yet Elizabeth is so very friendly, so *persuasive*. Just as her brot . . ." Her voice faded.

Esperanza plucked up the amethyst necklace and clasped it about Carmen's throat. "I did hear that

Lady Elizabeth has a very handsome bachelor brother," she said, just as if she had read Carmen's mind. "An earl. Perhaps she is intent on a bit of matchmaking."

Carmen looked up sharply. "Where did you hear this?"

"When I took Isabella walking in the park, I met nursemaids and governesses, all of them full of silly gossip. They say every single lady in Society has set her cap for this earl. But he is called the Ice Earl, because he pays scant attention to any of them . . ."

Carmen stood abruptly and reached for her gown, pulling the rustling purple folds over her head to disguise her bewilderment. "They say no one can hold his regard?" she said, muffled.

"So they say. Here, stop that, Carmencita! You are crushing your gown." Esperanza straightened the skirt and began to fasten the tiny amethyst buttons up the back. "Though Lady Dobbin's nursemaid said that she had heard that was soon to change, so perhaps Lady Elizabeth is not trying to matchmake after all."

Carmen's hand stilled on the sleeve she was adjusting. "Change in what way?"

"She said that this earl has been seen about with a certain Lady Deidra Clearbridge, daughter of the Earl of Chiswick. I believe we met him and his countess once in Vienna."

"Yes," Carmen murmured vaguely. "Perhaps. And Elizabeth's brother is going to make an offer for his daughter?"

"So she said. But maybe you will meet him yourself tonight!"

Before Carmen could answer, the heavy knocker at the front door sounded.

"That will be Elizabeth and her husband, come to collect me," she said. "You go down and make sure that the new housemaid answers the door, Esperanza. I can finish here."

"If you are certain . . ." Esperanza doubtfully eyed Carmen's stockinged feet. Then she nodded and hurried off, Carmen's evening cloak folded over her arm.

Carmen slid her feet into her satin slippers, and clasped her gold Etruscan bracelets over her arms, hardly knowing what she was doing.

Peter *betrothed*.

It was very foolish of her to have not even considered that he might have moved on with his life, romantically speaking. It had been many years since their romance and marriage. And a handsome, wealthy earl was a catch indeed.

Yet, since she had never forgotten, she had assumed that he had not. She had had chances, many of them, to form new attachments, both respectable and decidedly not so. She had even liked some of those men very much. But none of them had been Peter. None of them, no matter how handsome or how nice, had ever made her feel that warmth, that excitement, that full-of-joy way that he had.

The way he still did, despite everything.

She held out her hand and stared down at the mesmerizing green fire of her emerald for a long moment. She had worn it every day since he had placed it there. Would she soon have to remove it forever?

"You are a fool, Carmen," she told herself. "A silly, moonstruck fool, and you are too old for this behavior."

She took up her fan and her opera glasses, and went out onto the staircase landing.

Elizabeth and her husband awaited her down in the tiny foyer, Elizabeth chattering about something as she adjusted her attire in the gold-framed mirror hanging there. She was the first to see Carmen, and waved up at her. "Hello! Are we terribly early?"

Sir Nicholas Hollingsworth looked up at her then, a charming smile of greeting on his face. The smile disappeared when he saw her, and his face, bronzed from the Italian sun, turned rather grayish.

"Hello, Nicholas," Carmen said quietly, moving slowly down the stairs. "I am not a ghost, I do assure you." She paused on the last step and looked at him. She could have wept, he seemed so very familiar and dear. Yet different, just as Peter did.

A long white scar sliced across one cheek, and he leaned heavily on a carved walking stick. The spoils of war. But there was no lurking sadness in his eyes, as there was in Peter's. How could there be, married to Elizabeth? He still appeared the lighthearted young officer who had stood witness at her wedding.

"Oh, Nick," she said. "It is so good to see you again."

He reached out one shaking hand to touch her arm. "Carmen?"

"Yes, it is I."

Suddenly he caught her in his arms and twirled her around, laughing. "By Jove, *Carmen*! I knew *you* could never be dead. You were always far too wily for those Frenchies."

When he finally placed her back on her feet, Carmen reached out to lean on the newel post, giggling dizzily. "As, I see, were you!"

Elizabeth clapped her hands happily. "I knew you would be so happy, Nick! I could scarce keep it to myself."

Nicholas threw his arm around his wife's shoulders, still grinning at Carmen. "You knew about this, Lizzie? That the condesa was Carmen?"

"Oh, yes. I knew when I met her at the Dacey ball. But I also knew that you would never believe me, that you would have to see for yourself."

"Well, well," Nicholas mused. "What an interesting tale you must have, Carmen, of the past six years."

"Indeed I do. As, I am sure, do you." The clock in the foyer chimed the hour. Carmen reached for the cloak Esperanza had left draped over a chair, and allowed Nicholas to help her don it. "But you must tell it to me in the carriage, or we shall surely be late, and *Much Ado About Nothing* is my very favorite play."

"Oh, yes!" Elizabeth cried. "You must tell her the tale of how we met, dearest. She of all people should appreciate Peter's role in it."

The theater was quite full when Carmen, Elizabeth, and Nicholas made their way into their box. The houselights had not yet been lowered, but the boxes surrounding their own were filled with the glitter of jewels and satins and inquisitive opera glasses.

Elizabeth immediately seated herself in the center of the box, and turned her glass to examining the gowns of others.

Nicholas sat next to Carmen. "Tell me what you have been doing since the war," he said. "How you came to be alive! We all thought you dead."

Carmen smiled wryly. "Yes, so I have heard! But I thought all of you dead, as well. Tell me, are any of the regiment besides you and Peter alive?"

"There is Robert Means. Do you remember him?"

"Oh, yes! Lieutenant Means," she mused. "Such a dreadful cardplayer, he owes me a veritable fortune! Or would if we had played for stakes. And he is alive, you say?"

"Should be in Town any day now. His cousin is making her bow this Season, or so I heard. Usually he stays immured at his estate in farthest Cornwall." Nicholas grinned at her. "He always did have an appreciative eye for you, Carmen! I'm certain he will be more than happy to renew the acquaintance."

Carmen smiled and blushed. "He was a sweet man, as I recall, and quite handsome. But . . ." She turned away from Nicholas's forthright gaze.

"But you never saw anyone but Peter," he said quietly. "Nor he any but you."

She raised her gaze back to his, to find his dark eyes steady and serious. "No. I never saw any but him."

"Have you—met him yet?"

"Twice. Once at the Dacey ball, where I also met your wife." Carmen glanced at Elizabeth, who was still studying the audience. More to give them a chance to speak quietly than from any genuine interest, Carmen suspected. "I also saw him this very morning, when he came to my house to return an ivory comb I had lost."

"How, if I may be so bold as to ask, did these meetings proceed?"

Carmen twirled her opera glass through her fingers, watching the light dance on the mother-of-pearl. "As well as could be expected, I suppose. He has had so many years to be angry with me. I doubt we can ever be as we were in Spain."

"He believed you were in league with Chauvin."

"Yes," Carmen sighed.

"But you were not." It was a statement rather than a question.

"Of course I was not! I was riding to fetch reinforcements when I was shot down by Chauvin. It was a miracle that I and—that I survived." And the babe inside her, as well. "I am so very happy that *you* believe me, Nick."

"How could I do otherwise? No one could have been more loyal than you, to your country *and* to your husband. I still cannot fathom that Peter would condemn you on such flimsy evidence as the fact that you were seen with Chauvin at the battle. I was wounded, and even I could see you were in a stupor.''

"Then, why could Peter not see?'' Carmen cried. "He is—was my husband.''

"Peter is very stubborn, as you are no doubt well aware. He will not always listen to reason, as I do.''

Elizabeth snorted inelegantly at that.

"As I do,'' Nicholas repeated loudly. "He had a very difficult time indeed when he returned from Spain. He was not at all himself for a very long time. But I am certain that, between the three of us, we can make him see sense.''

"Do you think so?'' Carmen whispered. "Do you really think so, Nick?''

Elizabeth gave a small gasp. "Well! Speak of the devil and he shall appear, as my old nanny always used to say.''

Carmen looked over at Elizabeth, who had her glass trained on a box across the way. "What is it, Lizzie?''

She turned her own glass to the box.

And saw Peter, immaculately elegant in a deep burgundy velvet evening coat, matching brocade waistcoat, and perfectly tied snow-white cravat. His golden hair gleamed in the light.

He was not alone. He was assisting a lady into her seat. A very beautiful, very *young* lady, with red-gold curls framing a heart-shaped face. Her gown was the gown of a young girl, even, white tulle over a slip of pink silk, trimmed with tiny pink satin rosebuds.

Carmen never could abide pink.

"That looby!'' Elizabeth said with a hiss. "He never said he would be here tonight, let alone that he would be escorting Lady Deidra Clearbridge and her mama.''

Carmen watched the two bright heads bend together as the lady said something that made Peter smile gently.

Carmen's lips pressed together tightly. This must be the woman that Esperanza said the nursemaids giggled about. "Who is this Lady Deidra?"

Elizabeth's glass never wavered from her brother's box. "She is the youngest daughter of the Earl of Chiswick. This is her second Season, but not, from what I hear, for lack of offers. She has merely been waiting for—bigger fish." Lady Deidra laid her fan on Peter's arm, and peeked up at him from beneath her lashes. "And it appears that she thinks she has landed the largest trout of all. We shall soon see about that."

"Elizabeth," Carmen began, but she was interrupted as the curtain rose. "I don't want to cause a scene," she whispered. "Not yet, anyway."

"Quite right. Gather the troops, and all that. But in the end, Carmen, *you* are his wife, and your Isabella is his daughter. Lady Milquetoast hasn't a chance."

Nicholas, who had not heard all his wife's words but had certainly heard her tone, warned, "Lizzie . . ."

"I know, darling. I am being mean. But that Lady Deidra is completely wrong for my brother. I don't know what he could be thinking."

"That she is suitable and pretty? That it is time for him to set up his nursery, just as you have urged him?" Nicholas laughed, obviously intent on playing devil's advocate.

"If only he knew."

Nicholas threw a puzzled glance at his wife. "Knew what, dear?"

"We will tell you later," the women chorused.

As the overture finished and the actors appeared

onstage, Elizabeth leaned over and whispered in Carmen's ear. "I am having a house party next month at Evanstone Park, our new house in Derbyshire. You must come."

Carmen considered this. A quiet weekend in the country, far away from the clamor and glitter of the Season, where she could think and regroup, sounded just the thing. "I think I would enjoy that very much."

Elizabeth smiled. "I thought you might say that."

As the curtain closed for the interval, Elizabeth tapped her fan on her husband's arm. "Nick, I am quite parched. Do you think there might be some lemonade to be had? Or, better yet, champagne?"

"I shall go and see what I can find, my love," Nicholas answered.

Carmen glanced across the way where Peter and Lady Deidra Clearbridge were talking. "I know that ladies should really not go wandering about the theater, but may I come with you, Nicholas?" she said. "I find myself in need of some air."

"I shall come as well," Elizabeth said. "We shall promenade about and show off our gowns, rather than waiting for people to come to us!"

So the ladies left their box and, one on each of Nicholas's arms, made their way into the throng of the foyer in search of refreshment. Their mission successful, they ensconced themselves in a small nook to sip at their lemonade and watch the passersby.

"This must all seem very tame to you, Carmen, after the splendors of Paris and Vienna," Elizabeth commented as she waved to a diamond-draped dowager.

"Does it seem so to you, after living in Italy?" Carmen answered.

"Yes, at times. Certainly nothing can rival Venice

during Carneval for gaiety." Elizabeth smiled at her husband, soft and secret. "Can it, my dear?"

"Assuredly not."

"And, of course, there are a great many artists living there now. It is quite congenial," Elizabeth continued. "I miss my dear friend, Mrs. Georgina Beaumont, who you will perhaps have heard of. Her house is directly across the canal from ours, and she gives the loveliest parties! But then, you will meet her at our country house weekend. She is arriving in England any day."

"London will never be the same, after the havoc my wife and Georgina are sure to wreak on it!" Nicholas said with a laugh.

"I cannot wait," said Carmen.

"Shall we go back?" Nicholas asked. "I do believe the next act will be beginning directly."

No sooner had they disposed of their empty glasses and turned back toward their box when they came face-to-face with Peter.

And Lady Deidra Clearbridge, on his arm.

"Peter!" Elizabeth cried in surprise, quite as if she had not been watching them through her glass all evening. "I did not know *you* had planned a theater excursion, or we could have shared a carriage." She went up on tiptoe to kiss his cheek, and beamed from him to Carmen as if she had pulled some great coup.

Peter's gaze was steady on Carmen, his eyes calm and expressionless as blue ice. "Did I not say so, Lizzie? How remiss of me? I believe you have met Lady Deidra Clearbridge."

"Yes, of course." Elizabeth slowly held out her hand to the petite blonde. "How lovely to see you again, Lady Deidra."

"Yes," Deidra answered, her voice low and musical. "How do you do, Lady Elizabeth."

"This is Elizabeth's husband, Sir Nicholas Hollingsworth," Peter added. "And . . . the famous Condesa de Santiago."

Deidra inclined her red-gold head. "So lovely to meet both of you. And such a very pretty frock, Condesa. You must give me the name of your mantua-maker."

"Yes, of course," Carmen answered, hoping that her voice would remain steady and cool. "Your own gown is quite—delightful, Lady Deidra."

Deidra gave a small, rather tight smile. Perhaps she had read that ridiculous gossip about the Dacey ball and moonlit terraces. Confounded scandal-mongers.

Elizabeth gave her brother one long, speaking look. "I think the play is about to resume. Shall we see you later at Clifton House, Peter?"

"Of course. Shall I order a cold supper?"

"No, no, we—the three of us—are going out to supper."

"Then, I shall see you tomorrow."

"Yes," Elizabeth said. "We have so much to talk about, brother dear."

Elizabeth linked one arm in Nicholas's and the other in Carmen's, and led them away from the golden pair that was watching them walk away.

Elizabeth had a very thoughtful look on her face. Carmen felt sure she should be afraid.

The house was dark and silent when Carmen arrived back in the wee hours, the merest bit unsteady on her feet after the champagne supper she had enjoyed with Nicholas and Elizabeth. One candle had been left burning on the table in the foyer, and Carmen took it up and made her way to Isabella's room.

Her daughter was sleeping curled up on her side, one tiny fist under her cheek. Her golden curls were tangled on her lace-edged pillows, and her dreams were causing a frown to mar her fair brow.

She looked so like her father when she slept, fighting battles even in slumber.

Carmen put down the candle and bent to place a careful kiss on Isabella's cheek, to smooth the curls back from her face.

Isabella stirred, blinking her brown eyes open. "Mama? Is that you?"

"Yes, darling, it is me. I'm home."

"Were you with Lady Elizabeth?"

"Yes, and her husband. Did you have a good evening with Esperanza?"

"Um-hm. We had a blanc mange for dessert. I do like Lady Elizabeth, Mama."

"I am glad you liked her, dear. She is very nice, and I am sure she liked *you* a great deal."

"I never saw a grown-up eat *three* ices before. How does she not get very fat?"

Carmen laughed. "I don't know, darling!"

"Will I see her again soon?"

"On Thursday, if you like. We are going riding in the park."

"That is very good, Mama. You need a friend."

Oh, the wisdom of the young. Carmen smiled. "You are quite right, Bella. I think Lady Elizabeth and I will be very good friends. So you shall see her on Thursday. But now you must go back to sleep."

Isabella yawned hugely in agreement. "Good night, Mama."

"Good night, *querida*."

Carmen pressed one more kiss on her daughter's soft cheek, then left, closing the door gently behind her.

Her own room was warm with a banked fire in the grate, the bedclothes turned back invitingly. Carmen sighed wearily, and went to her dressing table to remove her jewels.

Propped there against the jewel case was the afternoon post, which she had missed in the excitement of preparing for the evening. She sifted listlessly through the new invitations and letters.

Then she froze.

In her hand was a cheap envelope, addressed to her in dark block letters and sealed with that ominous black wax.

Slowly, reluctantly, she broke the seal with the back of her brooch and read the words written there.

Chapter Eight

"Should you be spending so much time with the condesa, Elizabeth?"

Peter's voice was quiet and calm as he confronted his sister, yet there was steel in his words.

Elizabeth tossed her hat and riding crop onto a library chair, and began peeling off her gloves. "Indeed?"

"People may begin to think that—well, that your friendship, along with those gossiping articles in the papers, may give the impression that there could be something between our—our families."

"Why, Peter, never say you are stammering! I believe your infamous composure is rattled." Elizabeth grinned at him. "Are you afraid that Lady Deidra may decline your attentions if there are rumors about—your family and the condesa?"

"Elizabeth . . ."

"Surely it is only proper that your sister get to know your wife."

At that, his "infamous composure" shattered entirely. He shot up from his chair, his hands planted on his desk. "How did you know . . . ? Did she say . . . ?"

"Don't be so bacon-brained! Did you not show me her miniature only last year, and tell me of your marriage in Spain? I knew her the first—well, the second moment I saw her at the Dacey ball. She is quite distinctive."

Peter slowly sat back down, and rubbed his hand across his face. "Your memory is too sharp by half, Lizzie."

"I am an artist; it is my calling to remember faces. And I do truly like Carmen, since I have had a chance to know her. She is kind and tells such funny stories. And she is a bruising rider! She quite left me, and all her admirers, in the dust at the park this afternoon. *And*, furthermore, she is quite as intelligent as she is beautiful, unlike so many of your other chosen companions, who shall remain nameless. Truly a match for you, brother. Here I thought there could never be a woman in the world who could tolerate you!"

He smiled reluctantly. "I thought we were a match once, as well. Such did not prove to be the case. Now we have moved forward with our lives."

Elizabeth studied him quietly for a long moment. Then she slowly shook her head. "You are being a fool."

"I told you what happened in Spain, Lizzie!"

"With all respect, Peter, sometimes you cannot see past the end of your nose! I do not know exactly what happened in Spain, of course, but I know that Carmen would never have played you, or anyone, false. Nicholas feels the same as I, and he was there!"

"You do not know what you are speaking of. People said . . . I saw . . ." He broke off with a soft curse. "Nicholas was always charmed by her, and now so are you."

"There is no talking to you when you are in a mood." Elizabeth gathered up the train of her riding habit. "I am going to bathe and change. We are going to Lady Carstairs's rout tonight. Will you be there?"

"I do plan to attend."

"With Lady Deidra?"

"Perhaps. Are you and Nicholas bringing Carmen?"

"Of course. We are so 'charmed' by her, we want to spend every bit of time we can with her!" She smiled sweetly. "So we shall see you there."

"May I go, Mama?" Isabella leaned against Carmen's leg as she sat at her dressing table brushing her hair, one tiny hand stroking the soft satin of Carmen's deep burgundy-red gown.

Carmen laughed. "Not tonight! You are still too young for balls, Bella. When you are all grown-up, and make your bow, we shall have the grandest, most extravagant ball anyone has ever seen."

"And I'll have a satin gown? A pink one? And diamonds?" She reached for her mother's diamond bracelet and slid it over her own arm, admiring the flash of it against her nightgown sleeve.

"Whatever you like." Carmen held a ruby and diamond drop on a gold chain up to her throat. "This one, Bella?"

Isabella cocked her little head to one side. "Yes, that is pretty."

"I think so, too." Carmen fastened the necklace about her throat and reached for the matching earrings.

"Will Lady Elizabeth come to my ball?"

"Of course she will! As will hundreds of other people, everyone we have ever met."

Isabella's gaze fell as she fidgeted with Carmen's enameled pot of rice powder. "But there won't be . . ."

"Won't be what, darling?"

"Esperanza has been reading me a book where the princess dances with her father, the king, at a ball, and then she meets Prince Charming. But I won't have a father to dance with."

Carmen looked down at her daughter in shock.
She put her arm about her and hugged her close.
"Oh, Bella! I am certain that there will be many,
many men to dance with you at every ball you ever
attend, including a Prince Charming."

Isabella smiled, but it was rather watery. "Yes, of
course." The knocker on the front door sounded, and
she brightened. "That's Lady Elizabeth! May I go
down and say hello, Mama? She promised to come
in and say hello to me specially."

"Yes, of course, dear, if you will give me my bracelet back. Tell her I will be down directly."

Carmen watched Isabella scamper away before she
let her smile fade.

Isabella had very seldom asked about her father.
She had always been so content with Carmen's brief
explanation that her father had been a very brave
man who had died in the war, and gone to heaven
when Isabella was very small. And, despite a small
wistfulness on the very few occasions Carmen had
allowed a gentleman to come to their house to escort
her to a party, Isabella had seemed entirely content
to have her mother to herself.

Whatever could have brought on such questions
now? Could it be only the book that Esperanza was
reading to her?

Carmen only hoped that Esperanza was not putting too many ideas into Isabella's head with those
fairy stories. Kings did not suddenly appear on white
horses to set princesses lives aright in one fell swoop,
after all. As Carmen herself well knew.

The Carstairs rout was not the dreadful crush the
Dacey ball had been, but carriages were still lined up
around the street, waiting to disgorge their passengers. A few people, in their silks and jewels, had

become impatient and were now walking along the pavement to the front doors.

Carmen watched these pedestrians from her carriage window, fidgeting with the tiny buttons on her gloves. She was almost tempted to claim a megrim and ask the Hollingsworths to take her back home. It was sure to be a long, trying evening.

She knew, though, that Elizabeth would guess right away that Carmen was afraid of encountering Peter and his Lady Deidra again. It would be just too humiliating for her cowardice to be so exposed!

So she adjusted the small, burgundy-colored satin turban, fastened with a ruby brooch, that held her hair in place, and smiled brightly at Elizabeth and Nicholas.

Elizabeth beamed in return. She had been quite uncharacteristically quiet on the short drive, occasionally tapping one finger against her chin thoughtfully.

She reminded Carmen of Isabella, when she was plotting some mischief.

But all Elizabeth did was dig about in her reticule and come up with a letter, which she handed over to Carmen. "I have such a surprise for you!"

"A surprise?" Carmen looked down suspiciously at the paper. "What is it?"

"Just read it. It is not a snake; it will not bite you."

Carmen slowly unfolded it. "A voucher to Almack's?"

Elizabeth laughed and clapped her hands. "Isn't it too grand? I painted Lady Castlereagh's portrait last year, and she was very pleased with it. She was more than happy to give you a voucher. We can go the Wednesday after we return from the country."

"Oh, Lizzie!" Carmen giggled at the thought of a dull, socially correct evening at Almack's. Would she have to wear white? "Whyever would I want to go to Almack's? I am no young miss trying to snare a husband! I hear that the refreshments are abominable."

Elizabeth shrugged. "Perhaps. But then, a voucher to Almack's is essential to getting along in Society— even for a countess. It gives one such an air of respectability. And you never know who you will encounter there."

"You are up to something, Lizzie," Nicholas said sternly.

"I certainly am not! I am up to nothing but doing a small favor for a friend."

Carmen tucked the voucher away. "Well, thank you, Lizzie. I shall certainly go to Almack's with you, as you have been such a fine friend to me. If I am still in England then."

Elizabeth looked at her sharply. "Still in England? Never say you are planning to leave us already? I have so many plans!"

"I do not know. I have learned never to set definite plans in my life. They always seem to end up changing."

"But you cannot . . ." Elizabeth began.

Nicholas laid his hand on her arm. "Now, dearest, if you hound Carmen, she is sure to leave us! You must allow her, and Peter, to find their own way."

His voice was low, meant only for his wife's ears, but Carmen heard him still. She turned away, blushing.

She had not blushed since she was a schoolgirl, at the Carmelite convent, whispering with her friend Elena Granjero. That had been many, many years ago, and yet now she so often felt the telltale warmth in her cheeks again!

"Oh, look!" she cried in relief as the carriage halted at the doors. "We have arrived at last."

The dancing had already begun by the time they

made their way through the receiving line, and a stately pavane was forming on the dance floor. The crowd was of a goodly size, but the hum of conversation was still low.

"I do hope we can liven things up," Elizabeth said. "Or I will have wasted a new gown on a very dull evening!"

"A new gown is *never* wasted," Carmen answered. "Nicholas shall have to bribe the orchestra to play a waltz, and the two of you can scandalize everyone by dancing far too close. Perhaps you could even kiss!"

Elizabeth shook her head. "'Tis no good! We are an old married couple, and no one is shocked by what we do any longer. We shall have to find someone for *you* to waltz with."

"Such as who?" Carmen laughed. "Lord Stonehurst, perhaps?" She gestured with her closed fan to the portly little marquis, who was trying to wink at her in an alluring fashion. He looked a bit like a fish.

"Certainly not! The old hedgehog. He would never suit our purposes."

"Oh? And what are 'our' purposes?"

"To make certain parties sick with jealousy, of course."

The pavane ended, and sets began to form for a country-dance. Nicholas held out his arm to his wife.

"Come, my love," he said. "Dance with me, and let Carmen rest from all your scheming."

Elizabeth rolled her eyes in exasperation, but allowed him to lead her away.

Carmen waved them off, then looked about for acquaintances she should greet.

Her searching gaze fell on Peter, who had just entered the ballroom and stood conversing with a small group.

And Lady Deidra on his arm. With rather too much bosom showing in her white satin gown for such a *young* woman. Surely her mother, who stood nearby like a great battleship in gray silk, should have prevented her from so exposing herself.

Peter looked up then and caught Carmen staring at him. One corner at his lips quirked up, as if to smile at her.

Or as if to mock her sour thoughts.

She tilted up her chin and looked away. But it was almost as if she could still feel his gaze on her, warm against her skin.

She drew her fur-edged satin shawl closer about her shoulders.

"Carmen?" a quiet, incredulous voice said from behind her. "Carmen Montero?"

She looked over her shoulder to see a tall, handsome man with red, curling hair and wide green eyes. His face was a ghostly white as he looked at her.

She was becoming so familiar with that expression on people's faces as they looked at her. But this was a particularly welcome face.

"Robert Means!" she cried in delight. "How utterly wonderful to see you. Nicholas told me that you were in England, but that you seldom came to Town." She held out her hand to him.

He took it between both of his, holding it very tightly. "I don't, but I am very glad to be here now! Oh, Carmen, I never expected to see you again this side of the hereafter."

"Nor I you. Not after the battle we saw! But come, walk with me. Tell me what you have been doing all these years."

Robert offered her his arm. "Only if *you* will tell me all of what you have been doing. I am sure it must be more exciting than my tales of the wilds of Cornwall."

"I am certain not! Are you still a wicked cardplayer?"

"When I get the chance of it. There is little society where I live."

"But more than in Spain, I am certain!" Carmen smiled at him.

"Perhaps a tad more variety than in Spain, true!" he answered with a laugh. "But I had *your* society in Spain. That quite made up for any discomforts. I have thought of you so often over the years."

Carmen was not at all certain she was happy with the direction of their conversation.

She liked Robert Means; she always had. But she had always had the uncomfortable sense that his feelings for her went beyond friendship.

She had quite forgotten that, until now, with his warm gaze and soft smile on her.

She laughed lightly and tapped his arm with her fan. "I have thought of you, as well. But you cannot deny that there must be some pretty girl for you in Cornwall! You have always been far too nice to remain a bachelor."

He shook his head. "There was some talk in my family of a match with my cousin." He nodded toward a young brunette in pink silk across the room. "But we did not suit. I am afraid, Carmen, that I gave my heart away years ago, and there has been no one to compare since."

Carmen swallowed hard, her mouth suddenly dry. She forced another light laugh. "Oh, Robert! We should not be so serious at such a merry party."

He laughed ruefully. "How very right you are! Shall we dance instead?"

"Oh, yes. Let's."

Peter watched with narrowed eyes the progress of Carmen and Robert Means around the room.

Robert Means, of all people! Robert, the man who . . .

Robert had always proclaimed his love for Carmen, to Carmen herself, to any of the regiment who would listen. Indeed, Peter had once thought Robert as devastated by Carmen's betrayal as Peter himself was. He had thought that to be the reason Robert had buried himself in Cornwall.

Now, as he watched Robert laugh with Carmen, saw the light of avarice and lust in those green eyes, he knew that Robert's feelings did not come from love, but from a very deep hatred. For Carmen, perhaps, yet most assuredly for Peter. He could not say from whence it sprang. Was it jealousy?

Whatever it had been, and was, Peter knew one thing for very certain. He could not bear to leave Carmen in Robert's presence for an instant longer.

Carmen laughed at something Robert said to her, her dark head tilted back to reveal her swan-like throat. Peter remembered how he had loved to slide his arms around her waist and bend his head to nuzzle at that creamy skin. She had always smelled of jasmine, and sunshine . . .

His hand tightened on the champagne glass in his hand. Those days were long past, and if she wished to flirt with that bedamned Robert Means, or anyone else, then why should he even care?

Yet he did. He cared very much.

If only he could speak with her alone again, and discover what had truly happened in Spain and during her life after. Then perhaps he could cease thinking of her day and night. Cease pondering what she might be doing when he was meant to be going over estate accounts, or taking Lady Deidra driving in the park.

Lady Deidra.

She tugged lightly on his sleeve then, drawing his gaze away from Carmen and her attentive escort.

"Do you not agree, Lord Clifton?" she said, her voice soft and sweet. Her blue eyes gazed up at him steadily, a bit vacantly.

Such English eyes, pale and modest, framed in yellow lashes. They did not flash and fire like darker eyes, speaking of warm nights and fragrant gardens.

Peter pushed away such thoughts, and looked around at the small group they were conversing with. Political men from his club, and their proper wives. They all watched him expectantly.

"Oh, yes," he said. "Quite."

Apparently that was the correct answer, for Deidra smiled at him and nodded. The hum of conversation resumed around him, and he looked out at the ballroom again.

Carmen and Robert were still walking about the periphery of the party, their faces smiling as they spoke quietly together. As he watched, they turned their steps toward the dancing.

He felt his resolve to remove her from Robert's somehow-poisonous presence strengthen.

"Would you care for some punch, Lady Deidra?" he said, interrupting whatever old Lord Pinchon was saying.

She blinked up at him. "Why—yes. Some punch would be lovely. Is everything quite all right, Lord Clifton?"

"Yes, certainly. Now, if you will excuse me . . ."

As he moved away, Lady Deidra watched him for a moment, then turned her attention back to the conversation, nodding and asking Lord Pinchon a question.

She was so very poised, the perfect, polished political hostess.

Now, where the devil was Carmen?

Then he saw her, dancing now with Robert. Her tall, slim figure swirled through the figures, gracefully dipping and swaying as Robert twirled her about. Her slippers seemed to fly, barely touching the parquet floor. She laughed up at her partner, her face alight.

The sophisticated countess had vanished, and here was *his* Carmen again. The brave, laughing girl who had loved to dance around campfires, who he had kissed under Spanish stars and held in his arms.

Made love to.

The music ended, quite startling Peter, who had not realized he had spent so many minutes staring. Carmen was leaving the dance floor on Robert's arm.

Peter thrust his empty glass at a passing footman, and strode across the floor. He did not even see the many pairs of eyes that watched him with great interest, including those of Lady Deidra and her mother.

He halted at where Carmen stood, Robert Means's arm linked in hers.

"Condesa," he said quietly. "Dance with me."

Carmen gaped up at Peter. The music was beginning again, couples moving past them, but all she could see was him.

All she heard were his words, not the whispers and giggles of the other guests.

She closed her eyes tightly, and those words echoed in her mind. *Dance with me . . .*

"Dance with me, Carmen!"

She laughed up at her major. "You are moon-mad, Major Everdean! How can we dance here? Outdoors . . . with no music? And I am not wearing my ball gown!"

She pirouetted about in her trousers and boots.

"Can you not hear it?" His face, golden with the touch of sunlight, was merry as he looked down at her. The lines about his eyes deep with a smile.

"Hear what?"

"The music, of course. I believe it is a waltz."

Carmen heard only the rush of the river they were strolling beside, the sounds of voices and laughter from the nearby encampment. But she cocked her head to one side, pretending to hear the lilting notes. *"I do believe you are correct, querido! A waltz, indeed."*

He held out his hand. *"So—will you dance with me, Carmen?"*

"I would be honored, Peter." She dipped into an elaborate court curtsy, as if she wore the grandest satin ball gown and diamonds.

Then Peter swung her in a wide arc, his hand warm at her waist. They were much closer than would ever be proper in a fine ballroom; her very traditional mother would have fainted, had she been alive to see! Carmen cared not a whit. Peter whirled her around, around, until the sky tilted above them, and she leaned her forehead against his shoulder and laughed until she cried . . .

Carmen blinked quickly, back suddenly from her sunny riverback. Peter stood before her, not the dashing English officer who had waltzed with her beneath the branches of trees, but unsmiling and stern. His red coat was gone, replaced with elegant but austere dark green superfine.

This man would not dance with her on a grassy floor until she was dizzy with love and laughter and blossoming love and they collapsed, breathless, onto the ground.

She looked at him now, and saw all that she lost since that magical day. She burst into tears, breaking away from Robert and fleeing the ballroom. The crowd parted before her in utter silence, entranced by the possibility of a scene in their midst.

Peter moved not at all, staring directly before him, until he turned on his heel and left the room in her wake. He hurried past the gawking crowd, the footmen at the front doors, onto the pavement outside the Carstairs's house. But Carmen had vanished.

The street was quiet, except for rows of carriages waiting for the ball to cease and their owners to return.

Then he heard the faint click of shoe heels on pavement. He turned and saw a fur-trimmed burgundy satin train disappearing around a corner.

He dashed off down the street, calling after her. "Carmen! Carmen, please wait."

When he came around the corner after her, he found that she had halted at his cry, but had not turned back. She stood there on the pavement, one hand on the wrought-iron railings of a fence. Her shoulders shook a bit, as if she were breathing too deeply, but otherwise she was completely still.

Peter had the sudden, powerful urge to kiss the pale, vulnerable nape of her neck, exposed by her new cropped coiffure.

"Carmen," he said. "Why did you run away?"

"Why did you follow me?" she answered.

"Well, I . . ." Peter paused. Why *had* he run after her so impulsively? "I wanted to apologize."

"For asking me to dance?"

"It seemed to embarrass you. Perhaps you simply could not bring yourself to dance with the likes of me."

She turned around. Her eyes seemed too bright, but she was composed. "It would only do my reputation good and no ill to be seen dancing with the famous Ice Earl, aside from those silly gossipy articles. And, if you are as fine a dancer as you once were, I am sure it would have been most enjoyable."

"Then, why did you leave?" Peter was baffled.

"I was—startled."

"Startled?"

"Yes. That you would ask me to dance, a woman you dislike so. I suppose I questioned your motives."

"My motives were only to dance with you!" And to separate her from Robert Means. "To speak with you."

"Indeed?"

"Indeed. I have many questions I would like to ask you."

"I am here now. Ask me, Peter."

Peter looked about. The street they were standing on, wide and well lit, faced a small square where there were several benches. "We cannot talk standing here."

"I do not wish to return to the ball. No doubt it is buzzing with speculation."

"Then, will you sit with me over in that square? Just for a moment. When you are feeling more the thing, we can return to the ball. Or I can see you home."

Carmen glanced uncertainly at the square. "Are you sure it will be safe?"

"Carmen, you will be much safer sitting there with me than wandering the streets of London alone."

She nodded. "Of course. Yes, I will sit with you for a moment."

"Thank you." Peter took her arm to lead her across the street. There was a small patch of skin below her sleeve and above her glove that was bare, and that was where his hand fell. It was almost a shock to feel his palm against her warm flesh. It was as soft as velvet, just as he remembered that once all her body had been.

Once her hair had been long and had cloaked her sun-golden, soft nakedness like a shining black curtain, as she leaned forward to kiss him . . .

His hand jerked on her arm.

She turned her head to look at him. "Peter?"

He drew his coat closer about him, hoping it was too dark for her to see the new fullness at the front of his close-fitting trousers. "Shall we sit here?"

"Yes, certainly."

Carmen looked up at Peter as she settled herself on the bench, puzzled. He seemed so—discomposed suddenly. Almost as much as she was. "What did you wish to talk about?"

His eyes were wide as he looked down at her, almost as if he were rather startled to find her there. "What?"

"You asked me to dance because you wished to speak with me. I merely inquired what about. After all, when you came to call on me at my house, you seemed to have everything settled about me in your mind."

"No more than you have about me!" he snapped.

"I beg your pardon? I did not hurl accusations at *you*."

"No. You just think me capable of being cruel and close-minded. You think me bitter and implacable."

Carmen rather felt that was the gist of it. "Did you not accuse me of spying against your regiment?"

"Yes, of course. But—no." He shook his head. "Forgive me, Carmen. I am rather confused."

"Well, that makes two of us. I have been utterly bewildered ever since I saw you again."

Peter drew in a deep breath. "It is true that I have buried myself in regrets these past years. I did think those things of you, on the evidence I had at hand."

"The flimsy evidence of seeing me with Chauvin!"

"That, and—other things." But he did not want to bring Robert Means into it just at present. He only wanted Carmen to understand his own feelings. "Yes, flimsy evidence, as you say. But as the years passed, I clung to my anger, and it grew. Anger was so much preferable to grief." He laid his hand, very gently and tentatively, against her own. "Now, as I see you again, I remember other things."

"Things such as what?"

"How very brave you were. How outspoken, how valiant. How you made me laugh, made me want to dance, when it seemed I would never want those things again." His hand moved on hers, his fingers curling beneath her palm. "What a grand kisser you were."

Carmen gave a choked laugh. "Oh, Peter!"

"It is true that you were! Why, I recall that afternoon we went walking beside what you called a river, but what was really only a small creek . . ." He broke off and stared at her. "That was it, was it not? When I asked you to dance, you thought of that afternoon."

"Yes. I remembered how very happy we were that day, and how our lives have changed since then. I was—overcome."

"I remember that day, too."

"Do you?"

Their gazes met, clung, and a silence, deeper than words, fell around them.

Then a carriage clattered past in the street. Carmen pulled away from him and rose to her feet. "We should go back. It will already be a great *on-dit* that we are both missing, and Elizabeth will be looking for me."

Peter stood beside her. "Yes. Of course. But I still have so many questions, Carmen."

She was walking away from him, her train now caught up and tossed over her arm. "As do I," she called. "I am sure we will meet again, Peter. And then all questions will be answered."

Carmen shut her bedroom door firmly, and leaned back against the solid wood. Her ribs ached from her swift run up the stairs to the safety of her room, and something that felt suspiciously like tears was making her cheeks damp.

She wiped at them impatiently with her gloved hand, then tossed her wrap and reticule onto the turned-down bed. As she stripped off her gloves, she noticed that somewhere she had lost her painted silk fan. It seemed she was losing bits of apparel every time she went out in public, first her comb and now her fan. And not even for interesting, amorous causes.

"Ah, Peter," she sighed.

She sat down at her dressing table, and rested her chin in her hand. In the glass, she appeared a disgruntled, rumpled-haired schoolgirl, with an unflattering frown on her face.

Peter was as much a puzzle as he had ever been. Did he hate her? Or did he—and this was the truly frightening thought—love her still, deep in his heart?

As she still loved him. So very much.

There. She had thought it. She loved him.

She shook her head fiercely, and sat up straighter. There was nothing she could do about Peter, or her feelings for him, that night. A better subject to occupy her mind was her own silly behavior.

"What a nodcock you were!" she told her reflection sternly. "Dashing out of there simply because he asked you to dance. What were you thinking? Do you want to cause a scandal?"

And she had been having such a productive evening with Robert Means. Robert, so open, artless, and charming. So very happy to see her again.

He had been such an unlikely soldier all those years ago; more a gentleman farmer than a warrior. He seemed an unlikely blackmailer now. Yet Carmen had learned, in very difficult and painful ways, that

he way things *seemed* were so often not how they
vere.

Robert could very well be her letter writer. He
knew of her activities in wartime; now he knew of
her new place in Society. He was really her most
likely candidate, as painful as that was to confess.
But she would need more time to be sure.

Elizabeth's house party would be the perfect
chance to become better acquainted with Robert
Means. She would have to be sure he received an
invitation.

Carmen's bedroom door opened, interrupting her
thoughts. A tiny, white night-gowned figure appeared
there, clutching a favorite doll with one hand and
rubbing sleepily at her eyes with the other.

Carmen smiled at Isabella, and held out her hand.
"What is it, darling? Could you not sleep?"

"I had a bad dream. I was going to find Esperanza,
but I saw your light." Isabella glanced speculatively
at the bed. "Could I sleep with you, Mama? Just
for tonight?"

"Of course you may! Come to Mama, and tell her
all about your dream." Isabella rushed into her arms
then, and Carmen pressed kisses to her daughter's
sleep-warm curls. Spies and blackmailers were completely forgotten. "Telling about it makes it
disappear . . ."

Chapter Nine

"Well, you certainly jumped into the scandal broth last night, brother." Elizabeth stood before him, her face fierce and frowning in the harsh morning sunlight that flooded from the high library windows.

"Not now, Elizabeth," Peter bit out.

"Yes, now! Whatever were you thinking? It is not at all like you to behave so—so improperly. Embarrassing Carmen in front of everyone! Tell me what you were thinking."

"I was not thinking."

Elizabeth snorted. "That is obvious! I do not rightly understand you. You say you want nothing to do with her, that you have made a new life, then you accost her on the dance floor and cause quite an *on-dit*. Have you read the papers this morning? Are you trying to drive her back to the Continent? Do you love her, or do you not?"

"I—do not know," he said quietly.

Elizabeth shook her head at him. "Oh, Peter. Of course you know. You love her, despite everything. Just as I love Nicholas."

"But the past . . ."

"Bother the past! If I can move beyond what happened when I first met Nick, then you can surely find a way to be with the woman you love." She smoothed her hair back into its neat coiffure and ucked her shawl about her shoulders, her mind obviously now spoken. "I must go and finish packing for the journey to the country. We will see you this weekend at Evanstone Park, will we not?"

"Will Carmen be there?"

"Of course!" she answered blithely. "As will Lady Deidra Clearbridge and her *dear* mother. I received their note just yesterday."

Two days after the disastrous Carstairs rout, Robert Means came to call on Carmen.

Unfortunately, despite his cheering presence and conversation, Carmen was still distracted over her moonlit conversation with Peter.

What could it all mean, his sudden desire for peace between them? Could it mean he was at last willing to listen to her account of what had occurred in Spain? Did he merely wish to wed his proper Lady Deidra, without the dark cloud of his hasty marriage hovering over him?

Or did he desire that they be friends again? Or, perhaps, more than friends? And what did she feel about that?

Hm.

"Carmen," Robert said. Then, louder, "Condesa!"

She snapped her gaze back to him and smiled. "Yes?"

He shook his head ruefully. "You have not attended a word I have been saying."

"Indeed I have!"

"Then why, just now when I mentioned an orphanage my mother is sponsoring in Cornwall, did you smile?"

"Oh, Robert. I am sorry. I have been so tired these last days, so—distracted, by many things."

"Yes." He looked away from her, to the fire that was crackling in her drawing room grate, and to the mantel above it, crowded with many objects and pictures. "And I believe I could say what one of the chief distractions could be."

The blackmailing letters? Carmen leaned toward him. "Yes? And what is that?"

"Your husband."

"Oh." The word seemed to strike her physically and she leaned back in her chair. "Yes, it has been rather a shock to find him suddenly in my life again, after so many years."

"You still love him, do you not?"

"I—oh, Robert, really!" she protested.

"Forgive my informality. I still find it difficult to remember that I am no longer in an army billet! Especially with old friends such as you."

"I sometimes have the same problem. And, yes— I do still love Peter." And what a relief it was, to finally say it aloud.

"Does he love you?"

Carmen shrugged. "Perhaps not. We *have* been apart a long time."

"I doubt that very much. That he does not love you, that is. How could he not?"

"Do you really think so, Robert?"

"I do." His voice hardened just a bit, and he would not meet her eyes. "I never saw a man so in love as Peter was—is with you. We seldom saw each other when we returned from Spain, but I did hear that he was not doing well at all. I knew it was hopeless mourning."

Carmen could feel the hot pricking of tears behind her eyes, and she blinked very hard to hold them back. It would never do for her to suddenly become a watering pot, especially in front of someone she was not entirely certain of. "I mourned, as well. But that was a long time ago; Peter has a new life now. As do I."

"Now, that I do not believe." Robert still would not look at her directly, but he smiled. "I will confess, Carmen, that when we met again, I cherished a few hopes of my own."

"Robert!"

"Yes. I so admired you in Spain. I had never met anyone like you. Then I saw you again, here in England, and I thought perhaps . . ." He broke off on a short bark of laughter. "Now I see I was mistaken."

Carmen reached over and patted his hand gently. "You are a dear man, Robert. I am sure you will find happiness very soon, with a very proper English miss!"

He shook his head. "Such as Lady Deidra Clearbridge, mayhap?"

Carmen laughed. "How very convenient that would be! If only you could be so obliging, Robert."

"I am not certain even I could be so obliging, Carmen."

"Well, Elizabeth kindly obtained vouchers to Almack's for us. I am sure she could do the same for you, and then we could look over the newest crop of young misses and find you a lovely one."

"I will look forward to it. But now, I must be going."

"Of course. It was so kind of you to call. And I am sure we shall see more of each other in the future."

Robert bowed over her hand, lingering just an instant more than was proper. "I am sure we shall. Good day, Carmen."

"Good day, Robert." And she watched him leave, more puzzled than ever before.

But she did not have time that day to sit and ponder over Robert Means, and whether or not he could be the blackmailer or was just a lovestruck swain. She had packing to do.

*   *   *

Carmen carefully folded a soft Indian shawl and laid it atop the gowns already in her trunk. "I do believe that is everything I shall need."

Esperanza handed her a pair of satin dancing slippers. "You forgot these, Carmencita."

Carmen groaned. "Dancing! I do not think I'll want to do very much of that this weekend."

"You love to dance!" Esperanza's tone conveyed that she did not exactly approve of *dancing*, not for proper widowed ladies anyway.

"Yes, of course I do." She slid the shoes into the trunk, and shut the lid with a bang. "Under the right circumstances."

"Isabella is very disappointed not to be going to Lady Elizabeth's party."

Carmen sighed. "Yes, I know. She was inconsolable. But I told her there would be no other children there, and she would be very bored." She sat down at her dressing table and picked up a hairbrush, only to put it back down again. Her hands simply would not be still. "Do *you* mind staying in Town alone for a few days, Esperanza?"

Esperanza shook her head. "Not a bit! The little one and I will have a splendid time. I have promised her we could have ices at Gunter's again, and go to that Astley's you told her about."

"She will adore that!" Carmen picked up the brush again and ran it quickly through her hair. "I simply could not take her with me this time."

Peter was sure to be there, and she was not at all prepared to tell Isabella's father of her existence, even though she knew it would have to be done. If only she could be certain of Peter's reaction . . .

One day she would tell him. Just not yet.

"Pardon me, Condesa."

Carmen looked up to find Rose, their new housemaid, standing in the doorway, her arms filled with flowers. "What is it, Rose?"

"These just came for you, Condesa."

"Thank you. Just put them down by the bed."

There were two bouquets: one a large mass of deep red roses, one a posy of lilies in a delicate silver filigree holder. Carmen plucked the note from the roses.

"They are from Robert Means," she told Esperanza. "How very sweet!" Such a gentleman, even after a rebuff.

She placed the card down carefully on her dressing table, eyeing the looped handwriting thoughtfully. Robert did seem so very guileless, so full of admiration for her . . .

"Well?" Esperanza said, her voice impatient.

"Well, what?"

"Who are the others from?"

Carmen put aside the roses and reached for the other note.

The words were scrawled across the paper, bold and black. "I must speak with you—Peter."

"Rose," she said, not lifting her gaze from the note. "Can you have the footman take a message to Clifton House for me?"

"Yes, of course, Condesa."

"Have him tell the earl I will meet him at three o'clock in Green Park."

Chapter Ten

Peter saw her before she saw him, and he pulled his horse up, hidden behind a tree, to watch her.

She was perched sidesaddle on her gray mare, graceful in a deep purple velvet habit. Her face was half hidden by the small net veil of her tall-crowned hat, but she was smiling as she watched a group of children frolicking.

Peter remembered then the first time he had ever seen her. She had ridden her horse hell-for-leather through their encampment in the middle of a quiet afternoon, the plumes on her outrageous, wide-brimmed green hat flying. Never had he seen anyone more dazzlingly *alive*.

He had thought on the night he married her that no woman could ever be more lovely. Yet he had been wrong, because the years had only made Carmen more beautiful. More elegant, more alive.

She looked up then, and found him watching her. At first her gloved grip tightened on the reins, and he feared she would flee before he said what he had come to say. Then she raised one hand and beckoned him nearer.

"Hello, Peter," she said quietly as he drew up beside her.

"Hello, Carmen."

"I was rather surprised to receive your flowers and your note."

"I wanted to apologize," he said, watching her hands as she fidgeted with the reins.

"What? The famous Ice Earl is apologizing yet again?" She laughed. "Whatever for?"

"For my behavior at the Carstairs rout, of course. Causing such a ridiculous scene. It is not at all like me; I cannot fathom what came over me."

"No, it is not like you. But then, we find ourselves in such a very unusual situation. I am not at all certain what the proper behavior should be."

"Quite right. But Elizabeth has been at great pains to point out how foolish I have been. I have been rude to you, have endured sleepless nights trying to think what could have gone wrong all those years ago. Then I realized that Elizabeth's advice that I simply *ask* you makes a great deal of sense."

Carmen's dark gaze was wide and unwavering behind the veil. "So that is why you asked me to meet you? To ask me what happened?"

"Of course. What else could it be?"

"I—well, I thought you were here to obtain an annulment."

"An *annulment*?"

"Yes. In order to make a proper offer to Lady Deidra. It would be quite the scandal if the Earl of Clifton was discovered to be a bigamist, yes? And divorce is so protracted."

To his great horror, Peter felt a flush spreading across his face. He coughed and looked away from her steady regard. "Er, well, we should take things one step at a time, don't you think?"

"Certainly."

"And I think the first step ought to be a clearing of the air between us. We must let the past go before we can truly look to the future."

"Yes," she murmured. "The future. We cannot speak properly here, though."

He almost expected her to invite him to her town house, but she fell silent. "Would you care to come to Clifton House? Elizabeth has gone out shopping with her friend Georgina Beaumont, so we can talk quietly."

"I think that would be best."

Carmen was not exactly sure what she had been expecting of a house with such a grand name as Clifton House. Marble halls and gilded ceilings, perhaps. Yet what she found instead was a house she herself might have decorated and lived in.

It was large to be sure, but there was no gilding and very little marble. Instead, the floors were brightly polished parquet, overlaid with brilliant red and blue Persian rugs. The furnishings in the vast foyer were heavy carved medieval pieces. A large oversize Velazquez painting hung on the wall, no doubt a souvenir from the war. There were no dainty little gold and satin Parisian chairs, or Dresden shepherdesses.

She could almost have thought herself home again.

"Your home is lovely," she said as he led her down a small hall into his book-lined library.

"You sound surprised, as if you expected me to live in some dusty mausoleum of an ancestral pile." He held out a chair for her beside the fireplace.

"I am not surprised." Her gaze went to the portrait of Peter that hung above the mantel; it was a wonderful painting, completely lifelike, to the very glow in the ice-blue eyes. "Is that one of Elizabeth's works?"

"Indeed it is."

"She is very talented."

"My sister is the finest portraitist in England," he answered with a note of rare pride in his voice.

"Would you care for some sherry, Carmen? I have some particularly fine Amontillado."

She smiled. "You remember."

"Of course I remember you like sherry. Very dry, right?" He poured some of the brownish-red liquid into a crystal goblet and pressed it into her hands. "But then, I remember many things about you, Carmen."

She took a long sip of the sherry, relishing the warm bite of it at the back of her throat. She had a feeling she was going to be in great need of it for the afternoon ahead.

"So," she said, "you wish to know what happened in Spain, on the day we parted?"

"Please."

She looked up at him, at his serious, beautiful face. "Then, I will tell you. And after, you can believe what you will. You will know the truth—all of it."

Then she put aside her glass, folded her hands in her lap, closed her eyes, and told him the whole sorry tale of her capture by Chauvin. Of being shot and tortured. Of how she in turn killed Chauvin, and made her escape.

She relived every bit of the pain and despair of that dark afternoon.

She fell silent when her tale ended; she stared down at her hands, so neatly folded in her lap, and tried not to break down in helpless sobs. She had not thought of that time in a very long while; it had been almost the worst day of her life, and she had never, ever wanted to think of it, let alone speak of it, again.

The very worst had been that day, weeks after she had fled the French encampment, when she had stumbled into a hospital and discovered that her husband was dead. Then all the pride, all the fortitude that had kept her moving forward, had quite broken down, and she had almost wished that Chauvin had killed *her*.

If she had not carried Isabella, the most precious gift, inside her, she did not know what she would have done.

Only when she was very certain that she would not start crying, did she open her eyes and look up at Peter.

He stared out of the window, half facing away from her as he watched the street below. What she could see of his face was expressionless, as pale and perfect and composed as a Renaissance statue.

The faint, very faint hope that Carmen had allowed herself to feel, the hope that he would believe her and all would be right again, now tasted like cold ashes in her mouth. There was too much time, too much anger between them. They could never again be the couple who danced on riverbanks, made love on army cots.

She had known, of course, that those days could never return. But she had harbored the hope, so very deep inside that she had not even known it until now, that the people they had become could find a common ground. A place to begin again.

Now, in the face of his silence, that hope faded.

She schooled her own features into a careful, almost mocking smoothness, and reached for her gloves.

"Well," she said, rising to her feet. She was not at all certain her shaking legs could support her, but, through willpower, they did. She lowered the veil of her hat to cover her face again. "I will incommode you no longer, my lord. I certainly did not mean to bore you with my long tale."

"I looked for you."

His voice, low and thick, stopped her from leaving the room as she intended. She looked back at him, the sunlit room now hazy behind the veil. "What did you say?"

"I looked for you, after I recovered from my wound. I was meant to be invalided home to England, but I had to go back and see what had become of you."

He looked at her, piercing her with pale blue eyes that were now nothing like ice. They were pure blue flame.

Carmen fell back onto her chair. "What did you find?"

"I found the priest who had married us. He was the only person left within miles. He told me that the remains of the French regiment had been ambushed, wiped out by partisans after a Spanish woman died there. A Spanish noblewoman." His hands fisted on the window sash, his knuckles white. His gaze never wavered from her face. "You, I thought."

Carmen pressed her hand to her mouth. She had not known, had not wanted to know what occurred at Alvaro after she had left there.

"You did not know," Peter said.

"No. I went home to Seville. I was ill, I needed to recover." To give birth. "Then, when the war was over, I left Spain and began my travels. I could no longer bear the memories of my home."

"Did you find what you searched for on those travels?"

Carmen shrugged. "Not yet. But I do have one thing I would like to ask you, Peter."

"What is that?"

She pushed back her veil, and looked him full in the face. "If the Spanish partisans did not believe me to be in league with the French, and indeed sought vengeance for my death, then why did you?"

He came and sat down in the chair across from her, his golden hair haloed in the setting sun. "The fact that I saw you riding away with Chauvin was not the only evidence I had of treachery, Carmen," he said quietly.

"What else could there possibly have been?"

"Someone told me that you had—had been Chauvin's lover in Seville, that you had shared secrets with him, news of the British Army." His gaze fell away from her in shame. "I was drunk, grief-stricken. I fear I believed it true, and went on believing it for all these years."

Carmen's chalk-white fingers clutched at the arms of her chair. She shook her head, disbelieving. "Who? Who told you such vile lies?"

"It was—Robert Means," Peter whispered.

Carmen's jaw sagged. She fell back against the chair, no longer able to remain upright. "Robert? How can that be? He just called on me this morning, to express his—admiration. Why should he do such a thing?"

"I could not say. Jealousy, perhaps."

"Jealousy?"

"That you loved me, and not him, I suppose."

"But what proof did he present?"

"He had recently been to Seville. He said he had heard it from a friend of yours, Elena, oh, I cannot recall . . ."

Carmen's jaw tightened. "Granjero. Elena Granjero."

"Yes. He said she was your best friend, that she had told him because she so hated the French."

"Ha!" Carmen laughed humorlessly. "Elena did not have two thoughts to put together in her head. She thought the French so dashing in their blue uniforms. Oh, we were friends at school, but we hardly spoke after the French invaded Spain." She drummed her fingers on the arm of her chair, her mind racing with the thought of all the treachery that had surrounded her.

Yet even as she shook her head in disbelief, she could see the awful logic of it. A girl with no conscience who had been jealous of Carmen's young marriage to the Conde de Santiago, and a man jealous of her love for Peter.

She berated herself roundly for her utter lack of suspicion, her blindness—*she*, who had built her life on correct judgment of the motives of others had not seen Robert Mean's perfidy at all.

And it had cost her greatly.

In the silence that followed these revelations, Peter came to her and knelt on the floor beside her chair.

His hands, those long, elegant hands she had dreamed of for so many lonely years, reached for the tiny ebony buttons that marched up the front of her habit. He began to unfasten them, beginning with the one on the high collar. He paused at each button, as if to give her time to utter a protest, to stop him.

She did not protest.

He peeled back the close-fitting bodice and the thin silk of her chemise, to reveal the pink, puckered scar at her shoulder. The jagged mark of Chauvin's bullet.

Then, as she held her breath, he leaned forward and touched the scar with his warm, healing mouth.

Carmen cried then, hot tears that fell unchecked down her cheeks, dripping from her chin onto his bent head like a new baptism of truth. She placed her hands on his shoulders, felt their tremble beneath the wool of his jacket. And she felt love, love she had thought gone from her life forever.

"I am so sorry, Carmen," he said, his voice echoing against her skin. He leaned his cheek against her bare shoulder. "So very, very sorry. I can never say that to you enough."

"Peter," she murmured. "*Querido.* If only you knew how many things I must tell you . . ."

The library door opened, Elizabeth and Nicholas

standing on the threshold. They gaped at the tableau before them, Carmen half dressed, Peter kneeling before her with his face pressed to her bosom.

Carmen was so frozen she could not even pull her bodice closed. She could only gape at them in return.

She saw Elizabeth's face, grinning in delight, in the instant before they shut the door and left.

Soon after Carmen's ignominious departure from Clifton House, with her bodice buttoned crookedly and her cheeks stained with tears, Peter himself left the house. He meant to pay a very important call indeed.

On Robert Means.

When Robert opened the door to his lodgings, Peter wasted no time on preliminaries. He grabbed Robert by his shirtfront and shoved him back against the wall. Robert's booted feet dangled from the floor, and he flailed helplessly against Peter's iron grasp.

Robert was a strong man, from all the riding and walking he did in the country. But Peter had always been stronger, and now he had the fire of his fury behind him. He did not even notice the effort it took to keep Robert pinned against the wall.

"Wh-what is this, Clifton?" Robert gasped. His voice was rather faint, due to the fact that his shirtfront was pressed to his larynx.

"I have come to defend a lady's honor," Peter replied calmly. "Surely you have been expecting this."

"What lady?"

"Why, how many ladies have you so defamed? How many ladies have you spread vile falsehoods about?" Peter pressed harder, until Robert's face went quite purple. "Or have you lost count?"

"No, Clifton! I . . ."

"I refer, of course, to only one lady. My wife."

"Your *wife*? Carmen?"

"Just so." Peter released Robert, and watched as he fell into a heap on the floor, gasping. "I demand satisfaction."

Robert stared up at him. He struggled to his feet, but was careful to stay a goodly distance from Peter. "You are challenging me to a duel?"

"Did you, or did you not, tell me the lie that Carmen was Chauvin's lover and a French spy?"

Robert turned away. "I—I suppose I did. But I did not know it was a lie!"

"Then, I have no choice. Name your seconds."

Robert slid back down the wall to a seated position, his face hidden in his hands. His shoulders shook, and Peter suspected he was crying. Or shamming it.

That was a bit discomposing. What was a gentleman supposed to do when the man he had just challenged to a duel burst into tears? Peter was not at all certain, having never fought a duel before.

He reached for a straight-backed chair, swung it about, and straddled it, crossing his arms across the top. "Oh, for pity's sake, don't cry, Robert." He tossed him a handkerchief.

Robert wiped at his face and looked up, still not meeting Peter's gaze. "I never meant for it to be like this. I thought her dead."

"Oh, so it is quite all right to sully a *dead* woman's reputation?"

"No! It—I don't know what came over me that night."

"Do you not?"

"I—perhaps I do. I hated you for having her love. I wanted to hurt you."

Peter shook his head sadly. "And so you did. You ruined my life for six long years. Hers, as well."

"I never meant to hurt Carmen! I loved her. I thought she was dead—beyond pain."

"Well, now you know differently."

Robert began to cry again, sniffling into the handkerchief. "Are you going to shoot me?"

"Do you want me to?"

"Yes, please."

Despite all his pain and anger, Peter could not help but be a bit sorry for such a pitiful, jealousy-consumed creature. "I have a more effective solution."

Robert looked up damply. "What?"

"You will write a letter of apology to Carmen. Then you will leave London, and you will never speak to or of Carmen again. You will never come near any of my family. Do you agree? Or shall I shoot you?"

Robert looked back down again. "I agree. I will leave London, and go back to Cornwall."

"Very well, then. Write that letter, and I shall have it delivered at once. And—have a pleasant journey to Cornwall."

Chapter Eleven

Carmen stood in the doorway of Elizabeth's drawing room at Evanstone Park, and surveyed the crowd assembled there, taking tea, chatting, milling about.

Elizabeth and Nicholas had a very wide acquaintance, and it appeared that they were all gathered for the house party. Attending were Lord and Lady Rivers, an elderly couple who were well-known patrons of the arts. There was a Mrs. King, a very wealthy if somewhat silly widow, who was holding her yapping poodle tightly on her lap, no doubt to prevent it breaking free and biting every ankle in the room.

Elizabeth also included Lord Huntington, a young, handsome viscount, no doubt intended for Carmen. There was a Miss Mary Dixon, an excellent pianist and rather promising artist (Elizabeth was always on the watch for someone to be a mentor to). Miss Dixon was lecturing Lord Crane, a fashionable London beau, on some artistic point, splashing droplets of tea onto his fine green coat with every emphasis.

A vibrant redhead in a bright green silk tea gown held court in one corner, surrounded by laughing gentlemen. No doubt that was Elizabeth's good friend, Mrs. Georgina Beaumont, the famous artist.

And there was Lady Deidra Clearbridge and her

mother. They sat somewhat apart from the noisy fray, their lips slightly pursed.

Only Robert Means was nowhere to be seen. So he had kept the promises in his tearstained letter.

Carmen nodded politely at the Clearbridge ladies as she handed her muff and gloves to the butler. Then her smile widened as she saw Elizabeth hurrying toward her, tugging the redheaded woman along with her.

"My dear Carmen!" Elizabeth cried, kissing her on both cheeks. "You are here at last! You are quite the last to arrive, aside from my naughty brother."

"I do apologize, Lizzie. I had a very late start from Town."

"Well, you are here now, and that is all that matters. Now, you must meet my bosom bow, Mrs. Georgina Beaumont. I lived at her house in Italy before Nicholas and I were married."

"Of course! I have heard so much of the famous Mrs. Beaumont." Carmen turned her smile to the redhead.

Georgina laughed merrily. "Every bit of it true, I assure you!"

Elizabeth grinned. "Georgie quite prides herself on causing a stir everywhere she goes."

"Then, I can see why you are such good friends," Carmen said. "You have such a lot in common."

"*Touché!* But then, we are three of a kind, are we not? You yourself are always the center of attention."

Carmen laughed. "Perhaps you are right, Lizzie."

"I *am* right! What a dash the three of us will cut, now we are all together. But now you must come and have some tea." Elizabeth tucked one of her arms through Carmen's and one through Georgina's, and led them into the drawing room. "You must be parched after your journey. And then you must meet the Richardsons. Such charming people, so fond of art . . ."

Carmen, meant to be choosing a gown for supper, had instead been standing in front of her wardrobe for a full twenty minutes, dressed only in her chemise. She did not see any of the glittering array of garments hanging before her. She ran her hand absently over the skirt of a blue velvet gown, and thought how very much it looked like the blue of Peter's eyes.

She wondered if he would sit next to her at supper . . .

She snatched her hand back from the velvet as if burned. These were the very sort of soppy thoughts she had been trying *not* to have for days now.

The rogue had not called on her after their scene in his library. He had not even sent a note.

Had he forgotten about her the moment she fled his house in embarrassment? *She* had thought of nothing but him ever since that day. Her Ice Earl, her dashing English major. The man who had, once upon a time, held her, loved her, given her a daughter . . .

Isabella!

Carmen slammed the door of the wardrobe, and leaned her forehead against it. In all the tumult of the last few emotional days, she had forgotten the most perplexing problem of all. That Peter had a child he knew nothing about.

She had seen how very angry Peter could be when he felt he had been deceived.

"What to do, what to do?" she muttered, sinking down onto the bed.

"Carmen? Are you in there?" Elizabeth swept into the room without bothering to knock. She was already dressed for the evening, and was pulling on her silk gloves. "We must hurry, or we shall be quite late, and I faithfully promised Nicholas I would not leave him alone with the Riverses. Such bores, the pair of them, but such great ones for commissioning portraits of themselves. I did say that . . ." Then she looked up. "Why, Carmen! You are not even dressed. Where is the maid I sent up to you?"

"I sent her away," Carmen answered quietly.

"Was she unsatisfactory?"

"Not at all. I simply don't think I shall go down tonight, if you will forgive me. I am very tired after the journey."

Elizabeth sat down beside her, with a sigh. "It is my great lout of a brother, is it not? Did he not call after that little—tableau in the library?"

"That was not as it appeared!"

"Um-hm. I'm sure. Well, after you, er, left, he went straight out, and we never saw him again before we left for the country."

"Then, he is not here?" Carmen asked hopefully.

"Oh, he is here. He appeared only an hour ago, with not a word of apology for his lateness."

"Oh."

Elizabeth seized Carmen's hand and pulled her to her feet. "And you must come to dinner! Everyone knows I have the famous condesa here, and they will be quite put out if they do not catch a glimpse of you. My party shall be ruined."

Carmen smiled at that blatant piece of exaggeration. "Well, never have it be said I ruined a party."

"Excellent! And do not worry—I have seated you far from Peter, next to that very nice Viscount Huntington. So Peter can stew in his own envy. Now, what shall you wear?" Elizabeth opened up the wardrobe and began sorting through the gowns.

"I had thought the blue velvet."

"It is pretty, but if Peter is to stew, you need some-

-hing more—dashing." Elizabeth pulled out a pale gold satin. Carmen had never worn it; it had been purchased for a masked ball in Paris, but she had not been brave enough to wear it when it came to the day. It was cut high at the collarbone, but fluidly followed the lines of the figure.

"This one," said Elizabeth. "Most assuredly."

"Lizzie!" Carmen protested with a laugh. "If I wear that tonight, I will catch my death of cold."

"Not at all! I have plenty of fires lit. And it will make Peter very sorry he did not call."

Carmen giggled.

Peter stood beside the fireplace, and surveyed the crowd gathered in his sister's drawing room before supper.

He might as well have stayed in Town for all the difference it made. Here were so many of the same people he saw there, clustered in the same cliques, repeating the same gossip. Nicholas and a group of gentlemen were having a discussion about some horses that were up for sale in the neighborhood, which would usually have interested Peter at least moderately. But he had wandered away from them after five minutes.

Elizabeth's friend, the famous and dashing artist Mrs. Georgina Beaumont, was at the center of a more daring group, which was talking and laughing loudly, having already dipped into the port and brandy usually saved for after supper. Peter would have liked to join them, if only for the brandy, but they would hardly have welcomed him.

Lady Deidra was seated prettily upon a brocade settee with her mother, her pale pink skirts spread about her like rose petals. She had sent him several glances, but he had no desire to converse with her, either.

All he wanted was to see Carmen.

Then his sister the hostess at last entered her own party. He couldn't help but laugh at how she augmented her meager height with a new headdress of tall crimson plumes that accented her red and gold gown.

Then behind her appeared the very woman he had been longing to see.

She was, as always, in the first stare of fashion, her old trousers and men's shirts obviously left far behind her. Her golden gown modestly covered her collarbone and upper arms, but the fabric was as flowing and shimmering as liquid gold leaf, and followed the lines of her figure and her long legs.

Those long legs that had once wrapped about his own so perfectly . . .

He cursed softly and wished he had some of that brandy.

Then he cursed again, as Carmen turned, and it seemed that Peter—and the entire room—was gazing at her backside in the closely flowing gold satin.

He had such an urge to throw his own coat over her.

He moved behind her so quietly that she did not notice him, and he leaned forward to murmur in her ear.

"Good evening, Condesa," he murmured. His breath lightly stirred the curls at the nape of her neck.

The gold threads of the satin shimmered as she trembled.

But when she turned to face him, her features were perfectly composed, her faintly mocking smile in place. "Good evening, Lord Clifton. I do hope Elizabeth and I have not kept everyone waiting for their supper too long."

"My sister always keeps us waiting. It is her artist's prerogative." He smiled at her, and hoped it looked less like a lupine stretching of lips over teeth than it felt. He longed to be alone with her so very much that it was becoming difficult to display social politeness. "May I escort you in to supper?'

Elizabeth put her hand on her brother's arm. "Now, Peter, you know that is not the way! I have Carmen seated next to that handsome Viscount Huntington, and here he is now to escort her. Would you offer Lady Deidra your arm?" She went up on tiptoe to whisper in his ear. "I did invite her just for you, you know."

All Peter could do was watch helplessly as Carmen moved away from him on Huntington's arm, her soft laughter floating back to him, as if in some enticing dream.

Supper was interminable.

Carmen toyed with her roast duckling, nibbled at the apple compote, and drank more wine than was perhaps strictly prudent. She smiled and chatted with Viscount Huntington, who was most attentive and rather attractive, interested in her travels and her plans for the Season. She may even have flirted with him just the tiniest bit.

But her attention strayed often down the length of the flower-laden table, to where Peter sat between Lady Deidra and her orange satin–clad mother. Deidra spoke with him, quietly, earnestly, her bright head bent near his shoulder. Though he smiled and nodded at her words, Carmen couldn't help but notice that he, too, reached for his wineglass often. He seemed distant from all the merriment and chatter that flowed around them, preoccupied, but always unfailingly polite.

She wished she could read him, so cool and polite, so distant. She wished she could tell what he was thinking; most of all, what he was thinking of *her*. She wanted to tell him all about Isabella, the beautiful, delightful girl they had created together.

If only she could be certain . . .

Carmen sighed and took another sip of her wine.

". . . Would you, Condesa?"

Viscount Huntington's voice drew her back from her imaginings, into the gaiety of the supper table. She blinked up at him.

"I am sorry, Lord Huntington. I must have been woolgathering. Did you ask me something?"

He nodded understandingly. "Quite understandable, I'm sure. The trip from London is quite tiring. I just hope that you are not too tired for the charades after supper."

Carmen was appalled. "Ch-charades?"

"Yes. Lady Elizabeth was just saying that she planned for everyone to draw names for charade teams after supper. We will perform them on Sunday evening."

Now Carmen knew why she had truly never come to England before. It had not been grief. It had been the British propensity for party games. She had hoped to be safe at least at Elizabeth's house! "Well—no, of course not. One can never be too tired for charades."

"Excellent!" He smiled at her shyly. "I hope we are on the same team, Condesa."

She smiled at him, and took another sip of wine. Her gaze slid once again down the table, expecting to find Peter still conversing with Lady Deidra.

Yet Deidra had turned her attention to the gentleman on her left. And Peter was instead watching her, his eyes a warm turquoise in the candlelight. He raised his glass, and in a small, subtle gesture, tilted it in a salute.

Carmen almost choked on her wine.

*   *   *

After the ladies departed to take tea in the drawing room, Peter stayed at the supper table with the other men to sip his port and smoke his cigar. He even managed to engage in the discussion concerning politics and horses with a bit of coherence.

Yet his mind, as always of late, was elsewhere. It was in the drawing room, to be precise, with his wife and her damnably dashing gown!

She was hiding something, he thought. The Carmen he had known in Spain had been more than free with her views and opinions; she had argued with him heatedly on many topics, from politics to art and music, and had never hedged. He thought that it must have arisen from her careful, traditional upbringing; they had been tamped down inside for so long, just waiting to spring free. And he had adored that about her.

This new condesa had certainly learned subtlety. Age had lent her a new beauty and a new careful sophistication.

But she would not meet his gaze directly, would not smile at him with her old, open, sunny ways. Even after their revelations in his library.

What could it be she kept inside her? He burned to know, to understand this new Carmen.

No woman but Carmen, either before or after her, had ever stirred this wild need to *know*, to possess every secret and desire of her heart. After so many years of a frozen anger, his own heart had dared to begin to hope again. There were many things between them, good and terrible, but she still spoke to his soul as no one else ever could.

Yet she still held herself apart!

Could it be she had no feelings left for him, that he had killed them and there was not an ember left in her heart?

Could it be she cared for another? She was so beautiful, so unique. Many men surely desired her.

Men like—that Viscount Huntington Elizabeth had insisted on pairing Carmen with.

Peter looked at the man who was talking with Nicholas. He was a handsome man, Huntington, a wealthy man, so Peter had heard, who lived a quiet, content life in the country. He had been in Spain, as well, but had seemingly left the war behind the instant he returned to England, and had never lost his sweet ways.

Unlike Peter, the darkness had not swallowed him.

Huntington had smiled and talked with Carmen throughout supper, his face open and warm and a bit shy as he watched her. And she had laughed with him, the rich, brandy-dark laughter that Peter had not heard since their wedding night.

Damn Huntington.

Peter tossed back the last of his port and reached for the decanter.

"Well," Nicholas said, too cheerfully in Peter's opinion, as he rose from his chair. "Shall we rejoin the ladies, then? I think Elizabeth was planning some amusement."

"May I join you?"

Carmen looked up from her book, surprised, nay *shocked*, to see Lady Deidra Clearbridge standing beside her chair. The other woman's serene smile was in place, her blue-blue eyes placid, giving no clue as to her motivation in seeking out Carmen. She looked very pleasant, and bland, and English.

What a perfect Countess of Clifton she would make, Carmen reflected wryly.

She smiled in return and tucked away her book. "Of course, Lady Deidra. Please do."

As Deidra sat, her pale pink skirts fluttered about

ier like the petals of a dainty rose. She even smelled
oselike, and a wreath of white roses twined in her
ed-gold curls.

Carmen had thought she had long ago left behind
ier awkward schoolgirl days, towering like a gawky
giant over all the other girls at the convent. Now
hose days came back upon her in a rush.

"I do hope you are enjoying your stay in *our* coun-
ry, Condesa," Deidra said, her eyes wide and polite
over the edge of the teacup she raised to her lips.

"Oh, yes," Carmen answered. "I have found it
very charming."

"Though I am certain it cannot be as exciting as
Paris, or Italy. Or Spain." One dainty brow rose. "I
myself have never wanted to venture away from England. But I did hear you were lately in Paris?"

"Indeed. And before that in Italy, and in Vienna."

"Yes. The Continent is growing ever smaller, is it
not? Travel is so very much easier since the end of
he war. You must have found it so yourself, being
so very well traveled."

"Oh, yes," said Carmen, a bit puzzled. "I have
enjoyed great ease of travel. And the variety of company I have encountered is always a pleasure."

The drawing room doors opened then, to admit
he gentlemen who had concluded their rituals of
port and cigars. Deidra glanced at them briefly before
urning her smile back to Carmen. "I presume then
hat we must soon lose your delightful company to
he lure of travel and variety. What a great loss to
England."

Carmen eyed her companion impassively, think-
ng, *Why, the little baggage!* She almost laughed aloud
at these attempts to be rid of the foreign interloper.
"That is very kind of you to say, Lady Deidra."

"Well, I am very happy, Condesa, that we had this

chance to chat. I am certain we shall see each other again, before the weekend is concluded."

"I am sure we shall."

Deidra nodded and rose to cross the room in her graceful pink flutter. She took Peter's arm with her small hand, and stood on tiptoe to speak quietly in his ear.

Carmen looked away, into the flames that leap high in the marble grate. She could feel a headache forming behind her eyes, a sharp pain born of confusion, exhaustion, even apprehension. She was just gathering her book and shawl, to make her excuses to Elizabeth and then retire, when she felt a warm masculine hand alight briefly on her shoulder.

She turned, almost hopeful, to see Viscount Huntington standing behind her. Peter was still across the room, with Lady Deidra.

Carmen forced herself to smile in welcome, and patted the arm of the chair that had been recently vacated by Lady Deidra. Huntington, after all, was a very amiable gentleman.

He sat down shyly. "I saw that you were conversing with the Clearbridge Pearl, Condesa."

"Is that what she is called? I found her more of a . . ." Carmen paused. "Rose."

"Oh, yes. That, too. She is much admired. Young fops compose odes to her eyelashes, that sort of thing. They say she has had twenty offers."

Carmen laughed. "Was one of them yours, Lord Huntington?"

He looked affronted. "Lud, no. I couldn't tolerate being leg-shackled to such alabaster dignity my whole life, even if she would accept my addresses. Pardon my saying so, Condesa."

"Of course. But why would she not accept your addresses? You seem a very nice young man to me."

He blushed a bright pink, all the way into his cravat. "I'm not top-lofty enough for an earl's daughter!"

"Ah."

Then Elizabeth interrupted their conversation, swooping down upon them with folded bits of paper clutched in her hand.

"Oh, Carmen, there you are!" she cried. "Do forgive me, Huntington, for stealing her away, but I simply must beg her assistance in setting up my game."

"Elizabeth," Carmen protested, "if it is charades, I do not know how . . ."

"Not at all! I would not have *charades* at my party. This is *tableaux*."

Carmen did not see how that was any different. "Tableaux?"

"Yes. Here, hold these papers for me." Elizabeth had gathered a crowd with her enthusiasm, and she now clambered onto a chair to make her instructions heard. "Every team will be assigned a scene from Greek mythology to enact. The team which is the most dramatic, the most convincing, shall win the prize!" A small murmur of excitement arose, and she raised her hand for silence. She flashed a brilliant smile at Carmen, and then turned one onto her brother. "I shall assign the first scene to none other than my own brother, Lord Clifton, who, along with the Condesa de Santiago, shall enact Endymion and Selene!"

Carmen closed her eyes. She could hear Lady Deidra's hissing whisper, "Well, this is a most shocking pastime! I must say I had hoped Lady Elizabeth would show more propriety, despite being an *artist*."

Yet, even with her eyes squeezed shut and her ears trying to do so, Carmen could feel the weight of Peter's regard from across the room as he watched her. When she opened her eyes to look back at him, to beseech him to talk some sense into his sister, he *winked* at her!

"Psst! Carmen! Are you awake?"

Carmen rolled over in her bed and blinked sleepily, certain she must be dreaming. But when she pinched herself, it did not go away. Elizabeth still stood at her bedside, wrapped in a cloak, a lantern held aloft.

"I am now," Carmen said, sitting up and rubbing her eyes. "Whatever are you about, Lizzie?"

"Some of us are going out to look at the moon from the medieval ruins nearby. It is full tonight, you know. So romantic!"

"The ruins? But it must be after midnight!"

"Nearly two, I believe. Do you want to come?"

Carmen glanced at her window, at the bar of silvery moonlight that spilled from between the velvet drapes. She could feel the old excitement of adventure tingling in her fingertips again, something that had not happened for so very long.

The fact that this adventure was looking at the moon at two in the morning rather than facing French guns made it all the better.

"I may as well, since I am already awake." She climbed out of the bed and reached into the wardrobe for a plain muslin day dress and her cloak.

The others were already waiting for them on the drive. There was Georgina Beaumont, who carried a large picnic hamper; Nicholas, with a bottle of champagne; Lord Huntington, and Miss Dixon. And Peter.

Lady Deidra and her mother were nowhere in sight.

Elizabeth and Nicholas led the way down a narrow, tree-lined pathway that veered off of the main drive, closely followed by the chattering, laughing group. Carmen and Peter brought up the rear.

"I saw that Robert Means declined Elizabeth's invitation," she said quietly.

"Yes. I do believe that he has kept his word to me, and retired to the country for good. I went to see him after—well, after we spoke in my library. He promised he would leave London." Peter's hand sought hers, warm and reassuring in the chilly darkness. "He will not be bothering you again."

Carmen squeezed his hand. "He never *bothered* me. That is what makes his lies so very shocking."

"Perhaps even more shocking than that I would believe them?"

"Perhaps," Carmen whispered.

Peter jumped lightly over a fallen log, and reached back to assist Carmen, swinging her up into his arms.

When she was on the other side of the log, he did not release her, but held her against him. Carmen looped her arms about his neck and looked down at his lovely, patrician face, illuminated by moonlight.

"I can never say I am sorry enough, Carmen," he said softly. "I should have had more faith in you, in our feelings for one another."

"So you should have," she answered lightly. "But I have already forgiven you."

"Come along, you two!" called Elizabeth. "No lagging behind, if you please. What kind of chaperone do you think I am? Even if I *am* an artist!"

The others shrieked with laughter.

Peter placed Carmen on her feet and wordlessly offered his arm. She took it, and they walked together into the clearing where the medieval watch tower, half ruined, stood sentinel.

Some of the others were already climbing up inside the tower, and their laughter cast a warm golden glow over the ancient stones. A stream rushed along behind it, its gurgle and tumble mingling with that laughter.

The moon bathed the whole scene in a gentle, silvery luminescence, giving it the unreal atmosphere of a painting.

Carmen thought it the perfect setting for a reawakening love.

Georgina leaned out of a window at the very top of the tower, her long red hair falling over her shoulders. "Look!" she called. "I am Rapunzel!"

Carmen laughed as she took in the whole enchanted, fairy-tale scene. "Is it not wonderful?"

"Lovely," Peter said. "It is an enchanted night."

"That is exactly what I thought." Carmen looked up at him, to find he was watching her. "I am so happy we are sharing this together, Peter. I thought never to see such a thing with you again."

"Neither did I, Carmen," he answered. He raised her hand to his lips and pressed a tender, lingering kiss to her wrist. "Neither did I."

Chapter Twelve

"'Endymion the shepherd . . . the moon Selene, saw him, loved him sought him . . . Kissed him, lay beside him.' Hmph.''

Carmen tossed aside the volume of Theocritus she was perusing over her morning chocolate. She slid down among the mound of pillows on her bed, and turned her face into the lavender-scented linen with a giggle.

Nothing, not even hiding her face, could erase the persistent vision of Peter clad in nothing but a brief, a *very* brief, chiton. And perhaps a pair of sandals.

She was beginning to suspect that Elizabeth, seemingly so very charming and sweet, was nothing but an imp.

Endymion and Selene, indeed! Carmen shuddered to think of what Elizabeth might conjure up next, in her misguided scheming.

"Carmen?" Elizabeth knocked softly at the door, seemingly conjured by Carmen's thoughts. "Are you awake?"

"No," Carmen called.

Elizabeth came inside anyway, already carefully coiffed and dressed in blue muslin and a lacy shawl. "I so need your assistance in organizing today's excursion!"

Carmen pulled the bedclothes down from over her

head, and peered at Elizabeth over the edge. "Not if it involves bloody tableaux."

"Tsk tsk. Wherever did you learn such language? And the tableaux are our grand finale for Sunday." She paused. "Though today would be an excellent opportunity for rehearsal. I was thinking of a small picnic at the tower we went to last night. The day looks to be a wonderful, sunny one, and you should see the tower in the light!"

"That does sound delightful," Carmen answered reluctantly.

"I knew you would think so! Now, I must tell the others, so that we may be off directly after breakfast." Elizabeth began to turn away, then paused, reaching into her pocket for a small bundle of letters. "I very nearly forgot! These came for you with the morning post."

Carmen took the letters from her, but waited until she was alone again to peruse them. One was from Esperanza, with a carefully penned postscript from Isabella, detailing all they had been doing in Carmen's absence (a pantomime at the Sadler's Wells Theater seemed foremost among them). There were also two missives from friends in Paris, full of lively and amusing gossip.

And the last—the last was written on cheap, smudged paper and sealed with black wax.

Carmen dropped the letter, one hand pressed to her mouth to stifle a cry. How could they have found her. How could they have known where she was?

They were everywhere now. She was safe nowhere.

"I believe I owe you an apology, Carmen."

Carmen, who had deliberately wandered from the others on their picnic excursion in order to be quiet and think, whirled around with a gasp at the unexpected sound of Peter's voice. She crumpled the letter in her hand, pressing it tightly against the folds of her skirt.

He stood at the edge of the small circle of trees Carmen had found beside the stream, poised hesitantly, as if unsure of his welcome and prepared to instantly depart.

He was so achingly handsome, with the sunlight falling across his windswept golden hair, gilding it like a Greek icon. Carmen could almost have wept at his loveliness.

"Another apology?" she said. "What have you done this time?"

"For Lizzie's—overly eager behavior. She has the artistic temperament, you know, and once she has a goal in mind she will not relinquish it." He paused, watching the stream just beyond her figure. "I had the impression that she made you uncomfortable with her silly tableaux, which she no doubt learned about in Italy, and I wanted to be certain you knew you were under no obligation to go along with her. I could speak with her."

"Oh, no," Carmen protested. "I would not like to ruin Lizzie's plans. Unless, that is, *you* do not wish to participate in the tableaux." She glanced at him to gauge his reaction, but his expression was only very polite.

Then he smiled, the odd, crooked half smile that always made her stomach leap into her throat with no warning at all. "And forfeit the sight of you in a chiton, Carmen? Certainly not."

"How very strange."

"Strange? That a man should want to see you in a chiton?"

Carmen laughed, her mood instantly lightened. "I should hope not! Only odd because I had thought exactly the same about you. But I added sandals to the ensemble."

Peter's eyes widened, and Carmen feared she had ventured too far into flirting. It was early days yet, after all. She turned away to look at the water. "Is it not lovely here? So very peaceful."

"Beautiful." Peter moved to stand behind her, his breath warm on her cheek. "I used to come here often."

"I thought that Elizabeth and Nicholas only recently purchased the property?"

"Oh, yes. But it is only a short ride from here to Clifton Manor. Old Lord Mountebank, the former owner, never cared if we ran wild here as children."

"Clifton Manor. Your home." Peter had spoken to her often of Clifton Manor while they were in Spain. He had told her of the house, of how it began life as a Tudor manor, the long-ago dowry of an Elizabethan bride to the second earl, and of how each earl had added to it until it was a sprawling amalgamation. He had told her of the hidey-holes he and Elizabeth had found as children, of the great gardens, and the lake with its Oriental summerhouse.

She had always felt as if she could see it, touch it, feel its spell woven of so many generations of love and laughter, reaching out to enfold her in its history.

Once, for a brief while, she had thought to be its mistress. To belong there, as Peter and Elizabeth did. To watch her children playing in the gardens.

Then she had known she would never live there.

"Yes," said Peter. "My home."

Carmen sat down on the grassy bank of the stream, tucking the thick green velvet of her habit beneath her against the damp. "Was it still all you had dreamed of when you returned there after Spain?"

He sat beside her, his long legs in their fashionable doeskin breeches stretched out before him. "Clifton had not changed at all. That is the beauty of it. It was still as green and peaceful as ever. It even smelled the same, of wax candles and beeswax polish. But I had changed. So much, too much. That I had not counted on. I had foolishly thought that when I came home I would be the same as before I left. I would forget the war and be at peace."

"Yes," said Carmen with a sigh. "I felt the very same, when I went home to my family's house in Seville. I thought I could rejoin society, be a devout Spanish lady again."

"When did you go back?"

"After I learned that you were dead. I was so exhausted, so ill. I only wanted to go home. Though my parents were long dead, I still thought of that house, so dark and quiet, as home. The places I had known as a child. I, too, thought I could forget and be at peace. So I went back, and I never spoke of what had happened, not to anyone." Her fingers closed tighter about the crumpled letter she still held in her hand. The edges of the paper cut into her palm. "I only discovered, as we all must, that peace is only to be found in my heart. And my peace had gone."

Peter leaned back on his elbows to look up at the sky above them, covered by the interlocking branches of the tress. The laughter of the group could be heard faintly as they climbed up inside the tower. The two of them seemed enclosed in a world of their own, though.

"Did Elizabeth tell you how I was ill when I returned home?" Peter said.

Carmen looked down at him, at his beautiful, still face. "Nicholas said that it was difficult for you. That you were not at all yourself. Did you have a fever from your wounds?"

"I was ill in my mind. I could not forget you, never leave what had happened between us behind me. It made me cruel, especially to my poor sister. All I could ever think about, ever see, was you."

"Yes," she whispered. "And I you."

He touched her then, his hand warm on her arm, burning through the heavy fabric of her sleeve. She leaned against him and closed her eyes, letting herself feel, just for the moment, a measure of the security she had longed for for so long.

"This place," Peter said. "Does it not remind you of another we have seen?"

She smiled without opening her eyes. "That river in Spain, near your camp. Where you asked me to dance . . ."

"And asked you to be my wife."

"And I said yes, yes, yes!"

"And where I kissed you . . ."

Carmen laughed. "I do believe we did much more than kiss!"

Peter laughed, too, a rich sound rusty from disuse. "Oh, yes! I also recall that."

Carmen opened her eyes and smiled at him. How could anyone call him the *Ice* Earl, she mused, when he was as golden and alive as the sun.

He gently reached up and touched her face, cradling her cheek in his palm as if it were the most precious, fragile crystal. "Carmen. Are you truly here with me, alive, or are you another dream?"

"I could ask the same of you," she murmured. "I dreamed of a moment like this one so often during these years. Am I awake? Is this real?"

"Does this feel real to you?" Peter sat up and touched his lips softly to hers.

It was so strange, so familiar, so thrilling. Carmen leaned closer into the kiss, opening her lips under his inquisitive pressure. Her fingers reached to touch the satin of his hair, to feel him against her . . .

"Lord Clifton? Are you here?"

"I say, Clifton? Are you hiding from us?"

Carmen gasped at the sound of voices—Lady Deidra and Viscount Huntington. She pulled her mouth from Peter's, drew out of his reaching arms to scramble to her feet. She brushed at her skirts, frantically trying to disentangle leaves and grass from the velvet.

It was a hopeless cause. She simply looked too much like a woman who had been rolling about on the ground, right to the guilty flush she was sure must be staining her cheeks.

"What was I thinking of?" she muttered. "Anyone could have seen us! What a scandal! What if . . ."

Peter also rose to his feet, somewhat stiffly, and attempted to come to her aid. "Carmen, I never . . ."

He held out his hand to her, but she did not see it, stumbling back out of the clearing.

"Oh, Peter!" she cried. "Do not say you are sorry again! I couldn't bear it."

"Then please, let me . . ."

She turned away from him and scooped up her hat and gloves from where they lay on the ground. "I must be alone right now, must—think. But we will speak later, Peter, I promise. It is only that—oh, it is *nothing*!"

Then she rushed away to where the others were gathered beside the tower, brushing past Huntington and Deidra with only a distracted nod.

She did not even notice the balled-up, smeared note that had fallen from her hand, only to be found by a very puzzled Peter.

His face darkened as he read it, a rushing fury thundering in his ears. "By damn," he whispered.

"Lord Clifton?" Deidra asked softly. "Is something amiss?"

He forced himself to look up at her serene face,

and smiled tightly. "Not at all. Lady Deidra. Not at all."

"I do not understand women in the least!"

Elizabeth looked up from the menus she was perusing to blink at her brother in surprise. He very seldom came into her personal rooms at all, let alone unannounced, to throw himself into a chair and make odd pronouncements.

"You, Peter? Not understand women?" she said with a snort. "I can scarce fathom that. They are always flocking about you so."

"That does not mean I understand them; quite the opposite. The more I meet, the less I understand. And why should women want to *flock* at all?" He leaned his head back against the satin cushions of the chair, and closed his eyes. Yet he could still see Carmen by the stream, her dark hair tousled, her lips red from his kiss. The image seemed emblazoned on his eyelids, there for all time. "And Carmen de Santiago is the worst of the lot."

"Ah, yes." Elizabeth nodded sagely. "I often said the very same when I first met Nick—men are unfathomable, and Nicholas Hollingsworth is the very worst. I still think that, on occasion. That is what love does to a person, I suppose."

"Love!"

"Yes. You love Carmen. There is no use in denying it."

Peter could feel a blinding headache coming upon him, born of having to deal with *females*, whether they were mercurial wives-who-weren't-wives, or too wise sisters. He shook his head slowly. "I was not going to deny it. I do love her. I have since I first saw her, and I suppose I never truly stopped. Even when she was dead."

"Then, what is wrong?"

"I do not know!" Peter slapped his open palm against the arm of the chair. "It is Carmen. Every time it seems we may become close again, every time I try to understand her, she shies away like a skittish colt. She runs from me." He remembered Carmen in Spain, on that afternoon by the river. How she would spin away from his arms, laughing, beckoning, her long curtain of hair spilling about her. It seemed she was still doing that. "She was always elusive as water, so intent on her independence. She always said she would never be as helpless as she was with her dreadful first husband again. Perhaps it is only the same thing now."

"Hm. Perhaps."

"But she knows I am not him! And somehow it seems—different now. She seems rather desperate, in some way."

"Well, she *is* Spanish. You can hardly expect her to be a predictable little English rose, like Lady Deidra. She has had a very difficult time these last years, just as you have. She is not one to trust easily, especially in the appearance of happy times at last. You know what that is like, brother, because you are just the same." Elizabeth tapped her fingertips thoughtfully against her desk. "Perhaps your only real difficulty lies in a lack of communication. Perhaps Carmen thinks that you still mean to marry Lady Deidra, and that you are just trifling with her emotions."

Peter snorted. "How absurd! How can I possibly marry someone like Lady Deidra when Carmen is alive? There is no other woman for me in the world but her."

"Yes, but does Carmen know that? You were not very kind to her when she first appeared in London. You made it obvious that you had made a new life without her, that you had nothing but contempt for her."

"I never felt contempt," Peter protested. "I was only—confused. But that is all changed now! *Everything* has changed since she came back into my life. I felt frozen before, but now . . ." His voice fell away, unable to give words to his tumult of emotions. He held out his hands helplessly. "It has all changed because of her."

"I know that, Peter," said Elizabeth. "Does Carmen, though? She is as lost and confused as you are."

"Then, what can I do?"

"Talk to her, of course, you nodcock! Go to her, and tell her everything you have just told me. Hold nothing back. And, in exchange, you may hear some pleasant surprises of your own."

She held out her hand to him, and he clasped it tightly.

"Can I do that?" he murmured half to himself.

"You *must*. My brother, I know how you love to keep your own counsel, hide your emotions, but you must not do that now. Not if you want your wife, value your family. Do not be foolish, as I so very nearly was with my Nicholas."

"Of course you are right, as always." Peter stood and kissed his sister's cheek. "How did you ever become so wise, little Lizzie?"

"Oh, I have learned a great deal from the travails of marriage! As, I hope, have you."

"Marriage is indeed a travail. But I will do as you say, and go speak with Carmen now. We have a great deal to discuss." He reached into his coat pocket and touched the crumpled letter Carmen had lost. "A very great deal."

Elizabeth gave a small laugh. "Oh, Peter. If only you knew." She looked back to her menus, but then called after him. "If you need an excuse to go to her chamber, just say I sent you to rehearse for the tableaux!"

Chapter Thirteen

Carmen stared down into her trunk, at the jumble of gowns and underpinnings she had just tossed in. She hardly knew what she was doing, or why; she only had a desperate need to leave, to go to her daughter and hold her in her arms again, and know that she was safe.

Carmen leaned her forehead against the edge of the trunk lid, suddenly dizzy. What was *wrong* with her? Why was she suddenly dashing about like an escapee from Bedlam? Because Peter had kissed her?

It was not as if he had not done a great deal more than *kiss* her in the past!

But such had always been the way when she was with him. She had always considered herself rather levelheaded, yet when she saw him she was not herself, not the cool, sophisticated condesa. She became giddy, giggly, uncertain, wildly ecstatic.

She loved him, that was obvious. That had not, would never, change.

She also loved her daughter and feared more than anything to lose her. It was not at all a rational fear—the chances of Peter snatching her away were slim indeed. But there it was. Isabella had been an enormous, unasked for gift at a time in Carmen's life when she had seen nothing but fear and grief. Isabella had been her joy and her light for six years, and something in the back of Carmen's heart feared that light could be snatched away as suddenly as it had been bestowed.

She knew, of course, that Peter would have to be told of his child. She just did not know how.

A knock sounded at the door. Carmen, thinking it must be Elizabeth come to see how she was after her swift departure from their picnic, straightened and wiped at her damp cheeks. "Come in!"

It was not Elizabeth. It was Peter, utterly composed, unearthly handsome. Almost as if the untidy scene beside the stream had never occurred.

Then she looked into his eyes and saw that they were no longer ice blue, but a stormy gray.

As she just stared at him, unable to make her throat work to say a word, he stepped into the room and closed the door behind him.

"I . . ." he began, then stopped. His gaze dropped from hers, moved around the room restlessly.

The Ice Earl at a loss for words? Impossible! Carmen closed the lid of the trunk and sat down upon it, to await what he had come to say.

"Lizzy told me to say I have come to rehearse for the tableaux," he said at last.

Carmen laughed, all her fright and tension melting away at his absurdity. "Oh, Peter! Then, where is your tunic? No, you cannot fool me."

"No. Of course I did not come to discuss my sister's silly party games." He leaned back against the door, his eyes still wary as he watched her. "I wanted to say that if I did or said anything to offend you, then I am deeply sorry."

"We are a strange pair, Peter," she sighed. "After all we have been to each other, we should be beyond so very many apologies."

"So we should. But things are rather—complicated between us. I should not have rushed at you in that manner." He grinned at her halfheartedly. "You were always as changeable as the wind."

She smiled in return. "As were you. My unpredictable, dashing English major. It was why I married you."

"My unpredictability? And here I thought it was for my dashing regimentals."

"Because you understood me, as no one else, not even my parents, ever could! You never attempted to change me, to make me more ladylike or something." Carmen pleated the fabric of her skirt restlessly between her fingers, lost for a moment in memories of those heady days of first love. She looked up suddenly and saw from the rare softness on Peter's face that he, too, was thinking of the same things.

"I am sorry," she said, "that I dashed away from you this morning. I am tired, I suppose. I have been a bit, well, unsteady of late."

"I think I know why that may be, Carmen."

"Do you, indeed? As I said, you always were able to know me better than anyone else, but . . ."

He silently held out the letter she had lost beside the stream, now hopelessly crumpled and soiled.

Carmen bit her lip. Peter was the very last person she would want to know of her troubles! He knew all about that time in her life; he carried the darkness of the same time in his own heart. He had even suspected her of the same things the letter writer spoke of.

Could still suspect her, perhaps?

In the midst of her dismay, the thought flitted through her mind that perhaps *Peter* had written the letters. She dismissed that thought immediately. Not only had his shock on the night of the Dacey ball been very real, but she knew Peter as well as he knew her. If he believed that she had done those things, he would not have written foul, anonymous letters.

He would have faced her directly and shot her in the heart.

Carmen forced back the insistent urge to flee, and forced herself to remain where she was, seated on the closed trunk. She folded her hands carefully in her lap.

"Now you know why I came to England," she said softly.

"Do you mean to say that you were receiving these—these *things* even abroad?"

"Of course. Four of them in Paris, two here. I traced the ones I received in France to England, and I knew that I would have to come here if I was to find the culprit. I meant to track down every person I had met during the war, and hound them until I found the right one." Her gaze fell to her clasped hands, to the emerald that glowed on her finger. "Otherwise I would never have come to England."

"Why? Do you hate it here so very much?"

Carmen laughed, more a small hiccup than a true laugh. "Peter, what a true Englishman you are! I do not hate England. It is all these English voices. It was hard enough to hear them in France or Italy. I would hear an Englishman speaking behind me on the street sometimes, and I would turn, so full of hope, thinking it would be you." She pressed the back of her hand against her eyes, unwilling to look at him as she poured out these embarrassing confessions. "I knew it would be so much worse here, where I would see things and places you had told me about. That we had planned to see together. It would have been—awful."

She heard him move then, the soft rustle of his superfine coat as he came across the room to kneel beside her. His hand was cool as he laid it softly on hers, and she peeked up at him cautiously.

"When I came back from Spain," he said, "I saw you in every black-haired woman, every red flower, like the ones you carried at our wedding. Every emerald. I felt like my soul had been torn to shreds from losing you, and in such a terrible way. I could never have gone back to Spain."

Carmen had never so longed to weep in all her life. "Peter, *querido*," she said. Then she could say no more. She simply placed her other hand atop his, and they sat there in silence for several long, sweet moments.

Then Peter shook his head fiercely, as if clearing it of a dream, and gently drew away from her. He pulled a chair near to her trunk and sat down.

His eyes, so gray with roiling emotions only a moment before, were now ice blue with resolve. Carmen remembered just such a determined look on his face from military meetings during the war.

"You say you received four of these letters in Paris," he said.

Carmen drew in a deep breath. She had to focus on the business at hand now, not the bittersweet might-have-beens of her marriage. "Yes. And two since I came to England. One at my house in Town . . ."

"And one under my sister's very roof," Peter finished, steel in his voice.

"I knew that I would have to find whoever is doing this, and put a final stop to it. Or I will never be left in peace. I have not paid anything."

"Quite right. Do you have any idea at all of the villain's identity? Could it possibly be our friend Robert Means?"

"I had thought of Robert, of course. Especially after you told me of his perfidy. But, despite what he did,

I believe he truly thought me dead. And, if he truly was in Cornwall all this time, it would have taken much longer for me to receive the London letter." She shook her head. "So no, I do not think it is him. But I don't know who else it could be." Then she smiled teasingly. "It is only too bad it was *not* Robert. I could have ferreted him out so very easily, you know. I would simply have worn my most dashing gowns, laughed at all his witticisms, leaned subtly against his arm at supper, pressing my bosom . . ."

Peter seized her around the waist then and pulled her onto his lap, both of them laughing helplessly until tears ran down their faces. "I am glad, then, it was *not* Robert," he gasped, his breath soft on her hair. "If that is what you were planning, madam!"

Carmen leaned her forehead against his chest, still giggling. He smelled wonderful, of soap and clean starch and sunlight. She closed her eyes and tried to inhale him inside of her.

He pulled her even closer to him and pressed his lips against her temple. "We *will* find whoever is doing this, Carmen, and he will pay. I promise you are quite safe now."

"Yes," she murmured. "I cannot say how very many times I have longed to be a *we* again, not fighting the demons all alone."

"You are not alone."

"No." Carmen rested her head on his shoulder and smiled against the fine cloth of his coat. "Not anymore. And neither are you."

There was a rustle in the corridor, a hum of voices and laughter as a group passed her door and went down the staircase. Carmen looked at the window and saw to her surprise that it was full dark out. They would be expected at supper very soon.

She drew away from the warm shelter of Peter's arms and stood up. "We should be dressing for supper," she said. "Elizabeth will wonder what has become of us."

Peter also rose. "Not my sister! She will assume we are dutifully rehearsing for her dreaded tableaux and all her matchmaking efforts have been successful. But, yes, I should be going. We must put our plan of action in motion this evening, and find out the villain. Perhaps we could speak some more with Lord Crane. I understand that, despite his peacock ways, he was in Spain."

Carmen waved her hand airily. "Oh, yes! The plan of action. Low-cut gowns and bosoms. Do you think they would have an effect on Lord Crane?"

"Not *that* plan!" Peter took up her hand and pressed a lingering kiss on her palm. "I am very glad that you have confided in me, Carmen. Now there are no more secrets between us. We may begin afresh."

"Yes," she murmured as she watched him walk out the door. "No more secrets."

Only the greatest secret of all. His child.

Chapter Fourteen

Carmen sat on Nicholas's left at supper, half listening to him as he spoke of a planned balloon ascension from Hyde Park that he wanted to escort her and Elizabeth to when they returned to Town. She smiled and murmured at all the appropriate pauses, and even managed to ask pertinent questions every so often. She partook of the excellent dishes Elizabeth's new French chef had prepared, and tried not to partake too freely of the excellent French wines. Yet even the lobster patties may just as well have been sawdust.

Too many thoughts swirled in her mind for her to completely throw herself into the merry party the Hollingsworths had worked so hard to create. She was thinking of the cruel blackmailer, that could possibly hide behind a laughing and friendly facade just like the ones about her. She thought of Peter, and the tender scene they had shared. She thought of Elizabeth's announcement that Lady Deidra and her mother had been called home suddenly, and had left Evanstone Park. She wondered if that meant a final severing of Peter's old intentions toward Deidra and a new commitment toward herself.

She thought of her precious daughter, the daughter she had to tell Peter about very soon, and if she dared to hope such a thing.

Surely the man who had held her in his arms and

promised her she was no longer alone was someone she could trust Isabella with? Or was she being too hasty, too hopeful?

". . . don't you agree, Condesa?"

Carmen shook off her daze to smile at the woman seated across from her, who had apparently been speaking to her. A Mrs. King, if she was not mistaken, a lady who always seemed to favor grandiose headdresses of fruits and flowers.

"I do beg your pardon," Carmen said. "I fear I could not hear your question, Mrs. King."

"Oh, yes!" Mrs. King answered gaily. "Lady Elizabeth's parties are always so *loudly* delightful! I was only speaking of the tableaux planned for Sunday evening. Such a quiz! Do you not agree?"

"Oh, yes. Indeed. A quiz."

"Nicholas is in my little group." Mrs. King waggled flirtatious fingers at Nicholas. "As are the Richardsons. We are to enact Hermes and Athena coming to the aid of Perseus and Andromeda." She giggled. "I am to be Athena! I have found the most delightful armored breastplate in the attic."

"Ah," Carmen said, not entirely attending. "But your eyes are brown, Mrs. King."

Mrs. King blinked her brown eyes. "My eyes, Condesa?"

"Yes. They are not gray." When Mrs. King continued to look blank, she continued. " 'And gray-eyed Athena cried, Give the Greeks a bitter homecoming. Stir up your waters with wild whirlwinds—let dead men choke the bays and line the shores and reefs.' " So Theocritus had proved useful after all.

Mrs. King went a trifle pale at the mention of dead bodies, that could possibly clutter up her tableau. "Well. Yes, Condesa. But these are *silent* tableaux, you know. I needn't learn any lines. Need I?"

Carmen took a sip of her wine and smiled reassuringly. "I shouldn't think so. All you need do is look martial in your breastplate."

"Oh, good!" Mrs. King cried in relief. "You are to enact a tableau with Lord Clifton, are you not, Condesa?"

Carmen nodded. "Endymion and Selene."

"Yes. I did hear that that is the true reason Lady Deidra Clearbridge and her mother left." Mrs. King looked down the table at Peter, who was talking with his sister. "He is so very handsome. You are so *fortunate*. How I wish I could have been chosen for his team! If I did not have my dear Mr. King to think of . . ." She giggled.

Carmen was saved from replying by the arrival of dessert. She took a very large spoonful of the lemon trifle.

Ah, yes. Very fortunate indeed.

"We must have dancing!" Elizabeth announced. After supper, when the gentlemen had rejoined the ladies in the drawing room, small groups had begun to break off and drift away to various corners, but her words brought them back.

"Dancing?"

"What fun!"

"Yes," said Elizabeth. "The gentlemen will push back the furniture, so we needn't waste time by having the ballroom opened. Miss Dixon, if you could oblige us with your delightful playing? A country-dance, I think, since we *are* in the country."

As Miss Dixon struck up a lively tune at the pianoforte, Elizabeth took her brother's arm and drew him onto the cleared floor.

Georgina Beaumont and Lord Richardson followed, and soon ten couples had taken their places in the set. The drawing room was a blur of jewel-bright gowns, music, and laughter.

Carmen watched it all from her perch on a settee, laughing as Peter swung Elizabeth about so energetically in the turns that her small feet left the floor and her skirts flew out in a shining sea-green silk arc.

She thought, as she watched all the merriment and calling out that went on, how very much more comfortable a country party was than a London party. It was all good fun among friends. Perhaps, she reflected, a country life with a husband and children would not be such a terrible thing. Especially after the tumult of her travels.

As the country-dance wound to its rowdy finish, Georgina Beaumont clapped her hands and called, "We must now have a waltz!" The dramatic redhead lifted the hem of her purple satin gown and twirled about her partner, to the applause of the others.

Miss Dixon said, "But I have not permission to waltz, Mrs. Beaumont!"

"Pooh!" said Georgina with a laugh. "This is not Almack's, Miss Dixon dear. Lady Jersey will not catch you here. Will she, Lizzie? You do not have any patronesses lurking behind your curtains?"

"No, indeed!" Elizabeth answered. "Everyone is quite safe here. But perhaps you would prefer to continue playing to dancing, Miss Dixon? You played that last dance so beautifully."

With that, she took her husband's arm in one hand and Peter's in the other, and marched them over to Carmen's settee. "Here now, Carmen! Why are you sitting here all alone like such a matron? No one is allowed to be so serious and solitary at my party!"

"I do apologize, Lizzie," Carmen answered with a laugh. "I vow to be nothing but merry and gay for the rest of your weekend."

"That is more the thing," Elizabeth said. "Nick has promised to dance with me, so unfashionable to dance with one's wife, though I suppose we are allowed in our own home! So, Carmen dear, you must dance with Peter. We must not let him feel neglected, must we?"

Then, not giving her a chance to reply, she tugged on her husband's arm and led him onto the floor.

Nicholas grinned at them over his shoulder and shrugged.

Carmen started to plead exhaustion, but then she looked up at Peter's face. He looked positively— could it be *eager*? He was even smiling, without a hint of mockery.

That smile faded a bit as Carmen frowned in puzzlement. "We do not have to dance, you know," he said. "If you are too fatigued."

"Oh, I think we *must* dance, or Lizzie will surely have a fit and come *make* us dance!" She rose to her feet and laid her hand softly on his sleeve. "And I do so love a waltz. Remember?"

His smile returned. "Then, by all means . . ."

He led her onto the floor, just as Miss Dixon struck the opening chords of a Viennese waltz. His shoulder was warm and strong, the muscles tensed beneath the velvet of his coat as she touched him. His hand clasped hers firmly, and they swung into the dance, far closer than propriety allowed.

It was not a sunlit Spanish riverbank this time; Carmen's trousers and boots were now an elegant blue velvet gown, and Peter's regimentals were long gone. Years of pain and experience lay between the people they had been on that day, and the people that they were now.

But somehow that made this moment, this dance, all the more sweet. They had struggled long and hard to reach it, this instant of swaying together in a ballroom, her skirts wrapping about his legs as he twirled her around and around.

As Carmen looked up at Peter, into his sky-blue

eyes, she knew that he felt the same. She knew, without a doubt, that it would be safe to trust him with her most precious possessions, her daughter and her heart. For now, and for all the future to come.

As the music ended, she leaned forward to whisper in his ear.

"I must speak with you, Peter. There are things—many things I must tell you. Will you come to me tonight?"

His warm breath stirred the curls at her temple as he whispered back, "As you wish, Condesa."

Chapter Fifteen

Peter sat alone in his room for a long time after the rest of the household had retired, not lighting candles, just sitting beside the small, flickering fire. He sipped slowly on a snifter of brandy, and listened as a small group of late-goers talked and laughed in the corridor.

At last, in the very darkest part of the night, all was silent. Except for the soft, creeping sounds of people slipping illicitly toward bedrooms not their own.

As he should be doing, though it seemed a bit foolish to be sneaking into his own wife's room. He knew she was waiting for him, waiting to impart whatever dire secrets she was holding. And he fairly ached to go to her, to see her again, even if he had only been parted from her hours ago. He felt like some overeager schoolboy, hungry to hold her in his arms, to smell her perfume.

But he hesitated.

He poured himself another measure of brandy. So many things had changed since he had lost her, his beautiful Carmen, his dashing Spanish bride. He had never in his life before her thought he could love someone so intensely, find the presence of another person in the world to be so vital to his own existence. When he had lost her so horribly, it had been as if all light and beauty had left him forever, and he had known that he could never feel so strongly about a woman again.

So he had thought to contract a loveless, convenient union. Then Carmen had flown back into his life like a sparkling star, and he had seen how impossible such a bloodless life would be. He had known a great love; no convenience could ever compare.

The knowledge of her innocence, of Robert's lies, had freed him of the dreadful weight he had carried for so long, had made him finally cease to look back, to move forward into life.

Forward with her.

When they had danced that night, he had truly laughed, had felt free and light with her in his arms. He had felt truly alive, perhaps for the first time since their wedding night. He loved her; he wanted the life they had dreamed of together, at long last.

All of which made him reluctant to go to her. He took another sip of brandy.

He was not a man who easily trusted deep emotions, unlike his sister, who rushed into them headlong. They so often seemed the herald of disaster. And Carmen's eyes had been so dark and serious when she whispered that there was something she must tell him. Something that could not be kept from him for another night.

Peter was sick to death of secrets. He wanted nothing more than to move into the future fresh and free, and he knew that to do that Carmen must unburden herself of her last secret, whatever it was. And he would have to hear it—even if it was something dreadful, like she was in love with another man.

Carmen waited for Peter.

She waited while she listened to other guests slip from room to room, swift bars of light seen beneath her door then passing on, none of them stopping, no soft knock at her own door. Her own candles were growing shorter, and she had changed from her gown into a sensible nightrail and velvet wrapper.

She took Isabella's pearl-framed miniature from her jewel case, and laid it out carefully beside two glasses of wine.

Finally, as the small ormolu clock on the mantel chimed three, she knew that if she did not go to Peter herself and tell him the truth, she would lose all her courage. So she drank both glasses of wine herself, tucked the miniature into the pocket of her wrapper, and went to seek him out. She only prayed she would not have an awkward encounter with another guest seeking a rendezvous in the corridor!

At his door, she knocked softly, the light cast by her candle wavering as her hand trembled. "Peter?" she whispered. "It is Carmen. Are you asleep?"

There was a long silence on the other side of the door. She almost began to think he *had* fallen asleep. Then a low voice called, "The door is not locked."

She slid quickly inside the room, shutting the door carefully behind her. There were no candles lit, and the room was deep in shadows. So deep that at first her eyes could not make out anything; then she saw him, seated beside the dying fire. He was still dressed, having only removed his coat and loosened his cravat. A half-empty bottle of brandy was on the small table beside him.

Good, thought Carmen. Perhaps if they were both mildly foxed it would be easier to say what she must.

"I was just getting ready to come to you," he said. "I wanted to wait until the house settled."

"Yes. It would never do for the Earl of Clifton to cause a great scandal by slipping into his wife's room! Not the done thing at all!" said Carmen, making a weak attempt at humor. "Well, I could not wait. I had to come."

He leaned back in his chair and brought his steepled fingers to his chin. He regarded her steadily over their tips. "So, Carmen. Tell me your dreaded secrets."

She sighed. "You are not making this at all easy."

"I do apologize. Would you care for some brandy? It is excellent, some of the finest from Nick's cellar."

"Yes, please." She seated herself in the chair across from his and accepted the brandy, welcoming its calming warmth. She was suddenly very grateful for its smooth flow, for the darkness and intimacy of the room; it did seem to make painful confidences a modicum easier.

Peter leaned toward her, laid his hands lightly on her velvet covered knees. "You can tell me anything, Carmen. Surely I have proven that to you by now."

"Yes, you have."

"Then, if you are in love with someone else, if you wish to end our marriage . . ."

Carmen choked on her brandy. "In love with someone else!"

"Is that not what you wish to tell me?"

"Certainly not!" She reached into her pocket, quickly, before she could lose her courage, and drew out the miniature. She turned one of his hands over and pressed the ivory oval into his palm.

He turned it to the light of the fire, studying the painted image with a thoughtful frown. She hoped that the golden curls of the girl, the straight, small nose and stubborn chin, would tell him all he needed to know and her words could be kept to a minimum. She twisted her hands against the arms of her chair as the silence grew longer.

Then he looked up at her again, his face smooth and unreadable as marble. "What is this?"

She took a deep breath. "This is Isabella. My

daughter." He said nothing, only watched her. "She is six years old."

Peter looked back down at the painting. "She is—very lovely."

"Yes, she is."

"And what you are saying, I assume, is that she is mine."

Carmen bit her lip. "Yes. She is yours."

He closed his fingers tightly over his daughter's image. "Oh, Carmen."

Not certain what that could mean, she plunged on, telling him all she had longed to say for so long. "I think it happened on the night that we—we gave in to our feelings, after that kiss on the riverbank. Or perhaps on our wedding night. I did not realize until, well, until everything had happened and I was on my way back to Seville. I thought at first that I was ill from grief. Isabella was very tenacious to survive so much before she was even born! She stayed with me when I ran about the countryside, wounded and ill, hiding with friendly families and in gypsy camps." She paused, uncertain now what to say, what to tell next.

Without looking at her, Peter whispered, "Tell me more."

"She was born a bit early," Carmen continued, lost in her own bittersweet memories. "She was so very small. Esperanza, my old duenna, thought she would not live. She sent for the priest. But I knew, when I held her in my arms, that my girl would live and be strong. She *was* very small, but she was fierce, a true warrior; she would wave her little fists in the air both night and day, never silent. It was as if she knew what she faced, and she was fighting to live. I knew then that she was like you, with a will of iron, and that she would be fine."

A small smile touched Peter's lips. "A true Everdean."

"Oh, yes! She is very much your daughter, so stubborn, so certain of her own mind. But she is so very sweet and loving, so full of laughter. We have a grand time together." She paused. "When I thought you were dead, I wanted nothing more than to die myself. I thought I could never enjoy my life again. Isabella changed all that. She was a part of you, a gift from you, and that gave me the will to live on. Eventually I did come to enjoy my life, to appreciate a fine day, a ride on a good horse, a dance. That is entirely thanks to Isabella."

Suddenly exhausted, Carmen fell back onto her chair, trembling with emotion at all she had poured forth. Despite any lingering apprehension, she felt a very deep sense of relief. Peter knew everything, at last. Now, whatever was meant to happen could happen.

"For God's sake, Carmen!" Peter suddenly snapped. "I have a *daughter*. Why did you not tell me this sooner? Why did you not tell me the very instant we met again?"

Carmen laughed bitterly. "At the Dacey ball, you mean? And when should I have announced that we have a child together? When you were shaking me? Or when I slapped your face?"

Peter grimaced. "*Touché*, my dear. Yes, I was quite overcome with shock and anger when I first saw you again. But after we had come to an understanding, you could have told me at any time. This is so very enormous—why did you wait until now? You could have told me that day in my library."

"Elizabeth and Nicholas interrupted us, and . . ." Carmen broke off, shaking her head. "No, that is a mere excuse. I should have said something earlier, I know. I was frightened."

"Frightened? Of me?"

"You needn't look so incredulous, *querido*. You can be very intimidating, you know!"

He laughed reluctantly. "I suppose I deserve that."

"Indeed you do! And even though things appeared to be mended between us—well, disaster has come upon us unexpectedly before. Isabella was too important to risk." She reached for the bottle and poured herself another measure of brandy, taking a comforting amber swallow before she continued. "I swore to her on the day that she was born that I would always protect her, that she would never face the things I had seen. I was not certain of what you might do when you learned of her existence. You could have married Lady Deidra, and taken Isabella away to be raised by her, and I could have done little about it. Children, after all, legally belong to their fathers only. I could not risk that."

"Ah. What a sad pair we are, Carmen. I doubt even lovers in romantic novels could have been as wrapped up in half-truths and self-deceits as we have been." He held out his hand to her, and she slowly slid hers into its warmth. His fingers closed over hers. "Do you not know by now, my darling, that I could never, from the day I found you again, have wed Lady Deidra? Or indeed anyone else?"

"If it is because of our wedding, I am sure an annulment would be easy to obtain for a Catholic ceremony . . ."

His other hand came up, one finger pressed to her lips to stop the flow of words. "It is because I love you. There has never been another woman like you in the history of the world, I am sure, and no other could ever tolerate me." He grinned at her crookedly.

Carmen very much feared she would soon start crying again, and she had no handkerchief at hand.

he reached up and moved his finger from her lips.
Do you truly mean that? Do you still love me?"

"I do."

Carmen kissed his hand gently and disentangled
erself from his grasp. She rose and went to the win-
ow, leaning her cheek against the cool glass. Below
er, the garden slept all silvery beneath the moon,
n ocean of peace.

And, at last, her own heart knew just such a per-
ct tranquility.

"I love you, too," she answered. "I always have."

He came up behind her. "Then, you will marry me
gain? At Clifton Manor, in front of all our friends
nd our daughter?"

Carmen closed her eyes and thought. She loved
ie Peter she had married six years ago, and she
new that now she loved the man he had become.
s complicated and maddening as he could be! She
anted to quarrel with him and misunderstand him
nd kiss him until they were ninety and surrounded
y grandchildren.

She turned to face him. "Yes. I will marry you
gain."

"Carmen!" In one step he had her in his arms,
eld against him so tightly that her feet left the carpet
ntirely. She buried her face in the silk of his golden
air and laughed aloud.

"We *will* be happy now," he said fiercely. "As we
iould have been all these years."

"So you are *willing* happiness on us now?"

"I am. I believe we are richly deserving of it."

"I believe you are right! But I have dreamed of
iis moment so many times, only to have it vanish
the daylight. What if this is a dream?"

He lowered her slowly to her feet. His hands came
p to gently cradle the back of her head, his fingers
the soft curls. "My darling. Does this feel like a

dream?'' And he kissed her, his lips warm and so╱
on hers, as gentle as a spring day.

Carmen sighed and smiled as he lifted his head t╱
look down at her. "It feels like heaven."

"I want to meet Isabella. Soon."

"Of course. I will write to Esperanza tomorro╲
and ask her to bring her here. Isabella will be ecstat╱
to come and see Elizabeth, and she will *adore* you, ╱
am sure."

"And I will surely adore her." He laid his chee╱
against her hair and hugged her close. "Ah, Carmen╱
I can scarce fathom it! I am a father; I have a chil╱
a daughter."

"One who is the very image of you—tall, golder╱
and stubborn as a bull! I cannot wait for you t╱
meet." Carmen rested her head on Peter's shoulde╱
listening to the soft, ocean-wave sound of his breath╱
ing through the thin linen of his shirt.

She was sure she could feel the stirrings of som╲
long-buried emotion—joy.

Chapter Sixteen

"Carmen! Is it really true?" The door to the library flew open, and Elizabeth rushed in, the fringed ends of her shawl swinging.

Carmen looked up from the letter she was writing, and smiled a radiant welcome. All the world seemed gloriously sunlit to her that morning, despite the fact that it was raining outside. "Is what true?"

"Come now, do not tease me! I was just talking with my brother. Are you going to be my 'official' sister?"

Carmen giggled like a schoolgirl. "It is true—sister."

"Oh!" Elizabeth threw her arms about her 'sister.' "I simply knew how it would be! I knew it would all work out beautifully, and so it has. Nick told me not to fly into the boughs, that the two of you had been apart so long that perhaps you no longer wished to be married. I said that was fustian, that of course you wanted to be married! And you do!"

"Yes," Carmen interrupted happily. "We talked all last night, and everything is settled between us."

"I am glad. I would so much rather have *you* for a sister than that Lady Deidra Clearbridge! I never had a happier hour than when she went back to London. But only think what a dash you and I will cut together in Society! And now you *must* let me paint your portrait."

Carmen laughed. Surely life would never be dull

with such a sister and brother-in-law as Elizabeth
and Nicholas! "Indeed I shall! But not yet. We have
a wedding to plan. And you are not to say a word
to anyone yet. Peter wishes to wait to make an announcement until after he has met Isabella."

"I will be silent as tombs. Except to Nick." Elizabeth's expression turned suddenly serious. "Peter
does know about Isabella, then? That she is his
child?"

"Oh, yes. I told him last night."

"And was there a row?"

"Not at all. It was all much—simpler than I had
supposed. He was a bit angry at first, to be sure. But
I think that the happiness of the news quite overcame
his anger. He is most eager to meet his new
daughter."

"Well," Elizabeth breathed. "No tantrum. My
brother must be maturing."

"I believe so!"

"When is he to meet Isabella?"

"That is what I wished to speak with you about."
Carmen held up the letter she was writing. "I am
writing to Esperanza, asking her to bring Isabella
here for a few days. I thought perhaps it would be
easier for her and for Peter to meet here in the country, where it is quiet and they can talk, rather than
in Town."

"Yes, quite right."

"Of course, that means we must impose on your
hospitality for a few days longer. Esperanza could
not possibly arrive here before the end of your party.
I know you have your work to return to . . ."

Elizabeth waved away her apologies. "Not at all.
Nick and I were planning to stay here until next
month. I am sure he will be delighted to have you
and Peter and Isabella with us. And, of course, you
must visit Clifton when you are so near."

"That is so kind of you, Lizzie."

"Nonsense! It will be great fun. A family holiday." Elizabeth gathered up her shawl and prepared to depart. "This afternoon Georgina and I are going up to the attics to look for costumes. The former owners left simply piles of trunks and boxes! You must join us."

"That sounds delightful! I will see you later, Lizzie." Carmen waved to Elizabeth as she left the room, then turned back to seal and address her letter to Esperanza.

As she did so, she thought of the blackmailing letters she had tucked away in the bottom of her trunk, the ones sealed in black wax. She still had not found their writer, and that fact cast the one dark pall over her new happiness. She was always waiting for another missive to be delivered, for the sword of Damocles to drop on her head and all to be revealed to the scandal-loving *ton*.

A scandal, always to be avoided, was unthinkable now that she was soon to be presented as the Countess of Clifton, with her daughter the child of an English earl. Carmen could never bear to bring disgrace on Peter's head, of harming his promising political career and the name of his family.

She had, in her mind, ruled out Robert Means as the culprit. But if not him, then who?

The attics of Evanstone Park were not as Carmen remembered the attics at her home in Seville—dark, dusty, musty. They were wide and clean, with the smell of new wood and polish, lined with trunks left by the former owners, as well as a few that had belonged to Elizabeth's mother and grandmother.

Carmen, Elizabeth, and Georgina dug through this bounty, spreading silks, satins, and velvets across the floor in search of suitable costumes for the tableaux.

Georgina held up an elaborate gown of bright blue taffeta, its silk flower-trimmed skirts spreading wide in the style of the last century. "What do you think, ladies? Would this be quite suitable for Hera, descending from the heavens like a great bluebell?"

Elizabeth laughed and swirled a velvet cloak over her shoulders. "I like this one! I shall sweep onstage, covered from head to toe. Then I shall drop the cloak and reveal, hmm . . ." She pulled out a transparent chemise. "This! *Et voila!*"

"*Quel scandale!*" Georgina cried. She fanned herself with a large painted silk fan. "I declare I shall swoon from the shock. No vouchers for you!"

Elizabeth pushed her playfully. "You were never shocked in all your life, Georgie Beaumont! Remember that costume ball in Venice, where you wore a lady pirate gown with a skirt that ended quite at your knees?"

"I never!" Georgina gasped.

Carmen laughed at their antics, then turned back to the trunk she was excavating. It must have belonged to Elizabeth's mother rather than her grandmother, for it contained clothes of a slightly more recent vintage. And it seemed that Elizabeth's mother had been dashing indeed.

She took out a long, shimmering, one-shouldered column of silver tissue. It was almost of the right length on Carmen, and quite appropriately classical in appearance.

She held it up to her and examined the effect in the tall mirror set up in the corner.

It was beautiful, almost like a fall of liquid silver, flowing and sparkling.

She wondered what Peter would think, if he saw her in it.

She smiled softly.

Elizabeth came up beside her, to touch the magical

abric gently with her small hand. "My mother wore his to a masquerade ball when I was a small child," she said. "It was even before she married Peter's father. I remember watching her dress for the ball. She wore a mask of white feathers and long diamond earrings. I thought her such a magical creature in it, all gold and silver. Almost like a swan!"

"Oh." Carmen held the gown away from her. "Then, I must not wear it, not if it was a very special gown of your mother's."

"No, you *must* wear it, for that very reason. It should not be hidden away in a trunk forever." She smiled mischievously. "And just imagine the look on my brother's face when he sees you in it!"

Carmen laughed. "I was thinking that very thing!"

"Then, you will wear it?"

"Yes, of course."

"Excellent! Now, I am very thirsty. Digging about in dusty old trunks is tiring work."

Carmen carefully folded the gown and laid it aside. "I will go downstairs, then, and see about some tea and cakes."

As she went down the stairs, brushing dust from her hair, she caught a glimpse of Peter as he went into the conservatory. Tucked beneath his arm was a large, colorful book of children's fairy tales.

By noon, the morning's rain had paused, bringing out azure skies and glorious sunshine. So Elizabeth's luncheon moved out to tables set up on the terrace, where guests could look at the dew-damp gardens and chatter freely about their tableaux and the cards planned for that evening.

Carmen had only just finished the dessert, when a footman came to her and spoke quietly in her ear.

"I beg your pardon, my lady," he said. "A lady has arrived who is asking for you."

Carmen looked up at him, startled. A guest, for her? "Are you certain she is not looking for Lady Elizabeth?"

"Oh, no. She said most specifically the Condesa de Santiago. I have placed them in the library."

"Them?"

"Yes, my lady. She has a child with her."

Isabella. It had to be. Carmen quickly excused herself to her table companions, and followed the footman to the library, trying to still the trepidation in her heart.

As she stepped into the dim library, a small bundle of velvet cloak and satin hair ribbons flew across the room and hurled itself at her. Small arms flung about her waist, nearly pulling her off balance.

"Mama!" Isabella cried. "Mama, Mama, I've missed you so, so much!"

"Darling Bella!" For a glorious moment the bright joy of reunion overcame any misgivings. Carmen picked Isabella up and twirled her about until the little girl squealed with laughter. She kissed her daughter's small pink cheeks over and over, and nuzzled her nose into warm golden curls. "Um, you smell of roses and rain!"

"And you smell of Mama," Isabella giggled. "Are you happy to see us?"

Carmen glanced at Esperanza, who stood by the fire wrapped in her black traveling cloak. "I am happier than happy, dearest. And I know that Elizabeth and Nicholas will be happy to see you again. But I am surprised; you cannot possibly have received my letter, as I posted it only this morning."

"Letter?" said Esperanza. "No, Carmencita, we received no letter. I just thought it best to come to you, as Isabella has been ill."

"Ill!" Carmen framed her child's face in her hands and peered into it closely, searching for any sign of dreaded illness. Isabella's complexion was all pink and white, her dark eyes clear and bright. She *was* a bit flushed, but that could be attributed to the excitement of travel. Carmen laid the back of her hand against Isabella's brow; it was cool. "She looks well. What was amiss?"

"She is well now," Esperanza replied. "But only two days ago she was quite feverish and calling for you. I thought it best to bring her to you. If only you had been at home, where you belong . . ."

"Yes," Carmen interrupted firmly. "Just so. But you were right to bring her here."

"It was only a stomachache," Isabella said, her six-year-old voice quite as scornful as her father's. Then she leaned against her mother and whispered, "I wanted *you*, Mama, because you never make me swallow awful medicines when I'm ill, as Esperanza does. You tell better bedside stories, too."

Carmen laughed. "Well, I am happy my little imp is feeling better. I am also happy that you've come to me; I have a grand surprise for you!"

"A surprise? Really? What is it? A pony?"

"Better! But you shall have to wait and see. If I told you what it is, it would not be a surprise any longer."

Isabella made a moue. "Oh, all right! I can wait."

"Good girl! Now, you wait here while I go fetch Elizabeth. She can find you the very prettiest room and make sure you are settled while I talk to Esperanza . . ."

Elizabeth, as if conjured by the mention of her name, opened the door and poked her dark head inside. "Did I hear James say your maid was here, Carmen?"

"Yes. Esperanza has brought Isabella for a visit."

"Hello, Lady Elizabeth!" Isabella cried, running

forward to give her the same exuberant welcome she had given Carmen. "I have come to see you!"

"So I see!" Elizabeth kissed Isabella's cheek. "I shall have to tell Nick what a very charming guest has come to grace our house!"

"Can we go see him now?" asked Isabella.

"Well, I . . ." Elizabeth glanced questioningly at Carmen. At her nod she took Isabella's hand and led her out of the room. "Of course, dear. Then we will find you a chamber that suits so that your mother can talk with Esperanza."

Carmen closed the library door behind Elizabeth and Isabella, and leaned back against it. "Now, Esperanza," she said. "I wish to know what really happened."

"What really happened, Carmencita?" Esperanza sank down onto a chair, her lined features weary in the firelight. "Isabella was ill, she wanted her mother. It was a stomachache, as she sometimes gets, but I thought it best to bring her to you."

"She was probably eating too many lemon drops again. But why did you not send a messenger? I would have come back to London straight away. There was no need for you to make such a journey." Carmen went and sat on the arm of Esperanza's chair, taking her duenna's wrinkled hand in hers. "Did something else, of a more alarming nature, occur after I left?"

"Alarming, Carmencita? Such as what?"

"I do not know. A message, perhaps, or an odd visitor. A break-in. Did someone follow you while you were out shopping or walking in the park?"

Esperanza shook her head. "Oh, no, *niña*. Nothing of the sort. I only thought that Isabella would be better off with her mother."

Carmen was still uneasy. It was really not at all like Esperanza to act on impulse; she had spent almost six years following Carmen's travels stoically from city to city, but she had never enjoyed it. She had always wanted predictability, such as she had had with Carmen's mother.

Something *must* have happened in Town. But Esperanza's head was almost drooping with fatigue, and Carmen did not have the heart to press her. There would be time enough for talk later.

"I am sorry, Esperanza dear," she said. "You must be so tired from your journey. Let me see you settled, then later you and Isabella and I shall have tea together, and I will tell you all of what I have been doing here. And you must tell me what you and Isabella have been up to!"

"Yes." Esperanza allowed Carmen to help her to her feet, leaning heavily on her younger arm. "Yes. Yes, I am very tired."

What the devil was detaining Carmen?

Peter glanced at his watch. She had promised to meet him for a walk in the gardens, now that the rain had ceased.

But there was no sign of her: not in the drawing room, where small groups were preparing their tableaux for Sunday evening, not in the dining room, where an afternoon buffet was set. She was not even with Elizabeth and Georgina Beaumont, who were once again foraging for costumes in the attics.

He finally decided to wait for her in the library, where he was at least assured of quiet and a good fire. He borrowed a bottle of Nicholas's best claret and a book, and settled down to have a read until Carmen chose to show herself.

He had no sooner begun the first chapter, when he was distracted by a faint but persistent hissing noise. He glanced up and saw nothing. He wondered what Nicholas was putting in his claret these days, to cause people to hear things.

"Psst! Psst!"

There it was again, assuredly *not* a figment of the claret bottle. In point of fact, he believed it to be coming from beneath his very chair.

Peter looked down and saw a white lace flounce against the deep green carpet. There was also the tip of a tiny kid slipper.

It was far too small to belong to any of the female guests, even Miss Dixon, who prided herself on her very tiny hands and feet. So he knew he was not interrupting some bizarre tryst under the library furniture. One of the servant's children, perhaps?

"Oh, my," he said. "I do believe this library is haunted."

There was a giggle.

"I sincerely hope they are friendly ghosts."

"It is not a *ghost*," a small voice said. "It is I!"

"And who might I be?"

A head popped from beneath the chair. Peter leaned over to peer at the little porcelain face framed by a tangle of golden curls and untied pink hair ribbons.

He nearly fell from his chair.

He drew back from the sight of her. "Who—who are you, child?" he whispered. Though he did not have to ask—he knew. No one else but Carmen could possibly have a daughter with such eyes, chocolate dark and slightly tilted at the corners, full of laughter and mischief.

"I am Isabella."

Peter felt a pressure against his leg, and opened his eyes to see that she had emerged from beneath the chair and was now leaning against him. Her eyes were wide and curious as she looked up at him.

"Well," he said. "How do you, Miss Isabella. It is my very great honor to meet you."

"You did not introduce *yourself!*"

"Did I not? How very remiss of me. I am Peter Everdean."

Isabella held out one tiny, dusty hand. "How do you do."

Peter took her hand and raised it to his lips.

She giggled, then completely shocked him by clambering up into his lap. She was tall for her age, but as thin and delicate as a bird as she settled against his chest. Quite as if she had been sitting there all her life.

Peter was startled and, for one of the very rare times in his life, uncertain. He had never been around children, not since he himself had been a child, and had no idea of what the proper thing to do was in such a situation.

"Well, Miss Isabella," he said, "do you always greet strangers by climbing into their laps?"

"Oh, no," she answered blithely. "Never. That awful old Comte de Molyneux in Paris wanted me to hug him when he came to take Mama to a ball, but I wouldn't let him. He smelled vile, like onions. But you smell nice." She cuddled closer. "You must be a very nice man, not like the comte."

"No. Not like the comte," he said with a laugh. Then he carefully, tentatively, put his arm around her.

That was probably proper. After all, she was his daughter.

"Yes," she announced. "I do like you, Mr. Everdean."

What a quick judge she was. "Thank you, Miss Isabella. I quite like you, as well."

"Good. Then, you will not tell anyone I am here, will you?"

Peter could feel the twist as she turned her little finger. Yes, he was well and truly caught. "Are you meant to be someplace else?"

"Oh, yes. I am meant to be napping where Lady Elizabeth put me, so Mama and Esperanza can talk. But I am not tired! I wanted to see who was at the party."

"Well," he said consideringly. "I suppose we needn't tell your mama where you are, just yet. But won't she worry?"

"Oh, no. She and Esperanza are still talking. I know because I listened at the door." Her golden head drooped against his shoulder. "And you see, I am not at all sleepy . . ."

Chapter Seventeen

Carmen had settled Esperanza in the small dressing room adjoining her own bedchamber, and had stayed with her for over an hour. Esperanza had seemed quite exhausted, pale and drawn; Carmen wondered if perhaps it was *she* who had been ill and not Isabella. She at last managed to persuade Esperanza to take some tea and lie down for a rest.

Then she went off in search of Isabella. But the little girl was not in the bedroom where Elizabeth had left her, ostensibly napping. Nor was she in the long gallery looking at Elizabeth's paintings or in the drawing room or conservatory. Carmen even ventured into the kitchen, much to the shock of the chef and kitchen maids, hoping Isabella might have gone in search of sweets. But no sign of her was found.

Then Carmen went into the library, the last place she had to look before the attics. The large wood-paneled room was absolutely quiet, dim in the very late afternoon light. The fire had burned low, and no one had been in to light the candles yet.

She was backing out of the room when she saw the hint of golden hair above the top of an armchair drawn up before the fire. She tiptoed in closer.

And almost choked on a half sob, half laughter at the sight that greeted her. Her husband was asleep in the chair, with their daughter, also sleeping, leaning against his shoulder. Isabella's tiny mouth was open against the fine blue wool of his coat, and one little hand was curled in his cravat, hopelessly mangling the once pristine folds.

Carmen pinched her own arm to be certain she was not having one of the dreams that had so plagued her over the years. Dreams where she had seen the three of them together, sitting close beside their own fire. She had always awoke to a cold loneliness, an empty bed.

A small sound must have escaped her, for Peter's eyes opened and he looked up at her. He smiled slowly.

"Am I dreaming, Carmen?" he murmured.

"I thought the same thing," she whispered. "I see you have made Isabella's acquaintance."

"Oh, yes. The imp was hiding beneath my chair, trying to avoid a nap." Peter shifted in his chair. Isabella's head lolled a bit, but she did not wake. "She is rather more weighty than she appears."

"She gets heavier when she is asleep. But that is the only time she is quiet." Carmen sat down in the chair next to his. "Shall I take her?"

"No, no. I have six years to make up for. She is so very beautiful, Carmen." He looked down at his daughter's sleeping face. "So very beautiful."

"The most beautiful girl in the world."

"She looks very much like you."

"Not at all! She looks like you."

They sat quietly together while the shadows lengthened on the floor, the only sounds the soft breaths Isabella drew in her sleep. It grew a bit chilled as the fire died away, but Carmen did not feel cold even in the thin muslin of her gown. Indeed, she had never felt warmer in all her life.

"We will have to go change for supper soon," she said at last when the sounds of people leaving the drawing room could be heard.

"Yes, of course. And the little one should be in er bed." He stood slowly, careful not to jostle the hild in his arms. Isabella murmured a little and vined her arms about his neck.

"Not sleepy," she muttered, then fell back to snor- ng against him.

"Shall I take her to her nursery?" said Peter.

"I will go with you. Elizabeth put her in the floral hamber, just down from mine." Carmen went ahead) open the library door.

Peter kissed her cheek as he went past her. "Thank ou, Carmen," he said.

"Thank you for what?"

"For giving me Isabella. For being here again."

"You are very welcome, *querido*. And this time we rill not be parted again!"

"Never. I promise you that."

"I will hold you to that promise."

Isabella did not even wake when her father placed er on her small bed, removed her slippers, and rew the bedclothes about her snugly. Carmen icked her favorite doll next to her, and kissed the)p of her tumbled curls.

"Will she sleep the night through?" Peter /hispered.

"Of course! She is not an infant. But if she cries ut, the maid Elizabeth sent up will hear her. We ally should go now, or we shall be too late."

"Yes, certainly." With a last glance at his daughter, eter offered Carmen his arm and escorted her to the oor of her own chamber. "Will you walk with me the gardens after supper, for a quiet talk?"

"I would love nothing more. Well—*almost* nothing ore!" She made certain no one was hanging about the corridor, then kissed him lingeringly. When is arms reached out to draw her closer, she pulled way with a laugh. "Remember supper!"

"Bother supper! I am not hungry for *food*," he mu*
tered, and reached for her again.

Carmen ducked under his arm into her room an*
closed the door on him. "Supper!" she called.

He protested, but soon she heard his footstep*
move away down the corridor.

There was no time to ring for a maid, so Carme*
quickly chose an evening gown that required sma*
effort, a lilac satin that buttoned up the side of th*
low-cut bodice with tiny pearl buttons. It was on*
after she had pulled it on that she noticed one of th*
buttons was hanging on only by a thread, and he*
white silk chemise could be seen through the gap.

"Oh, bother!" she cried. "I will never make it t*
supper until the dessert." She pattered in her stock*
inged feet to Esperanza's dressing room chamber, in*
tending to ask her to sew up the button.

But Esperanza was not there. The bedclothes wer*
rumpled, and candles were lit on the dressing tabl*
yet no one was there.

Carmen went quickly to the dressing table wher*
Esperanza's valise was placed, intending to find *
needle and make the repair herself.

What she found there was far more shocking tha*
needles and cotton.

In the valise, beneath carefully folded shawls an*
caps, was a small wooden box. But instead of th*
sewing paraphernalia that Carmen expected to fin*
there was a small sheaf of cheap stationery, a clutc*
of pencils, a wax jack, and a few sticks of wax.

Black wax. Carmen knew for certain that Esperar*
za's usual wax, used to seal all her letters, was red*

A knot of ice formed in her stomach, freezing a*
the delicious anticipation of the evening, all th*
warm *life* she had begun to feel again. As she opene*
the jack to look at the little bits of ominous blac*
wax still inside, the woman she had been during th*

var seemed to take her over again. Calm, calculating, emoved from the horrible things that were really happening around her. That distance had always erved her so well through war and widowhood.

Through betrayal.

But Esperanza had been with her since she was orn! She had been Carmen's mother's duenna, her own companion through her terrible first marriage, through the birth of Isabella, and all her wanderings. How could she have written those letters, those ugly letters?

Carmen had suspected Robert Means, when all along it had been her own Esperanza!

She sank down onto the dressing table stool, her knees suddenly like water. She had seen betrayal before, of course, had seen hatred and rage. Yet this was a woman she had shared her life with, had let her near her own child.

It was all so awful, so unfathomable.

Carmen threw the jack onto the floor in a flash of pain and anger, all her cold distance gone.

"Oh, Carmencita," a sad, soft voice said from the open doorway. "I am so very sorry you saw that."

Chapter Eighteen

Carmen slowly stepped backward, until she fel her hips bump against the edge of the table, and she leaned against it weakly. She knew her mouth was inelegantly agape, but somehow her mind would not connect with her jaw and tell it to close. She just stared at Esperanza, enveloped in a haz cloud of unreality.

Esperanza looked the same tidy, efficient lady Car men had known since childhood. Her neat black sill gown was fastened at the throat with an ivory brooch that had been a long-ago gift from Carmen's mother The lace cap atop coiled gray braids. It was all th very same. Yet something in her faded brown eye was very different. They were sad and calm, even bit cool, as they regarded Carmen and her shocked face.

"Carmencita," she said quietly, moving a bi nearer. "I did not mean for it to be this way."

"It—it was you," Carmen managed to whisper "All this time. You were the one writing those let ters." She sat back down slowly, her ankles suddenl unbearably wobbling.

"Yes. When we were in Paris, I gave them to friend who was traveling to England to post at regu lar intervals, so you would not suspect. Very cleve of old Esperanza, sí?" She chuckled, but her de meanor remained soft and regretful. "It was careless of me to leave these things about."

"But, Esperanza! How could you do such things?" Carmen cried. She pounded her fists against her satin-covered thighs, like the lost child she felt inside. "You were like a dear aunt to me, even like a mother after Mama died. Why do you hate me so?"

"Carmencita, I *love* you! That is why I did this."

"No. Those letters were full of hatred. No one who loved me could have written them. If you needed money, you know I would have given you anything . . ."

"Do you not see, *querida*? I did not do this for money. I had to save you and Isabella from yourselves."

Carmen stared at Esperanza, utterly aghast that she had been so blind to such madness for so long. It had been beneath her very roof, and she had not seen it. Slowly, she held out one hand to Esperanza, trembling so much that the emerald on her finger flashed and danced merrily.

"Esperanza," she said slowly, forcing herself to remain placid and quiet as she once had with battle-mad soldiers. "You are not at all yourself. You are tired from all our travels, I know, and that is all my fault. You must have rest, a permanent home. Let me help you . . ."

"No!" Esperanza suddenly cried. She moved closer, her fists in their innocuous black lace mitts opening and closing against her skirts. "It was *you* who were not yourself, Carmencita! That is why I did what I did. To make you see. I could find no other way."

Carmen shook her head, bewildered. She was still reeling; she longed to scream, to cry. Instead, she stayed very still. "Tell me, then, Esperanza. Tell me what I must see."

"That you have not lived your life in a way that your sainted mama and the Blessed Virgin would deem proper. That you must repent and change before it is too late."

"Not proper?"

"No. In Spain, during the war, your mother and I knew that you were not with the Santiago family in Toledo, as you claimed. We knew what you were really about, riding around the countryside, associating with peasants and with English soldiers." Esperanza practically spat those words out, making "English" sound the vilest curse. "You were messing about in war and politics, as no proper woman should. I knew you were caught in evil when you came home heavy with child and with no husband. And when you had not given your lawful Spanish husband an heir as you should have!"

Carmen pressed her fist against her mouth. She felt horribly like a chastened schoolgirl, awaiting some dreadful punishment from the Mother Superior. "I told you my husband had died!"

"What husband? I saw no marriage lines!"

"Esperanza, please . . ."

Esperanza continued, unhearing. "I knew when I saw Isabella that *she* could be saved, if only you could be brought to see how wrong you were. If you could be brought to repent, to send the child to a convent to be raised." She stepped up half behind Carmen, almost concealed. "She is so like you when you were a child, Carmencita. So lovely, but so very willful. And you never discipline her as you should . . ."

Carmen closed her eyes, but she could not shut out dreadful reality. It still hung heavy about her, no dream at all. "Esperanza, please, let me help you . . ." She half rose from her stool.

The next thing she felt was a sharp, heavy pain

ainst the back of her head. There was a shower of
ght, a strange stickiness.

Then—nothing.

"I am worried about Carmen, Peter." Elizabeth
gged on her brother's coat sleeve, making him
nd closer to hear her hurried whisper. She cast a
ick look around at the guests gathered in the
awing room for cards after supper. "I do not wish
be a hovering hostess, but when she did not ap-
ar for supper . . ."

Peter frowned. "I am worried as well, Lizzie. It is
t at all like her to not send a message if she meant
absent herself. And she said she was going to
ess for supper when we parted."

"Do you think she could be ill?"

"She seemed well enough earlier. I will go and
eak with her."

"Yes," Elizabeth said with a sigh of relief. "Thank
u, Peter dear. I am sure all is well, and there is
me easy explanation."

As Peter left the bright, chatter-filled drawing
om and climbed up the dim staircase, the cold knot
at had formed in his stomach as supper went on
ith no Carmen grew. He felt almost a sense of fore-
ding, an intuition that had served him well in
ttle.

Something was amiss with his wife.

Carmen's bedroom door was slightly ajar, a sliver
light spilling into the corridor. Wishing he had his
istol, or at least a knife, Peter slowly opened the
oor completely and stepped inside.

Her shawl, gloves, and fan were laid out on the
ed. On the dressing table, a jewel case sat open, but,
om the wealth of gems that tumbled there, he
dged that nothing had been burgled. The fire had

almost died away, but candles still burned brightl
The faint scent of jasmine perfume hung in the air

It was so very quiet.

Then he heard a small sound, a rustling, comin
from behind the half-closed door of the adjoinin
dressing room, which he knew had been made int
a bedroom for Carmen's maid. Peter caught up th
only weapon at hand, the fireplace poker, and wei
inside.

At first glance he thought the room as empty a
the bedroom. Then he saw a flash of lilac sati
against the floor, heard a low moan from behind th
dressing table.

"Carmen!" he shouted, dropping down onto th
carpet beside her prone body. Her black curls wei
sticky with blood, and she was alarmingly pale. Fc
one sickening moment, he feared she was gone froi
him again.

But she moaned again, a bit louder, and her han
moved on the carpet.

He took that cold hand and pressed it against hi
chest. "Carmen?" he said urgently. "Can you hea
me, love?"

"Peter?" She tried to turn her head and cried ou

"Do not move," he said. "Just try to lie still."

"Cold," she murmured.

Peter stripped off his coat and tucked it aroun
her. "I shall have Lizzie fetch a doctor."

"Not yet! Not until . . ."

"What happened here? Can you tell me?"

Her eyes opened, unfocused and dilated until the
were completely black. They darted frantically abou
the room. "It was Esperanza. All the time."

Peter was shocked. That frail old lady he ha
glimpsed earlier that day had bashed Carmen, wh
was a tall, athletic woman, over the head? He wor
dered fleetingly if Carmen was having delusion

rought on by her head wound. "Your maid did
his?"

"Yes!" Tears spilled down Carmen's cheeks. "She
wrote all those letters. It was Esperanza all the time!"
Her voice rose sharply. "I confronted her, and she
hit me on the head."

He looked up at the table they were crouched behind, and saw the jumble of papers and pencils and
sticks of black wax. A heavy silver candlestick,
flecked with blood, was carelessly tossed there on
its side.

He shuddered at the palpable sense of evil that
surrounded them, as strongly as he had once felt it
in battle. He carefully gathered Carmen into his arms,
surrounding her with his body as if he could thus
ward off anything bad from touching her. She was
trembling.

"My poor dear," he whispered. "Why would she
do such a thing to you?"

"I don't know!" Carmen cried. "She just went on
and on about how wicked I was, how I have lived
my life sinfully, and now Isabella . . ." She gasped
suddenly and struggled to sit up, clawing at Peter's
hands when he pressed her back down. "Isabella!"

"What is it? Did she threaten Isabella?" Peter felt
such a burning rage, uncontrollable as a house fire,
rising up in him. He forced himself to stay quiet as
he held Carmen, to not frighten her further. "Did
she?"

"I do not know! I can't remember. It is all such a
jumble in my mind. But if she could do *this*, she is
capable of anything!" She seized his hand, her grip
painful as she pressed the bones together. "You must
find Isabella, Peter. Find her, and keep her safe."

"I will, I swear. But you must stay here, and not
move until a physician can get here."

"No! I must go with you . . ."

"Carmen!" Unmistakable authority rang in hi
voice. He pressed her gently but firmly back agains
the floor. "You will start to bleed again if you mov
about. Either you wait here for me to return, or I wi
not leave you."

Carmen moistened her cracked lips with the tip o
her tongue, indecision flickering in her eyes. Finall
she gave a small nod. "Yes."

"Good. I will not be gone long."

He kissed her on her forehead and went in searc
of his daughter. But in Isabella's bedroom, he foun
precisely what he had feared to find—nothing.

Her small bed had been slept in, the sheets turne
back and rumpled. Yet they were cold, and the do
Carmen had tucked in so carefully beside thei
daughter was tossed to the floor. Isabella's little ve'
vet dressing gown was still folded across the foot o
the bed.

Peter picked it up, feeling the soft fabric beneat
his hands; the milky-sweet little girl smell still clun,
to its folds. He had only just found her; how coul
he lose her so quickly?

"She is gone?"

He turned to see Carmen leaning weakly agains
the door frame, clinging to the wood to keep fror
falling. Her eyes were huge as she took in th
empty room.

"Esperanza took her," she whispered.

"Perhaps. Or she might have simply wandered o
somewhere, perhaps to find you or to look for some
thing to drink. I do not know where her maid is, bu
when I find the stupid girl . . ." Carmen swaye
precariously, so he swept her up into his arms an
laid her on the bed before she could injure hersel
further. She turned her face away, weeping.

"No!" she sobbed. "Esperanza took her, I know

She is not in her right mind! What if she does an injury to Isabella?"

Peter was quite terrified. He had never seen Carmen, his brave Carmen, so helplessly hysterical. His own fragile hold on calm was quickly slipping away. He knew that if he did not *do* something, he would soon be as frantic as Carmen and they would never find Isabella.

He sat up, drawing Major Everdean around him once again. He had a battle, the most decisive of his life, to plot.

"Carmen," he snapped. "You must cease this at once. Tell me what Esperanza said to you, if she gave you some hint as to where she would have gone."

Something in Carmen seemed to respond to the crisp authority in his voice. She sniffed and slowly sat up against the pillows. "No," she said thoughtfully. "Nothing. She said something about a convent, but there are no convents near here."

"Are you sure that was all?" .

"Of course. I . . ."

"Peter! What has happened?"

Elizabeth swept into the room, holding a shrinking housemaid by the wrist. Elizabeth took in the scene of a bloodied and tearstained Carmen, a pale and grim Peter, and nodded.

"So something did happen," she said. "It was Carmen's Spanish maid?"

"How did you know?" Carmen murmured.

Elizabeth drew the maid forward. "Molly came to me with quite an odd tale. Tell them, Molly!"

"Oh, no, my lady, I can't . . ." The maid was obviously terrified, afeard she had done something wrong and was probably about to be dismissed.

"It is quite all right, Molly," Elizabeth urged. "This is terribly important. Do you not want to help that little girl?"

"Oh, yes, my lady!"

"Then, go on, please, Molly," Peter urged.

"Well, my lord, I was up here putting the bed warmers in the guest rooms, see, when I heard a bit of a set-too."

"A set-too?"

"Yes, my lord. Loud, like. Then I heard the young lady crying and saying, 'No, no.' So I came out into the corridor, and I saw the old lady. I beg pardon, your maid, Condesa. She was carrying the young lady off down the stairs, but she didn't want to go.'

"The child did not?" Peter asked.

"Yes, the young lady." Molly was warming to her tale. "She tried to get away. I heard her call for her mama."

Carmen gave a choked cry.

Molly went on. "I knew this wasn't right, so I followed at a bit of a distance to see where they went.'

"You were not seen?" Peter asked.

"Oh, no, my lord. I saw them go out the back doors, to the garden, and across the way to those trees. I daren't leave the house, my lord, without the butler knowing. So I told him what I seen."

"When was this, Molly?"

"Oh, my lord, 'bout an hour ago, I'd say."

"Damn!" Peter raked trembling fingers through his hair. "They could be anywhere by now."

Carmen reached for his hand. "We must make up a search party, quickly."

"Of course. Lizzie, will you help me?"

"I will go down now and tell Nick to have some horses readied." She started to turn away, then snapped her fingers. "The ruins?"

Peter looked at her sharply. "What ruins?"

"That old medieval tower, of course!" Elizabeth said, excited. "You follow the path through those trees to get to the tower on foot, remember? The

tler does like to brag of the local sights to guests.
rhaps he told Esperanza of the tower, and she
ought it a fine hiding place."

"Surely that is where they have gone!" said Car-
en. "Esperanza is fascinated by romantic old ruins;
ey are the only things she has enjoyed on our trav-
s. And it is beginning to rain, so I am sure they
ill have sought shelter."

"I will go there at once," Peter answered. "Lizzie,
ll Nick and Viscount Huntington to come after me,
it quietly. There must be no charging ahead full
rce like some cavalry, not when dealing with so
hinged a person."

"Of course, at once." Elizabeth hurried away, pull-
g the now-grinning maid behind her.

"I will come with you," Carmen announced.

"No!" Peter said firmly. "There is no knowing
hat will be found, Carmen. If something terrible
is happened, or if I am forced to take some dras-
c action . . ."

"Do you think I have no stomach for whatever
ight happen?" She grasped his arm and forced him
 look at her. She was pale as snow, her eyes huge
id dark, but she was utterly composed now. Her
irlier hysterics were gone, and in her face could be
en only steely resolve.

"Peter," she said, "you know the horrible things I
ave seen in my life, and that I have always done
hat was necessary, without flinching."

He nodded slowly. "Indeed you did. You were the
est shot I have ever seen."

"Then, take me with you now! I will go whether
ou say aye or nay, but we would be so much more
fective if we work together." Her grip tightened.
She is my *child*. I cannot sit here idly while she is
 danger. After all is finished, I promise I will rest
id see the doctor, and whatever else you like."

Peter sighed, resigned. "Very well. But put on cloak! It is cold and wet outside."

She smiled faintly. "Of course, Major."

"Carmen . . ."

"Yes?"

"We will find her." His voice was implacable, y somehow searching for reassurance.

"Oh, yes. We must."

The alternative was completely unthinkable.

Chapter Nineteen

It was a misty night, foggy and damp, not at all like the night they had their midnight picnic. The moon was almost completely obscured by clouds, casting the landscape into a dangerous darkness. Carmen and Peter had been forced to leave their horses and proceed down the narrow path on foot. They kept the lantern they had brought shuttered, so as not to reveal their progress. The only saving grace was that it had not yet begun to rain in earnest, just spitting little dribbles at them.

Carmen marveled that such a landscape, so pastoral and idyllic only days before, could look like the setting of the darkest nightmare now.

She held tightly to Peter's hand as they walked along the path. In her other hand she clutched the cold steel of her loaded pistol. As the cold air swept up her legs, she wished vaguely that there had been time to change into trousers. The thin satin of her evening gown, even covered by a heavy cloak, hardly seemed the proper armor for going into battle.

But the only thought that could stay in her mind was of Isabella. Where was she? Was she cold? Was she frightened? Did she call out for her mama?

Carmen bit her lip until she tasted blood to keep from crying out. This was not the time for panic; this was a time for cold, rational calm.

She looked at Peter and was reassured by the hard

set of his jaw, the icy light in his eyes. Here was not the English earl, who danced so gallantly in ballrooms, but the warrior she had first met. He would get their daughter back for her, no matter the obstacles. She was sure of that.

"There it is," he whispered.

The trees thinned out, and the path widened, revealing the ruined tower set atop its bluff. The stream beside which Carmen and Peter had talked ran behind it, swollen now with the rain.

Peter drew his field glasses from inside his greatcoat and examined the tower. Carmen remembered that, though the stones were crumbling, the stairs that curved up the center of the tower were intact and passable. They led to a small room at the very top of the structure, where medieval warriors had kept watch for their enemies.

"Do you see anything?" she whispered.

"No. It is too confounded dark."

Yet even as they spoke, they saw a small light flicker and die, then flicker again in the windows at the top of the tower.

"Did you see that?" she hissed. "It must be them!"

"Perhaps. Or perhaps it is merely vagrants."

"We must find out."

"Yes. Remember to stay behind me at all times, Carmen. Do you understand? No matter what we may see?"

"Of course."

"Do you have your pistol?"

"Yes, loaded and ready."

"Excellent." Peter turned suddenly and pulled her into his arms for a brief, hard kiss. "Then, once more into the breach, eh, Carmen?"

"Peter . . ."

"Yes?"

"I love you."

"And I love you. After tonight, my dear, shall we strive to live the dullest lives imaginable?"

"Oh, yes, please!"

He smiled down at her, then released her to walk off across the clearing toward the tower. He looked every bit the nonchalant Englishman, off for a bit of an evening stroll, but Carmen knew that concealed beneath his stylish many-caped greatcoat was a sword and two pistols.

Praying that no one was watching their approach, Carmen followed him, her own pistol primed and ready. Despite the enveloping warmth of her fur-lined cloak, she shivered.

It was when she slipped inside the open doorway of the tower and reached for Peter's hand for assistance ascending the crumbling stairs, that she heard it. A faint cry, a rumble of low, hurried, feminine voices. There was a golden spill of light from above.

Her eyes met Peter's. "Go," she mouthed.

He nodded, and quickly, nimbly ran up the stairs, his soft-soled boots silent on the old stone. He turned a corner, and was gone from her sight.

As per their agreement, she would wait a full minute before following. The longest minute of her life.

She leaned against the cold stone wall, the chill damp seeming to seep into her very bones. She held the pistol against her side. If only this were all over, her daughter in her arms . . .

Just as she thought she could not bear to wait another instant, she heard the deeper tones of Peter's voice, echoing from above. The rising, heavily accented voice of a woman. A shrill cry, a sob.

Carmen pushed away from the wall and ran up the stairs as quickly as she could over the stones rumbling beneath her half boots. She kept one gloved hand on the slimy wall for balance.

At the top of the stairs, she did not give in to

her longing to rush headlong into the lamp-lit room
Instead, she held back to the shadows, peering
around the sharp corner of the wall.

Esperanza was there. Her usually immaculate
black gown was dusty and torn, her cap gone and
hair straggling from its pins. She stood near the window, her back to the night. One hand held a long
dagger; the other clutched Isabella's arm.

Carmen bit her lip. He daughter was shivering in
only her nightrail, her tangled blonde curls falling
over her shaking shoulders. She was crying, her little
face pale and streaked with tears and dirt.

Peter stood just inside the doorway, his arms held
out as if to show surrender. His voice was very low
and soft as he spoke.

"Please, Esperanza," he said slowly. "Please,
have not come to hurt you. I have only come to take
you and Isabella back to the house. It is very cold
here; this is not a place for a child."

Esperanza backed up another step, pulling Isabella
with her. She was now almost leaning on the low sill
of the window. "No!" she cried. "You need not pretend innocence with me, *your lordship*. I know who
you are."

"Who am I, Esperanza?"

"It was you who spoiled my Carmencita, my innocent girl! Who lured her into wickedness."

"I do not know what you mean." Peter's voice was
soft, almost tender. He took a very small step forward, then immediately halted as Esperanza backed
up, sending a shower of stones from the window to
the cobbles below.

"You *do* know what I mean! You were the English
soldier who seduced Carmen, encouraged her in un-
seemly actions when she should have been at home
I know, because you are the image of Isabella! You
are this child's father! You abandoned them to sin."

"You are wrong. Carmen was, is, my wife. There was never anything sinful about it."

"So she claimed." Esperanza pulled Isabella closer against her. She was shaking as if in a hurricane gale. "You pulled Carmen down into evil, and now she is lost. Now you are trying to do the same to Isabella. But I will save her!"

"She is my daughter. I would never do anything to hurt her, Esperanza. Now, please let me take you back to the house."

Isabella stared at him with huge, bewildered dark eyes. She strained against Esperanza's grasp. "You— are my papa?"

Peter took another step toward them. Esperanza stepped back again, sending another clatter of stones below. Carmen could hear the pounding of horses' hooves, coming closer to the tower.

Esperanza obviously heard them, as well. She glanced back over her shoulder and gasped.

Carmen sensed that their time was growing short. Esperanza was perilously near the edge of the unstable window frame, and her eyes were wilder and more unfocused than ever before. Slowly, Carmen pushed back her cloak and lifted the pistol. She stepped away from the wall to take aim . . .

"Mama!" Isabella's sudden scream made Esperanza whip her head back around. Her wide, startled gaze took in Carmen and the gun.

"Demon!" Esperanza whispered.

Then Isabella tugged hard on her arm, catching Esperanza by surprise. The soles of her shoes skidded on the stone floor, and she began to lose her balance. As Carmen watched, horrified, Esperanza fell backward, toward the windowsill, her hand still gripping Isabella.

"Papa, help!" Isabella screamed, her free hand

flailing in midair as she was pulled toward the window, her bare feet dangling off the floor.

Carmen screamed as well, and rushed forward
even though she knew she was much too far away
to catch her in time. Her feet seemed made of lead.

Peter, though, was much closer to them. Sleek and
swift as a tiger, he lunged at his daughter, and
caught her small hand, pulling her back from the
brink along with Esperanza.

The momentum of their weight sent him skidding
backward, to land on his back with Isabella atop him.
For a moment they both lay still.

Esperanza slumped on the floor near the window, sobbing.

"*Madre de Dios*," Carmen whispered. She tossed
aside the pistol and fell to her knees beside her family. She could not even feel the bite of the sharp
stones through the thin satin of her gown as she
watched them stir. Isabella, sobbing, fell into her
mother's arms.

"Sh, my darling," Carmen murmured. "It is well
now. You are safe."

Across the room, Esperanza stirred, her shoulder
shuddering as she took a deep, shivering breath. Carmen put Isabella into Peter's arms and went to her,
crouching down at her side.

"Esperanza," she said very quietly. "Are you
hurt?"

Esperanza began sobbing in earnest at the sound
of her voice. Great tears fell from her wrinkled
cheeks onto her dusty black skirts. She covered her
face with her hands. "What have I done? What have
I done?"

"Sh," Carmen said, just as she had with Isabella.
She drew Esperanza carefully into her arms, cradling
her against her shoulder, as Esperanza had done so

often for her when she was a child. "It is quite all right now. Everyone is safe."

"No!" Esperanza lifted her head to stare frantically up at Carmen. Her twisted, thin hands clutched at Carmen's hand. "I would never have hurt Isabella, *niña*, never! You must believe me."

"I believe you. I know you would not want to hurt Isabella."

"She is like my own child, just as you were." Esperanza's grip tightened. "Just as my Isabella was."

"Yes. My mother loved you very much, Esperanza."

"As I loved her! I did this for her."

"For my mother?" Carmen still kept her voice soft and steady, despite her own bewilderment and sorrow.

"Before she went to the angels, she charged me to look after you. She said she feared you had a wild soul, that you would not live your life in a manner befitting your station. A manner the Blessed Mother would approve." Esperanza's head drooped against Carmen's shoulder, and Carmen's arms clasped closer about her. "I saw that her fears were correct when you came back to us so heavy with child, and so silent. You laid in bed all day, with your face turned to the wall, refusing to speak. You said nothing about the Englishman you claimed had been your husband. I thought your silence was shame at your disgrace."

"It was not shame. It was grief."

"I only wanted to save you, Carmencita!" Esperanza wailed. "Never harm you. You must believe me! You must!"

"I do believe you, Esperanza. Of course I believe you."

"Do you, Carmencita? Truly?"

"I do."

Then, as Esperanza subsided back into tears, Carmen became aware of other voices.

"Mama!" Isabella sobbed. She left Peter's arms and crawled onto her mother's lap, burying her face against her shoulder. She was shaking and scared, but seemed physically unharmed. "Why did Esperanza do that? Why? I was so scared!"

"My poor angel." Carmen kissed the top of Isabella's head and held her very, very tightly. "Esperanza is very ill. She did not know what she was doing or saying. But all is well now; Mama has you safe."

Isabella clutched at her cloak. "Is Peter safe, too? Is he hurt?"

Carmen looked over at Peter, who had laid back down on the stones. He seemed rather stunned by his fall, but his eyes were open and focused as he watched them, his chest rising and falling steadily.

"I don't think he's hurt, dearest," she said. "You see, he is getting up now."

Isabella watched as Peter painfully climbed to his feet, leaning against the wall. "He said he was my papa."

Carmen sighed. "Yes, darling. He is. But I shall explain it all to you tomorrow, when you are warm and rested."

Isabella, however, seemed to require no explanations just at present. She just nodded and cuddled closer to her mother. Her eyelids were drooping in exhaustion.

Peter came to them then, wincing as he tried to put his weight on his left leg. "Carmen," he murmured, "we should go."

"Yes, of course. The others should be here any moment; perhaps they have brought horses for us. You should not walk on that leg."

"I am quite all right. Here, let me have Isabella. You should see to Esperanza. I think that . . ."

Whatever he was going to say was lost in a shout from below. "Peter!" Nicholas called. "What has happened? Are you all right? Is Isabella with you?"

Peter limped to the ruined window, a sleeping Isabella against his shoulder, and peered out. "Yes, and we are all well, if a bit shaken. I think I have sprained my ankle."

"We'll be up to help you!" Nicholas answered. "Don't go anywhere!"

"Ha! This is no time for witticisms." Then Peter turned to look at his Carmen and Esperanza, huddled on the stone floor. "*Are* you well, Carmen?"

It seemed such an insane thing to say at such a moment, but he could think of nothing else. What did one say after all the people one loves most have faced death and madness? No words could possibly articulate all the vast emotions roiling inside of him. Rage, battle exhilaration, relief, hope—love.

Above all, love.

"Oh, yes. No. I am not sure." She laughed, a bit hysterically, then rose to her feet, holding Esperanza against her. Her old duenna was in a stupor now, murmuring in Spanish as she went with Carmen without a protest. "But we must go now. We must get help for Esperanza."

Nicholas came up the tower steps then, his gaze darting sharply about the room, taking in the four weary, battle-scarred figures. He went to Carmen and took the weight of Esperanza from her arm.

"*Señora*," he murmured solicitously. "Please allow me to escort you someplace warm."

Esperanza nodded vaguely and went with him without a murmur. It was painfully obvious that she was no longer at all aware of where she was. She had unburdened her heart, been granted forgiveness,

and now she had retreated to someplace very fa
away.

Peter went to Carmen as she watched Esperanz
leave with Nicholas. He wrapped his arms about he
and their child, precious treasures, and tried to wil
warmth into them. "Do not worry now, my love. Al
will be well now. All will be well."

Carmen sobbed against his shoulder.

Chapter Twenty

It was late afternoon of the next day by the time Peter managed to conclude his business. With Elizabeth's help, he had seen Esperanza settled with a local woman, a former army nurse, in her cottage at Clifton. He had not had time to bathe or eat or sleep, but he went directly to Carmen's room after he returned from the woman's cottage.

She was asleep in her bed, Isabella curled against her, also deep in slumber. A dinner tray on a nearby table was mostly untouched; but Isabella sported smears of candy on her little chin and clean nightdress, so he knew they were not entirely unnourished.

Peter smiled at the lovely sight. He drew a chair to the bedside, very quietly so as not to wake them, and settled down to the very important job of watching them.

Dark purple marred the delicate skin beneath Carmen's eyes, but she seemed a trifle less pale than she had last night. The tousled black curls that fell across her brow made her appear almost as young as her daughter.

But Peter felt himself to be positively ancient. He had lived a lifetime in one night, a life of such joy and terror and pain. He had spent so many years completely alone, trapped in a hell of guilt that had been of his own making. Then there had been a miracle. He had been given a family, the one love of his life and a beautiful child. He had experienced the most glorious feeling in life, the feeling of not being alone any longer, of knowing he would never be alone again.

He had watched his sister and her husband, had seen the life they were making together, and he had been envious. He had thought he could never find a love such as they had again; it was surely a onetime only gift, and his was gone. Then he had found Carmen again, and could see a future for them that was quite as rosy as the one awaiting Elizabeth and Nicholas. He could make love to his wife, not the mechanical physical release he had known with his mistresses, but to truly lose himself in her warmth, her love. He could play and laugh with his daughter, perhaps even hold new babies in his arms. More golden little girls and a dark-haired heir.

And he had almost lost all of that, all his fragile dreams, in one shattering second.

But here they were, safe and alive.

Peter reached for Carmen's hand, the one wearing the wedding ring she had kept so faithfully all their years apart. He raised it to his lips.

"Oh, Lord," he murmured. "I know I have been a wretched pagan. I only pray that I am worthy of all these gifts You have given me."

And let our lives be peaceful and dull now, he added silently. At least for the next forty or fifty years.

Carmen stirred and blinked up at him. "Peter? Who are you talking to?"

"I am praying."

"*You?*"

"Yes, love, me."

"I do not think I have ever heard you pray before. Not even before a battle."

"I do not think I ever have. Until now."

"Why now?"

"I merely thought I should give thanks for the wonderful miracles bestowed on us. And I was humbly asking for a very dull life in our years to come; I have had quite a surfeit of adventure now."

"Amen to that! Do you think He will grant your request?"

"Hm, at least until it is time to marry Isabella off. I have the sense that that will be no easy task."

"No, indeed!" Carmen looked down fondly at her sleeping daughter. "Fortunately, we will not have to worry about it for many years yet."

"But what if we have more? What if we have six daughters, and have to deal with six betrothals?"

"God forbid!" Carmen laughed. Then her gaze turned serious as she looked at him. "Oh, Peter. How could I have made such a dreadful mistake? How could I have left my child in the care of a madwoman? We could all have been killed last night, all because I was so blind."

"How could you have known? You knew Esperanza your whole life; you trusted her. Of course you could not have believed that of an old woman. No one would have."

"I *should* have seen it!"

Peter slid onto the bed next to her, boots and all, and drew her and Isabella into the warm circle of his arms. Her hair was soft against his beard-roughened cheek, and she still smelled of jasmine even after their long night.

"My dear," he said. "You are not culpable in this. Some people are not—not *right* in their minds, for whatever reason. Esperanza is one of them. I was one when I came home from Spain. I did some dreadful things. I could not see reality, just as Esperanza could not. Does that, then, make my sister at fault, for not seeing my illness and dispatching me directly to Bedlam?''

Carmen shook her head. "Certainly not!''

"No. Certainly not. It is the same for you. Isabella is safe. We are all here, together. So we can move into the future now, free of doubt and guilt.'' For the first time in years, Peter himself knew that to be true.

The past was gone, and they were free.

Carmen nodded then, and turned her face up to his. There were tears in her dark eyes, sparkling like crystals, but they could not rival the brilliance of her smile.

Chapter Twenty-One

"Carmen? May I come in?"

Carmen smiled at her reflection in the dressing table mirror at the sound of her husband's voice.

Her husband. How her heart thrilled at those words, at knowing they were true at last, and not a mere futile wish.

"Come in!" she called. She rose to her feet, straightening the folds of her silver tissue gown.

"I was coming to see if you were quite prepared for this ridiculous tableau . . ." His words trailed away, and he came to an abrupt halt inside the bedroom door at the sight of her. "Carmen. You look—entrancing."

"Do you like it?" She twirled about, displaying the full effect of the gown, the laced sandals, the diamond bandeau in her hair. "I found it in Elizabeth's trunk in the attic. She said it once belonged to your stepmother."

"I am certain that Isobel, as lovely as she was, could never have looked half so beautiful in it." He came to her and took her in his arms. His kiss was warm and lingering, a healing touch, a benediction, on all they had faced and overcome.

"If you continue like this," Carmen murmured against his lips, "we will never make it to the tableaux."

"Hang the tableaux," he answered, and reached his hand toward her bodice.

She stepped back with a laugh. "Lizzie would be very vexed with us! And Isabella would be so disappointed. She is looking forward to showing you her Cupid costume."

"Then, I suppose we must not miss it," he sighed. "I do look forward to seeing our daughter attired as Cupid. She is very likely darling in it."

"Yes, she is. And, speaking of costumes, is that cloak you are muffled in yours?"

"Er, no. But I think I may keep it on."

"Oh, no! That, sir, is not allowed. You must let me see your costume. You have seen mine."

"Very well. But first close your eyes."

Carmen squeezed her eyes shut. "They are closed."

There was a rustle of cloth, another long-suffering sigh, then, "All right. You may look now."

Carmen opened her eyes. And gave a great shout of laughter.

Peter stood before her attired in a rather brief white muslin, gold trimmed tunic. His legs, muscled and dusted with fine, blond hairs, were bare from the knee down to his laced gold sandals.

His face, usually so very cool and haughty, was bright cherry red as he tugged at the tunic's hem.

Carmen sat down on the edge of her bed, as she feared she might otherwise fall over with the force of her mirth. "Oh!" she gasped. "It—it is wondrous."

"Elizabeth made me wear it," he muttered.

"I adore it! You should dress in this fashion every day."

Isabella burst into the room, trailed by her harried new maid. She wore a miniature of her mother's gown, only made of a heavier silver satin. A crown of silver leaves perched atop her curls, and she held a tiny bow and arrow.

"Oh!" she cried. "You look *beautiful*, Mama." Then she looked at Peter. "And so do you, Papa. Though I have never seen a man's *legs* before."

Carmen buried her giggles behind her hand.

Isabella came to her mother and leaned against her happily. "What a very nice looking family we are!" she proclaimed with great satisfaction.

"Endymion the shepherd, as his flock he guarded, she the moon Selene . . ."

Isabella, perched atop a short marble column, angelic in her silver gown, faltered, and glanced uncertainly at her mother.

Carmen struggled to hold her pose without laughing. Her lovely gown was proving too thin for the rather chilly night, and goose bumps had popped out on her shoulders. Her arms ached from holding aloft her wooden, silver-painted moon. And Peter, stretched out on the floor of the makeshift stage as the sleeping shepherd, kept surreptitiously reaching out to grab her ankle.

It was the grandest fun she had had in years. So very welcome after such dreadful events.

Without turning her head, she whispered, "Selene saw him, loved him, sought him . . ."

Isabella frowned and lowered her little bow. There was actually no Cupid in the myth, but the role had been invented for her at the last moment, and she wanted to play it to the hilt. "Must I say that, Mama?" she said very loudly.

The audience laughed.

"Yes, dear," said Carmen. "It is part of the speech."

"Very well," Isabella sighed. "But since you have already said it, I don't think I ought to repeat it." She lifted her bow again. "And coming down from heaven, kissed him and lay beside him."

Carmen knelt down beside Peter and loudly kissed him on the cheek.

Isabella laughed. "You have lip rouge on your cheek, Peter!"

The audience, already warm with champagne and the general hilarity of all the tableaux (especially the one where Elizabeth, as Hera, had entered trailing twenty feet of blue velvet curtain behind her) collapsed in mirth.

Isabella faced the merrymakers with a fierce scowl on her little face. "We are not finished yet!"

Elizabeth, her own whoops concealed behind her hand, waved her fan at her guests. "Yes, do let them finish!"

Isabella nodded in satisfaction. "Evermore he slumbers, Endymion the shepherd."

There was silence.

"*Now* we are finished," she said, and jumped off her column perch to curtsy.

There was wild applause, and everyone rose from their chairs in ovation.

"Bravo!" cried Georgina, her red curls twisted wildly in her guise of Medusa. "What an actress you have here, Carmen. Bring her to Italy one day, and we shall put her on the stage at La Fenice."

Isabella's eyes widened in delight. "Really?"

Carmen swung her daughter up in her arms. She kissed her little cheek, leaving the second smudge of lip rouge of the evening. "No stage for you, dearest! But you did do a very fine job tonight, Bella."

Peter rose from the floor, tugged the rather brief skirt of his toga down again, and came to stand beside his wife and daughter. "So fine I believe it merits staying up for supper."

"Bravo!" Isabella crowed.

Carmen looked up at Peter as he took her arm.

She raised her brown eyes inquiringly. "Now do you think?" she whispered.

"Now is quite as good a time as any other. Don't you agree—Lady Clifton?"

Carmen smiled. "Once more into the breach!"

Peter faced the chattering crowd and raised his hand for their attention. A silence fell.

"My friends," he said. "I—we have a rather surprising announcement to make . . ."

Epilogue

"And I pronounce that you be man and wife. Amen."

Carmen's hand, newly adorned with a band of diamonds as well as her emerald, trembled in her bridegroom's grasp, and she was certain she was about to cry. But she blinked the tears away and smiled as she lifted her face for Peter's kiss.

A kiss that went on for so long, that the good vicar coughed in a delicate disapproval, and Elizabeth and Isabella could be heard giggling from the first pew.

Peter finally drew back and gazed down at her warmly. "Well, Carmen. Do you feel *more* married than you did ten minutes ago?"

"Not a bit. But this *is* a lovely moment. Do you feel more married?"

"No. But I did hear that Lizzie's excellent chef has prepared a lovely lemon cake, so that should make all this wedding folderol worthwhile."

"Folderol? Do you not recall that this was all *your* idea?"

"Was it? Hm. Perhaps it was." He stepped back and very politely offered his arm. "Shall we move forth, Lady Clifton?"

"Thank you, Lord Clifton. We shall."

So they processed down the aisle to the booming strains of the church organ, amid the cheers of the few good friends gathered there in the old Norman church of Clifton Village. In the sunny churchyard, they were quickly surrounded and showered with a fall of rose petals.

"Oh, Carmen!" Elizabeth cried, wiping at her eyes with her lacy handkerchief. "I have never seen a bride so lovely." She straightened the folds of Carmen's ivory-colored lace mantilla, which fell from her high comb over her simple ivory satin gown.

"I should be," Carmen said. "You and Georgina spent hours fussing over me this morning!"

"My mama is the loveliest woman in the world!" Isabella announced, leaning against her father's leg. She was quite pretty herself, in a new white dress with a pink silk sash. Even her curls were tidy for once, brushed and threaded with a wreath of pink rosebuds.

"Indeed, she is one of the loveliest women in the world," said Peter, catching his daughter up in his arms and kissing her cheek. "You and your Aunt Elizabeth are the others!"

Isabella giggled.

Elizabeth beamed. "Shall we go back to Evanstone, then? Pierre will pout so if his magnificent wedding breakfast grows cold."

"Ah, yes. The famous lemon cake. What do you say, my loves?" Peter said. "Shall you ride with us, Bella?"

"Yes!" Isabella shouted. She wriggled down from her father's arms, and ran toward the flower-bedecked open carriage that awaited them outside the churchyard gates. "Come on!" she called. "All the villagers are lined up along the road to wave to us!"

And Peter and Carmen looked at each other then ran down the pathway amid more rose petals and laughter, to join their daughter and be carried forward to their new life.

ALSO AVAILABLE FROM

Amanda McCabe

Spirited Brides

In this beautiful omnibus, two heartwarming
stories of magic and matrimony from
popular Signet Regency author Amanda McCabe
are brought together for the first time.

One Touch of Magic
Lady Iverson has taken up the haunted archeological
dig her late husband left half-finished. When she
meets the estate's lord, Miles Rutledge, he feels an
otherworldly connection with her—and he prays she
feels the same...

A Loving Spirit
When Cassie Richards visits the haunted castle of the
Earl of Royce, she bewitches the bookish royal. But
for the two to embrace their love, they're going to
need a little spiritual guidance...

**Available wherever books are sold or at
penguin.com**